the
Mistletoe
Pact

BOOKS BY JO LOVETT

The First Time We Met
The House Swap

the Mistletoe Pact

JO LOVETT

Bookouture

Published by Bookouture in 2021

An imprint of Storyfire Ltd.
Carmelite House
50 Victoria Embankment
London EC4Y 0DZ

www.bookouture.com

ISBN: 978-1-80019-796-1
eBook ISBN: 978-1-80019-795-4

This book is a work of fiction. Names, characters, businesses,
organizations, places and events other than those clearly in the
public domain, are either the product of the author's imagination
or are used fictitiously. Any resemblance to actual persons, living or
dead, events or locales is entirely coincidental.

To William

Chapter One

NOW – CHRISTMAS EVE 2021

EVIE

Evie opened her eyes and squinted upwards.

Pink. She was in a very, very pink room, with a lot of hearts. The ceiling was pink. The wallpaper was pink with padded hearts on it. The cushion on the (pink) chair opposite was pink and heart-shaped.

What room was this? Why was she here? She was definitely awake, not dreaming. This was definitely a *real* pink room.

She shook her head slightly.

Ow. It was like there was a band clamped across her forehead.

Her neck hurt too. There were a lot of lumps in her pillow.

She turned her head to the right.

Oh no.

Oh no, oh no, oh no.

She was in bed with Dan. Oh, no, no, no, no, no.

Drink. Sex.

A lot of drink and a lot of sex.

No, no, no.

Although also, yes, yes, *yessss*, because from what she remembered, the sex had been good, *really* good. *Amazing.*

But mainly, no. Because Dan was Dan and they'd snogged once, a long time ago, and they flirted a bit, but they didn't sleep together; they just didn't do that. Maybe they should have done, though, because the more she remembered the more she knew that last night had been *fantastic*.

The memories were flooding back now.

They'd talked about their fallback pact.

Oh God. A wedding chapel. A wedding *service*.

Oh no.

Nooooo.

She and Dan had got married. Disaster. Married. *Married*.

They'd got drunk-married in Vegas. Who actually did that?

Bloody hell.

And now, God, they were obviously going to have to get divorced. *Divorced*. They'd managed to change their marital status without ever really having been married. And *how* were they going to get divorced? Would it be expensive? Would it involve a lot of admin?

God.

She turned her head carefully and took another look at Dan. He was still asleep, facing her, his head nestled on his own lumpy, pink, heart-shaped pillow. Funny how someone's face could look different when they were asleep. Awake, he laughed a lot. In repose, his features looked quite harsh. Still gorgeous, though.

And still lovely, kind, funny Dan. She really hoped that last night wouldn't have ruined their friendship.

Unbelievable that, after all these years, they'd had actual sex. It had been *so* good. She wished she'd been sober enough to remember all the good bits properly.

And what was wrong with her? It wasn't the not-having-been-sober-enough-to-remember-all-the-sex she should be worrying about, it was the *marriage*.

Dan's eyes pinged open very suddenly and he did the lying down equivalent of leaping backwards. Yep, she might have had her face a bit too close to his. Her head and neck weren't feeling very mobile though, so it was hard to move.

'Evie,' he barked. 'Oh my *God*.' He was simultaneously staring and frowning, like he'd just seen something truly horrifying. Her.

'I know,' Evie said, scrunching her face up. Her head was *really* hurting now. The lights were far too bright. Getting from here – lying in a random hotel bed next to *Dan* – to being back in her own hotel, showered and in clean clothes, ready to start her day – her birthday for God's sake – was suddenly feeling like an insurmountable obstacle. And actually, why were they here and not in their own hotel? She frowned, trying to sift through last night's memories. Something about them having bought a special honeymoon hotel package?

'What are we...?' It was amazing how, with bloodshot eyes that he couldn't fully open and serious stubble, Dan still looked so good.

Evie just raised her eyebrows and did some more face scrunching. It would probably be better for him to remember things for himself gradually.

Dan did a manic patting motion under the sheets and the cerise, nylonny velour bedspread covering them nearly fell onto the floor.

'Oh my *God*. Naked,' he said. Maybe he didn't remember all the sex. Maybe he wasn't going to remember that they were married. Again, God, *married*.

If he didn't remember, she was going to have to tell him. Not immediately, though. It would be hard to find the right words. Hopefully he'd remember for himself eventually, if she waited.

'I know.' Evie nodded. Ouch.

'Oh my God.'

'Yeah.'

'Oh my *God*.' It sounded like he was starting to remember.

He turned away from her and looked over the side of the bed and did more patting around.

'I can't see my clothes,' he said. He suddenly froze. 'Oh my *God*.' There it was; that had to be him remembering everything.

Evie just lay there. She couldn't think of any words that would do justice to the magnitude of the situation.

Dan unfroze after a few seconds and slid off the bed, taking the bedspread with him and wrapping it round his waist in one impressively athletic motion.

Evie's shoulders were cold. Because they were bare. She dragged the bedclothes up so that they were tucked round her neck.

'Um, married,' Dan said. Croaked, really.

Evie nodded and screwed her face up further.

'Do you think we can get divorced today?' Dan adjusted the bedspread so that it covered more of him. At any other time, Evie would have been disappointed, because he had a *great* chest and it didn't seem that likely that she was ever going to see it again at close quarters.

'Probably. I mean, a lot of people probably get married in Vegas and regret it.' She'd said that in a really normal voice, which was surprising, because *married in Vegas*; it was really hard not to *freak* about the fact that they were married.

'Yeah. We can google it.' Dan was shuffling himself and the bed-spread around the room now, gathering up clothing.

'Yep. Good plan.' Evie stayed put, holding the sheets up to her chin. It *was* a good plan. Definitely. Google had an answer for everything. Hopefully.

Eventually, Dan sat down on the other side of the bed and, with his left hand holding the bedspread in place, began to sort through their clothes with his right.

He placed her lovely new red dress – which she couldn't really imagine wearing again now because of the memories – on the bed next to her, followed by her tights, her bra (quite a nice black one) and her pants (beige, huge and stomach-flattening because she had not been expecting to pull last night). Dan folded the pants in four as he put them down and Evie winced. And then winced more at the memory of when he'd tried to pull them off and she'd had to help him and it had taken ages and they'd both got quite out of breath because the pants were seriously tight.

'Would you like to use the bathroom first?' Dan asked.

Nope. It might not be soundproof and she didn't fancy weeing with him sitting just outside. Plus, would she realistically be able to get herself out of bed with the sheets still wrapped round her without flashing any more flesh? She'd be a lot better off waiting until he'd gone.

'You go first,' she said.

'Sure? Okay, thanks.'

Evie watched Dan shuffle himself and the bedspread into the bathroom, and then resumed staring at the pink ceiling, trying very hard not to let any tears squeeze out.

Happy birthday, me, she thought. Thirty years old today. She had a lot to be thankful for, like how she'd definitely ticked a lot of the boxes you wanted to tick by your thirtieth. A wonderful family, yes. Great friends, yes. A career that she loved, yes.

No hint of a proper love life and about to be divorced, not so much. Friendship with Dan possibly ruined, also not so much.

In a parallel life, if she was honest, she'd have loved this marriage to have been planned and to have involved all their family and friends and been meant to last forever. Like her occasional fantasies over the years when she thought about their fallback pact.

But this wasn't a parallel life, it was her actual life, and clearly the pact was never going to have played out like that.

Chapter Two

THEN – 23RD DECEMBER 2013

EVIE

Evie's mother pouted at herself in the hall mirror, applied another coat of glossy red Chanel lipstick, pouted again, and scrunched her fingers into her long blonde hair for a bit more volumising.

'You look gorgeous, Mum.' Evie smiled at her. 'Very glamorous.' Her mother was a lot more glamorous than all Evie's friends' mums, and not just because she was a good ten years younger than most of them. Evie was pretty sure that she was the kind of woman who'd still be glamorous when she was in her seventies and eighties.

Her mum turned round and smiled back at her. '*You're* gorgeous. I am *so* proud of myself having given birth to you. Look at your beautiful eyebrows. Honestly, *who* doesn't ever need to pluck? Only my perfect daughter. And your amazing hair. And your beautiful brown eyes. I can't actually believe you're twenty-two tomorrow. It's only five minutes since you were a baby.' She narrowed her eyes. 'Evie. I do like that top, and it looks great with your jeans, and you have the perfect figure for what you're wearing, but I'm thinking if you just undid another button, or maybe even two more, you'd look a lot more *available.*'

'Honestly.' Evie took a step backwards and batted her mum's hands away from the buttons on her blouse. 'Available is a grim word.'

'You *are* available, though. And I'm not sure the boys realise that.'

'Mum. *Honestly.*' Evie couldn't say that it didn't matter if no-one realised straight off that she was available, because what she wanted was a serious relationship, with someone very sensible, who she could eventually get married to and have children with and stay with forever. That might hurt her mum's feelings, given that it was the exact opposite of all her relationships.

'I just worry about you, that's all. You're turning twenty-two, not sixty-two. You should be having *fun*.'

It was lovely that her mother cared so much about her, but Evie could really do without the constant questioning – in person, and by text when she was away in Birmingham at uni – about whether she was *sure* she was happy and whether she thought she might have more fun if she 'let her hair down' a bit more, specifically with regard to boys and big nights out. It wasn't like she didn't enjoy a little drink; she just didn't like spending the morning after with her head over a toilet bowl. And it wasn't like she didn't like boys, just not too many of them and not ones who'd make her cry after they'd slept together once. 'Maybe you'll meet someone nice this evening.'

'Honestly,' Evie said again, trying really hard not to sigh loudly and roll her eyes.

'Maybe just one button?' Her mum was looking at her top again. 'You have such gorgeous skin and such a fab cleavage. You should be showing that off. Especially in the winter when everyone else is so pale.' Oh, God. Cleavage. Any minute the conversation would be veering in the direction of actual sex chat. Evie adored her mother and she loved spending time with her, but, if she was honest, she could do without all the openness. She was pretty sure that there were zero sex discussions between her best friend Sasha and her mother, for example. 'You know your boobs probably won't be this amazing forever. They lose a bit of bounce over time,' her mum added.

'Fine. One button.' Anything to stop the conversation. She could do it up again in a minute.

Her mum reached forward and tugged Evie's blouse down away from her shoulder and adjusted her camisole top. 'Perfect,' she said. 'Now, while we're on the subject...' No, no, no. This was where her mum was going to start on some advice about sex.

'We should go,' Evie said, taking her coat off the hook next to the front door and putting it on. 'We're going to be late.'

'Better to make an entrance than to be boringly on time,' her mum said as they stepped out of the front door of their cottage.

They walked arm in arm down the little lane from their house to the green in the middle of their village, Melting Bishop, and then round the edge of the green – Evie's mum didn't want to ruin her heels on the grass – and up to Sasha's parents' wide Cotswold stone house in the middle of the opposite side, arriving at the same time as another family from Melting and a couple who Evie thought she recognised as friends of Sasha's older sister Lucie.

Sasha's mother, Fiona – wearing a knee-length, velvet dress, nude court shoes and pale-pink lipstick, and holding a full champagne glass – opened the door. 'Welcome, everyone. Happy Christmas.'

Two hours later, Evie's dancing companion gave her one last twirl, let go of her, boogied himself a couple of steps backwards, and started some impressive arm-popping, his eyes locked on hers the whole time. Evie pushed her tinsel headband out of her eyes, smiled at him and decided to stick with some bog-standard swaying and hand clapping. There was a time and a place for pulling serious moves on the dance floor, and that was not here, at her best friend's parents' annual Christmas party, with her mother only a few feet away.

Because whatever moves Evie produced, there was every chance her mother would join in and go one better, like she had last year. She'd dropped into the splits, pulled a hamstring, fallen forwards in agony, landed hard on her arm and broken her wrist, and Evie had had to cart her off to A&E in Cheltenham.

The arm popper was very good-looking. Light-brown skin, similar to Evie's, a lot of dark curly hair, and nice eyes. He was still smiling at her. Evie clapped herself round in a little circle, firstly to give her face a break from smiling back at him, and secondly to check whether her mum had noticed that it looked like she was on the brink of pulling.

If Evie publicly snogged a good-looking stranger this evening, she'd hopefully get her mum off her back for at least the next month or two. Evie would have to make sure there were witnesses, so that her mum heard about it on the village grapevine if she didn't see it with her own eyes. She could kiss him just outside as they were leaving. She should probably start chatting to him now.

It would be nice to know his name. She wasn't big on snogging anonymous strangers.

Her mum was right: Evie wasn't always very good at spontaneity when it came to men.

She clapped herself a little closer to him, widened her smile and said, 'I'm Evie.'

'Well, hello, Evie. I'm Jack.' Jack looked her up and down, very deliberately, from head to toe, which, if she was honest, made her a bit uncomfortable, and then, with a slow smile, started to bend his head towards hers. Oh, okay, the kiss was going to happen right here. Under bright lights. In front of lots of people. In Sasha's parents' house. Well, at least her mother would *definitely* see, and it was *definitely* spontaneous. And she did know his name. It was definitely the right thing to do.

She inched closer to Jack.

God. She hoped her mum couldn't actually see her now. If she could, there was every chance that she'd have some tips for Evie on kissing technique tomorrow.

Evie looked at Jack. His gaze was roving up and down her body again. She really wasn't up for this. She kind of just wanted to do her blouse buttons up to her neck, fold her arms over her chest and glare at him.

No, it would be fine. It would probably be *nice*.

She moved even closer to him, and he moved closer to her, so close that she could smell the beer on his breath. They were going to kiss, any second.

And *then*, they did not kiss. Because Jack lifted his head and smiled at someone beyond Evie. He took Evie's hand, lifted it high above her head and spun her until she was breathless, kissed her cheek, said, 'Thank you for the dance,' and strut-walked himself over to speak to the person who had clearly caught his eye just as he'd been about to kiss Evie.

Which would have been kind of a relief, really, had it not been for the fact that that person was Evie's *mum*.

Evie's mum did a serious shimmy, adjusted her gold, ruched boob tube, pouted her still very scarlet lips – that lipstick was good – and twirled her hair with her finger and then did a *cringe* beckoning thing with the same finger. And Jack, *who Evie had been about to kiss*, followed her, very closely, right into the middle of all the dancing, with a mega shimmy of his own.

Evie was pretty sure that his crotch connected with her mum's bottom at the apex of the shimmy.

'No *way*,' she said, out loud. The only saving grace was that she was pretty sure that her mum would never have realised that Jack had binned Evie for her because there had been tall people in between them and she wouldn't have been able to see that Jack had been dancing with Evie before he spotted her.

'No way what?' Sasha's older brother Dan put a glass of mulled wine into her hand. Evie downed half of it in one and started coughing. Dan whacked her on the back. 'Are you okay?'

'There are a *lot* of cloves in there.' Evie's eyes were still watering. She wasn't *totally* sure that all the watering was due to the near-choking – it was seriously humiliating realising that you were so bad at spontaneously snogging people that, when you'd finally decided to go for it with a stranger, the stranger in question ditched you in favour of your own mother – but Dan wouldn't realise that. Thank goodness. She didn't need her gorgeous secret crush to know about her humiliation at the hands of a different man.

What was actually wrong with her? Jack had danced very enthusiastically with her for three songs running. Her mum was beautiful and glamorous and lively, but she was twenty years older than Evie, and Jack was quite *young*. How square-looking *was* Evie?

'Who's the man my mum's dancing with?' she asked Dan.

'Old friend of Lucie's from uni. Moved to Cheltenham recently for work. Seems like a nice guy.' Lucie was Sasha and Dan's older sister. Evie was pretty sure that she was about twenty-seven, which presumably meant that Jack was a similar age. Five years older than Evie and fifteen years younger than her mother. And much more attracted to her mother than to her. Right.

There had to be a lesson there somewhere. Like, don't decide to snog someone just to keep your mother happy. Evie downed the rest of the contents of her glass and started coughing again.

Dan hit her on the back again. 'Still too many cloves?'

'Yep.'

'So how are you doing? Apart from nearly choking to death?'

'Good, thank you.' Evie nodded, still coughing slightly.

'Hello, hello, two of my most favourite people.' Sasha had danced over to them with a plate of mince pies. 'Wow. Look at your mum. Is that Lucie's friend Jack?'

'Yep.' Evie finished coughing and took a mince pie.

'I know I've said it before, but your mum's got amazing legs. And great boobs.' Sasha put the mince pies down on a side table. 'I'm bored with handing these round.' She grabbed Evie and Dan's hands. 'Let's dance.'

'Maybe not *right* next to my mum.' Evie eye-swivelled and head-indicated towards where her mum and Jack were slow dancing with hands going in far too many places for Evie's liking.

'Oops, yes. Love you, Evie Green,' Sasha told her as the three of them moved to the opposite edge of the dancing group.

'Love you too, Sasha Marshall, but are you *pity*-loving me because my mum's pulled and I haven't?' Evie dodged round one of Sasha's uncles and into a space next to the holly-and-berry-decorated fireplace, where four stockings were hanging neatly in a row, despite the fact that Sasha, the youngest in the family, was turning twenty-two in April. Sasha's mum kept the house in a state of permanent perfect tidiness and preparedness for any given holiday festival. Evie *loved* all the tidiness and preparedness.

'No pity.' Sasha went for an all-the-way-down-to-the-floor-shaking-her-thing move and Evie joined in, safe in the knowledge that her mother definitely currently had eyes only for Jack and would therefore not also be joining in. 'Just appreciation for my oldest and best friend and your adorable mother.'

Evie's mother *was* adorable. Just slightly different from everyone else's mothers. Good job that Sasha didn't know that Evie had had plans to kiss Jack herself this evening. Her pity would be off the scale.

A lot of dancing later, Evie and Sasha flopped onto a sofa at the far side of the double reception room as people put on coats, gloves and scarves and hugged Sasha's parents goodbye. Only about twenty minutes ago the room had been full to bursting but then one of the guests had noticed that it was midnight and had gathered up their family of five and left, and that had started a domino effect of departures.

'I should get going too,' Evie said. It'd be nice to get a good night's sleep so that she enjoyed her birthday tomorrow.

And then her mother and Jack emerged from the door at the end of the room and walked past Evie and Sasha, holding hands, eyes only for each other, very joined-at-the-hip. And thigh… and chest. They stopped under the mistletoe at the front door for a quick smooch, and then giggled themselves out of the house.

'He's going to stay over with us, isn't he?' Evie said, trying to pull her face out of a disappointed ruck.

Sasha nodded. 'Looks like it. Want to stay here tonight?'

'That's such a lovely offer but I'll be fine at home. More than fine. I'll have a birthday lie-in and he'll be gone by the time I get up.' Evie really wanted to be in her own bed tonight with her own pillows and duvet. And to have her traditional birthday breakfast with her mum. Which would definitely happen. Her mum would kick Jack out at about nine; she was like clockwork when it came to men staying over. She never wanted them around during the day and she definitely wouldn't want someone else there on Evie's birthday. 'And we're seeing you for lunch tomorrow. I might stay here for another half hour, though.' That should definitely give her mum and Jack time to have the bedroom door firmly closed behind them.

Two hours, the rest of the mulled wine and two coffees later, Evie pushed her chair back and told the others round Sasha's parents' kitchen table – Sasha, Dan, Lucie, their brother Max and a couple of other village friends – that she had to go home.

'Nooooo. Stay.' Sasha reached out to pull Evie's arm but missed and banged her own arm on the table. 'Ow. That table's *hard*.'

Evie nodded. Sasha had made a good point there. She was *clever*. 'Tables *are* hard. And I know that because I'm old. It's after midnight. I'm *twenty-two* today. Two little ducks.'

'Did you say duck?' Sasha asked.

'Bingo speak for twenty-two,' Evie said. 'You know Mum's last partner owned a bingo hall in Cheltenham and we went a few times. I love it, if I'm honest.'

Sasha nodded. 'Happy birthday,' she said.

'Happy birthday,' the others chorused.

'Thank you.' Evie beamed at them. 'And I *am* going to go now and get some sleep because I don't want to spend my whole birthday feeling awful.' She pushed her chair further back, and somehow it knocked some spoons on the floor and they landed with a *really loud* clatter. 'Whoops.' She put her finger on her lips and shushed, twice, to make sure everyone heard her. 'We might wake your parents up.'

Sasha's older sister Lucie stood up too and went over to the sink. 'I think we should all have some water first. Just to make sure you actually make it across the green in one piece and so that you don't spend your birthday with a hangover.'

'Everyone should take two paracetamol with their water,' said Dan. 'Or three. Tried and tested anti-hangover.'

'Let's definitely do that,' Evie said. 'Doctors know *everything* about paracetamol.' Dan had recently finished medical school.

'Okay, so I'm definitely going now.' Evie finished hugging everyone a few minutes later and they all followed her towards the front door.

'I'll walk you back,' Dan said, joining her on the doorstep.

'Oh, no, honestly,' Evie said, suppressing a little shiver of pleasure at the idea of a moonlit walk with Dan. 'I'm not going to get lost between here and home.'

'Nope, I'm coming.' Dan shrugged into a Puffa jacket. 'Dad was saying yesterday that there've been a couple of attempted burglaries in the village recently. And it's very quiet at this time of night, no-one else up except us. You don't want to bump into a burglar on your own.'

'Well, thank you, that's very kind.' It was slightly surprising that Sasha wasn't having a go at Dan about not being feminist but, if there *were* burglars around, Evie would definitely rather not be on her own when she bumped into them, and Dan was a lot larger than her. Bugger feminism, frankly, if there were burglars out and about.

As Evie started to step through the front door, Sasha pointed upwards and squealed, '*Mistletoe*. Dan and Evie. You have to kiss now.'

Evie stopped and turned to look at Dan, in a bit of a panic, which was definitely a mistake, because it clearly made it look as though she *wanted* Dan to kiss her. Which, in a very secret way, she might do, but not in *front* of people. Although you didn't *kiss* kiss under mistletoe.

You *peck* kissed. Oh, God, she was still looking at him. Like she *totally* wanted to do the mistletoe-kiss.

Dan smiled at her, rolled his eyes in the direction of Sasha, and leaned down and brushed his lips to Evie's *lips*, not her cheek, or anywhere else, but her *lips*, very fleetingly. His lips were warm, but not too warm, and nice and firm, but not too firm. And Evie felt the tiny kiss all the way to her centre. What would a *proper* kiss from Dan be like?

Shit. She had her eyes closed. She pinged them open, fast. Hopefully no-one would have noticed because Sasha was clapping and happy-birthdaying again.

'Let's go.' Dan started walking and Evie followed.

'So have you decided what branch of medicine you want to specialise in?' she asked, fast, to prove that her mind was *totally* off the fact that *their lips had just touched*.

'I'm pretty sure I want to do emergency medicine.'

'I think you'd be great at that. You're very good at staying calm. Remember when Sasha got her head stuck between those railings and all the rest of us were panicking but you got her out.' And he was fantastic with people, which would have to help.

'You weren't panicking, you were *laughing*.'

'Well, yes, because it was hilarious.'

'What about you? Did Sasha tell me you've started teacher training?'

'Yep. Hoping to be a secondary school geography teacher.'

'I think you'll be a great teacher.' Dan stopped. 'What's that?' He bent down to pick something up. 'Someone's dropped a scarf. Maybe someone who was at the party. I'll hang onto it and Mum can ask around tomorrow.'

Evie peered at the scarf in the moonlight.

'I think it's actually mine.' She took it from Dan. Yep, pink and gold faux fur. Her mum had borrowed it this evening. She'd probably dropped it mid-passionate al fresco embrace with Jack. Not what Evie wanted to think about. She kind of felt like she was never going to want to wear it again herself. She was imagining the scarf being involved in the embrace in some way. Maybe her mum had flirtatiously twirled it round both their necks at once.

No, no, no. She needed to stop with the imagining.

What had they been talking about?

'So, yes, I'm planning to be a teacher.' Bugger. Now she sounded like she wanted Dan to elaborate on why he thought she'd make a great teacher. That was what he'd been in the middle of saying. She *would* like him to elaborate but she would *not* like to look like she was fishing for compliments. 'It's cold. Do you think we'll get a white Christmas?'

'Doubt it. I mean, you never know. Maybe. But also, we never do, so no.'

'That's very pessimistic. Although probably right. Oh. My. Goodness.' Evie stopped in the middle of the lane opposite her house. The sitting room curtains were open and her mother and Jack were in the middle of the room, wearing not nearly enough clothes. And doing *stuff*.

Neither she nor Dan moved for far too long, very rabbit-in-headlights, and then Dan said, 'Right, so here's a plan. You're going to go back round the corner and I'm going to knock on the door and shout "Oo-er" – they won't recognise me, I'm sure, given that they're, um, busy – and then we're going to walk round the green for a few minutes and then I'm sure when you get back they'll have gone upstairs.'

Evie nodded. 'Thank you. That's an excellent plan.'

She'd just got round the corner when she heard Dan knock and shout, and then his footsteps *sprinting* down the road. She was already sniggering when he got to her and when she saw his face she full-on snorted, and then Dan laughed too, and then they were both doubled up, staggering around, almost crying with laughter.

'My *eyes*,' Evie said when she could talk. 'I can't believe we saw that.' Did it make it better or worse that her mother was in seriously good shape body-wise? 'Why did you decide to shout *Oo-er*? I mean, why not just *Good evening* or something?'

'I was too overcome to think straight.'

'Yeah. Oh God.' And they both started sniggering again.

'This is so ridiculous,' Evie said, when they'd finally recovered. 'It's like we're naughty kids. But my forty-two-year-old *mum* was practically having sex in full view of the whole village.'

'Well, not really. I mean, it's two thirty in the morning. No-one's around.'

'*We're* around. Anyway. I love my mum. She's amazing. I don't want to sound like I'm criticising her, but, when *I'm* a mother, I'm going to be a boring mother. No sex in the sitting room. I say *when*. If. Obviously I might never have kids.'

'I reckon you'll totally have kids. If you want them.' They'd reached the bench in the middle of the green. 'Want to sit here for a few minutes to give them time to get to bed?'

Evie nodded and they sat down.

'I know it's not something everyone would say at twenty-two, but I *would* like kids one day. Once I've established my career, obviously. But I feel like I'd much prefer to have children within a serious relationship.' She didn't fancy being a single mother like her mum had been – it looked very difficult – so, man-wise, she was going to need someone solid. She did keep trying but they never worked out. Which you could also say about her mother; she definitely kept trying and the men definitely never worked out. 'So there's every chance it will never happen.'

'Yeah, I mean, you're already twenty-two. You only have about twenty-odd years left to start a family and then that's it. No chance of meeting someone and having kids. I mean, you need to *rush*. You're so *old*.'

Evie shook her head. 'You mock, but, you know, time passes quickly. One of those famous facts of life. Anyway, I want to have at least two kids and I want to have them well before I'm forty. So I need to meet someone by the time I'm thirty.'

'Well, shit. Only eight years to go. That's a tight deadline.'

'I'll remind you of this if I'm single on my thirtieth birthday. Which, now I say it, I probably will be.'

'Evie Green, you will not be. But if you are, I'll marry you myself. If you'll have me.' He nudged her in the ribs.

'Dan Marshall. That's a lovely offer.' She nudged him back. 'I will totally have you if we're both still single in eight years' time.'

Dan held out his hand. 'So that's a deal then. We'll get married on your thirtieth birthday if we're both still single.' Evie put her hand in his and they shook.

'I'm genuinely excited to have a fallback pact,' she said. 'You know I'm going to hold you to it.' A part of her registered that in a parallel universe where they hadn't known each other forever she'd genuinely *like* to hold him to it.

'You'll be coupled up with a baby on the way by then, but, if you aren't, I'll be there like a shot.'

They both laughed and then Evie felt something on her face and looked up.

'You were wrong,' she said. 'It *is* snowing. Look. And look at that.' She pointed upwards. 'Isn't that mistletoe growing on this tree? I've never noticed it before. Mistletoe and snow. The perfect Christmas scene for the perfect fallback pact. A mistletoe pact.' She looked back at Dan, at his eyes and his cheekbones and his mouth, and suddenly her own mouth felt dry. She wished she hadn't spotted the mistletoe and mentioned it. Awkward. 'Good job Sasha isn't here to make us kiss.' Oh, for God's sake. *Way* more awkward. She stood up. 'The coast's probably clear at home now.'

'Yep.' Dan stood up too.

'Goodnight, then.'

'Hey, no. Remember those possible marauding burglars. Come on.' He held his arm out and she took it.

'Well, thank you.'

They didn't say much as they crunched their way across the frost that was already starting on the green, Evie getting serious butterflies every time their hips bumped as they walked.

She glanced up at Dan and he looked down at her at the same moment, half-smiling in the moonlight, which made her want to smile too.

What was it about him that made all the other men in any given room seem *less*? His hair was what some people would call red and Sasha, whose hair was the same colour, called strawberry blond. He had blue eyes and fairly average features. But the combination of them all was just so *sexy*, basically. Maybe because of his personality. Kind. Capable. Very funny. And the fact that he wasn't that much taller than average but he was satisfyingly solid and nicely in shape – she'd seen him in sports kit a few times, and he looked *good*.

She felt herself smile more. She looked up again and saw that he was watching her and his smile was growing too.

Neither of them had said anything for ages now. Evie should probably speak, except she was having a mind blank.

She licked her lips and Dan's eyes went to her mouth.

Oh, wow.

Chapter Three

THEN – CHRISTMAS EVE 2013

DAN

What was he on?

Dan dragged his eyes away from Evie's gorgeous, full lips and cleared his throat.

For a moment back there, when Evie had mentioned the mistletoe and reminded him about their peck on the lips earlier on, and he'd looked at her smiling face turned up to his, Dan had wished that he *could* kiss her. Properly, not like the tiny kiss they'd had under the mistletoe. Which, now he thought about it, could easily have been a cheek kiss. Why had he kissed her on the lips?

He shook his head. This was middle-of-the-night madness.

'So what are you hoping to get for your birthday?' he asked, to break the silence now stretching uncomfortably between them. Ridiculous to suddenly be lost for conversation. And ridiculous to suddenly have noticed, properly, how attractive Evie was. She was his little sister's best friend, who he'd known for years. You didn't find your younger sister's friends attractive. Although the two-year age gap was nothing when you were adults. She was still his sister's best friend, though. She was talking. She seemed to be listing items of clothing.

'Yes, so in summary,' she said, 'clothes, clothes and more clothes. I do love student life but I'm actually looking forward to having a job and being able to afford stuff. What about you? What do you want for Christmas?'

Good question. If he was honest, the biggest thing he'd like for Christmas would be to be away from his family. There was too much tension in the air. He'd love just to spend the day with friends. Which you absolutely could not do on Christmas Day when your whole family, you included, persisted in their 'We are the perfect family' charade. Obviously he wasn't going to say that, though.

'Money for Glastonbury this summer,' he said. 'And, yeah, clothes too. Some obscure medical textbooks that cost a fortune. The usual.'

They were nearly at Evie's cottage now.

'I'm kind of feeling guilty,' she said. 'My mum's fab. And she's single and she's still quite young. If she wants to have men over, I should totally not object. I mean, I don't object. I just *really* don't like having to have breakfast with strangers in my own kitchen, or bumping into strangers on my way to the bathroom. And, at the risk of sounding like a five-year-old, I *really* don't want to have to do that on my *birthday*, but it's fine, I won't have to, because he'll be gone by the time I get up. I shouldn't be laughing about my mum.'

'I know.' Dan had felt guilty too. 'We weren't laughing at her, though; we were laughing at the situation. Which *was* farcical.' Dan really wanted to make Evie feel better. 'And clichés are there for a reason. It's true that no-one wants to know about their own parents having sex. I walked in on my parents doing it once, when I was about ten.'

'*Really*? Selfishly, I'm *very* pleased. Also, weirded out to think of *your* parents having sex.' Evie clapped her hands over her mouth. 'Sorry. I didn't mean that the way it sounded.'

She was right, actually. Dan would be astonished if they did nowadays. He'd stumbled upon some texts on his father's phone a few years ago which had indicated that he was having an affair, and he was sure there'd been others; there was a definite ongoing polite distance between his parents. He'd always been pretty sure that his father had known that he'd seen the texts, but nothing had ever been mentioned. In Dan's family, no-one ever talked about anything bad, like, if they ignored it, it wouldn't be true. It didn't work.

'Hey,' he said, 'it didn't sound bad. I know what you mean. Everything in my house is always so neat and tidy. Clinical.' That sounded bitter, and Evie was shaking her head. He needed to try for something a bit lighter. 'I mean, they're in their fifties. And they've been married for thirty years.' Evie was still looking unsure. He needed to be jokey. 'When *we've* been married for thirty years it'll be your sixtieth birthday.'

Evie laughed. 'That's true. Wow. It really isn't going to be that long until we're old.'

'You're right. One minute it's the early hours of your twenty-second birthday and the next it's your ninetieth.'

'Yeah. In fact, I'd better get inside and get my nearly-elderly self upstairs. It sounds quiet, like they've gone to bed. Thank you so much for walking me back.' She fumbled in her pocket for her key.

'Hey. Not a problem. Happy birthday again.'

'Got it.' Evie held her key up and smiled at him.

Dan smiled back.

And neither of them moved.

And then, like some invisible force was propelling him, he lifted his hand and traced the line of her cheek, carefully, because it felt like she was precious. Her beautiful smile grew and her lips parted. She tipped her face up towards his, and, slowly, he lowered his head and kissed her, like there was no other possible course of action.

The kiss was only fleeting, and it wasn't enough. He leaned down again, and she reached up to meet him.

He pulled her into him, one hand on her back and the other in her thick, soft hair, and felt her arms go round his neck.

They kissed for a long time. So good.

He wished she didn't have her coat done up so tightly or such a thick scarf around her neck. He moved backwards a little and started to unwind the scarf and undo her coat buttons. Evie sighed and slid her arms around him, inside his open jacket.

He let her scarf fall to the ground and kissed her lips again, and then kissed across her jawline, and inside the curve of her neck. He heard her gasp a little as his hands moved up, and felt her grip his back.

He shifted a little so that they could reach each other better, and heard something.

It took him a moment to focus, and then he realised that someone was calling, 'Good evening,' from somewhere quite high. He looked up and saw a face at an upstairs window of the cottage at the bottom of the lane, the house on the corner. That would be Mrs Bird.

Evie moaned slightly, reached up to kiss his lips again and began to loosen his belt.

'Mmhmm,' he said, and pulled away.

Evie opened her eyes, but didn't stop with the belt-loosening. She had the most gorgeous just-been-kissed look on her face.

'Evening, Mrs Bird,' Dan said loudly, letting go of Evie and putting his hands on hers over his belt, to stop her.

Evie froze. Dan indicated towards the corner with his head.

Evie pulled her hands away from his jeans, really fast, and then turned round, really slowly.

'Don't let me disturb you.' Mrs Bird's cackle carried very well in the still air. 'Happy Christmas.'

Evie turned back round to face him again and screwed her face up. 'Oof,' she said.

'Yep.'

'So.' Evie didn't move. She looked dazed. Like he felt. It was hugely tempting to suggest going for a walk somewhere a little less overlooked, to carry on where they'd left off. It was also hugely ridiculous, because Evie was Sasha's best friend and he'd known her forever, and in three days' time he was going back to London. Plus he really wasn't up for any kind of relationship right now, and she'd pretty much just said that she only wanted serious relationships. So they should just say goodnight to each other now.

'Happy birthday for tomorrow,' he said.

'Thank you,' she said after a pause. 'Goodnight, then.'

'Goodnight.' He bent down and picked up her scarf and gave it to her.

'Thank you.' Evie took it and started to feel in all her pockets. 'What did I do with my key?'

'You were holding it when we…'

She nodded. 'Yep. Maybe I dropped it.'

Dan pulled his phone out of his pocket and switched the torch on and they both crouched down.

'It isn't here,' he said eventually. He looked closely at Evie. She had her lips clamped together like she was trying not to laugh. 'What?'

'I think it might be…' She stood up and covered her face with her hands. 'I think it might be inside your clothes somewhere.'

'Oh.' Dan stood up too. 'Um, okay. Well, I'll just check.'

In the end, he found it tucked between the top of his jeans and trunks waistbands. Evie still had her lips pressed together when he handed it to her.

'Thank you,' she said, and then she started giggling. How was this the first time that he'd ever noticed the dimple on the right-hand side of her mouth?

He laughed back at her. *God*, he wanted to kiss her again. And a lot more.

And now she wasn't laughing any more and nor was he.

They stood and looked at each other, Evie smiling a little, and Dan's lips, he was pretty sure, mirroring the curve of hers.

Time to go.

'Goodnight,' he said. He needed to say something light, to break the tension. 'Only eight years to go until our wedding day.' Maybe not *the* best weak joke to have made, actually, given the circumstances.

Evie nodded, put her key in the door, turned it, opened the door and said, 'Already planning my wedding dress. Night,' before slipping inside.

Lucie and Sasha were still up when he got back to the house.

'I went for a walk,' he said. 'After I saw Evie home.'

'Right,' said Sasha, like he was being weird. Yep, he was acting like someone who had something to be guilty about, over-explaining things.

'Goodnight, then,' he said. Any other evening it would have been nice to share a nightcap with Lucie and Sasha in the absence of the rest of their family, but right now wasn't the moment for it.

As he passed the sitting room on his way to bed, he heard his mother speaking. Hissing, actually. He caught the words *her* and *attractive*.

His father's reply was indistinct but he had a very snappish tone to his voice. Dan took a deep breath and got himself up the stairs, fast, to his childhood bedroom, to lie awake for hours feeling angry with his father and sad for his mother, like he'd done too many nights in the past. This was why he didn't come home much any more.

*

Two and a half days later, Dan crunched across the snowy green with the rest of his family. Evie had been right about the white Christmas. It had snowed properly yesterday, Christmas Day, and again this morning.

Since he'd started at university, Dan had always been relieved to get to Boxing Day, because it meant that he could leave the next day without comment. He just had this walk and one more family meal this evening to get out of the way, and that was it; he'd be off first thing in the morning.

'Helloooo.' Mrs Bird from the corner house was doing huge whole-arm waves at them. 'How wonderful to see you all together. Let me take a photo of you. Wait, wait, wait where you are.' She stepped outside her front door, wobbled, saved herself on the doorframe, and said, 'I might just get my stick.'

'Be careful.' Dan's father jogged over to her, ever the perfect gentleman, externally, anyway. 'You don't want to fall on ice and have to have another hip operation.'

The six of them stood for the photo, in front of the tree in the middle of the green, arranged by Mrs Bird with Dan's parents in the middle, Lucie and Sasha on either side of them, and Dan and his older brother Max on the ends. Portrait of a perfect family.

'What a wonderful picture you make,' said Mrs Bird. She waved her camera at them. 'Would you like a copy of the photo?'

'Thank you; we'd love one.' Dan's father smiled at her and she visibly fluttered while Dan gritted his teeth. His father held his arm out to escort her back to her house, while the rest of the family waited next to the tree.

Dan was laughing at something Lucie had said when a snowball landed squarely in his chest. Sasha cheered and Dan looked over to see Evie on the other side of the green at the corner of her lane, outside Mrs Bird's house, doing what looked like a victory haka.

'Seriously?' he said, bending down to collect snow. 'I don't think so.'

Dan's throw missed Evie, who was as good at dodging as she was at throwing, it turned out, and hit her mum, who'd just rounded the corner onto the green, holding hands with Jack.

'Good God,' said Dan's father from behind him, having safely deposited Mrs Bird. 'Three days. And only about fifteen years younger than her. For Jenny, that's a serious relationship.'

Dan felt his shoulders go rigid. He was pretty sure that Evie and her mum would both have been really hurt if they'd heard his words. And his father's patients would be very surprised by their dependable, lovable local GP being snide. Plus, the hypocrisy: how could a man who seemingly regularly cheated on his wife criticise someone who had a lot of short-term relationships where no-one got hurt?

Dan walked away from his father, towards Evie, her mother and Jack, and said, 'Morning. Sorry about the snowball, Jenny. It was meant for Evie.'

'No problem,' Jenny said. Dan turned to speak to Evie in response to some boasting about how she'd been right about the snow, and Jenny whipped a huge snowball down his neck.

'Okay. War,' Dan said.

Twenty minutes later, they'd trashed the previously beautifully white-snow-carpeted green and they were all soaking wet and laughing except for Dan's father, who was standing to one side, checking his watch and his phone.

And Dan had realised a few things. One, it was really nice to see his mother having actual fun. Two, even in the middle of a snowball fight he couldn't help registering Max's limp when he ran, and feeling the familiar crushing guilt. It was eight years ago now, when Max was eighteen and he was sixteen, and still he hated being reminded of the accident and its impact on Max. And three, Evie really didn't seem like just his younger sister's best friend any more.

Their pact from the other night popped into his head again and he wondered briefly what they'd both be doing on Evie's thirtieth and whether they'd still see each other much by then.

Chapter Four

NOW – CHRISTMAS EVE 2021

DAN

Dan stared at himself in one of the twin heart-shaped mirrors above the twin heart-shaped basins in the pinkest bathroom he'd ever been in.

God.

God.

He turned the, yes, heart-shaped tap on and splashed cold water onto his face.

Didn't help.

He put his head down under the tap. Still didn't help.

He lifted his head and shook water out of his eyes.

This was a very, very bad morning after.

He and Evie had definitely got married last night. *Married*, for God's sake.

What a nightmare. Despite some phenomenal hangover brain-fog, he could still see that unravelling even a one-night marriage would involve a lot of hassle.

Also: sex. He'd had sex with Evie. And it had been amazing. Like he'd always known it would be.

But Evie was Sasha's best friend. He and Evie were friends too. They'd had moments, but nothing physical had happened between them since that kiss years ago when they'd made their stupid pact, which had led to where they were this morning.

It wasn't a good idea to sleep with your friends, especially a friend who you *really* liked and whose friendship you didn't want to lose. He couldn't see himself sustaining a serious relationship, even with someone as amazing as Evie; he messed up too often. He'd definitely rather stay single than end up like his parents several years down the line, with all the hurt that entailed. He didn't want Evie to get hurt and he didn't want to get hurt himself and he didn't want to jeopardise his friendship with her any further, so it was a no-brainer. Nothing more should happen between them.

Actually, he was probably flattering himself. Evie probably wouldn't be interested anyway.

He shook his head again. Quite painful. He could do with a couple of paracetamol.

Right. So. He and Evie needed to get an annulment or a divorce. And maybe then pretend that this had never happened. Should they talk about it first? Hard to know, because he didn't normally sleep with old friends who he really liked.

It felt like this was the culmination of years of attraction and it felt a lot bigger than your average one-night stand.

He splashed more water on his face.

Oh, shit. It was Evie's *birthday* today. Her *thirtieth* birthday. Not a great day for it given that she was going to be seriously hungover and clearly full of regret. She hadn't looked at all happy just now.

He really wished he'd said no to Sasha's offer of joining them on this trip. At least he was only here for another couple of days because the friend he'd replaced had had to get back for work earlier than everyone else. It felt like it was going to be a long couple of days, though.

Okay. He needed to do something. Have his shower. Get dressed. Leave the room so that Evie could get dressed. The longer he just stood here, thinking, the longer she'd be waiting out there.

Okay. Quick shower.

The (heart-shaped) shower was good. Powerful and hot. Until he was just about to get out and the water turned tepid. He turned the temperature knob as high as he could. Didn't help. The water was getting colder.

Bloody *hell*. He hoped Evie wasn't going to have to have a cold shower.

He dried himself fast, with one of the pink towels hanging on the refreshingly non-heart-shaped – just your bog-standard rectangular ladder-shaped – towel rail, and started to sort through his clothes. Jeans. Shirt. Socks. Jacket. No boxers. Jeans. Shirt. Socks. Jacket. Definitely no boxers.

Two choices. Go back out into the room wrapped in his towel and hunt around for his pants while Evie lay in the bed, if that's what she was still doing. Or go commando.

Commando it was.

He'd literally never worn jeans without boxers before, and it wasn't that comfortable. It was nothing compared to his mounting headache, though, and *really* nothing compared to the cock-up of currently being *married*.

He ran his tongue around his mouth over his teeth – it wasn't great not being able to brush your teeth, although, again, that was a tiny issue compared to everything else – and put his hand on the doorknob.

He should knock. Let Evie know he was leaving the bathroom.

He knocked hard a couple of times, and then again, and heard Evie say, 'Um, come out?'

He opened the door and saw that she was lying where he'd left her, straight as a rod in the bed, on her back, with the sheets pulled up to her chin and tucked in. Her lovely corkscrew curls were spread out on the Pepto-Bismol-coloured pillow and her beautiful dark-brown eyes looked huge in her unsmiling face. No sign of her dimple this morning.

'Morning again,' he said, aiming for cheery, but pretty sure that he'd landed on over-friendly-children's-TV-presenter mode. When you'd essentially had a thing for someone for years and then finally slept with them, and it had been out of this world, but you didn't want a repeat of it, and you weren't sure how the other person felt, it was really bloody awkward. 'I'm so sorry but I'm worried that I used all the hot water. You might end up having a cold shower. Or it might be re-heating now. Maybe they have an immersion heater-type system. You never know.'

'Never mind,' said Evie. 'Thanks for letting me know.' Yeah, she probably didn't want to chat about hot water. Her voice sounded a lot thinner than usual and she wasn't totally meeting his eye.

'So I'll get going then. I'll probably see you later.' Well, of course he would unless he avoided everyone for the rest of his stay. 'I'll find out about the annulment or divorce today. Probably easy to get it sorted out on the grounds of extreme drunkenness. Hopefully.'

'Yep. Great. Thank you.' No smile. This was horrible. Maybe he should try to make a joke out of it.

'I think we took "having the full Vegas experience" a little too far. And the fallback pact thing,' he said. 'What a pair of muppets.'

'Yep.' Evie wasn't raising a smile. Maybe it was too soon to laugh about it. Maybe she was regretting the sex and not just the marriage.

Maybe she hadn't *enjoyed* the sex. Maybe she'd never liked him as much as he liked her.

Probably better if he didn't stay and look for his boxers now, on balance.

'Okay, so I'll see you later.' He opened the door to the room and said, 'Happy birthday,' as he went out, and then immediately regretted it.

The cold air that hit him when he got outside the hotel helped his head at least.

He pulled his phone out to google the annulment question. Maybe he should also try to change his flight home, pretend there was a work emergency; maybe that would be the best thing for both him and Evie. Give them both a bit of space and then they could hopefully laugh this off next time they saw each other with Sasha or in Melting.

Ten minutes on his phone told him a few things:

A *lot* of people knew about the wedding because they'd taken some photos of themselves and posted them on Facebook. It was going to take a long time to wade through all the congratulations and set everyone straight. He'd better do it this morning – clearly it was a the-sooner-the-better matter.

It looked like if you got married in Nevada there was a fair chance you could get your marriage annulled if you stated that you were suffering at the time of the wedding from a 'want of understanding', which included being intoxicated. If not, it'd be the divorce route. Whichever, they were going to have to appoint an attorney and sign some forms together and fork out way more cash than you'd normally spend on even a seriously big night out.

And he wasn't going to be able to change his flight at all given that he didn't have tens of thousands of dollars to spare for a first-class Christmas Eve flight. Well, now he thought about it, that was probably for the best. In fact, it definitely was. What had he been thinking? Evie would probably have felt mortified if he'd just scarpered. Far better to stay here and laugh the whole thing off with her as soon as possible. And he was going home on Boxing Day anyway. Only forty-eight hours to go.

Chapter Five

NOW – CHRISTMAS EVE 2021

EVIE

The water was so cold. *So bloody cold.* Evie was going to freeze to death. *Why* had she on autopilot shampooed her hair? *Why*? And why had the water gone so quickly from manageable to tepid to painfully freezing just after she'd rubbed all the shampoo in?

Her headache was getting better, though. Maybe she should tell Dan about this. No need for paracetamol, just take a freezing shower.

Dan. Gaaah. It was going to be so embarrassing seeing him later. Sleeping with someone you'd known and liked for so many years was completely different from sleeping with someone you'd met recently.

So embarrassing, especially given how extremely vocal she remembered having been last night about how much she was enjoying things. She was pretty sure she was blushing just thinking about it. To be fair, he'd been pretty vocal too, even if he hadn't seemed that happy this morning.

She took the hand-held shower attachment off the wall and turned her head upside down to wash the shampoo out of the underneath of her hair.

Ow, ow, ow, freezing. It was like the water was stabbing her. Why had she even had a shower here, actually? It was because Dan had mentioned it, so she'd just hopped in. She was too suggestible. She should have just dragged her clothes on and gone back to her actual hotel where all her stuff was.

She screeched as the water got even colder, if that were possible. So unpleasant. Not as unpleasant as her thoughts, though.

She was basically Rachel from *Friends*. She was thirty today and she had a broken engagement and a failed one-night marriage under her belt. How. Bloody. Ridiculous.

And, again, embarrassing. How was she going to face Dan later? She kind of wanted to just jump on a plane and escape home today. No, she was being ridiculous. She and the others had all saved up for this trip for over a year, and she couldn't leave. And this had just been a one-night stand – only with a marriage thrown in. And the fact that it had been with her best friend's brother, who was her long-term crush. But no-one knew that. It would be fine. They'd be a bit red-faced around each other briefly and then that would be that; they'd move on and Evie would accept that *clearly* they'd never really been going to come good on their fallback pact.

Right. It was too cold to carry on washing shampoo out of her hair. She was going to leave it, towel it dry as it was, walk-of-shame herself back to her hotel and have a nice hot shower there.

Last night's clothes back on, she folded the velour bedspread that Dan had wrapped himself in this morning into four and placed it at the bottom of the bed. The staff were obviously going to strip the bed, but she could never actually bring herself to leave a hotel room anything other than tidy.

There was something on the floor half under the bed. She bent down to pick it up. Dan's boxers. Black, stretchy trunks, which she remembered had fitted him *very* well. They were nice ones, Calvin Kleins, but no way was she going to give them back to him. That would be one step too far on the rising-above-their-one-night-stand thing. She took them into the bathroom and binned them.

Right. Time to go.

Except – disaster – she had no idea how to get back to her own hotel. No. It was fine. She could Google-Map it.

She opened the clutch that she'd brought with her and took her phone out.

It was stone-cold dead.

Okay, not a problem. They'd be able to give her directions at the hotel reception downstairs.

'Yeah, we can't help with directions. Where's your new *husband*?' Susan looked around the hotel foyer like Dan might be hiding behind one of the large pot plants, or the cardboard Elvis.

'Not really my husband. Just a drunken joke.' Evie winced as she said it, even to a woman who she'd only met briefly last night and who she would never see again. And who was *mean*.

Susan shook her head sorrowfully. 'You seemed great together,' she said. 'I thought you were one of the for-real couples. Anyway, yeah, I can't help you. I'm very busy.' She picked up an emery board and started filing her nails. 'I can offer you a charger so you can use your phone. Five dollars for fifteen minutes.' She pointed her nail file in the direction of a charger hanging out of the wall beyond the desk.

'Right. Thank you,' Evie said, actually mildly impressed at Susan's hard-nosed business instincts. To be fair, right now she'd have paid a lot more than five dollars to get her phone working.

Evie plugged the phone in and sat down on the floor next to it, put her arms round her knees and closed her eyes. The positive physical effects of her cold shower had worn off. Now she felt sick, headachy and tired, and really miserable, and she just wanted *so* much to be back in her own hotel room.

Gaaah. Her alarm was going off. No, it wasn't her alarm, but it was definitely her phone making that noise. Oh, okay, she'd nodded off and, now that the phone was slightly charged, about a billion messages and calls had pinged through. Probably birthday messages. She wasn't going to read them right now. She was too hungover and shellshocked about last night to have the capacity to send lots of *Thank you* replies at the moment.

'Your phone charged enough yet? You gonna call your husband? Try to patch things up?' Susan's cackle was *loud*.

Evie rolled her eyes, which hurt her head, and typed her hotel's name into Google Maps, which told her that it was only a fifteen-minute walk from here. Yesssss.

It was the most immense relief to get back to her actual room in her actual hotel. Evie put the 'Do Not Disturb' sign on the handle outside *and* double-locked the door, put her phone – still without having read any of her messages – on her charger and then sank down into the room's armchair.

Before another shower, she could really do with a lot of coffee and a lot of water and some breakfast. There was a menu on the bedside table and, yes, thank goodness, they did room service at any time of day.

While she was on the phone to Reception asking for an all-day pastry breakfast, her phone carried on pinging periodically. She couldn't remember a time when she'd received so many messages. Thirty was obviously a big milestone age, but she didn't actually know hundreds of people. Were her friends sending multiple messages or was it possible that they'd got wind of what she and Dan had done last night?

Okay. Deep breath. She was going to find out.

She opened up her messages. There were literally hundreds. Yeah, a lot of them were of the 'OMG you got MARRIED' and 'Details NOW please' variety. People had found out from the photos that she and Dan had apparently posted on social media. Eek. She'd better check them.

Oh no. No, no, no, no, no. They'd posted a *lot* of photos including selfies.

Oh *God*. They'd posted *semi-naked* photos.

Evie closed her eyes and leaned back in the chair as a wave of nausea washed over her.

When her stomach had settled, she opened her eyes and took another look.

Wow. She and Dan had been *active* on social media last night. They'd slapped 'Married tonight' stuff all over Facebook and Instagram. Everyone, literally *everyone* that Evie could think of, had seen, loved and commented on the posts.

Some of the photos featured Dan looking devour-me-now sexy in only his jeans with no top. He did have a very nice six-pack. Some of the photos featured Evie sprawled across the bed with the skirt of her dress up *high* – not quite showing her pants, thank goodness – and her neckline down *low* – showing her bra – and looking like she was about to have sex. And some of the photos – oh *God* – showed the two of them in various poses, apparently at various stages of the night. There were photos of their bare legs tangled together. There were photos of them with their heads very close together with both of them with bare shoulders. There were photos of them kissing.

They'd also carefully photographed their marriage certificate and posted it.

The one positive thing about the photos – and given how trigger-happy they'd been on the posting-suggestive-photos front, it was clearly a genuine win – was that none of them were actually pornographic.

The other positive thing was that neither of their mums were on social media.

Dan had already, thank goodness, been back on this morning and had slapped a lot more posts on, all basically saying *Joke, ha ha*. Evie posted some *Joke* messages of her own. Then she messaged Sasha and their schoolfriends Anita, Tola and Millie, who they were on this thirtieth-birthday mega-trip with, telling them she was totally fine but wasn't going to manage to meet them for sightseeing this morning because she was too hungover but would see them at lunchtime. Then she googled how to get a divorce in Vegas. Yep, totally doable but a lot of hassle and quite expensive.

Bloody hell.

Once she had an almond and raisin croissant, a pain au chocolat, two cups of coffee and some painkillers inside her, Evie spent a very long time in the shower, and then a lot more time drying her hair and doing her make-up. It felt like she needed to look as good as she could manage for facing Dan and the world today. Dan, mainly, actually.

Obviously pretty much anyone in her position would be feeling embarrassed. But they wouldn't necessarily be feeling like someone had taken their heart out, screwed it up and stamped on it, and then put it back in slightly the wrong place.

The thing was, though, when you'd slept with someone who you'd had a big thing for, since basically forever, and it had been amazing, but obviously a one-off, it felt like it might take a bit longer than it ought to to get over it.

And in the meantime, you wanted to avoid them, or look good for them if you did have to see them.

'Happy birthday!' Sasha swept Evie into a huge hug as she arrived in the hotel foyer to meet the rest of their group of friends for lunch, and whispered in her ear, 'Are you okay?'

'Thank you,' Evie said, as chirpily as she could. She returned Sasha's hug and whispered back, 'Yes, totally fine.' Utterly ridiculous that her eyes were pricking in reaction to Sasha's concern.

'So Angus, Dan and Rav are playing golf all day while we're at the spa,' Sasha said as they walked over to join Anita, Millie and Tola. Angus was Sasha's truly lovely boyfriend – they were both vets, working in the same practice, and had been going out for years now – and Rav was Anita's husband. They'd being planning this trip for a good year and a half to celebrate all their thirtieth birthdays happening over the next few months. Another schoolfriend had been coming but had unfortunately broken her leg last week and Sasha had persuaded Dan to join them instead because they couldn't get a refund.

'That sounds nice,' Evie said. And a great relief, frankly. This evening, they'd booked to go to the Fremont Street Light Show in Vegas's downtown, which hopefully would distract them all and mean that she and Dan wouldn't end up having to talk to each other at all today. Evie felt like she needed a bit of time to process what had happened, and she didn't want her first post-sex proper chat with Dan to be in front of all the others.

'Happy birthday,' chorused Anita, Millie and Tola.

'Good *night* last night?' Tola asked as they all piled in for birthday hugs.

'Thank you. Yes, thanks. I mean, you know, too much to drink.' Evie emerged from the hug and stood back and looked at the others. When you'd known people for a good twenty years, you knew when they had stuff they wanted to say. Especially Millie. She always looked as though her cheeks were going to burst when she was trying to be tactful. Her cheeks were so full-looking. 'So I'm quite hungover today,' Evie said. 'But I'm powering on through with coffee, carbs and painkillers.'

'You have to tell us everything,' Millie said, having clearly given up on tact. 'About Dan, not your hangover.'

'Nothing to tell.' Evie went for a nothing-to-see-here shrug. 'I mean, beyond what we posted on Facebook. We got married for a joke and now we need to get divorced. That's it.'

'How was the sex?' Tola said, waggling her eyebrows.

'Noooo.' Sasha put her hands over her ears. 'One, Evie never really wants to talk about sex and it's her birthday so we should leave her alone, and two, Dan's my *brother* and I do *not* want to know. *Please* don't tell us, Evie.'

'There's hardly anything to tell and you're right, I *really* don't want to. I mean, I can't even remember most of it because we were so drunk,' Evie lied.

'Okay, great,' Sasha said. 'So no more Evie-and-Dan chat then.'

The other three nodded, with some eye rolling.

It would probably be best to stick to Sasha like glue for the rest of their stay so that the others wouldn't ask her anything else. Evie was *never* going to want to talk about last night. Because it was Dan.

Against all the odds, she really enjoyed their afternoon getting massages and pedicures together. She did stick glue-like to Sasha, and through a *lot* of gossip none of the others mentioned Dan more than about five times each. Evie ignored them every time and Millie continued to look as though her cheeks were going to burst.

Evie had a lot more messages on her phone when she checked it again as they left the spa. One of them was from Dan saying maybe they should have a quick chat about getting an annulment or a divorce. And happy birthday again. Evie was so physically relaxed after her last massage that she just kind of thought, *Yep*, when she read his message.

*

Evie was the last down to meet the others in the hotel foyer in the evening because she'd been on the phone to her mum for a long time – it had taken ages to move the conversation on from the *OMG you did WHAT* exclamations about the Vegas marriage thing – plus she had to re-do her make-up because she was seeing Dan this evening. And it was actually always better to arrive last to a tricky group situation, so that you could choose who to stand with.

She stepped out of the lift and immediately saw Dan on the other side of the foyer, waiting with all the others. Either he was much more noticeable than every other person around, or she had some serious Dan-radar going. She also had serious butterflies going, the ones she always got when she saw him for the first time after a while, except now massively magnified by the memory of last night.

She smoothed her jumper down and, pretending to have her attention drawn by the extravagantly decorated Christmas tree next to the reception desk, started to walk towards the others. The tree's baubles were genuinely very striking, if not tasteful, in various neon shades. It wasn't that hard to find it interesting.

Aaargh. Her heel caught in something and she went flying.

Dan, Rav and Anita all dived forwards at once to catch her, so they ended up in an awkward four-way hug. And, weirdly, it was like she knew, without looking, that Dan was the person holding her arm and waist.

'Thank you,' she said, moving towards Anita and away from Dan. 'Don't know what happened there.'

'I think you were stunned by the tree,' Anita said.

'Yeah, or still ridiculously hungover,' Sasha said. 'Come on. I think our taxis are here and the light show starts in half an hour. Happy birthday again, lovely Evie.' She put her arm round Evie's waist and gave her a squeeze.

Evie managed to manoeuvre herself into a taxi with Sasha, Angus and Millie, definitely helped by some similar manoeuvring in the opposite direction from Dan, and they were on Fremont Street about ten minutes later.

The light show was amazing, actually, and Evie would have been completely absorbed by it if she hadn't spent the whole time being far too aware of Dan, standing on the opposite edge of their little group.

They took taxis back in the same two groups as before, and got back to the hotel just before eight thirty, in time for the table they had booked in the hotel's restaurant.

'Your birthday dinner,' said Sasha as they got out of the cab. 'We have to have something sparkly.'

Evie's stomach rolled. There was no way she was drinking this evening. Hair of the dog never worked for her.

The others' cab pulled up next to them and Tola, Anita, Rav and Dan spilled out. And Evie's stomach rolled some more, but this time because her entire mind and all her senses seemed suddenly to be filled with Dan again.

Right. Enough was enough. It was her *birthday*. She didn't need this torture. What she needed was a little break from Dan and the others this evening and a lot of sleep, so that she could pull herself together and get over last night. She was going to pull a social sickie.

'Last night was my real birthday dinner, and I'm feeling *rough*,' she told the others. 'Turns out thirty's too old for getting really plastered. I think I need to go and crawl into bed and watch TV with a room service sandwich, and then sleep for a very long time. As a little birthday present to myself.'

'You can't do that on your *birthday*,' several of the others said at once.

'I really can.' Now she'd thought of it, Evie *really* wanted to do it. She held her arms out to hug her friends goodnight. 'I'll see you in the morning for Christmas Day and Secret Santa. Don't eat and drink too much tonight. Make sure you save space for your Christmas lunch tomorrow.' She gave Tola and Millie, the two nearest to her, a final squeeze, and started a purposeful walk towards the lift, watching where her feet went this time.

Up the escalator and inside her room, with the Do Not Disturb sign on and the door double-locked for the second time that day, she sank into her armchair and put her head in her hands.

Her phone rang about ten seconds later. It was Dan. She stared at the screen for a second and then swiped. She was going to have to talk to him at some point.

'Hi,' he said. 'I've left the others to it as well. Do you have time for a quick chat about next steps now? I totally understand if not, obviously.'

Evie looked longingly at her bed and the TV and thought about the awkwardness of talking to Dan. It would probably be better to get the chat out of the way, though, to get things back to normal.

'Yep, great,' she said. 'Want to come to my room? Number one-thirty.' They didn't need to have this talk in the bar and risk the others joining them.

'Cool, thanks. There in a couple of minutes.'

Evie sprinted into her en suite, re-did her hair and finished applying more lipstick just as there was a knock on her door.

'Evening again,' she said as she opened it. Dan's eyes went straight to her lips. *So* stupid of her to have put more lipstick on for him. He'd clearly *noticed*. Maybe she should mention it. No, she'd sound ridiculous. 'Drink?' she said. 'From the minibar?' *Drink?* She'd actually just suggested that they drink alcohol again. In a room just the two of them. When she'd clearly just reapplied her lipstick. And he was looking jump-me-now gorgeous and all she could think of was how much she'd *like* to jump him now. 'Or tea or coffee?'

'A coffee would be great, thanks.'

'White, three sugars?'

'Nope. I've gone on a health drive recently. Only two sugars.'

'Ha.' Evie filled the kettle and switched it on.

'That's a really loud kettle,' Dan said.

'Yeah.' They stood in silence for a moment and then Evie said, 'Why don't you sit on the chair? I'll take the bed.'

When she'd made Dan's coffee and a tea for herself, she sat down on the edge of the bed and said, 'So I was going to google how to get divorced this evening. *Really* not how I imagined spending my thirtieth.'

'No. We were supposed to be on our honeymoon this evening after coming good on our fallback pact.'

'Exactly.' Evie *loved* how expressive Dan's eyes were. And mild jokes were clearly the way forward here. 'And then have our two point five kids,' she said, and then gasped. 'Oh my God.' What if she'd got *pregnant* last night?

'No, I think it's okay. I mean, I'm sure it is. We were definitely careful.'

Evie thought back and hoped she wasn't blushing. 'Yup,' she said. 'Pity we couldn't have been a bit more careful when it came to avoiding wedding chapels.'

'Yeah.' Dan nodded.

'Bloody Susan,' Evie said.

'Yeah.'

And then they stared at each other for ages and then Evie sniggered and then Dan did and then they both properly laughed until Dan was leaning back in the armchair snorting and holding his sides and Evie was lying on her side on the bed gasping and honking.

Eventually they were both sitting up straight again, and Dan said, 'If I'm honest, that's not normally the effect I'm hoping for when I sleep with someone.'

Evie looked at him and smiled, but not a lot. That didn't seem so funny, actually. Right now she didn't want to think of Dan sleeping with other people, or the fact that it didn't seem like the two of them would sleep together ever again.

'Yeah, too soon for jokes,' Dan said. 'Sorry.'

'No, don't say sorry.' Evie picked her cup up from her bedside table. 'My tea's gone cold. I'm going to make more for both of us. Have you managed to do any divorce googling yet? I did a little bit this morning but nothing concrete because my head hurt.'

'Yep, same. I've done a bit. What I've gleaned so far is that an annulment would be better than a divorce because then legally it would be like the marriage never happened, and that you can get an annulment based on being completely off your faces but you have to have evidence. And the sooner we do it the better. And I think we'll need to pay an attorney because there are a lot of forms. But I think it'll be okay. Although quite expensive.'

'Yes, that's what I thought too. So annoying,' Evie said, stirring their milk in. 'Why couldn't we have just stolen a couple of road signs or something? Why did we have to get *married*?'

'I know.'

She handed him his new coffee and sat back down on the bed. 'So maybe we should both do a bit more googling and come up with a shortlist of attorneys and check them out and then approach the best one. I'm pretty sure it'll be okay to do it once we're both back in London and we won't need to stay on longer here.'

'Good plan.' Dan took a sip of coffee and shook his head. 'Not enough sugar. What kind of a wife are you?' He looked up at her and said, 'Still too soon for jokes?'

Evie rolled her eyes. 'I'm a great wife. I'm trying to stop your teeth falling out. Want to spend ten minutes googling now so that we have a plan? And then we can try calling them on Monday?'

Ten minutes later they had a shortlist and their plan. Dan drank the last bit of his coffee and stood up.

'So, good,' he said, 'I think it'll be okay. Just a very expensive and admin-heavy experience. Maybe not one to repeat in a hurry.' He moved over to the door. 'Happy birthday again. Goodnight.'

'Night.' Evie waited for him to close the door behind him before doing an enormous sniff to try to get rid of the tears that had suddenly formed. She really shouldn't feel sad now, or bereft that Dan had left.

This was going to be fine.

She was totally going to get over last night; she just needed a little bit of space to process it, that was all.

Chapter Six

NOW – CHRISTMAS DAY 2021

DAN

At lunchtime the next day – Christmas Day – Dan dodged a couple of waitresses in – surely very demeaning – skimpy elf outfits, rounded a pillar covered in mini Santas climbing tinsel, and scoured the hotel dining room for the others.

They were all, including Evie, who was looking stunning in a sparkly green jumper, already sitting at a circular table on the far side of the room. Evie was directly opposite the one remaining empty chair, which was ideal because the table was big so they wouldn't be able to talk much. His night with her had felt like a much bigger deal than your average one-night stand, and he'd enjoyed her company yesterday evening way too much for comfort. He didn't really want to spend too much time with her again until things felt back to normal.

'Happy Christmas,' everyone chorused as Dan sat down. He'd opted for a lie-in and a swim this morning so this was the first time he'd seen any of the others today.

'We're thinking lunch now, obviously,' Sasha told him, 'and then Secret Santas in the lounge with coffees, and then a slow walk to work off some of the food.'

'Great plan,' Dan said. And he was going home tomorrow, and then next time he saw Evie they'd be divorced and have almost forgotten about this and be completely back to normal with each other. And why did that thought cause him a little twinge of misery? It would be *great* to have forgotten about it. He'd moved on very easily from his last relationship, with a woman called Hannah who he'd gone out with for a few weeks in the autumn. A one-night thing was nothing. Not a relationship at all. Although it didn't feel like nothing.

An hour and a half later, they'd all agreed that Vegas could definitely do a good Christmas turkey and that they were far too full to have pudding yet.

'Crackers and joke-reading?' said Angus.

'We're joke-reading?' Dan said.

'*Yes*, we're joke-reading.' Angus was looking at Dan like he'd grown two heads. 'You have to treat Christmas crackers with respect or it isn't a proper Christmas.' Yeah, so Christmas lunch was probably a lot more relaxed and a lot less fraught in Angus's family. The Marshalls had learned young that their father wasn't that tolerant of weak jokes. 'I hope you aren't a cracker philistine, Sasha. I want us to do Christmas properly when we're married.' They all whipped their heads round to stare at Angus and he went bright red. 'Sash, could I just have a word with you outside?' Wow. It seemed like Angus had tripped himself into a surprise proposal right in the middle of Christmas lunch.

'Oh-kay.' Sasha mouthed *OMG* behind Angus's back as she stood up.

All the rest of them turned to watch Sasha and Angus make their way across the room, and then they all turned back to each other, with varying degrees of wide eyes and slack jaws.

No-one spoke for a couple of beats and then Evie said to the whole table, 'So what are everyone's New Year plans?'

'Well, *maybe* celebrating Sasha and Angus's engagement,' said Millie.

Evie shook her head. 'I don't think we should talk about that,' she said. 'Just in case one or both of them comes back in here upset.'

Dan suddenly worried that might have a broader meaning, so he picked up his cracker and inspected it.

'If anyone would like to join us,' Evie persisted, 'Sasha and I will be in the pub in the village on New Year's Eve.'

'And Angus too, I'm guessing,' Millie said.

'I'm not sure about this year but I often work on New Year's Eve,' Dan said. 'It's a busy night for us.' You could always turn a conversation with a few medical anecdotes, and Evie was right; they shouldn't gossip about what Sasha and Angus might be doing. He really hoped that Angus *was* proposing and Sasha was accepting, because Angus was loyal and decent and they blatantly adored each other, and if anyone could make each other happy, it was those two.

He was busy fielding questions from Millie about cosmetic surgery and, specifically, boob jobs, and genuinely worried that she was about to lift her top and invite some very personal advice, when Sasha and Angus came back into the restaurant, holding hands.

'We're engaged,' Sasha started squealing from about halfway across the room.

Through the, frankly, insane restaurant-wide congratulations and ring-viewing that followed, Dan focused all his attention on his sister and her new fiancé – again, wow, his younger sister was getting married, to a very nice man – and carefully avoided looking at Evie, in case she was finding the group chat about weddings anywhere near as awkward as Dan, ridiculously, was.

Angus was just finishing explaining how he'd been planning to propose during the trip, maybe later today, just not during Christmas-cracker-pulling or in front of an audience, so he'd handily had the ring in his pocket, when one of the waiters hurried over and pressed a card into Angus's hand. 'You get engaged in Vegas, you gotta get married in Vegas. This is the best wedding chapel in town. Run by my sister.'

'Is that the one you two got married at?' Millie raised her eyebrows and looked from Dan to Evie and back again.

Neither Dan nor Evie replied.

Why had Sasha and Evie been friends with Millie for so many years? She was really annoying.

'Oh, wow. When did you two get married? Which chapel was it?' the waiter said.

Dan took a sideways glance at Evie. She was rolling her eyes and shaking her head and laughing a little.

'Um,' he said.

'They aren't really married,' Sasha said. 'It was a joke. *We*, however, *are* getting married. In England, in the Cotswolds. *Anyway*, everyone, we all need to *look at my ring* again.'

The congratulations and ring admiration were followed by the crackers.

'As the new Mrs Angus-to-be,' Sasha said, 'I'm going to be really strict about joke-telling. We're all going to take it in turns to read them, and we're going to do guessing and everything.'

'Steady on,' said Angus, smiling at her besottedly.

Evie was third up. 'I have a medical joke,' she said, holding her piece of paper up. 'Why did Santa's helper see the doctor?'

'Nope,' she said a couple of minutes later. 'You're all wrong. Wait for it. It was because he had low elf esteem. Ba boom.' Nice delivery.

You could see how she'd make a good teacher. She was smiling at everyone and there was that dimple again that Dan had first noticed all those years ago.

An hour later, they were all in the hotel lounge drinking house champagne to toast Sasha and Angus before doing their secret Santas. Sasha had told them that they had to spend as close to £20 as possible and that they had to buy proper presents, and had drawn them all out of a hat to decide who gave to whom. Dan had got Rav, who he'd only met a couple of times. After an initial total lack of inspiration, he'd bought him a pair of 3 kg dumb-bells for £21.

Following the cracker jokes, Sasha was going big on everyone taking turns, and no-one was going to contradict her. She was fairly bossy at the best of times, but when she was on a high from getting engaged, you'd be mad to mess with her if you didn't have to.

'Thanks, mate. Genuinely a good present,' Rav said when it was his turn.

'No problem,' Dan replied. 'I was pretty pleased with my brainwave until I realised that it'd take me over my baggage allowance for the flight. Had to leave my heaviest pair of shoes at home. I can take them back in my bag if you have the same issue. Best to go light on presents when you're travelling.'

'My present for Evie *is* light,' said Sasha, bringing out a fancily wrapped square, flat, soft present. Clearly clothing.

'It's gorgeous,' said Evie, beaming, when she'd unwrapped it and pulled out a cream scarf. 'Linen and silk. Hmm. Pretty sure you cheated on the price criterion.' Good present, actually. Now Dan thought about it, Evie wore a lot of scarves in different colours.

'Organiser's prerogative,' Sasha said. 'And I'm *engaged*. I can do *anything I like.*'

'You are so right,' said Evie. 'Engaged people can do literally anything. Thank you again, lovely Sasha.'

Dan was last on the present opening. His present was clearly going to be from Evie, because she was the only person left.

She stood up to hand it to him and then sat back down between Millie and Tola on their sofa.

'I'm going to apologise in advance,' she said. 'I was completely out of good present ideas. And every other secret Santa I've ever been involved in was at least partly a joke. So, yeah, I'm kind of sorry. But also not.'

'Can't wait to find out what's inside,' Dan said, raising his eyebrows.

Evie covered her face with her hands while he unwrapped. The paper was nice – gold Santas on a green background – and she'd wrapped it very neatly.

She'd bought him the *Home Alone* film collection and a pair of Christmas novelty socks. Not that controversial, surely.

'You said you'd never seen *Home Alone* that time you drove me from London to Melting,' she said, 'and DVDs of old films are very cheap nowadays, because no-one buys them, so I had money left over. So I bought the socks. They're very cool. You see the folded bit, like the cuff at the top. Lift it up.'

Dan lifted one of them and choked. '*Evie Green.* That's outrageous. And clever. That's some serious Santa sock pornography.'

'Did you say Santa sock or Santa sack, ooh-er?' Rav asked while Anita play-smacked him and Evie covered her face again.

'Thank you very much,' Dan told Evie. 'I'll watch the film and marvel that I've never seen it before, and I'll wear the socks with pride.'

Evie uncovered her face and smiled at him and Dan felt something inside him falter.

They all went for a stroll late afternoon, before their next eating fest, Dan careful to avoid walking next to Evie, because he didn't want any more strange feelings. He did the same over their evening buffet meal in the hotel restaurant.

'Christmas-engagement-last-night-of-your-stay cocktails in the bar,' pleaded Sasha as they finished dinner, waving her ring in his face again, when he said he was going to get an early night before his flight the next day.

Dan looked around the group. Everyone except Evie was watching him. Yep, he couldn't be a party pooper. Of course he couldn't. His sister had got engaged today.

'Sure,' he said.

Chapter Seven

NOW – CHRISTMAS DAY 2021

EVIE

At least Dan was going home tomorrow. Evie really didn't fancy spending any more time with him in the near future, especially not surrounded by other people who knew about the wedding. She wanted some time to – what was the word – recover, probably.

What was wrong with the two of them? Most people could manage to drink a few too many cocktails without getting married and posting dozens of TMI photos of themselves on social media. Anyway, at least he seemed to be as keen to avoid her as she was to avoid him. And that should not feel unbearably sad, because it wasn't like they were regular features of each other's daily lives.

'Great,' she said, and trooped with the others into the bar. She couldn't possibly not join drinks on the night Sasha had got engaged to lovely Angus.

'Jugs again, I'm thinking,' Sasha said. Angus whispered something in her ear and she giggled and said, 'Yep, not *too* much to drink. Let's get some water too.'

Evie did not enjoy the evening despite how happy she was for Sasha and Angus. She nursed one Screwdriver – not as nice as the cocktails they'd had the other night, especially the bright-green one – the entire time and tried not to watch Dan looking ruggedly handsome while he chatted to Millie and Tola at the opposite side of the table. She was pretty sure that Millie had a bit of a thing for him. She was making far too much – in Evie's opinion – OTT eye contact with him while she chatted. Obviously, Evie and Dan weren't together, but equally they were currently married and they'd had a very big night together and right now, if she was honest, she really wouldn't appreciate it if anything happened between him and anyone else.

It was actually a struggle not to glare at Millie when she practically batted her eyelashes at Dan when he excused himself to go to the loo, and not to beam when he sat himself down next to Rav and Anita on the opposite side of the group from Millie when he got back.

'Evie?' Sasha said. Evie jumped slightly and looked at her. She had a big, expectant-looking smile on her face, of the type where you felt like you just had to say a big 'Yes!' even when you had no idea what the person was talking about. Best not, though, or she could be saying that she'd milk a cow or go on a six-week belly-dancing course, both of which she'd done with Sasha in the past and regretted.

'I'm so sorry, I missed what you said.' Because she'd been obsessing over Sasha's brother.

'Will you be my bridesmaid?' Sasha said surprisingly quietly.

'Oh, wow.'

'Shhh.' Sasha eye-swivelled at the others and shook her head slightly.

'I'd be honoured,' Evie whispered.

'Thank you so much,' Sasha whispered back. 'I should have waited until we were alone but I really wanted to ask you immediately. We're going to have a lot of work to do. I want to get married *soon*. We're thinking a marquee in Mum's garden because then we won't have venue problems. Hopefully this summer at the latest. We need to start making plans as soon as we get home.'

'Wow again,' said Evie. 'So exciting. I can't wait to start the planning.' She pushed away a miserable thought about how Sasha's fairy tale 'meet your Prince Charming, fall in love, go out for a few years and then get ecstatically engaged' was light years from her own pathetic 'make a fallback pact with your secret crush, have a lot of other rubbish relationships and then get stupidly drunk and marry and divorce the secret crush on your thirtieth' history. This evening should be all about Sasha and Angus, not thoughts about Evie's pathetic, non-existent love life.

Eating and drinking huge amounts pretty much non-stop all day had taken its toll, and by ten o'clock they were all leaning back in their chairs, yawning and not talking that much. Evie wasn't sure who the first person to suggest bed was, but everyone leapt (slowly) at the idea.

They all heaved themselves to their feet, and wandered out of the bar, through the foyer and over to the lift lobby, where Dan did a lot of handshaking and air-kissing, saying that he might not see anyone before he left in the morning, because his flight was just after midday so he was going to be on his way early.

Dan got to Evie last. She was very aware of at least a couple of the others watching them with what felt like avid curiosity. And then she was only aware of Dan, standing quite close to her.

He gave her a small smile and said, 'So goodbye then. We'll speak soon about the…'

'Documents. Yep.' Evie was sure her voice didn't normally sound like that, but she felt very self-conscious having this weird goodbye in front of a little audience. She cleared her throat. 'Great. Yes.'

'Goodnight.' Dan leaned in very slightly in for an air-kiss with at least six inches between their cheeks.

'Night then,' Evie said.

The doors of one of the lifts pinged open at that point. Dan stood back and gestured for some of the others to go. Evie stepped in with Tola and Sasha and Angus. It felt like a much bigger effort than it should have done to maintain cheery small talk until she could leave them.

When she was finally inside her bedroom, she plonked herself face down on her bed and let the tears that she'd been holding in spill out. It shouldn't feel this miserable saying goodbye to Dan. Nothing that meaningful had actually happened between them. People had one-night stands all the time, and some of those people had them in Vegas and – if they were stupid – ended up briefly married.

Dan was Dan, though. He wasn't just anyone.

*

Evie decided to skip Boxing Day breakfast. She was still full from all the Christmas Day food plus she didn't fancy possibly bumping into Dan in the dining room. Each time she'd seen him yesterday she'd felt too emotional for comfort. It would be better not to be looking over her shoulder the whole time. Probably best to stay in her room until lunchtime and relax.

She got a text from him mid-morning saying he hoped she enjoyed the rest of the stay and he'd be in touch ASAP about the annulment, which made her feel tearful again, so she switched the TV on and found an episode of *Schitt's Creek* to watch.

By lunchtime, she was really bored and very pleased to be meeting the rest of the group. And, really, it was lovely for it to be calm and relaxed with no awkwardness around Dan, or being constantly aware of him. Yes, it felt a *tiny* bit flat, but overall it *was* lovely, especially with the ongoing excitement about Sasha and Angus. It was a little bit annoying that she kept wondering what Dan would say about things, but, really, it was way better without him.

'There's nothing actually going on between you and Dan, is there?' Millie asked over their pre-sightseeing salads.

Evie chewed her lettuce very thoroughly to give herself time to think of a good reply, and then ended up saying, 'No, nothing.'

'Great,' said Millie, with a suggestive pout.

Evie shoved some more lettuce in her mouth and chewed hard again. It felt like Millie had changed since they were at school, and not for the better.

*

'Evie, over here,' Sasha hollered across the main room of the Duck and Grapes, the pub in Melting Bishop, as Evie made her way across to her on New Year's Eve.

Evie said hello to everyone she recognised and tried hard to keep her attention on the people she was speaking to rather than combing the room with her eyes for any sight of Dan. She'd spent the whole week fantasising slightly – okay a lot – that maybe something might happen between them *sober*. Given that he'd been away for Christmas, there had to be a good chance that he'd come home for New Year to see his mum. He'd said he didn't know whether or not he'd be working. She'd been *so* tempted to ask Sasha whether or not he'd be there. It was actually really hard to decide whether or not she wanted to see him.

'Evening,' she said to Sasha when she'd finally made it over to where she was sitting with Angus and several local friends and Max. And not Dan. So maybe he wasn't coming. Or maybe he was late.

'I love your top,' Sasha said. 'Is it new?' It was new. Just in case she saw Dan. 'Should we look at my ring just one more time?' She waggled her engagement finger and Evie laughed. 'Oh, look, there's Millie.'

Millie, looking remarkably glammed up, was standing in the doorway.

'Hello,' she said when she got to their table. 'Thought I'd come after all.'

'Let me buy you a drink,' Angus said.

Millie sat herself down in his place next to Sasha, and said, 'So when's Dan coming?'

Really, Evie should be pleased that she'd asked that question, so that she could hear the answer too, rather than having an urge to slap her.

'He isn't,' Sasha said. 'He's working tonight. I think it's often a busy one in A&E and he had to swap shifts with someone apparently.'

'Right,' said Millie. She laced her fingers together and tapped her forefingers against each other a few times and then said, 'I'm not going to be able to stay long. I have a party in Cheltenham as well this evening.'

Angus put her glass of white wine down in front of her, and she said, 'Thank you so much.'

About three sips of her wine later, and while Evie was right in the middle of telling them about the Year Eight ski trip she was going on at February half-term, Millie stood up abruptly and said, 'So it's been great to see you. Happy New Year.' And off she went.

'She asked for a large glass,' said Evie, indignant on behalf of Angus and generally furious with Millie. 'She could have had a small one and saved you a good fiver.'

'It actually really annoys me that she's so blatantly got her eye on Dan,' Sasha said. 'I mean, I know you don't want to talk about it and

I know that what happened in Vegas was just a one-off and everything, but it still feels rude to you.'

'It really does.' Evie nodded, delighted that Sasha wanted to bitch about Millie, because she *really* wanted to.

'I don't think Dan's at all interested in her,' Sasha said.

'Yeah, no, I mean, it's just the principle. It doesn't actually matter to me at all,' Evie lied. It did matter, though. It was one thing him not having been in touch with her after their doorstep snog many years ago, but it would be another him dating one of her school friends right now. If she was honest, she wouldn't like to think of him dating anyone at the moment, even though there was no reason whatsoever that he shouldn't. They were both clearly free to do whatever they liked with whomever they liked.

Chapter Eight

THEN – DECEMBER 2014

EVIE

Evie locked her Renault Clio – nicely nestled in the last space in Cirencester's biggest car park – and beamed at the middle-aged man in the un-parked bottle green Jaguar who'd arrived literally minutes after she'd started waiting – with her indicator on – for this parking bay and had then tried to angry-gesture her into giving the space up to him.

She checked her watch. She was actually nearly half an hour early for brunch with Jed. She could go shopping but she didn't have any spare money so that was clearly a bad idea. She could go and sit in the café and wait for him and read. *Or*, she could go to his flat and surprise him and they could have a lovely hand-in-hand walk along the river together to get to the café.

That would be nice. It was maybe taking things slightly to the next level, just turning up unannounced at his flat, but it felt like things were getting serious between them. They'd been going out since the middle of September, just after Evie had started her job at the big comprehensive in Cirencester where he worked as a games teacher. Some Year Elevens had seen them together walking through a park a couple of weeks ago and had done the whole 'Ooh, Miss Green and

Mr Rafferty *holding hands*' thing and Jed had been cool about it; he'd just laughed. And he'd mentioned maybe going to the staff Christmas party together.

Jed's flat was on the ground floor of a Victorian house a little way out of the town centre. She could see from along the road that the curtains at the front were closed, so he must be having a slow start this morning.

When Evie got to the house, the main front door was open. She went in and knocked on the door of his flat.

He didn't come to the door immediately but he was definitely in there, because she could hear voices. He was probably watching TV in the sitting room, which his front door opened directly onto.

Eventually, he opened the door, wearing a dressing gown tied very haphazardly and showing a lot of bare chest.

'Evie!' he said, his voice a lot higher than usual, and pushed the door so that it wasn't so wide open, but not before she'd seen Laura Carter, one of the history teachers at school, on the other side of the room, wearing a large t-shirt over long – and gorgeous – bare legs and feet.

Evie reflexively pushed the door back towards him and stepped into the room.

'Morning, Laura,' she said. 'Morning, Jed.' Something was whooshing loudly in her ears and her eyes were filling and she had no idea what to say next.

Jed tightened the belt on his dressing gown and said, 'Evie, could you give us a moment?'

Give them a moment? Like *she*, his supposed girlfriend of nearly three months, was intruding? With the implication that she was being almost slightly rude? Piss *off*.

'I'll give you as long as you like.' Evie was pleased that she'd found her voice and, hopefully, her dignity, since her tears had receded. 'Just so you know, Laura, Jed slept with me, in his bed here, two nights ago. Jed, just so *you* know, you're a two-timing bastard.'

She turned round and marched herself back out into the hall, feeling slightly shaky with adrenalin. It took her three fumbles to get the main front door open but finally she was outside and had walked far enough along the road that Jed and Laura wouldn't be able to see her out of the sitting room's bay window if they were looking.

How unbelievably humiliating. God, how *stupid*, that, after Jed had mentioned the Christmas party date, she'd been on the brink of telling several other teachers that she and Jed were an item. Thank goodness the only person at school that she'd told was her friend Anita, who she'd known forever since they were at school themselves before they then ended up working in the same school.

What had he actually been planning for the Christmas party? How could he have gone with her if he was also sleeping with Laura? Maybe it was a one-off with Laura.

Now she thought about it, she and Jed hadn't actually been out anywhere within sight of anyone from school apart from bumping into those Year Elevens in the park. There'd been a couple of group evenings out and he'd made excuses not to go each time. Again, bastard.

Okay. She should stop wasting her life thinking about him *right now*. Although what else was she going to do with her morning? God. She was *so* stupid. She'd *really* liked him. Not *really* really. Not like *love* really. But he'd seemed like a good long-term prospect. He was good company and good-looking and he was a teacher. And he had a lovely, neat flat.

Hopefully it wasn't just neat because he'd always just cleared up after other women. Eurgh, if he'd done this before, she really hoped he'd changed his sheets in between.

It felt so bad to have been two-timed. And it was what so many men had done to her mum.

Evie stopped in the middle of the pavement and put her hands over her face.

What. An. Idiot.

She should have been a better judge of character.

Right. She wasn't going to waste her morning. She was going to call Anita and see if she was around for coffee, and moan to her about Jed.

Her phone pinged with a message from Jed while she was waiting for Anita. *No hard feelings? Jx*

No hard feelings? Was he insane? She had very hard feelings. Completely rigid feelings. She sent a reply saying *Piss off* and then deleted his number.

Which was clearly a pretty pathetic response from a spurned woman. She should probably have done something spectacular, like spray-paint his pride-and-joy kit car with something very sweary, or cut up all his designer trainers or, no, she couldn't even think of anything else. And painting a car and cutting up trainers weren't really spectacular; they were just petty. Better to have walked away with *some* pride intact.

Forty-five minutes later, Evie and Anita were in the coffee shop in Middle Bishop, the village where Anita lived, a couple of miles from Melting, and Anita was shaking her head for the umpteenth time and saying, also for the umpteenth time, 'Bastard.' She poured herself another cup of tea and forked up another big mouthful of coffee and walnut cake. 'I know it's only been an hour or two, but I feel that you're ready to move on to the next phase of your break-up.'

Evie wasn't so sure. 'What is that phase?'

'The phase where you hear gossip about Jed and realise that you've had a very lucky escape.'

Evie did want to hear any gossip going about Jed, although she still wasn't so sure that she was going to deal with it well. 'Hmm. What's the gossip?'

'He's been working his way through Humanities. Reliable rumour has it that he shagged Kaye Jones during the summer.' Kaye was an RS teacher. 'Which makes sense, because last year he slept with half of Languages. I'm going to be prepared if he moves on to Science next year.' Anita taught chemistry. She was doing her teaching degree on the job and had started working at the school a year before Evie, so she was Evie's go-to woman for gossip.

'You're engaged,' Evie said. 'You don't need to be prepared. Why didn't you *tell* me about all the others?'

'He was your new boyfriend and you seemed so loved up, I didn't want to upset you, and I hoped he'd turned over a new leaf.'

Evie nodded. Not upsetting her hadn't worked out, but fair enough. And, if she was honest, the worst thing about it all was feeling so *stupid*. Jed had seemed *perfect* on paper. The good news was that imagining him sleeping his way through half the female staff under fifty pissed her off more than it made her sad. The bad news was that she was *crap* at choosing the right man.

'You know what you need to do,' Anita said, still scoffing carrot and walnut cake. 'You need to turn up to the staff party with a *gorgeous* man. Someone from outside school.'

Evie shook her head. 'Nope. I need to avoid men for a bit. Regroup.' Why was it that Dan had popped into her head at the mention of a gorgeous man? Maybe it was the fact that she'd been massively humiliated this morning that had made her think of him. After they'd kissed last Christmas – and it hadn't been just any old kiss, it had been a big one, which could have led to a lot more if they hadn't been on her doorstep with Mrs Bird watching – he'd effectively run a mile; she hadn't seen him once since. Which was almost worse, really, because it sounded like Jed was just a bastard, who did this to lots of women, whereas Dan was not a bastard. He had just obviously wanted to make it very clear by avoiding her that the kiss had been an aberration.

Or maybe he'd just been very busy. Everyone knew that junior doctors were run off their feet. Maybe he hadn't regretted the kiss. Maybe something might happen this Christmas with him. Maybe at his parents' Christmas party again. Maybe it would turn out to be a blessing in disguise that she'd found out about Jed now. Seven years until their mistletoe pact deadline. You never knew.

'Evie? Are you alright?' Anita asked.

'Yep. Let's get some more coffee.'

*

A couple of weeks later, Evie was at Sasha's parents' Christmas party, sitting on a sofa, cuddling her new baby sister, when Dan – wearing a Christmas jumper and jeans – plonked himself down next to her.

'Hi, Dan,' she said, ridiculously pleased to see him. She actually had very sudden full-on butterflies. She hadn't seen him since The Kiss; she knew from Sasha that he was so busy with work that he'd only been home a couple of times during the year, both times just for the day. Good job she'd worn her new dress. 'How are you? Liking your jumper.'

'I'm good, thanks. I've come straight from work. The jumper was for the benefit of the kids. I'm working on a paediatric ward at the moment.' He jiggled Santa's eyebrows and ears, and Evie nodded, impressed. It was a *great* jumper. 'Way more to the point, how are you? I can't believe Sasha didn't tell me. There was no need for our pact, was there? You were worrying you wouldn't be in a relationship by the time you were thirty and now look at you. Congratulations. What's her name?'

'Her name is Autumn and she's my baby sister and I am *totally* going to need that pact. No way are you off the hook so lightly.' Even though Evie knew it was just banter, she felt a little thrill that he'd remembered.

'She's… Oh. Wow. Well, congratulations again. And I still can't believe no-one told me. Goes to show I've been far too busy this year. Autumn's a pretty name.'

'Yes, and not a surprise. My mum likes a name that tells everyone when you were born.'

'*Oh.* Is that why you're called Eve?'

'Yep.'

'And how did I never know that either? Well, wow again. Autumn's so cute. And very sound asleep. Where's your mum?'

'Dancing.' Evie indicated with her head. Dan followed her eyes towards where her mum was dancing with someone Evie didn't recognise at all, and then looked back at her, his eyebrows raised. 'Yep. Jack from your parents' party last year is Autumn's father but he basically scarpered within days of my mum doing her pregnancy test. And then he *really* scarpered. Changed jobs and everything so that he could move back to London. And keeps saying that he'd like to meet his daughter but hasn't got round to it.'

'Nice.'

'Yeah, but you know, Autumn *is* cute, and perfect and adorable, and my mum wouldn't have things any other way. And nor would I. I almost can't remember before Autumn was born.' Which was true, but if Evie had children herself, she was definitely going to be aiming for a conventional relationship first. It felt like it would be a lot easier, a lot calmer, a lot more ordered. For a start, how would her mum have managed without Evie around now? In fact, how *had* she managed when Evie was little?

'So how's she doing? Is she managing to carry on with her millinery around looking after Autumn? Are you living nearby now?'

'Yep. I'm teaching at a school in Cirencester, and I'm living at home with Mum and Autumn. Mum's fine for money because Husband Three was loaded, and she made a lot of extra hats while she was pregnant so she'd have a bit of leeway now, for Christmas, and she should be up and running in the new year before all the Cheltenham festival requests come in.'

'So is Autumn a good sleeper?'

'No. But luckily I'm a truly excellent sleeper so she hardly ever wakes me up.'

'Your mum's lucky to have you.'

'No.' Evie shook her head. 'I'm just as lucky to have her. And Autumn. Honestly, I'm loving our expanded family unit.' Although right at this moment she did have serious pins and needles in her arm. 'I've been looking after her all day as a little break for my mum and she's just a delight. I mean, hard work, but delightful.'

'Why don't I hold her while you dance? Or just go and chat to some other people? Give you a little break of your own?'

'That's so sweet of you, but I'm fine, honestly.' Now that Dan was here, he was really the only person in the room she'd like to dance with. 'It's quite nice sitting and watching the world go by.'

Dan grinned at her. 'Old before your time. Next thing you'll be saying you can't hear yourself speak and slippers are ever so warm and comfortable and that your neck's feeling a lot better now you've found the perfect pillow and from now on you're going to take it on holiday with you.'

'I *do* have the perfect pillow and I would *totally* take it on holiday with me if I weren't scared that I'd lose it.' Evie rubbed Autumn's back again in response to a gurgle but it was no good. Autumn lifted her head and yelled.

'Good lungs,' Dan said.

'Let me take my daughter.' Evie's mum had supersonic hearing when it came to Autumn; she could hear her cry from several hundred metres away, so a loud party was nothing. She reached down, picked Autumn up and started rocking. 'Hi, Dan. Why don't you two go and dance now?' She did a huge pantomime wink and eyebrow wiggle as Dan pulled Evie to her feet.

'Good job she doesn't know about our pact,' Evie said to Dan as they walked away from her mum. A joke was always the best way to deflect her mother's unsubtle attempts at setting her up with people. Although at least Dan was *nice*, unlike a lot of the men her mum chose for herself and tried to choose for Evie. Sometimes, Evie could really do with her mum having a more conventional love life.

'Hah,' Dan said. 'At least she'll have no problem finding a hat for the wedding.'

Evie felt a smile spread over her face as they walked towards a group of people near the fireplace. She loved Dan's company. She loved talking to him. She loved his sense of humour. And his kindness. And he was gorgeous in his own rugged way. Maybe something would happen between them tonight.

They reached the group and a tall, blonde and beautiful woman who Evie didn't recognise took Dan's hand.

Oh. *Oh.* They were quite clearly together.

Why hadn't Evie thought of this? Mortifying. Although at least no-one would ever know what she'd been hoping for this evening.

Dan turned to the woman he was holding hands with and said, 'Manda, this is Evie, Sasha's best friend; Evie, this is Manda.'

'Hi, Manda!' Evie realised immediately that that had not come out of her mouth the way she'd wanted it to. She'd been aiming for nonchalant but she'd just sounded peculiar. Manda was smiling and blinking her very long eyelashes a bit too much, like she thought Evie was a bit weird. What Evie needed to do now was sound completely natural, not like she was mentally kissing goodbye, with real sadness, her mythical marriage to Dan in seven years' time. And remembering their kiss last year and thinking with distaste of him kissing Manda. 'So where did you two meet?'

'Just at a party,' Dan said.

'Great,' Evie said. 'Well, I should go and say hi to a couple of friends over there who I haven't seen for a while. Good to meet you, Manda.' She fake-wide-smiled at them both. Bloody Manda did not return her smile.

'I don't like her,' Sasha said a few minutes later.

'Why not?'

'She's really unfriendly and kind of scornful. Not to sound incredibly judgemental about someone I've barely met. I don't know. I just get negative vibes from her.'

Evie nodded. She didn't like the look of Manda either, but she was pretty sure that she wouldn't have liked the look of any woman who was with Dan.

But, really, what did she expect? Dan was amazing. He was gorgeous, funny, kind and a doctor. He could have any woman. *Obviously* he'd never have more than a passing interest in Evie, at the most. God, she actually felt slightly tearful, and like she'd rather be anywhere but here. Frankly, she'd rather just go home and have a hot bath and get into bed with a good book. But this dress was dry-clean only, so she wasn't going home now. That would be a waste of at least a tenner's cleaning bill.

She was going to ignore Dan and Manda and have a good evening anyway.

Chapter Nine

THEN – DECEMBER 2014

DAN

Dan kept his arm round Manda's shoulders and tried hard not to watch Evie dancing. She looked amazing in her sparkly blue dress.

The last time he'd seen her they'd been doing some pretty intense – and pretty amazing – kissing on her front doorstep.

He'd thought about that night far too much afterwards, and then he'd managed to put it out of his mind, because Evie was absolutely not someone he should date but, now he was in the same room as her for the first time for a year, it was difficult not to remember again.

Manda turned to look at him. 'Shall we get out of here? Kind of boring?' she said.

Shit. He'd been standing next to Manda, thinking about Evie. Terrible behaviour, although clearly no-one could read his thoughts.

'I'd quite like to stay,' he said. 'There are a lot of people here I'd like to talk to. Old friends who I haven't seen for a while.' Other than his father. He'd happily avoid one-on-one father-son time.

'But what about me?' Manda pouted. And then her whole demeanour brightened and she smiled at someone beyond Dan. He turned to see who'd caught her eye.

It was his father. The man was strutting towards them, wearing a flirtatious smile and holding eye contact with Manda. Dan hadn't really thought before about his father's walk, but, yes, it was definitely a strut. Like a peacock.

He hadn't actually seen him for a whole year before today. He'd only been home a couple of times, both of them day trips to have lunch with his mother when he knew that his father was away. *Playing* away.

'I think it's my turn for a dance.' His father had reached them and was holding out his hand to Manda.

Manda took the hand, visibly flattered. For God's sake. Dan couldn't even be bothered to try to smile.

'Have fun,' he said. 'I'm going to go and find Mum.'

'She'll be in the kitchen,' his father said, 'fussing over mince pies or something.' That sounded very dismissive.

On his way to the kitchen, Dan passed Evie, chatting now, in a group. She looked lovely, her eyes sparkling and her hands gesticulating as she told a story. One of the men in the group definitely had his eye on her. Dan didn't really like the look of him if he was honest. Smarmy.

By the end of the evening, Dan had really had enough. Manda was alternating between obvious boredom and flirting with Dan's father, the 'silver fox', as she called him. His mother was being her usual kind and great-hostess self and clearly pretending that she couldn't see the flirting between her husband and her son's girlfriend. His father was just himself. His brother Max was himself too, and being around him nearly always made Dan stressed. He always felt so guilty remembering the accident and its aftermath. And Max was always open and friendly, which just made Dan feel even guiltier, like he was pushing him away. Which he was, really, but he couldn't help it.

His sisters were great, as always, but he couldn't talk to them properly without Manda blatantly trying to turn his attention away from them. Similarly, he wasn't able to chat to his friends unless Manda was being entertained by his father. And then there was Evie, looking stunning in that blue dress, surrounded by admirers, which made him feel more jealous than he'd care to admit. He suddenly desperately wanted to speak to her again.

When he saw that she, her mum and the baby were on their way to the front door, he inserted himself and Manda into a conversation with a group of his father's male friends, and then slipped away and positioned himself near the door.

As Evie and her mum were leaving the sitting room, Dan caught Evie's eye and smiled at her. She pressed her lips together for a moment and then began to smile back until her attention was caught by two men – both friends of Max's, Dan thought – who started chatting animatedly to her and her mother. There was a lot of laughter and then one of the men pointed at the mistletoe above them and next thing the man was planting a kiss on Evie's lips. Dan felt his own lips twist. He really did not want to see Evie kiss someone else. Which he had no right whatsoever to be thinking, especially given that he was here with Manda.

Evie glanced in Dan's direction, and he looked away quickly.

Evie, her mother and the two men walked slowly through the hall together, talking and laughing.

Dan really wanted to say goodbye to Evie at least. He busied himself with some other guests who were leaving while he waited for Evie's little group to be ready to go.

When they finally got to the door, Dan hugged and air-kissed Evie's mum very heartily, and then hugged and air-kissed Evie even more heartily.

'Happy birthday and happy Christmas,' he told her.

'Thank you.' She smiled. 'Happy Christmas.'

And that was it. Off they went.

As he said goodbye to some more people, he saw over their shoulders Evie and her mum begin the walk round the green, her mum carrying the baby, the two women's heads close together as though they were sharing anecdotes. Their laughter carried back to him on the night air. He loved that they had such a close relationship. He should spend more time with his own mother; he shouldn't let his feelings about his father keep him away so much. Maybe he shouldn't leave first thing tomorrow after all. He'd volunteered to work Christmas Day, to avoid his parents, and had unsurprisingly had his hand bitten off by his colleagues, but he could stick around for a few extra hours.

*

Dan snuck out of bed early the next morning, leaving Manda asleep, to go for a run. He found Max and his newish boyfriend Greggy in the kitchen, back from a run themselves.

He still, after all these years, hated seeing Max in running kit. He hated being reminded of the outstanding sportsman Max had been and the glittering future he'd missed out on. He hated seeing the scars on his legs and his limp. Because it was all Dan's fault. The guilt was crushing. Every time. Nearly ten years now.

It felt particularly harsh because Dan – broadly – loved his job, while Max was a sports physio, and realistically who wanted to be a physio *to* the stars when you should have been one of those stars yourself?

His heart twisted and he started backing out of the kitchen, and then Max said, 'Morning, stranger. Want some breakfast? Hardly ever see you now.'

Dammit.

He was clearly going to have to stay and chat.

'I'm about to go for a run myself,' Dan said, 'but a cup of coffee would be great if you're putting the kettle on.'

'I'm making my legendary pancakes,' Max said. 'Just one. With maybe a bit of sugar and lemon? Give it fifteen minutes to digest and you'll be good for your run?' Not really possible to say no without looking purposely unfriendly. Shocking, actually, that Dan had no real idea whether Max could cook or not.

'You've twisted my arm.' He pulled a chair out and sat down with Greggy at the table in the middle of the room.

'So where do you normally go for your runs when you're here?' Greggy asked. 'We just did a circular one via Little Bishop.'

'That's a great one,' Dan said. 'I hadn't decided. I was going to do either that one or one from the opposite end of the village past the church that follows the little stream and some more gentle hills. I was going to wait and see how I felt once I got going.'

'Not a lot of hills where you are in London?' Greggy smiled up at Max as Max put a pancake down in front of him, and Max ruffled Greggy's hair when he'd let go of the plate.

'Exactly. I live between Earl's Court and Fulham, which is very flat.'

'Great area, though.'

'Yeah, it is. My flat's a shoebox and it's above a very fragrant Indian restaurant, which is the only way I could afford to buy in the area, but I love it. And luckily I love curry, and theirs are all delicious.'

'We should come over and visit you some time. And you should come to us. We can tempt you with hills.' Greggy and Max had recently moved into a flat together near Alexandra Palace in North London. 'And Max's cooking of course.'

'Or a barbecue when it's a bit warmer. That's Greggy's speciality,' Max said, flipping the next pancake.

'That's a nice way of saying that I'm a rubbish cook in an actual kitchen,' Greggy said.

'Hey, probably better than me.' Dan stood up and took his plate over to Max. 'I seem to have fallen into the cliché junior-doctor-bad-diet trap recently.' Amazing how much less difficult it was talking to Max with Greggy around.

Half an hour later, he'd stayed chatting for a lot longer than he'd thought he would and had had three pancakes and had realised that he was going to have to postpone his run for another half hour or get some serious indigestion.

If he was honest, he was looking forward to Manda leaving later this morning to spend Christmas with her parents, and maybe he'd stay around after that for a while, spend some more time with his mother and siblings.

Greggy put another cup of coffee in front of him and he took a sip. Yeah, maybe he should actually stay until this evening instead of leaving this morning. This was really nice.

'Morning, morning.' His father strode into the room, doing his usual lord-of-the-manor impression. He clapped his hands together and said, 'So who's in for a family game of golf today?'

Dan looked at him briefly, decided that he was leaving this morning after all, chugged half of his too-hot coffee and burned his mouth – he wasn't going to be able to taste anything properly for days now – and stood up to leave the room.

Chapter Ten

NOW – JANUARY 2022

EVIE

'Miss, have you taken your husband's surname?' Jake, one of Evie's Year Ten pupils, yelled as she walked into the classroom on the first morning of term. Yep, there was nothing like a drunken Vegas one-night marriage for making the first day back at work after the holidays even more of a joy than usual. *Why* had she and Dan posted so much stuff on social media and *why* had the mother of one of her pupils had to stumble across it via a mutual friend and tell the world about it?

'No husband, just a joke,' she said, giving Jake the evil eye. 'And can I ask why you were *yelling*?' Evie had developed an *amazing* glare over the years, and, thank *God*, it was working right now. She glared at everyone else, for good measure, and then clapped her hands. 'Right. I'd like to see everyone's Christmas coursework, *now*.'

Unfortunately, she couldn't glare at her colleagues in the same way.

'Oh my *God*, Evie,' her friend Priya said, really *loudly*, as soon as she set foot inside the staff room at morning break, '*no-one* gets pissed-married in Vegas. He was total sex-on-legs. Who is he?' The heads of the majority of the people in the room, including two of the three deputy heads, turned in their direction.

'Ha,' Evie said, thinking *Shut up*. 'Old friend. Just one of those things. You know.'

'No, I don't know. You're the first person I've ever known to get married in Vegas. And *pissed*-married. That had to have been a big morning after.'

'Yeah, it was,' Evie said. 'But, you know.' She moved in nearer to Priya and hissed, 'Shhh.'

'Oops, sorry,' Priya said, grinning in a very un-sorry-like way. She pulled Evie over to a table in a corner and, at least speaking at normal – instead of fog-horn – volume, said, 'So tell me everything. Your messages were far too short.' Priya had been one of the many people who'd WhatsApped Evie asking for details and Evie had gone very succinct on her replies.

'Honestly, there's nothing to tell. Just a one-night stand that involved a ridiculous joke marriage that turned out to be legal so we have a bit of admin to do to sort it out and that's all.'

'So are you seeing him again?' Bloody hell. Good job Evie liked Priya a lot, otherwise right now she'd be finding her *really* irritating.

*

It was a relief to get to Friday evening after what had felt like a very long four-day first-week-back full of drizzle, over-lively kids and staffroom gossip about Evie. Hopefully by Monday morning they'd have stopped talking about her, because *surely* there was nothing more to say now.

Evie was going out tomorrow evening, to a Mexican restaurant with some old university friends who also lived in London. This evening, she was knackered and she was going to be firmly on the sofa in the sitting room of her shared flat, with the remote, a takeaway and a large glass of wine, hoping that her flatmate Josh wouldn't get home with his latest 'shag-for-the-night', as he called his succession of very handsome boyfriends, before she'd gone to bed. Their other flatmate, Mia, was away on business.

Her phone rang as she was grappling with Netflix decision-making: film or start a drama series. She picked it up and saw Dan's name on the screen. And, pathetically, she felt it right to her centre. Literally. Just reading his name. A tiny flicker of hope and warmth.

She swiped right and said, 'Hi, Dan.'

'Hey, Evie. How are you? How's your week been?'

'Good, thanks. Happy New Year. How are you?'

'Also good. And happy New Year to you too.' Dan paused and Evie curled her legs under her so that she was more comfortable. She always enjoyed talking to Dan and it was nice to hear from him. That was an understatement, actually. 'I'm calling with good news.'

'Okay, great.' News. The annulment, obviously. He hadn't called for a chat after all. It had been stupid of her to think that he would have done.

'The attorney just called me and we just need to sign some documents, which he's sent over, and then he'll submit everything and the courts should decide within hopefully a couple of weeks and then we should officially be no longer married. I'll sign them and send them on to you.'

Evie uncurled her legs, sat up straight, and said, 'That's fantastic. Great. Thank you for letting me know.'

'No problem. So, yep, I just wanted to set your mind at rest. I'll let you get on with your evening now. I hear that Sasha's planning a big engagement party, so I might see you there.'

'Yep, probably. Thanks again. Have a lovely weekend.'

'Bye, then.'

'Bye.'

And that was that.

Evie felt really lonely all of a sudden. Why had she thought it would be a good idea to stay in by herself this evening?

She shook her head and pointed the remote again. She could totally find something absorbing and uplifting to watch on Netflix.

The front door crashed open and the sounds of Josh's voice and another man's filled the hall. Evie turned the sound up on the TV. She *really* wasn't up for being around two people on a first date right now.

'Hi, Evie.' Josh and his partner – a tall, slim man wearing a well-fitting navy suit and a well-trimmed beard – walked into the room. 'I thought you were out this evening. This is Marc.'

'Hi, Josh, hi, Marc. In this evening, out tomorrow.'

'Oh, okay, well, in that case we'll take ourselves into my bedroom. Don't mind us.'

'See you in the morning,' Evie said. She did love Josh – they'd been friends since uni and she'd lucked out massively when, a few months after she'd moved to London, he'd offered her the single bedroom in his Wimbledon flat at well below market rent. He'd been fantastic to live with during lockdown, because never a dull moment, but also he was kind of similar to her mum as a housemate; she'd basically gone frying pan to fire when she'd moved to London from her mum's. Josh was not tidy and he went through men at about the same rate Evie went through magazines (and she liked a magazine).

Right now, she could really do with a celibate, anally tidy flatmate.

Especially because Josh's success with men reminded her that she really, really did not have a man herself, and that she was really, really bad at one-night stands, because she was still feeling bereft after the Vegas-Dan thing. She needed to move on from it as soon as possible.

*

The following Tuesday, Evie arrived slightly late for the regular weekly badminton group session that she'd started in September on a get-fit drive for the new school year. If she was honest, it hadn't had much of an impact on her fitness, but it was strangely addictive. There was a seventy-two-year-old ex-GB player in her group, and Evie was going to beat her one day if it killed her.

There was also a lovely man called Matthew, who had an astonishing memory for not-that-funny-but-very-clever one-liners – literally at least five of them on the subject of badminton alone – and wore pristine and – as far as Evie could see – different kit every single week. He'd asked her out before Christmas, which was lovely of him, but she'd turned him down because she didn't really feel a spark with him. Maybe she'd been too hasty, though. He was nice, very nice; going by the pristine kit and his extreme punctuality for their sessions he didn't live a remotely chaotic life; and he was very good-looking in a classic way. Maybe she should have gone out with him. The whole love-at-first-sight thing was clearly nonsense. Attraction and love grew as you got to know people.

He'd been very sweet to her when she'd said she wasn't sure about a date. And he was smiling away at her now from the other side of the court.

'We're going to practise volleying today,' their coach told them when they'd finished warming up. 'Evie, I want you to focus on hitting the shuttlecock harder and more cleanly.'

Matthew manoeuvred things so that they were partnering each other for the volleying, which gave Evie a little thrill, like, actually, she *was* desirable. If she was honest, Dan's blatant horror at how things had panned out in Vegas had dented her confidence quite a lot.

'Harder, Evie,' yelled the coach.

Matthew fed the shuttlecock gently to her and she whacked it back in as aggressive a volley as she could manage.

'Ow,' he howled, as it hit him squarely in the eye.

'Oh, no.' Evie sprinted round the net to see if he was okay. 'I'm *so* sorry.' This was reminding her of the time she'd inadvertently headbutted her ex-fiancé.

Matthew, his hand over his eye socket, shook his head. 'It's fine. Don't worry.'

'Are you sure? I think we should put ice on it.'

'I'm sure I'll be fine.'

'Ice is a good idea,' the coach said.

A couple of minutes later, Evie was sitting with Matthew by the side of the court while he held an ice pack over his eye area.

'You don't need to sit here with me,' Matthew said. 'I'll be completely fine in a minute. I don't want you to miss the session.'

'Don't be silly.' Evie smiled at him. Thoughtfulness could really make someone a lot more attractive. 'Probably better if I stay here anyway until the volleying practice has finished. I don't want to injure anyone else.'

'You did whack it impressively hard. When we do our matchplay, can I be your partner so there's no risk of you hitting me again?'

Evie laughed. 'It's a deal.'

An hour later, at the end of their session, they strolled outside together.

'I'm *so* excited to have beaten Ruth,' Evie said. 'I mean, I know it was all down to you and the fact that she was partnered with Gerald.'

Ruth was the seventy-two-year-old ex-GB player and Gerald was well into his seventies too, and by the signs of things, not an ex-GB player. 'But still very satisfying.'

'It absolutely wasn't down to me. You played a couple of killer winners. Fancy a quick drink now in the pub over there to celebrate our stunning win?'

'I actually would,' said Evie, banishing thoughts of drinking with Dan in Vegas. 'That would be lovely.' A good way of celebrating the fact that their annulment had come through yesterday. She'd felt a bit low since then, and going for a drink with a nice man would be a good thing to do.

Chapter Eleven

NOW – FEBRUARY 2022

DAN

Dan sucked in a big gulp of cold February evening air as he left the hospital by its wide revolving doors. That was a welcome head-clearer. He'd spent the last couple of hours with the parents of a girl with suspected leukaemia and it was hard not to take some of their devastation home with him. They'd caught it early and the prognosis was fairly good, but it was still not news that you ever wanted to have to share with anyone.

He could do with a drink. He pulled out his phone to call his friend Zubin, one of the other emergency doctors at the hospital, who he'd trained with. Thursday evening: he'd hopefully be free.

He had a couple of email notifications and a message from his ex, Hannah. Odd. He was vaguely surprised that he still had her number in his phone; they'd literally only dated for a few weeks, in the autumn, and then they'd split up by what had felt like very mutual agreement and hadn't been in touch since. Hannah had actually been the one to say that she wasn't sure things were going anywhere, but Dan had just been relieved, really.

Maybe she'd messaged him by mistake.

Dan, hi, it's Hannah. I have something important to tell you.
Could you call me?

She must know more than one Dan, and have texted the wrong one. She clearly didn't have anything important to tell him.

Hi Hannah. Just to let you know that I think you sent your message to the wrong Dan

She pinged straight back before he'd even managed to find Zubin in his contacts to call him.

Not the wrong Dan. I have something to tell you, Dan Marshall.
Is now good for you to talk? Hannah

Shit. It felt like there weren't many things an ex who you'd only been with briefly might have to tell you. All of them related to sex and none of them were good.

He pressed the call button.

'Hi, Dan.'

'Hi, Hannah. Is everything alright?'

'Yes, it is, actually, from my perspective. There's no obvious easy way to say this, so I'm just going to launch straight in.'

'Okay.'

'I appreciate that you won't necessarily be particularly happy about this, but I'd like you to know that I don't want or need anything from you. I'm just over three months pregnant with your baby. I'm keeping it.'

'Okay. Um.' *Shit.* 'Congratulations.' Wow. Huge. Better than some terrible disease but really not what he wanted right now. Ever. God. A baby. She was pregnant. He was going to be a father.

'I can understand that it's a huge shock. I was shocked myself when I found out. And surprised that I wanted to keep it. I never saw myself as a mother, you know?'

Dan did know, because he'd never seen himself as a father.

'So I assumed that I'd terminate it, except I just couldn't. I want this baby. I'm thirty-eight and this might be my only chance to have a baby and so I've decided to go ahead with it.' Thirty-eight. He'd thought she was younger than that. And that was very much a side-issue here.

'Yeah, I get that.' Dan moved out of the way of a group of teenagers walking several abreast on the pavement. 'I mean, of course. And I'd like to be involved.' Gut reaction. He'd never imagined that he'd be a father, but now that he was going to be, he already couldn't imagine not being involved.

'Well, that's great. Thank you.'

'Well, thank you for letting me know.' Stupid thing to say, but life hadn't prepared him for this moment.

'Okay, well, I'm not sure there's much else to say now, but I'll be in touch. Obviously you're welcome to call me if you'd like to talk when you've had a chance to digest things.'

'Great.' Dan moved again to avoid yet another group of people out for the evening. 'Yes, I'll probably be in touch again soon. I'd like to join you at your anomaly scan, if that's alright.'

'Of course.'

When they'd ended the call, Dan carried on staring at the pavement for a while before he decided that right now he just wanted to go home and be by himself this evening and, as Hannah had said, digest the news.

*

Forty-eight hours later, Dan was in his car on the way to the Cotswolds for Sasha and Angus's engagement party and nowhere near having digested the baby news. He'd texted Hannah to congratulate her again and reiterate how keen he was to be involved in the baby's life but beyond that he hadn't got his head round it at all.

When he finally arrived at his mother's house, she opened the front door wide and said, 'Dan. I'm so pleased to see you. Darling, you look tired. Are you alright?'

Dan opened his mouth to reply, wondering if he was going to tell her right now that she was going to be a grandmother again (his older sister Lucie already had two little boys). And then she looked at her watch and said, 'Goodness, we're quite late.' Yep, now wasn't the time. In fact, what had he been thinking? Of course he shouldn't tell anyone the weekend of Sasha's engagement party. No-one appreciated their thunder being stolen.

'Why don't you go ahead and I'll follow you?' he said. 'I need to get changed and I might grab a quick shower first if that's okay.' Sasha was torturing them all with a fancy-dress party.

Half an hour later, he stuck his Henry VIII hat on his head and pushed open the door to the pub function room where Sasha and Angus were holding the party. The room was boiling. He was going to fry in this synthetic-fur-lined cloak. Bloody fancy dress. Probably good, though, for taking his mind off everything else.

'Dan.' Sasha flung her arms round him. 'Hello. You make a *great* Henry the Eighth.'

Dan bowed his head gravely. 'Thank you. And you make an even better Cleopatra. Huge congratulations to both of you.'

'Thank you so much. Good to see you.' Angus pumped Dan's hand up and down a few times, grinning. 'And before you ask, the costume was Sasha's idea.' Angus was dressed as an Egyptian pharaoh, complete with headpiece, bare chest, snake armband and a staff. Dan had never seen him in anything other than jeans and a checked shirt before. He was so conservative in his dress taste that he practically made Dan look like a boy band member.

Dan battled laughter for a few seconds before he managed to say, 'You look great, Angus.'

'Thanks.' Angus nodded and his headpiece wobbled. He set it straight. 'God. The things you do for the woman you love.'

'Yeah.' Dan caught sight of Evie chatting to friends on the other side of the room and suddenly felt less mirthful. They hadn't spoken much since Vegas and he wasn't totally sure they were back on track friendship-wise even though they'd kind of laughed it off the next day. He wondered what she'd think about his baby news. 'Congratulations again. I'll let you greet the rest of your guests. Catch up with you later.'

Twenty minutes later, he was managing not to worry about the baby and was enjoying the party, if he ignored the fact that he practically had a crick in his neck from spending the entire time surreptitiously keeping an eye on where Evie was. He wasn't even sure whether it was because he wanted to talk to her or avoid her. Also, was she *with* that tall, blond man? He glanced over again to where she was talking in a group in the opposite corner of the room. The blond man wasn't there now.

She was looking sideways at him at exactly that moment. He smiled a little and looked away.

'Stop looking at her but avoiding her,' Sasha hissed in his ear. Dan jumped slightly. 'It's really obvious. There'll be a lot more gossip if you *don't* speak to her than if you do.'

'I'm not avoiding her,' he said. He kind of was.

'So go and speak to her.'

Dan closed his eyes for a second. He really didn't need this from his sister. He'd *like* to snap at her, but it was her engagement party, and also they were now adults, not bickering children.

'Please?' She gestured with her sceptre, narrowly missing his eye. 'Not for my sake, or your sake, but for *Evie's*.' Her voice was very piercing and several people turned to look. Fantastic. 'Once you've had a chat in public, that will be that. It will all have blown over.'

Dan nodded. 'Good plan,' he said. It probably wasn't, but it didn't feel like he had a lot of choice now.

He started walking across the room towards Evie, aiming for a saunter, which didn't work well, it turned out, when you were dressed as a Tudor king.

'Hey, Evie.'

'Hello.' She gave him a small smile.

'Great costume.' Always a failsafe conversation starter at a fancy-dress party. Evie was dressed in an incredible all-in-one flared trouser and top thing, in bright-blue satiny stuff, and high platform boots. 'ABBA?'

Evie gave him a slightly bigger smile. 'Yes. Liking yours, actually. I'm a little bit surprised by it if I'm honest.'

'Yeah, my initial instinct was to wear my one and only ten-year-old dinner suit, and get myself a toy gun.'

'James Bond?'

'Yup. And that was the plan I was going with until I realised that Sasha would be loudly disappointed in me, and, more importantly, that she might find a costume for me herself.'

'Definitely safer to choose your own.'

'Indeed. Although I'd like to make it clear right now that this wouldn't have been my number one choice. There were only three options in my size and the other two were Superman and Harry Potter.'

Evie sniggered. 'I'd have liked to have seen you in a Superman costume.'

'Yeah. I decided to embrace my inner wife-murderer instead.' Oh, for God's sake. Why had he mentioned the word *wife*? This was the effect Evie had on him. She made him lose his mind slightly. 'Can I get you another drink?' He gestured at her nearly full glass.

'Hi.' The blond man had reappeared and put his left arm round Evie's waist as she was opening her mouth to reply to Dan's question. He held his right hand out to Dan. 'I'm Matthew.'

'Dan,' said Dan, shaking Matthew's hand. He looked between the two of them. 'So you're…?' How long had they been together? And did he have any right to be angry however long it was? No, he didn't, so he should try to act like he didn't want to punch Matthew or shout at Evie right now. What a ridiculous reaction, actually. And, now he thought about it, of *course* she hadn't already been with Matthew at Christmas. He was sure she wouldn't do that, and also Matthew would have found out about their Vegas trip on social media.

'Yeah,' said Matthew, apparently impervious to what Dan felt simmering between himself and Evie. 'Been seeing each other for about three weeks now, haven't we?' He smiled down at Evie. 'Although we've known each other for a few months. She finally consented to go out with me after she'd hit me in the eye.'

'With a shuttlecock.' Evie smiled at Matthew and didn't completely meet Dan's eye. 'By mistake.'

'Aw,' said Dan. 'That's sweet. Well, great to meet you, Matthew.' He was pretty sure his voice was almost shaking with insincerity. 'Good to see you, Evie.'

Evie murmured, 'Lovely to see you too,' while Matthew shook Dan's hand enthusiastically again.

Dan turned round and walked away, tempted to shake his head.

He made himself busy chatting to old friends and relatives and he had a perfectly pleasant evening. Except for the fact that he actually had a physical pain now in his neck from surreptitiously eyeing Evie and Matthew the whole time. He really hadn't been expecting her to be with anyone tonight. No reason she shouldn't be, of course, but it still felt off.

Matthew seemed like a nice enough guy. Much better than the man she'd been with at Lucie's wedding a few years ago. Not a great guy, though. Not good enough for Evie. Not someone she'd necessarily have a lot of fun with.

God. The way he was thinking, it was like he was *jealous*.

Chapter Twelve

THEN – OCTOBER 2016

EVIE

The beauty of having to wear a large (purple velvet) penis-and-accompanying-balls deely bopper ('Double meat and two veg all round,' Sasha's sister Lucie's very posh friend Tara had yelled when she'd distributed them) was that when you leaned forwards it obscured most of what you did.

Evie waited for Lucie's friend Nags to finish sloshing tequila into everyone's shot glasses.

'Right,' Nags said, sitting down. Oops, she'd missed her chair. Up she got. 'Chair moved,' she said. 'Okay. On the count of three. One. Two. *Three.*'

While everyone else tipped their heads back and downed their shots, Evie poured hers into the pot of the large yucca plant behind her. She'd spotted the yucca when they'd arrived at the restaurant and had manoeuvred herself into the closest seat to it. She'd now tipped three out of five shots in there and was a lot more sober than everyone else. It was lovely that Sasha and Tara had invited her – along with thirty-seven other women – to Lucie's hen night, but she was helping out with a school Duke of Edinburgh training day tomorrow, and it would be torture with a hangover. Plus she wasn't that keen generally on getting over-pissed.

Nags stood up again and banged the table with a fork. Oh, God. If there was one thing the last hour had taught Evie, it was that Nags had a lot of ideas that Evie didn't like.

'It's time for Truth or Dare,' Nags announced. Exactly. Evie didn't like that idea.

Fifteen minutes later, it was Evie's turn.

'Truth,' she said. There was no choice. The first three victims had gone Dare. Nags had a big list that she was ticking off. The first three had been: ask a man at the bar for his number (that had been Lucie and she'd gone for someone with a wedding ring and he'd still given her his number and tucked it into her bra top – Lucie had been free with the champagne before the tequila and she'd found that *hilarious*, where Evie wouldn't have been quite so pleased); let the rest of the group sign you up to Tinder with your real details (the woman who'd got that one had just got engaged and wasn't happy); and go braless for the rest of the evening (and the woman who'd got that one was wearing quite a see-through top and also wasn't happy). Truth had to be safer. And what did she have to hide? Absolutely nothing.

'Oooh, I have a big question for you,' Sasha screech-slurred before anyone else could speak. Everyone went quiet and leaned in. 'I always want to ask you this and I never do.' Really? Evie and Sasha didn't have secrets from each other, surely? 'Do you fancy Dan? Like really fancy him? Because I love you both and I think you'd be perfect together. And I've thought for the past few years that maybe you like each other. Do you?'

Okay. The whole Dan thing was the one big secret Evie *did* have from Sasha. The kiss the night before her twenty-second birthday. The very full-on, amazing kiss, since when she'd hardly seen Dan. And the fact that for a long time Dan had been her secret crush. She thought about him much less now, because she hardly ever saw him, so it shouldn't be too difficult to lie, especially since she was a lot soberer than everyone else.

'I mean, he's lovely,' she said. Good start. 'Really nice. Of course he is. And good-looking. Of course. But he's your *brother*. I've known him forever. I mean, he's almost like a *cousin* to me or something.' He really wasn't. 'I don't think there'd ever be any kind of spark.' She was going on too much. She needed to stop talking. Pretty good lying, though, if she said so herself.

'Hmm. I'm not sure.' Lucie waved a dildo wand in Evie's direction. She was slurring even more than her sister. 'People *always* fancy their friends' siblings.'

'That's what I think. And you looked all *dreamy* when he kissed you under the mistletoe that time,' Sasha said. 'I didn't mention it because I didn't want to embarrass you.'

Very restrained of Sasha. Unfortunate that her restraint had gone out the window now, though.

'Ha,' Evie said. 'Dreamy. I was probably a bit pissed.' She remembered it well and, yes, she had had a bit too much mulled wine, but it had been more than that. She'd *definitely* felt a bit dreamy. 'Also, if you remember, I have a boyfriend?' So silly. She should have mentioned Euan immediately rather than wittering on about why she could never fancy Dan. That would have been the end of the conversation. And probably a lot more convincing.

'Is he the one for you, though?' Sasha said. 'I know you *think* you want boring, but do you *actually* want boring? Oh.' She clapped her hands over her mouth. 'Oops. Did I say that out loud? Evie, I'm really sorry. I love you and I'm so sorry.'

'It's fine.' Evie shook her head and smiled. It wasn't *that* fine. This was one of the downsides of being the sober one. Drunk people said brutally honest things and you remembered all of them. At least her mum didn't say stuff while drunk that she wouldn't say while sober. Other people really did, though.

Maybe Evie should just abandon caution and get plastered herself.

'Isabel. Truth or Dare.' Nags had turned her attention to the woman on Evie's left, hooray.

Was Euan boring?

No, he wasn't. He was just sensible. And sensible was great. Sensible didn't force you to wear huge penis deely boppers, drink too much and play Truth or Dare.

Evie looked around the table. Everyone else was having a lot of fun, screaming in delight at Isabel's dare (twerking her way round the restaurant – the best one so far – Isabel was having fun too).

Arguably, Evie would have more fun if she binned all the sensibleness.

Maybe she wouldn't chuck her next drink in the yucca pot.

'So this is nice. BFF,' Sasha said three hours later.

It really wasn't.

They were sitting on the floor together in a loo cubicle in a not-very-nice nightclub in Cheltenham. Evie had been vomiting into the toilet basin and Sasha had been holding her hair out of her face.

'I feel guilty,' Sasha said. 'I was drinking a lot faster than you but you're the one vomiting. I'm kind of thinking you should practise drinking a bit more.'

'Or never ever touch alcohol again,' Evie croaked. Her mouth tasted beyond disgusting, her head was killing her and things were spinning around her. This hadn't been boringly sensible but it wasn't fun either. 'I have to be at D of E practice at school at eight thirty tomorrow morning.'

'That's bad.' Sasha hugged Evie's shoulders. 'Sorry you feel rough.'

Evie closed her eyes while the tiles of the loo cubicle spun round and round her and her stomach heaved. The tiles were cream, she knew that, but when they were spinning they got a lot darker. Weird.

'You okay?' Sasha rubbed her back and Evie's stomach heaved again and she threw up some more. Sasha looked into the loo. 'Bile. I think that's good news. I think your stomach's pretty much empty now. I think you might be okay to sip some water soon.'

Evie turned her head, slowly, because fast movement wasn't good, and did her best to smile at Sasha. 'Thank you so much for being with me here. This would be a lot worse without you. Sorry you aren't out there with everyone else.' Oh no. Sasha *should* be out there with everyone else. 'You should go and dance again. I'm ruining your evening.'

'You aren't ruining my evening. This is nice.'

'This is not nice.' The underneath of the toilet bowl definitely hadn't seen any form of cleaning product recently. 'I want to get some Marigolds on and chuck some bleach around.'

Sasha sniggered. 'I love you, Evie Green. I love all your tidiness and the way you like everything to be so perfect. Sorry about what I said about Euan and sorry for asking you about Dan. Obviously Euan's great and obviously you don't have a thing for Dan. And you're bringing Euan to Lucie's wedding and Dan's bringing his latest girlfriend. Another new one. Ignore what I said. It was just the drink talking.'

Evie shook her head, slowly, waited for her stomach to settle, and said, 'You were kind of right.' It felt mean to be lying to Sasha, who really was an amazing friend. 'Euan is a bit boring.'

'Oh, Evie, I'm even more sorry now.' Sasha took some loo paper and folded it round some of Evie's hair and pulled gently. 'Vomit in your hair. I wasn't holding it properly. Sorry. Anyway. I don't think we should talk about this now. But I would say that I don't believe you need boring and I don't believe you should settle for boring. Maybe you need *sensible*, or *steady* or *dependable*, but you do not need boring. You're under-selling yourself. Anyway. When you're ready, let's get a taxi and go home. You should maybe wash your hair before you go to bed. Or wash your pillowcase in the morning. Maybe both.'

*

Sitting in the Melting Bishop village church a fortnight later, Evie looked over her shoulder with everyone else to see Lucie as she walked sedately down the aisle on her father Robert's arm, her bridesmaids Sasha, Tara and Nags behind her. Lucie looked stunning, and a completely different woman from the penis-accessory-holding, boobs-spilling-out-of-tiny-top, cackling hen she'd been two weeks ago. The bridesmaids also looked beautiful, particularly Sasha. Evie beamed at her best friend as they all glided past the end of her pew.

Euan reached for Evie's hand with his own as the wedding party took up their position at the front of the church. Evie tried not to frown. Lucie had gone for a big wedding, with a lot of family and local friends present. There were a lot of people here that Evie knew very well and liked a lot. She loved the village. She loved the village church, beautifully decorated today with autumn foliage. And, if she was honest, she wanted to enjoy it all without being distracted by Euan's presence. He was doing some – slightly annoying – finger rubbing. She was pretty sure that he thought it was erotic, because he usually finger-rubbed at the end of an evening when she was going back to his and it looked like sex was on the cards. Right now, it was a struggle not to slap his fingers away.

Euan whispered something in her ear that she didn't catch. Simultaneously, the vicar started talking. Evie hadn't been to that many weddings in recent years, since her mum had stopped getting married – she'd had three short-lived marriages when Evie was at school – and she wanted to hear what the vicar had to say. And this was a nice traditional one and a relative biggie: someone she *knew*, who she'd known most of her life, her best friend's older sister, was getting married, and hopefully she was going to stay married a lot longer than Evie's mum used to.

She edged away from Euan so that she could hear the vicar better. He edged after her. She edged more. He followed. Evie gave up and stayed put and Euan spoke in her ear again.

'I can imagine us at the altar maybe next year or the year after,' he said.

Evie froze. What? It sounded almost like he was *proposing*. They'd only been going out for just over a year. And no-one said things like this in the middle of someone *else's* wedding.

'Will you marry me?' he whispered. Good heavens.

Evie shot her head round to look at him and the top left of her forehead connected hard with his chin.

'Ow,' she said.

'Umph,' Euan said.

Both really loudly.

A lot of people turned to look at them.

Evie screwed her face up. 'Sorry,' she mouthed.

Oh, for God's sake. Euan was mumbling something else now. Yes, it was lovely and very kind of him to have proposed, very flattering, yes, but *honestly*. What was wrong with him? No-one proposed in the middle of a wedding service and the way he was carrying on everyone was going to be staring at *him* when their attention should be focused on the actual ceremony. Her head hurt too but she wasn't mumbling.

'What?' she said out of the side of her mouth, staring straight ahead, and trying not to hiss *Shut up*.

'Blood,' he said, his consonants very dulled.

Evie turned with reluctance to look at him. Yep, quite a lot of blood actually, dripping out of his mouth and onto his pristine white shirt and pale-yellow silk with little foxes – not very nice actually; the foxes looked evil – tie.

'Oh my goodness, I'm so sorry,' she said.

He opened his mouth and showed her more blood and his tongue, which looked almost bitten-through, and she nearly gagged.

She shouldn't have gagged. It looked awful, so painful. Poor Euan.

She took tissues out of her handbag – she'd taken to carrying all sorts in there because with a two-year-old in the family you never knew what might happen and her mum usually forgot practical stuff – and passed them to him. He pressed them to his mouth and made a kind of *eech* sound, very quietly but quite persistently. Not surprising; it must be *so* sore. She put her hand on his knee and squeezed, hoping that that might feel comforting.

Had he actually just proposed to her?

The vicar was going through the marriage ceremony. She should listen. Hard to concentrate, though, with Euan's ongoing *eech*ing in her ear.

Euan had actually just proposed.

What if this was the only proposal she ever got and it was a) inappropriately timed, because *surely* it was rude to propose to someone at someone else's wedding in case the proposee told someone and stole the bride and groom's thunder; and b) rubbish, because shouldn't a proposal be romantic in some way, like on a famous bridge in the moonlight, or on a beautiful beach, or in a lovely restaurant? Or just out for a quiet walk. Anywhere, basically, other than in the middle of a crowded church during someone else's wedding ceremony.

It *would* be a good story for the grandchildren: *I was so shocked when your grandfather proposed that I inadvertently headbutted him.*

Grandchildren. With Euan.

They'd be very sensible grandchildren.

Euan made a weird gurgling sound. Evie turned back towards him to see what was wrong.

'I think my tooth's loose,' he whispered, as the vicar asked the groom if he'd take Lucie to be his wife.

'Oh my goodness. I'm so sorry. I hope not,' Evie whispered back, trying simultaneously to look at Euan's mouth and watch the ring exchange that was now happening at the front of the church.

It was one of his front teeth. Clearly, an important tooth. Well, all teeth were important. But front teeth were *really* important. If it *was* loose they should do something about it immediately. But they couldn't stand up and go anywhere because they'd disrupt the whole ceremony. They'd have to make a dash for it at the end.

Euan gurgled and moaned away – very understandably – next to her during the remainder of the service until Lucie and her new husband processed down the aisle, hand in hand, looking both gorgeous and gorgeously in love.

As they walked past the end of Evie and Euan's pew, Evie's mind conjured up an image of herself walking down an aisle hand in hand with Euan. It was a stretch to imagine either of them having eyes only for the other in quite such a besotted way. Euan would probably be finessing some financial calculations in his head, maybe discussing aspects of them with Evie, and Evie would probably be... a bit bored.

No. She was being unfair. He was lovely. Sensibleness and prudence were great attributes.

'Can we *do* something about my tooth?' he said, dribbling a bit more blood.

It was totally understandable thing to say, and Evie should *not* find the whiny tone to his voice at *all* annoying. And yet... She could see Max, Sasha's other brother, out of the corner of her eye. He'd had the most horrendous accident in his late teens, and Evie had never heard anyone in the family whine about it, ever.

But Euan was clearly in a lot of pain and everyone reacted differently to things and probably a lot of people would be whining right now. And they did need to do something about it as soon as possible.

'Let's find a loo and clean you up a bit and check your mouth properly and then we'll go and find a doctor or dentist as quickly as we can,' she said.

'It's definitely loose,' Euan said five minutes later, peering at himself in the cracked mirror outside the church's one – brown-carpeted – loo, as he touched his tooth gingerly.

'Okay. Why don't I call your dentist and ask them what to do?'

'Fine.'

An answer machine message told Evie that Euan's dentist was closed on Saturdays.

'Okay. We need to do something. I'll order a taxi. Do you think we should go to A&E?' Evie tried very hard to squash any feeling of

disappointment about missing the rest of the wedding, which she'd
been looking forward to. Obviously, her possible-fiancé's loose tooth
was infinitely more important than a wedding, even if the bride was
Lucie, who she'd known practically her whole life.

'I don't know. Can't you google it?' She understood why Euan was
tetchy, but did he have to sound *quite* so irritable? It wasn't like she'd
headbutted him on purpose.

When she and her mum had been moving a big chest in the summer
and Evie had dropped her end and it had landed on her mum's foot and
broken a bone, her mum hadn't been tetchy at all. Evie had apologised a
lot and her mum had told her a *lot* that it hadn't been her fault and it was
just one of those things. Euan clearly did not feel like that. But maybe
it was different between mother and daughter. Maybe you'd always be
reasonable with respect to your daughter because you loved her so much.

Although, shouldn't a man *really* love the woman he'd just proposed
to and not blame her for something that she obviously hadn't done
on purpose? If your relationship with your husband was going to be
worse than your relationship with your mother, what was the point
of getting married? Not a comfortable thought to be having as you
googled broken teeth.

'What does it *say?*' Euan said.

'Well, Google isn't conclusive,' Evie told him. 'I'm not sure.'

'This is ridiculous. It's *Google.* Did you even look properly?'

Evie took a big breath and didn't snap back at him. He was in pain,
after all. She had a sudden brainwave.

'Why don't I ask Sasha's brother Dan?' she said. 'He's an A&E
doctor.'

'*Thank* you,' Euan said. 'I'll wait here. I can't go outside looking
like this.'

*

Dan – apparently without the girlfriend Sasha had thought would be coming – had just finished doing family photos and was talking to some people who Evie thought she recognised as his aunts and uncles.

'Hello,' she said. 'Sorry to interrupt.'

'Hey, Evie. How are you?'

'Hi, Dan. Good thank you. How are you? Your sister's a married woman!'

'I know. Very grown-up.'

'I have a question for you.'

'Oh-kay? I'm intrigued.' Dan's smile made Evie want to smile too.

Evie suddenly remembered their pact – weddings, marriage, word association – and shoved the thought away.

She started talking rapidly. 'Basically, during the service, I headbutted my boyfriend Euan, by mistake, *obviously*, and there's lots of blood and his tooth's loose. I think he might need a stitch in his lip or his tongue or both, and I'm not sure where I should take him to get his tooth seen. Do we take him to A&E?'

'Where is he? He'll need to get his tooth seen by an emergency dentist rather than A&E. Why don't I take a look to see if I think he needs any stitches?' There was something very sexy about how Dan had just flipped straight into doctor mode.

It was difficult not to compare Dan and Euan while Dan checked out Euan's mouth. Obviously she shouldn't be comparing anyone with anyone. *But.* Dan was slightly shorter and quite a lot wider and a lot more fun to be with. Euan was more kind of classically handsome, but – to quote Sasha – in quite a boring way. Euan's smile – when he was smiling, which he certainly wasn't this afternoon, understandably, of course – was not infectious.

Dan was speaking right now and, totally inappropriately for the situation, Evie now wanted to smile too. 'I think you'll be okay without stitches but you do need to get your tooth seen. Don't go to A&E because you'll be wasting your time – you'll have to wait and then they'll send you to a dentist anyway. I'm sure you'll find one that's open on a Saturday afternoon.'

'Thank you so much,' said Evie. 'I'm so sorry that we've dragged you away from Lucie's reception. I'm sure we can sort things from here.'

'Do you know of a dentist?' Euan said.

Dan took his phone out of his pocket. 'I'm sure I can call a couple of people.'

'No, honestly, we've already taken up a lot of your time and you need to get back to the wedding party. I'm sure we can find somewhere.' Evie took her own phone out of her clutch.

'It would be great if you could give us a couple of names,' Euan said to Dan.

Dan knew a lot of people, via his father's GP surgery, and after three calls had found a dentist who could see Euan within the hour.

'Right,' Euan said, 'we'd better get going.'

'Thank you so, so much for all your help,' said Evie. Was it bad to find your boyfriend embarrassing? Obviously it was awful to have a loose tooth, *really* awful, so it was *totally* understandable that he wouldn't be that effusive with his thanks, but equally Dan had definitely gone above and beyond and it wasn't *hard* to say a proper thank you.

*

Ten minutes into their – silent until then – journey in the back of the cab to the dentist in Cheltenham, Euan sneezed three times in a row.

'Bless you,' Evie said.

'There must have been a cat somewhere.' Euan looked around him, like one might be clinging to the taxi upholstery.

'Oh dear,' said Evie, horrified that her lips were twitching a bit. It was *awful* to be tempted to laugh, but Euan had been a county-level athlete when he was younger and he always put his speed and jumping ability to good use whenever they were within about a hundred metres of a cat, and now every time he mentioned the allergies Evie struggled not to snigger at memories of him vaulting fences and sprinting *miles* if he suspected a feline presence. Even though Evie had twice witnessed him unknowingly being in the same garden as a cat and completely unaffected by it.

If she married him, she was going to have to live forever with his – possibly imaginary – cat allergy. What if he developed new imaginary allergies? What if he developed *real* allergies? How would he behave if something *genuinely* affected him?

Euan harumphed and they spent the rest of the journey alternating between looking out of the windows on their sides of the taxi and at their phones.

They'd been in the dentist's waiting room for a few minutes, still not doing a lot of chatting, when Euan's mother turned up.

She rushed over to Euan. 'Darling, how are you?'

When Euan's mother had finished inspecting his mouth and she and Euan had had a chat about his week at work, his work dinner last night and his breakfast this morning – yes, really – Evie said, 'Hi, Elspeth.'

'Evie and I are engaged,' Euan said. Evie's head shot round for the second time in one day. Good job his head was safely beyond butting distance this time. Had she *replied* to his proposal? Absent-mindedly? Had she said *yes* at any point? She was pretty sure she hadn't. In front of his mother, in a dentist's waiting room, wasn't the time or the place to discuss it, though.

She looked back at Elspeth, who was as open-mouthed as Evie felt.

There was a long pause before Elspeth said, 'Wonderful news.' She adjusted her pearls and smoothed her skirt, opened her mouth and then closed it again. Not smilingly.

'Why don't you go back to the wedding?' Euan told Evie, then dabbed at his mouth again. 'We can manage without you.'

'Are you sure?'

'Definitely,' Euan said.

'Absolutely,' Elspeth said, a lot more enthusiastically than when she'd been talking about her son's supposed engagement.

This was very good news for the rest of Evie's day. She snuck a look at the clock above the reception desk. Yep, if she got her skates on, she'd be back in the middle of the pre-dinner champagne reception at the hotel where the wedding dinner and dance were.

'Are you sure?' she repeated, trying very hard not to beam in delight.

Euan nodded, winced and put his hand to his mouth. 'Ow. Yes, certain.'

'Okay. Well. I hope you're alright. I'll call you later.' It felt like she should say something loving and maybe kiss the top of his head or hug him or something at this point, except it felt awkward in front of Elspeth, plus he wasn't even looking at Evie any more.

*

'What happened?' Sasha asked her about half an hour after she'd got back. 'Where did you go? Where's Euan?'

Telling the story took quite a long time because they both started laughing halfway through, which they really, really shouldn't have done – and Evie obviously *really* hoped Euan would be okay – but aspects of it *were* funny, and he'd never know that they'd laughed.

'Soooo, congratulations?' Sasha said.

'I mean, maybe,' Evie said. 'Except I don't totally remember accepting his proposal.'

'But you're going to?'

'I mean, maybe. Probably.' Evie adored her mum, obviously, but since as far back as she could remember it had been like she was the adult and her mum was a teenager, and she wanted a calmer adult life than that. Less chaos. Euan was very calm and unchaotic. He had a nice, tidy house. He was very pleasant when he wasn't stressed about a loose tooth. 'Yep, I think so.'

'Well, that's *great*,' said Sasha, far too over-heartily, like a parent at sports day pretending that coming second-from-last in a race was *amazing*. She clinked her champagne flute against Evie's. 'Congratulations.'

Chapter Thirteen

THEN – OCTOBER 2016

DAN

'Congratulations on what?' asked Dan. Maybe Evie had a new job or was moving house.

'Evie's engaged,' Sasha said.

'Nothing,' said Evie, simultaneously, swivelling her eyes and shaking her head at Sasha.

Sasha mouthed, 'Sorry,' at Evie, and then, a moment later, said, 'I was joking,' to Dan.

Wow. Evie blatantly *was* engaged. Secretly, apparently. To Euan, presumably. His tooth must have been alright for them to be back so quickly. Good news. He must be in the loos or something right now.

The engagement seemed a shame. If he was honest, Dan hadn't really taken to the man. He'd seemed a little petulant and lacking in humour. Although to be fair he had just been smacked in the mouth. And it was clearly nothing to do with Dan. In fact, he was pleased for Evie. It had to be three years now since the Christmas when she'd told him that she wanted marriage and babies. So this was great for her. It didn't feel like that man was the right one for her, though. She deserved someone better. Not that it was any of his business.

Maybe he'd leave Sasha and Evie to their conversation now.

'I'll catch you later. Evie, I think we're on the same table at dinner.'

He left them and meandered over towards the bar, smiling and nodding at various people as he went.

This was the way to enjoy a wedding. Knowing a lot of the people there but having no duties beyond that of usher, which he'd now fulfilled.

'Hey, Dan.' His cousin Harry slapped him on the back. 'Saw you earlier at the church doors but no time to chat. It's been too long.'

'It has.' Dan nodded. 'Got to be a couple of years? You were working out in New Zealand, Mum said?'

'Yep. Back for good now. I've taken a job in Edinburgh, in ortho-paedics. We should catch up properly soon. I'm staying in London for the next couple of weeks. I saw your mum and dad in London the other day, too. Thursday, I think.'

'Really?' Odd that his mother would visit London without mention-ing it to him. And hadn't Lucie said that they'd been doing last-minute bride, bridesmaid and mother-of-the-bride dress fittings and other weddingy things on Thursday before he and Max arrived yesterday? 'Day before yesterday?'

'Yep. I didn't speak to them, just saw them in the distance, in the middle of the concourse at Paddington station. I have to say, it was sweet. They were hugging; in fact, at the risk of making you vom, they were full-on snogging, like teenagers. It was definitely them. I saw your dad very clearly.'

Dan felt his features freeze.

He should smile, or something. Speak.

'Small world,' he managed. No-one mistook their uncle, did they, when they'd spent so many family holidays together. And he was pretty sure his mother had mentioned that his father had indeed been in London on business this week.

'Here's the man himself,' Harry said, moving a little to the side to intercept Dan's father on his way past them.

'Harry, Dan.' Dan's father shook both their hands.

'I was just telling Dan that I saw you at Paddington station on Thursday afternoon,' said Harry. 'Presume you were about to catch the five thirty train back here.'

'That's right. Small world,' his father said, echoing Dan. 'Yes, I've been working in London a fair amount recently. Back and forth from Kemble to Paddington. I have a role with the Royal College of General Practitioners.'

'Nice that Aunt Fiona can go with you too,' Harry said.

'I don't think Mum went on Thursday,' Dan said.

'No, she doesn't often come with me. Busy at home.' Dan's father wasn't so much falling into a trap, he was leaping into it. 'Particularly in the run-up to the wedding.'

'Really?' Maybe Harry's senses were dulled by all the champagne he was knocking back. 'I definitely saw her. On the platform.'

'No, I...' Dan's father looked at Dan, and visibly paled. Then he returned his gaze to Harry. 'You must have seen someone else, Harry.' He shook Harry's hand again. 'Good to see you. Let's speak again later. I'd better go and fulfil some of my father-of-the-bride duties now.'

Pity he'd apparently lost the ability to fulfil his husband-of-the-mother-of-the-bride duties some years ago.

Dan could feel heat rising up his head. He really wanted to confront his father there and then. Tell him to stop the charade, that everyone knew that he was having an affair, indeed multiple affairs, and just to be honest. But he couldn't do that now, not in the middle of Lucie's wedding.

'You look hot. Very red. You alright?' Harry was peering at him.

'Yeah, I'm great,' Dan said. 'It is hot in here, though. I might step outside for a minute.'

Dan had himself back under control by the time he sat down for dinner. Normally, he was great at controlling himself around his father. He'd had enough practice; he'd been silently angry with him since he was sixteen, just before Max's accident.

He shouldn't have let his father's behaviour get to him earlier. It wasn't like it was new information; it was more a reminder of what he already knew. And from snippets of arguments that he'd heard over the years, he was sure that his mother knew too. If she didn't want to kick his father out, Dan really shouldn't interfere. He barely even went home now; it was their relationship, nothing to do with him.

'Looks like the food's going to be fantastic,' Evie said, showing him the menu. They were now a table of nine, due to Euan's absence; apparently his mother was staying with him at the dentist, which was why Evie had been able to come back to the reception. Dan couldn't say he was displeased with the result, though it was just because Evie was good company. That was what he was telling himself anyway. She was *engaged,* after all.

'That does look good,' he agreed.

'So what would be your dream banquet meal?'

'Good question. At least four courses, obviously. You know, now I think about it, it's actually really hard to say what your favourite food is, when you can only have one thing for each course.'

'Really? I think it's quite easy. Like, for the starter, truffle risotto, *obviously*.'

Dan shook his head. 'That isn't obvious. What about a really nice lobster dish? Or a pâté? Or scallops? There are a lot of options.'

'That's true. You've got me completely doubting myself.' Evie shook her own head. 'I've honestly got no idea now.'

'What about a soufflé?' said Greggy, from Evie's other side.

'Damn, I love a soufflé. I think I need to re-evaluate my choices,' Evie said.

Ten minutes later, when they'd all got their – tuna carpaccio – starter, Evie said, 'Oh my goodness. It's a good job that this looks delicious, isn't it, or I could have just done a very bad thing and made everyone dissatisfied with this meal talking about all those other starters.'

'I eat a lot of my meals in the hospital canteen,' Dan told her. 'I'd be happy with pretty much anything that doesn't taste of cabbage.'

'So how is your work? Is it stressful?'

'Yup.' Dan speared some asparagus. 'You see death and heartbreak, obviously, and it gets to you at times. You know: with all our fantastic twenty-first century medicine, we can't save everyone, and we can't prevent bad things still happening to some of the people we save. You have to learn to accept it as part of life and rise above it, or you couldn't carry on, but equally I think that if you were to be completely unaffected by the bad stuff, maybe you'd have lost your humanity.'

'It must help to have colleagues you can share stuff with?'

'Yeah, definitely.' Bit of a lie, actually. He did have some great colleagues, who'd become great friends, but they usually kept the chat light. He'd be more likely to talk to Evie about how sometimes he felt like he just couldn't cope with the tragedy of it all. But not now. 'You get your funny ones too,' he said. 'I had a pea-up-the-nose kid in yesterday. That was an easy one. I just pressed his other nostril and told him to blow hard and it came out on the second blow. His mother asked me what she should do with it.'

'Did you tell her she could bin it or take it home as a souvenir, her choice?'

'I actually did,' Dan said, pleased. 'You're a mind-reader.'

An hour and a half later, Evie placed her knife and fork neatly on the side of her plate and said, 'That was *so* good. I *love* trout.'

'Thinking about making changes to your dream banquet meal?'

Evie nodded. 'Yup.'

Dan shook his head, sorrowfully. 'So suggestible.'

'You can talk. Remember that summer where we made you laugh, *all* the time, just by telling you that you were going to?'

'I do remember that. You were so annoying. Anyway, I'm an adult now. No longer suggestible. Unlike you.'

'Fair enough.' Evie nodded and then a couple of seconds later did an enormous yawn.

Dan felt his own mouth gape in response.

'Hah,' Evie crowed. 'Made you yawn. I think that's practically the actual definition of suggestibility. Not so adult after all.'

Dan shook his head again. 'Still *so* annoying.' He slid his gaze to the side and smiled at her and she grinned back. So beautiful. Gorgeous brown eyes, gleaming with triumph right now.

*

Twenty minutes later, it felt like an intrusion into his and Evie's little world of happy chat when, as the waiters cleared their dessert plates and everyone raved about the lemon tart they'd had, there was a lot of clapping and cutlery banging from the top table. Everyone turned round to see Lucie standing behind her chair.

'I'm doing the first speech,' she said. 'Screw the patriarchy!'

Dan joined in with the cheering and whistling that followed, and when it had died down, turned back to the table to pick up his glass, in time to see Evie putting her phone back in her bag.

'Just texted Euan to check he's okay,' she said. Euan. He really hadn't seemed right for Evie.

'How's he doing?' Dan fought to keep his expression neutral.

'Apparently the dentist moved his tooth back into place and it's going to be fine, thank goodness. He's recovering at home with his mum at the moment. Thank you again for all your help earlier.'

'Hey, really, I did nothing. I just hope he's okay.'

'Well, thank you.' She leaned back down to tuck her bag under her chair and Dan caught a glimpse of her cleavage – which he really shouldn't be noticing given that he'd just been reminded that she was engaged to someone else – and a glimpse of her forehead – with a very green bruised lump on it – as her masses of hair swung back. That had to be where her head had connected with Euan's chin and it had to hurt.

He opened his mouth to ask if she was, in fact, okay, but Lucie started her speech so he couldn't speak.

As the clapping was dying down after the final speech, he turned to Evie and said, 'Going back to the tooth incident, how are *you* doing? Is your head aching?'

'Are you telling me the large lump on my forehead is noticeable?' Evie deadpanned.

'I mean, only a tiny bit,' Dan told her, smiling.

'Yeah, it's huge. I keep having to resist the temptation to go to the loos again to check it out in the mirrors. It was big this afternoon and *humungous* when I checked it between the main course and pudding. And it was starting to change colour.'

'Huge is an exaggeration,' Dan said. It really wasn't. 'But you're definitely going to have some seriously impressive bruising there tomorrow. Everyone's going to be asking if you walked into a door.'

'So, Doctor Dan, is there anything I can do to reduce the bruising?'

'Well, you'd normally want to put an ice pack on it but I'm not sure that there's a lot of point eight hours after the event.'

'Yeah, and it might trash my hair and make-up.'

'Yep, I think you're just going to have to style it out. Or wear a lot of make-up for the next few days.'

'Tricky to do anything to flatten the lump itself, though.' She raised her eyebrows and wiggled them a little. 'Ouch.'

Dan winced on her behalf. 'Not surprised it's a bit sore. I'd recommend…'

'Paracetamol before bed with at least a pint of water?'

'Exactly. Do I say that a lot?'

'Not a *lot*. Just every time anyone has a drink in their hand after ten p.m. In my experience.'

'You know what, the best sayings are always worth repeating.'

'Maybe a *slight* stretch to call it a "best saying".' Evie smiled at him. She had a gorgeous smile. She always had done.

The others from their table were all making their way to the dance floor, but Dan had quite a strong urge to stay here, talking to Evie.

Plus, she didn't look like she was as keen as she normally was to dance. Maybe her head hurt too much.

He took a big slug of the port that had come round with the cheese and coughed. 'Woah, that's strong. How's your head feeling now?'

'It's *fine*,' she said. 'I mean, totally fine. Though, speaking of, do you happen to have any painkillers on you? Just as a preventative measure?'

'I do in the car. Lame, I know, but I keep a first aid kit there now. You wouldn't believe the number of injuries you see in Casualty that could have been mitigated by some basic on-the-spot treatment. I'll go and get it.'

'No, honestly, don't worry, I'll be fine. I'll just take some later.'

Dan felt eyes on him and looked up to see his father snatching his gaze from their direction and walking away towards the dance floor. He ran his finger round the inside of his collar, immediately hot again.

'I'll get it now,' he said. 'I wouldn't mind a bit of fresh air—' that was an understatement – anything to get out of the same room as his father for a few minutes '—and the car park's just round the corner of the front of the hotel.' The wedding reception was in a country house hotel a few miles from Melting, and they were currently in a large function room on the ground floor, just off the main foyer.

'Okay, if you're sure, that's very kind. Would you mind if I came with you? I also wouldn't mind some fresh air.'

'Sure.' It'd be nice to have her company. Keep his mind off his parents.

'Wow,' Evie said as they went through the double doors out of the room and into the hotel foyer. It was absolutely heaving with people wearing very bright flares, mini-dresses and platform boots. Some moderately tasteful and some not so much. As they dodged round the hordes of seventies-garb devotees, Evie tugged Dan's arm gently, indicated a board on the wall a few feet away and said, 'Look, I think that's a seating plan.' She scooted over to it before coming back to him.

'It's an ABBA-themed wedding,' she told him when they were outside and out of earshot.

'What? Really?'

'Definitely. The tables all had names like "Fernando", "Money, Money, Money" and "Waterloo". So *cool*.'

'Cool? Really? I mean, *would* you?' Dan didn't think she would. She was a lot of fun, always had been, but from what he knew of her, she was also quite conservative in her tastes. Like, she'd dance manically to ABBA at her wedding reception, but she wouldn't go for an actual ABBA theme. And if you could make an assumption about a man's wedding reception taste from a two-minute acquaintance, he'd assume that Euan would go conservative every time, including on the dancing front.

'Yeah, totally. I mean, maybe not ABBA.' Evie was silent for a moment, maybe also thinking about Euan. 'No, definitely not at my own wedding. But I'd love to *go* to a themed wedding involving costumes. I do like a fancy-dress party. You can always turn it into an excuse to wear an amazing outfit of some kind.'

'I don't *hate* fancy dress. I mean, I'll join in if you twist my arm. But I don't love it. And I definitely wouldn't do it at my own wedding. Were I to have one. Which I won't.'

'Really? Why not?'

For a mad moment, Dan had the urge to tell her about his family, about himself, his knowledge that every important relationship he touched, he broke, how it killed him that he couldn't save every damaged child he encountered at work. And how he was scared that if he ever loved someone he'd get hurt like his father had hurt his mother.

He opened his mouth and then shook his head slightly. That would have been that last glass of port talking.

'Just. You know. Not for me. Various reasons. Here's the car.' He opened the boot. 'And here's my trusty first aid kit and here are the paracetamol.'

When Evie had glugged two tablets with the bottle of the water they'd brought out with them, she looked over to the other side of the car park.

'Look at that.' She started walking towards an old car, sitting in a pool of light from the lamp above it. 'I love a vintage car. And this is a lovely colour. Is it a Rolls?'

'Not sure,' Dan said. 'I've never been a big fancy car fanatic. I'm all about getting from A to B and never breaking down.' He peered at the little ornament on the bonnet of a woman outstretched. 'That's the Rolls thing, isn't it?'

Evie peered too. 'Yep. Spirit of Ecstasy. Beautiful. I'd love to own one. Although obviously you'd have to have a modern, reliable car too, as you say.'

Dan smiled at her. She was a woman of contradictions, and he liked that.

'You finished drooling over the car?' he asked.

'Yep. Ready to go back. Thank you for your magic medicine.'

When they got back inside, the ABBA crowd were still milling around but now starting to head back into the function room opposite Lucie's.

'Ooh, let's just get a look at the bride and groom,' Evie said.

'Really?' Dan said, but he couldn't help smiling. She started edging towards the doors to the room and he followed. She was peeping round the corner of the room, with Dan just behind her, when the band on the stage at the far end of the room suddenly struck up 'Dancing Queen' and there was cheering and a stampede from the crowd in the foyer. Evie got swept up in the swirl of people into the room, and Dan really had no option but to follow her since it didn't feel right to abandon her.

The crowd around them thinned out once they were a few feet beyond the bottleneck of the doors, so they were free to edge back out again, except Evie was pointing at all the décor.

'It's all so shiny and sequinny,' she said. 'Oh my goodness. Look at the glitterballs hanging from the ceiling. And there's so much *purple*. It's fabulous.' She really didn't look like she had plans to leave.

'We should go.' Dan indicated towards the door with his head.

The band were belting out 'Super Trouper' with serious enthusiasm.

'Just one dance?' Evie said. 'I *love* this song.'

'This isn't our wedding,' Dan said. Although it was tempting to stay in here. His parents, Max, Harry – who might or might not have realised by now that something was amiss – were all in the other room. In here there were a lot of strangers, and Evie, who was already swaying in time to the music. *Our wedding*. That reminded him of their fallback pact. He'd mention it now as a joke if she weren't engaged to Euan.

'I know but we're already in here and this is a *great* song.'

Dan rolled his eyes at her but allowed her to lead him right onto the dance floor. Evie was immediately Travolta-style pointing, arm rolling and stepping with the best of the actual wedding guests. Oh, God. She had some of them lined up and they were all following her moves.

Evie eventually nodded at them all and did a circular clap before moving closer to Dan.

'This is the hustle,' she yelled in his ear. Dan nodded. He had no idea what she was talking about, but, if he was honest, he was enjoying this and he was getting more into it. There was always something quite joyous about strutting your stuff with huge gusto.

'Mamma Mia' was up next, followed by 'Take a Chance on Me'. Evie just kept on laughing and dancing away, and Dan just kept on boogying with her. Evie was right; ABBA was great. You just needed to suspend all music snobbery and take things as they came.

Evie was really going for it and Dan was pretty sure that he wasn't far behind. A group of equally enthusiastic dancers had formed around them and Evie was smiling away at people and exchanging the odd word here and there.

During a breather between songs, as they all waited, some people panting slightly, a man in a very bold electric-blue velvet flared suit and kipper tie said to them, 'So how do you two know Dom and Clara? I see you didn't get the memo about the dress code.'

Evie frowned. She opened her mouth and Dan *knew* she was about to argue. He swivelled his eyes at her and nodded his head slightly in the direction of the doors.

'*Fine,*' she said to him.

'Friends. Recent ones,' she said to the velvet-suited man.

'I think we need some air,' Dan said.

Evie bent down and picked up her very high-heeled shoes, which she'd kicked off midway through the first song, and Dan grabbed her hand and started walking.

'Lovely to meet you,' Evie called over her shoulder.

'Honestly,' she said to Dan. 'He was far too unappreciative of the effort we've made. You're wearing *tails*.' Lucie had nagged every man at the wedding she had any influence over into wearing them. 'And this dress is from LK Bennett and it cost a fortune even in the sale.'

'You're right. That's a very nice dress, as I think I mentioned earlier in the evening.' Evie looked stunning. The dress was a bright green and quite fitted on the top half and then swirled out into a knee-length skirt that swished a lot when she walked or danced. 'And I did have to visit two separate Moss Bros shops to hire this suit.'

'Exactly. The only thing wrong with our outfits is that they're a few decades too modern.'

They closed the ABBA wedding function room doors behind them and Dan said, 'We just bloody gatecrashed a wedding – I mean, who *does* that?'

'I know,' Evie said, and giggled. *Really* giggled. Dan started laughing too.

'Oh my God,' Evie said eventually. 'What were we *thinking*? Okay, it was me. What was *I* thinking? Although it isn't like we ate or drank anything. And we got the dancing going really well. I mean, some of those guests really weren't putting their heart and soul into it before I showed them the hustle. *And*, if anyone mentions us, it'll be an interesting talking point for the bride and groom afterwards.'

'You mean when they're bored on their honeymoon?'

'*Exactly*. Who *were* those very elegantly dressed and enthusiastic dancers?'

'I actually think they will see us. Did you see those people going round with the disposable cameras taking pictures of everyone dancing?'

'Really? No, I didn't. Oh well. I think they'll be pleased. I'm pretty sure everyone would like a mystery wedding guest as long as they only stayed for three dances.'

'Yep, you're right.' Dan nodded. 'We were doing them a favour. And now we should probably go and show them how it's done at the wedding we're actually supposed to be at.'

They were both still sniggering slightly when they got back inside Lucie's function room.

'"Grease"!' Evie said, pointing at the dance floor.

'Let me guess,' Dan said. 'Up there with ABBA?'

'Well, duh.'

Sasha danced her way over to them while Evie was squealing that her chills were *mult*iplying. 'Where have you *been*? You just missed "I Gotta Feeling".'

'How do you know *all* the words?' Dan asked five minutes later.

'Er, from our musicals phase?' Sasha said, like he was stupid.

'And, also, you've literally just sung every single word to "Summer Nights" correctly?' Evie pointed out.

'Yeah, well, you know, you hear them,' Dan said.

Half an hour later, he was still dancing with Evie and Sasha, and more because he was having fun than because he wanted to be sure to avoid his father. He twirled a laughing Evie under his arm and looked down – quite a long way down, because she was dancing shoeless again – and, as the twirl finished, their gazes caught. And suddenly it was only the two of them. He was still holding her hand. He could draw her in. It would be so easy, so natural now to kiss her. Her eyes were on his. She smiled a little and there was that dimple again. So beautiful. He moved his head slightly closer to hers. He couldn't look away from her. He knew how good it felt to hold her, taste her. Memories.

And she was engaged to another man.

He let go of her hand and started a bit of half-hearted clapping with everyone else.

Chapter Fourteen

THEN – OCTOBER 2016

EVIE

Even having to share a taxi home with her mum and the man she'd met at the wedding – Grant, a newly divorced friend of Lucie's new father-in-law and the landlord of the pub in Little Bishop, a neighbouring village – didn't dent Evie's mood.

'My other daughter's staying with my sister for the night and not due back until ten tomorrow.' Evie's mum ran her hand up Grant's thigh while Evie tried not to gag and wished that her mum had stopped drinking a lot earlier in the evening. And then she thought about her own evening and started smiling again. She'd had fun; her mum had had fun. It looked like her mum's night was likely to end with sex, and Evie's clearly was not, but it would have done if Euan hadn't got injured. Although then, if she was honest, she'd have had a lot less fun at the wedding.

That was something to think about.

It was actually something she didn't want to think about.

Another thing she did and didn't want to think about was what had happened at the end of that dance with Dan. They'd had a definite moment. Engaged people weren't supposed to have moments with third parties. They weren't supposed to *adore* dancing for hours with another man.

Her mum and Grant were looking into each other's eyes. Evie *really* didn't want them to kiss until she wasn't there.

She needed somewhere to look that wasn't at them or their reflection in the windows backed by the dark country night. Her phone. She pulled it out of her bag and discovered that Euan had finally replied to her last text asking how he was doing. He'd said *Fine*. Okay, well, good. You couldn't expect him to send a long text. He'd had a bad day.

When the taxi finally arrived at their house – thank goodness; Evie's mum and Grant were now *way* beyond the limit as to how much canoodling you could happily be around – Grant hopped out first and opened the door wide for Evie and her mum.

'Hang on a minute, mate,' he said to the taxi driver. 'I'd love to get your number,' he told Evie's open-mouthed mum, getting his phone out.

Wow. So he wasn't coming in.

Evie started letting herself into the house to get out of their way and as she went in heard Grant say, 'I'd love to take you out for dinner.' Wow. This was unusual.

Her mum came in very soon afterwards, definitely within under a minute, and said, 'So that was weird. I thought he really liked me.'

'Well, maybe he does. Maybe he just wants to take things slowly.' Maybe Grant was interested in more than just sex, unlike the vast majority of men her mum was attracted to.

'Hmm. I'm not sure.'

*

Evie went round to see Euan a couple of days later, after work. When she arrived, he opened the front door, wrapped in a blanket, led her into his sitting room and sat himself down on the sofa. The contents of his side table – three remote controls, two books (on *Financial Management* and *Getting Ahead in Business*), an empty coffee mug and a plate with two empty fruit compote tubs and a spoon placed neatly in the middle, the biggest mess Evie had ever seen in his house – indicated that he'd been on the sofa for a while.

'How are you feeling?' Evie asked.

'A little bit delicate,' he said. He touched his mouth very lightly and moaned a little.

Evie nodded. 'I'm really sorry. Can I get you something to eat?'

'Thank you. Maybe some soup. Or perhaps an omelette for some strength. Could you go and buy me some eggs? And I think perhaps some tomatoes and a little shredded ham. Perhaps some cheese. Stilton. All in the omelette, not on the side. Chopped and well-cooked so that I can manage them. Maybe with some chives. Fresh, obviously, not dried.'

'Of course.' Evie wasn't as particular about her herbs as Euan was. 'So shall I buy all of that for both of us? And then we can eat together?'

'If you like.' Euan leaned his head back and closed his eyes.

Not that romantic for people who were supposedly engaged, but it was understandable that he'd be feeling rough with all that tooth pain.

A couple of hours later, when they'd finished their omelettes, plus some chocolate mousses Evie had bought for a treat, Euan said, 'Thank you. That was very nice.' He reached out and held Evie's hand for a moment. 'We should go engagement ring shopping together when I'm better.'

'That would be lovely.' Evie smiled at him and tried to push a tiny feeling of doubt out of her mind. Euan was perfect. She looked round his lovely, tidy, tasteful pale-grey sitting room. He'd be a wonderful husband.

*

By Saturday, he was well enough to go for a walk, which was very nice, but not well enough for ring shopping, he said.

Midway through their walk in a nearby wood, he put his arm round Evie's shoulders and pulled her close to him.

'I'm lucky to have you,' he said. He leaned his head down towards Evie's upturned face and then pulled back, saying, 'No, I don't think my mouth's sufficiently recovered to kiss yet.' He pulled a little mirror out of the pocket of his – very well-ironed – chinos and inspected his face while Evie waited.

Euan was tired after their walk, so Evie went home after agreeing a shopping trip and lunch in two weeks' time – when Euan thought he'd definitely be better – to buy the ring. Which was very exciting. Quite exciting, anyway. Well, a bit exciting.

Maybe it should feel more exciting than it actually did.

*

'I'm going for the bullseye,' Sasha said the following Thursday evening, holding her third dart horizontally ahead of her between her forefinger and thumb.

'You look like an actual darts player,' Evie said, nodding encouragingly.

They were in The Crown, Grant's pub in Little Bishop. He'd just set up a darts league and had invited Evie's mum to get a team of four together for it. She'd been a little bit upset that he didn't seem interested in her romantically – Evie suspected he *was* interested but was maybe keen to take things slowly after his nasty divorce – and had then decided it sounded like fun and had asked Evie and Sasha and Sasha's mum Fiona to join her. Grant had provided them with large, pale-blue men's team t-shirts to wear, so both Evie and Sasha's mothers were looking very different from their usual respective low-cut dressy-topped and twin-setted selves, which was still making Evie giggle slightly every time she focused on one of them. The four of them were also wearing matching little pale-blue hats, knocked up in two evenings by Evie's mum, which were lovely but, frankly, weird-looking with the t-shirts.

'I *am* an actual darts player.' Sasha let fly, with a lot of force, and her dart hit the board's wooden surround, ricocheted off and just missed an elderly man nursing a pint at the bar.

'Good try, darling,' Fiona said as the man clutched his heart.

Grant hurried out from behind the bar, saying, 'Great enthusiasm, Sasha,' and helped the man to a bar stool further away.

Evie's mum turned and glared at their (orange-t-shirted) opponents, who had clapped. She turned back to her team, frowning. 'So unsporting. Right. I think we need to take this more seriously. I'm thinking we need to get some practice in before our next fixture. If you're going to do something, do it properly. Could you all do next Wednesday evening?'

Fiona and Sasha both said they could, while Evie thought. She was *supposed* to be seeing Euan. But she'd *so much* rather play darts with her mum, her best friend and her best friend's mum. What did that say about her relationship with Euan?

'I'm free too,' she said. She and Euan could go to the cinema another evening.

They stayed for another drink after they'd finished losing their match, and finally spilled out of the pub at about eleven, escorted to the door by Grant.

'He's *lovely*,' Fiona said, when he'd finally kissed all their cheeks and gone back inside.

'Just a friend,' Evie's mum said. 'Blatantly not interested in sleeping with me. But, yes, a very nice man.'

'I've just got a text from Millie asking about Dan,' Sasha said, scrolling through her phone. 'She's so obvious about liking him.'

Evie could see where Millie was coming from. Her heart had literally just leapt at the mention of Dan's name. She took her own phone out. And there was a message from Euan replying to hers about postponing their cinema date. And the sight of his name caused her no heart leap at all; in fact, it made her feel vaguely flat, like her mood was suffering from a slow puncture. If she was honest, she didn't want to postpone the cinema trip; she wanted to cancel it forever. And she even more didn't want to go engagement ring shopping with him.

Because, if she was honest, she really didn't want to marry him.

She'd better tell him tomorrow. Shortest engagement ever. Just under two weeks. Like her mother, she made some rubbish choices when it came to men. Although in a different way.

Chapter Fifteen

NOW – MARCH 2022

DAN

'Happy St Patrick's.' Dan adjusted his leprechaun hat, handed a packet of chocolate buttons to Minnie, the little girl in the bed next to the window, and smiled at her. 'Your special challenge is to not eat all your chocolate at once.' The paediatric ward had had a big donation of chocolates, and they'd decided to use any excuse to cheer the kids and their families up by dressing up and doling treats out.

'Thank you, Mr Leprechaun.' Minnie's mother smiled a bit tearily at him. 'It's so nice that you can visit all the children.'

'I'll tell you a secret, Minnie,' Dan said. 'Soon my friend the Easter bunny will be visiting too.' Minnie had a chronic condition, which meant that she'd be in hospital for a while.

'That's wonderful,' Minnie's mum said.

'It's our pleasure,' Dan told her. It was true. It wasn't great for anyone at the best of times if a child had to visit A&E or be admitted to the paediatric ward, and it seemed even worse over holiday periods, especially if it meant that a family was separated.

Of course, he was separated from his own family pretty much every holiday season, by choice. He wasn't six years old, though, and since he was that age he'd learned that his father was a total arse.

'You make a superb leprechaun,' Zubin told him fifteen minutes later as he peeled the costume off.

'Thank you.' Dan bowed. 'Couldn't do it without my magical carrot helper.'

Zubin, who'd squeezed himself into a random carrot costume that he'd found in the store cupboard – and that was meant for someone a lot smaller – and followed Dan round with the bag of chocolates, grinned. 'I'll take any excuse to wear a pair of orange tights. Time for a quick pint later?'

'Definitely.'

*

Twenty-four hours later, Dan was in a place far removed from the convivial fish-and-chips and beers evening he and Zubin had ended up having last night with another couple of friends at the pub along the road from the hospital.

He closed his eyes and took a deep breath as he felt bile reach his throat and his palms grow clammy.

He needed to rise above this.

Zachy, the boy on the other side of the door Dan had just closed, needed him. Zachy's family needed him. Dan needed to shove all memories of Max's accident back in the compartment they normally rested in and focus on the here and now.

God, though.

Zachy was about five years younger than Max had been when he'd had his accident, but the backstory was hideously similar – he'd been rugby tackling his cousin on a pavement and had fallen into the road. His main injury appeared to be a very badly fractured leg, as Max's had been. And his mother had mentioned several times that he was a talented footballer – training with a top club – as Max had been at Zachy's age. And there was every chance that his future in football would now be in doubt. Or possibly ended, as Max's athletics career had been.

God, the memories. The screeching of brakes. The screaming. The terror that Max might be dead. The terror that Max's brain might have been injured. The terror that Max would never walk again. The realisation that he would walk again but he'd never go back to the exact way he had been physically.

And the knowledge that it was all Dan's fault and the realisation that their mother couldn't deal with the fact that one of her sons had maimed the other, so she was going to pretend for the rest of time that it hadn't happened the way it did.

He took a glance at the clock on the other side of the paediatric emergency waiting area. It was nearly the end of his shift. He *could* hand Zachy over to someone else and turn round and walk out. Grab a beer with a friend and re-bury those memories.

He shouldn't, though. He should stay.

He took another big breath and turned the handle of the door.

He pulled a phenomenal effort out of the bag and smiled over at Zachy, lying on the bed against the opposite wall.

'Right, mate,' he told him, 'we're going to give you something for the pain and then cart you off for an X-ray and get you sorted once we know the exact damage. It hurts now but you're going to be fine.'

Three hours later, two and a half hours after he should have ended his shift, Dan left the hospital, not confident that Zachy was going to recover fully, but at least confident that he was in good hands, in surgery for his leg. Lisa, the orthopaedic surgeon doing the operation, was going to message Dan later and let him know how things were.

It could have been worse. Zachy could have been more severely injured. But *God*. You went into medicine to try to help people and make them better. And it was shit that sometimes you couldn't work miracles and you couldn't do everything you wanted to.

He aimed a vicious kick at an empty can littering the pavement. The can flew into the air and clattered against the railings separating the pavement from the road. He walked over and picked it up and shoved it into the top of an overflowing rubbish bin just along the road.

He was pretty sure that there was some kind of metaphor for his life in there but he was too tired to work out what it was.

Anyway, he needed to stop wallowing, go home, eat something vaguely healthy – now he thought about it, he was starving – and get some sleep.

*

Late morning the next day, Dan squeezed in a quick visit to the paediatric inpatient ward to check on Zachy. The operation had been a success and he'd definitely walk again, but he probably wouldn't be back to football at the same standard ever again, and he might need more surgery. Heartbreaking.

And Dan didn't have as much time as he'd like to spend with Zachy, because over lunchtime he was meeting Hannah and her mother at a fancy private clinic along the road for Hannah's anomaly scan.

'Good afternoon, Dan.' Hannah's mother, a slim woman with shoulder-length, very sleek, grey-blonde hair and wearing a pale pink jacket over a black jumper and black trousers, put her hand out. 'I'm Julia. How do you do?'

'I'm very well, thank you. It's good to meet you. How are you?' If he'd ever planned to have a baby, he'd probably have planned to meet its grandmother well in advance of conception rather than halfway through the pregnancy. Better than not meeting her until the birth, though.

'Very well, thank you. I'm looking forward to becoming a grandmother. Hannah tells me that you're a doctor.' Her manner was brisk but pleasant.

After only five minutes of forced small talk – thank God for private appointments running to time – they were ushered in for the scan.

Hannah raised her top and lowered the waistband of her trousers – both black and very sophisticated, very Hannah – and the sonographer rubbed gel onto her tummy.

Dan felt his heart rate pick up slightly. What if something was wrong with the baby?

Hannah, staring with extreme intensity at the sonographer's screen, clearly felt the same way.

'And everything's fine,' the sonographer concluded fifteen minutes later. 'Your daughter looks perfect.'

Hannah, Julia and Dan all beamed at each other and inside his head Dan yelled, again, *It's a girl*.

'Do you both have time for a coffee?' Julia asked as they left the clinic.

'I do,' Dan said quickly. This felt like a good opportunity to make it clear in person that he'd like to be involved in the baby's life.

Hannah checked what looked like a slim Rolex. 'Yep, I can do a quick one,' she said. 'I have a meeting in an hour but the traffic looks good and I can hop in a cab.'

Julia was one of those women who had a way with waiters, and indeed probably with everyone, Dan suspected. They were at a table in a very nice open-all-day wine bar within only a couple of minutes of leaving the clinic and a waiter was taking their order within only about a minute of them sitting down.

'Decaf latte,' Hannah said, rubbing her tummy.

'The same for me,' Julia said.

Dan looked at them both and at the menu. He could murder a caffeinated coffee right now. But was it rude to the pregnant mother of your child to drink caffeine when she couldn't? He really didn't know and he really didn't know her well enough to ask her.

'And the same for me too,' he said.

'So I've been very pleased to meet you, Dan,' Julia said. 'I wondered whether you two thought it would be a good idea to discuss before the baby's born how much time you each want to spend with her.' Dan wanted to high five her. Of course it would be a good idea, but Hannah had been busy with work and not available to chat since she'd dropped the pregnancy news bombshell. 'I don't want to interfere but, for the sake of my granddaughter, I do think that you should have these conversations sooner rather than later.' Dan didn't just want to high five, he wanted to kiss her. Of *course* they should discuss things now.

'Mum!' Hannah gave her mother the evil eye. 'I think we're probably adult enough to work that out for ourselves.' Although she hadn't managed to engage with Dan so far.

'I'd love to be involved and I'd love to hear your thoughts on how much time you thought she might spend with me?' he said.

Hannah cleared her throat and said, 'If I stay in London, I'd be very happy for her to spend close to half her time with you, however you'd like to play it, as long as we both think it will work well for her emotional needs.'

'Great,' said Dan. That was a *lot* better than he'd been expecting. It was fantastic, actually.

'But there's a possibility—' Hannah folded her hands together and looked at Dan's left ear '—there's a possibility that I – we – will be moving to New York, for work.'

What?

God. *God.* Not so fantastic.

'When would that be, darling?' Julia was frowning.

'An opportunity's come up at work recently.' Hannah was some kind of high-flying investment banker. Corporate finance. Dan wasn't totally sure what that involved other than apparently insane working hours, almost longer than a junior doctor's. 'We're restructuring our team globally later in the year and I might move to New York with the baby to head up our team there after my maternity leave.'

'What's the...' Dan paused, to give his voice a chance to stop sounding so croaky. 'What's the likelihood that you'll make the move?'

'I don't know.' Hannah was looking at his right ear now. 'It's a great opportunity. But of course it might not be the best thing for the baby, and I have to think of her too now.'

Of course it won't bloody be the best thing for the baby, Dan wanted to yell. *How will she spend time with her father if you move to America?* 'Okay,' he said. 'Well, I would of course very much appreciate an update as soon as you've decided.'

'Of course.' She took a long sip of her coffee and then looked at her mother rather than back at Dan.

'I will of course be very sad if you move to New York,' Julia said. Dan looked between the two of them. Julia was twisting her hands together, looking at her daughter, and Hannah was looking at her coffee cup. 'But I will of course support you. And I'd love to see my granddaughter as much as possible. I would visit and I presume that Dan would too?'

'Yes, of course,' Dan said. 'And…' God, he needed to phrase this well. 'This is a bit of a shock. I wondered if we could perhaps discuss your decision together, a little at least, for the baby's sake?'

'Yes, definitely. Absolutely.' Hannah pulled her sleeve up and checked her watch again. 'I think I ought to go now. The traffic's looking worse.' There were literally no moving cars on the road outside.

'Of course.' Dan would have another go at speaking to her another time. He got his wallet out. 'I'll get these.'

Julia shook her head. 'My treat.'

'Well, thank you,' Dan said. 'It's been great.' It hadn't. It had been shit. He was pretty sure that he was going to be absolutely devastated if he had to live on the opposite side of the Atlantic from his daughter.

Chapter Sixteen

NOW – APRIL 2022

EVIE

'Evie, this egg's got a present inside it.' Autumn shook it hard. It did sound like there was something clunking around inside there. 'Look.' Autumn pointed at the side of the personalised box. 'It says "gift". That means "present".' Very good point. Evie hadn't spotted that earlier. She looked at her watch.

'I'm late,' she said. 'I'll open it later. Thank you for pointing that out. Night. Love you. See you in the morning.'

Evie gave Autumn a hug, grabbed her phone, purse and keys, and sprinted out of the house. Her phone rang as she was walking down the lane.

'Hi, Matthew. Happy Easter.'

'Hey. Happy Easter to you too. I'm missing you.'

'Missing you too.' Eek. She wasn't really, if she was honest. She'd had a lovely day with her mum and Autumn, and now she was on the way to the pub for a pre-wedding summit with Sasha and Lucie and Sasha's other bridesmaid, Dervla, a university friend of Sasha's. They were planning to discuss all things weddingy, eat pub food and drink a lot of Prosecco, with the bonus of not having to get up early tomorrow because it was Easter Monday, and Evie was really looking forward to it. It was lovely going out with Matthew, but it was nice to have the opportunity to see her mum and Autumn and her friends on her own sometimes, so it felt like it had worked out well that he'd had a golf weekend planned for ages.

Matthew had a *lot* of golf trips planned. He wasn't going to be able to make it to Sasha's wedding because he had a golf week in Tenerife arranged for then.

He also had a *lot* of golf stories, like the one he was telling now, not as interesting to your non-golfer as they probably were to people who had *any* idea about the rules and under-par and irons and all those things. It was nice listening to his enthusiasm, though, and watching his eyes twinkle when he joked when they were together in person.

'Ha, hilarious,' she said when he'd stopped talking after what she was pretty sure was a punchline.

'Yeah, I know. Golf's a fantastic game. Different every time. Anyway, enough about me. Have you opened your Easter egg yet?'

Evie screwed up her face as she rounded the next corner along the green to go up the lane past the church towards the pub. Autumn must have been right. Clearly, there was a present in there, and she couldn't thank him for it without knowing what it was.

'Not yet,' she said. 'I've had a really busy day with Mum and Autumn and I thought I'd save it. I'm going to open it this evening when I get home from the pub.'

'Okay, well I hope you like it. The egg. Have fun this evening.'

'Thank you.' Wow. If he was like this over an Easter egg, what would he be like over a birthday present?

*

'Okay,' Sasha said three hours later. She put her pen and notebook down and glugged more Prosecco. 'So that's favours sorted. Thank you so much for doing those, Dervla. And Evie, I'll let you know what dates they have available for menu tasting. And Lucie, thank you so much for sorting all the place settings.'

'I know what I was going to ask,' Lucie said. 'What have you decided about Max and Dan?'

'We drew lots. Dan's walking me down the aisle and Max is doing the reading and the speech.' Sasha and her siblings still had very frosty relations with their father since he'd left their mother for another (older) woman three or four years ago.

'Perfect,' Lucie said. 'Okay, I've got to go. I'll be up at the crack of dawn with the kids.'

'Me too, actually,' Dervla said.

'Stay for another one, Evie?' Sasha said.

'Definitely,' Evie said.

When the others had gone, Sasha said, 'There's something I thought I should tell you, about Dan.'

'Mmm?'

'He's expecting a baby with his ex.'

Evie choked on her Pringle and Sasha whacked her hard on the back.

'Ow,' Evie said.

'Sorry. Are you okay?'

'Yes, you didn't hit me *that* hard.'

'I meant about Dan,' Sasha said. Yep, Evie had known that she'd meant about Dan. And she was not okay about it but she didn't want to say that. Because why wouldn't she be okay? It was nothing to do with her.

'So, um, what's the due date and how long were they going out and… everything, really?' she said, trying to sound normally gossipy rather than suddenly desperately miserable.

'I'm not sure about dates. And apparently they only went out for a few weeks, so it was a huge shock. And Dan wants to be involved in the baby's life but the mother, Hannah, might move to New York.'

'Wow,' Evie said.

'Yeah, bit of a nightmare for him. Not how you want to start a family in an ideal world.'

'Happens to a lot of people, though.'

'Yes. Oh, God, Evie, I'm sorry,' Sasha said. Evie's mum had never known who Evie's father was and Autumn's father, Jack, wasn't exactly around.

Evie *really* didn't mind about Sasha saying that wasn't the way you wanted to start a family. She was right; it wasn't. She really *did* mind about the fact that Dan had had a relationship straight before he came out to Vegas by the sounds of it. Or maybe even while he was there. No, surely not.

'Honestly, nothing to be sorry about. I know you didn't mean that in a bad way. Of course it isn't what he'd have planned. So when did he and Hannah split up?'

'Definitely before Vegas. I think that might have been why he was keen to go.'

Right. *Right.* So Evie had been a rebound one-night stand. And there was *totally* no reason that she shouldn't have been. He'd been single. She'd been single. Nothing wrong with it *whatsoever*. Clearly there was nothing wrong with it.

She was still *really* pissed off, though.

Why, though?

They'd both been single. He'd done nothing wrong. End of.

She shouldn't be pissed off.

'Game of darts for old time's sake?' she said.

'Wow,' Sasha said ten minutes later. 'You're chucking those darts like they're murder weapons.'

Evie nodded. Yup. She was feeling murderous. She flung another one.

'OMG,' she squealed. 'Bloody bullseye.'

'You're a darts superstar,' Sasha said. 'We're going to have to get you back from London as a secret weapon.' Sasha had periodically been putting serious effort into trying to persuade Evie to return to the Cotswolds from London ever since she moved a couple of years ago. 'Maybe you should have drunk more Prosecco when you were playing regularly.'

Nope. It wasn't the Prosecco. It was anger. And the anger, Evie realised as she pulled her darts out of the board, was fuelled by hurt. That Dan had had something big with someone else. Jealousy, maybe. Which was absolutely ridiculous, because she was with Matthew and he was lovely. And any jealousy wasn't just ridiculous, it was stupid. Nothing serious was ever going to happen between her and Dan, so she couldn't let any feelings she might have for him ruin her relationships with other people.

*

'Close the curtains, Autumn,' Evie groaned the next morning. 'What time is it?'

'Seven. You said I could wake you up at seven.'

'Did I?' Why hadn't she said eight? Or nine? Or ten?

'Will you open your Easter egg present now?'

'I'll open it at eight. Come back then. Love you.'

Autumn was back what felt like about three minutes later, brandishing the egg and a big plate.

'Is it really already eight?' Evie asked.

'Yes. Look, I brought you a plate so that you don't make a mess if the chocolate cracks.'

'You're very clever.' Evie sat up in bed and took the egg while Autumn bounced up and down on the end of her bed. She took the egg out of its blue foil and gave it a little smack against the plate. 'Oh.'

'It's a key,' Autumn said. 'Why has he given you a key?' She bounced herself down onto her bottom and shuffled forwards and inspected the plate. 'It's got a message on it. "Twenty-two A Hartfield Road". What's that?'

That was Matthew's address. On the back of the address message he'd written, *So that you can come and go as you like.*

Wow. Giving someone a key was huge. And unnerving.

Nice, of course.

But very unnerving.

At least he hadn't asked her to move in with him. She definitely wasn't ready for that.

Evie thought about Dan and his baby and about Matthew and how *nice* he was.

'That's a strange present,' Autumn said. 'Grown-ups do boring things.'

'Mmm.'

Chapter Seventeen

NOW – MAY 2022

DAN

Dan's phone buzzed. Sasha. She was up in London for the May bank holiday weekend and he'd seen her for lunch yesterday.

'Hi, it's me,' she said. 'You got any plans for this evening? Working? Going out?'

'No. Why?'

'Perfect, perfect, perfect. We need someone extra for a quiz night. I'll text you the details. It starts at seven. See you then. There's curry. Don't eat.'

He experienced a wave of annoyance that reminded him of being about twelve and furious with his bossy little sister. He should text her and say he wasn't going.

Although, Sunday evening. It had been raining all day, he'd had a depressing text from Hannah earlier, saying that she was still thinking about next steps but that New York in the autumn was looking likely, and he'd been planning to catch up on some admin this evening but really didn't fancy it right now. A quiz night wouldn't hurt to take his mind off things.

'Okay,' he said. 'See you later.'

Sasha's text with the details pinged through. It was in an upstairs function room at a pub in Kew. He could drive out there.

Would Evie be there? She might be. Did he want to see her? It depended. It was always nice to catch up with her but he wasn't really up for watching her with her boyfriend.

By the looks of things, i.e. the one empty seat at their table of eight, Dan was the last to arrive. There was no sign of the blond guy Evie had taken to Sasha's engagement party. Maybe they weren't together any more.

'Thank you for coming,' Sasha said. 'You can only ask a sibling at really short notice. Evie's boyfriend got a migraine. We couldn't really ask anyone else because it would have sounded rude, like they weren't our first choice.'

'I can only say I'm honoured,' Dan said, rolling his eyes at her, more pissed off than he should be at being the stand-in for Evie's boyfriend.

'Yeah, you should be,' Sasha said. 'We could have decided an empty seat was better than you.'

'Might well be,' Dan said. 'I might feed you all the wrong answers.'

'I'm Josh, Evie's flatmate,' said a man on the other side of the table. 'We have beers, red and white.'

'A beer would be great, thanks.' Dan remembered Evie talking about Josh at a picnic last year.

'Sorry, I should have introduced you,' Evie said, passing a bottle of beer and a glass to Dan. 'This is Josh's partner, Tom. And these are my colleagues and friends Priya, Claire and Sara. How are you on dingbats?'

'I want to say I'm a genius but I can't actually remember what they are and I'm fairly sure I'm not.'

'You have to make well-known phrases from pictures,' Evie said, pushing a piece of paper towards Dan. 'Josh is really good at them *if* they involve sex.'

'I'm really good at anything if it involves sex.' Josh did a suggestive pout in Evie's direction and she laughed and made a face back at him, looking a lot more relaxed than she had just now talking to Dan. Maybe she'd sensed his initial irritation about the boyfriend.

'Okay.' A sound like gunshot came over the speakers and a lot of people, including most of their table, half-screamed. 'Apologies. I'm Dr Blue, your quizmaster, and apparently I just clapped too loudly. Time to start the questions.'

Three rounds out of eight down, they were coming third out of about twenty tables, they were *all* taking it a lot more seriously than possibly any of them had been expecting, and Dan was *loving* Evie's quiz persona.

'No, no, no,' she was saying, waving both her forefingers at the others for emphasis. 'We need to think it through. We can't just *waste* our joker. This could be the difference between winning and losing. I mean, it probably will be.'

'I just think sport's safer than music,' said Dan. 'Music could be *anything*. It could be classical. It could be country and western. Can we cover all of that?'

'But can we cover every sport?' Evie said. 'Like, who here knows who the current dodgeball world champions are?' They all shook their heads. '*Exactly*. I think we go music.'

'Or,' said Dan, 'and I know this is controversial, but maybe we go world capitals.'

'Dodgy,' Evie said.

'You're a bloody geography teacher,' Josh said. 'What do you teach kids at school now?' Evie glared at him and he said, 'Sorry.'

'I think we should go music,' Evie said.

*

Music turned out to have been a good call – although they'd done equally well on sport, Dan kept reminding everyone – and two hours, a very nice chicken biryani followed by choc ices and a lot of questions later, they were the winners.

'This is literally like a village pub,' said Sasha when they piled out with their victory case of wine. 'Apart from the planes. It's lovely.' It was near Kew Green and surrounded by a surprising number of trees. 'I'm going to hug you and leave you so that I don't get home too late.'

'Text me when you arrive,' Evie said.

'And me,' Dan agreed. Sasha was driving back to Melting this evening. It should be fine, under two hours, on a Sunday evening, but you wanted to make sure that people were okay.

'We're going to head off too,' Josh said. 'I'm staying at Tom's tonight, Evie.'

Priya, Claire and Sara were walking to the train station together.

'Evie must be pretty much on your way back, Dan,' Sasha said, jiggling her own car keys.

'Yes, pretty much,' Dan said. Not really. 'I'll give you a lift.' He wasn't totally keen, if he was honest. He'd enjoyed her company this evening, as he always did, but there was something intimate about being alone in a car with someone, and they hadn't been alone together since Vegas, and she had a boyfriend.

'No, honestly,' she said, looking about as thrilled as he felt, 'I can get an Uber.'

'Really not a problem,' Dan told her insincerely. No option, because Sasha was looking at him.

'Okay, well, great, thank you.'

Now that they didn't have the quiz to talk about, silence stretched between them as he reversed out of his parking space and into the road. On Dan's part, he was suddenly – ridiculously – thinking about Vegas again. Should he mention it, to break the ice? No, maybe not.

'So that was a great evening,' he said eventually. 'Good to know that we're quizzing superstars.'

'You were very impressive on your weird niche sports,' Evie said.

'Ice hockey is not weird or niche. I will admit that bossaball *is* niche. As is knowing the names of every celebrity ever who's had twins by a surrogate, though.'

'Niche in a good way. I'm *proud* of my celebrity twins knowledge. And also my rice knowledge.'

Dan nodded. 'That was seriously impressive.' Their table had been the only one in the room who'd got full marks in the 'Name what type of rice grain this is' round, courtesy of Evie.

Dan slowed down for a red traffic light and the conversation slowed too. Stalled completely in fact. They'd never struggled to talk before.

'I should have congratulated you before now on your baby news,' Evie said after a few moments.

'Um, thanks. Yeah. It was a bit of a surprise. But I'm obviously delighted now.'

'Yes, wonderful news.' More silence. Then Evie said, 'What's the due date?'

'Late July or early August.' Dan negotiated a right turn onto a main road followed by a sharp left.

'Wow, so… wow.' Her voice was suddenly very cold.

Dan could say nothing, or he could say something. It felt like this was another one of those make or break moments in terms of a friendship. If he said nothing, maybe Evie was going to think he'd still been with Hannah when he was in Vegas. He actually couldn't let her think that.

'Hannah, the baby's mother, and I went out briefly in the autumn,' he said. 'We split up before I came to Vegas.'

'Great,' Evie said, very over-brightly. 'I mean, I wasn't suggesting you hadn't.'

Dan gripped the steering wheel. He shouldn't react to that.

He was going to react to it. He didn't like the implication that she would think that he might do that.

'You know, I would never cheat on anyone,' he said. 'Never have, and I'd really like to believe that I never will.' When your father had cheated on your mother a *lot*, you knew you never wanted to be that kind of arsehole yourself.

'No, I really wasn't suggesting that you would.' They'd slowed down for more lights, so Dan was able to turn to look at Evie. She was staring straight ahead. 'I suppose I was a rebound thing.' She turned slightly and looked at him for a moment before resuming her straight-ahead stare.

'No.' Dan shook his head. 'No. Definitely not. No rebound. Hannah and I weren't serious. I mean, we're having a baby and that's serious, but we weren't serious as a couple. I wasn't upset when we split up. There was no rebound. You weren't a rebound.' He eased forward as the lights went green. 'You, our night in Vegas, that was…' What was it? Amazing? Perfect? Incredibly special? A complete one-off. 'It happened. In the moment. Because, I suppose, at the time it felt… right.' He should really not have said that. Except, he liked Evie. He liked her a lot. She was a lovely person. He'd known her most of his life and she was Sasha's best friend and he didn't want things to be awkward. 'I mean, that was a great night. I really enjoyed it.' Oh, God. What was wrong with him? Was he making things better or worse?

'Yep.' Yeah, she sounded very clipped. He'd made things worse. 'Yep, no, it just sounded as though it was very soon after. But obviously you and Hannah had split up first.'

'Yes, we had.' It *really* annoyed him that Evie had thought for even a moment that he'd cheat on someone. Especially her, actually. Because it would have been cheating on her too if he'd already been with someone. He just wouldn't do that. 'Frankly, I can't see much of a difference, if any, between me splitting up with someone and then sleeping with you, and you sleeping with me and beginning shortly afterwards to go out with Matthew. Assuming you weren't going out with him at the time.' Of course she hadn't been going out with him at the time; he was being ridiculous. It was like he was trying to pick an argument with her for no good reason at all. Other than the fact that he really hadn't taken to Matthew. Which wasn't a good reason. She could go out with who she liked.

'I wasn't. And, yes, sorry, I shouldn't have said that.'

'No worries. Nor should I.' Dan didn't take his eyes away from the road.

They drove the rest of the way in silence.

When they got to Evie's road, Dan stopped the car and double-parked.

'Thank you for the lift,' said Evie, only half-looking at him. 'It was really kind of you. And thank you for coming to the quiz. That was kind of you too.'

'I enjoyed it,' said Dan truthfully. It was just the drive back here that hadn't been so good. He turned so that he was facing her full-on, and she turned a little bit more towards him. God, he loved the line of her neck. So elegant. 'I'm not sure what happened during that conversation, but I'm sorry.'

'I'm sorry too.' She looked up at him and he saw that her eyes were glistening.

They were sitting so close to each other that he could see her lips trembling, the rise and fall of her chest. He saw one tear dribble out. He lifted his hand and wiped it carefully away with his thumb. Evie bit her lip.

Oh, God.

He slid his hand into her hair and she leaned slightly towards him.

Their lips were only inches apart now. He loved her skin, the shape of her cheek, the feel of her hair. He leaned further towards her. He wanted to taste her again, learn the shape of her body again. He wanted a repeat of that night in Vegas, except sober.

She turned her head towards his. They were going to kiss. This had been building for years, really. He moved a little closer.

Evie sighed and parted her lips.

And then very suddenly pulled away from him.

And, Christ, rightly so. She had a boyfriend apart from anything else.

He let go of her and drew back and she shook her head and fumbled for the door handle behind her.

She practically fell out of the car in her hurry to get out.

'Goodnight,' she said. 'And thank you again.'

Dan sat and watched until she was safely inside her front door and then smacked a palm to his forehead. What the hell had that been? Again, she had a boyfriend, for Christ's sake. If you had a partner, you didn't kiss someone else. And you didn't kiss someone – however briefly – who you knew had a partner. That moment had almost become something that they'd both said they'd never do. God.

He wasn't going to be giving Evie a lift anywhere again in a hurry. Far too intimate. There was something about him and Evie in a car together.

Chapter Eighteen

THEN – CHRISTMAS 2019

EVIE

Bloody London. Bloody car. Bloody British Rail. Bloody Christmas bloody presents. Bloody bloody everything.

Obviously, some might say that Evie should have checked that her car would start before she'd spent one and a half *bloody* hours traipsing backwards and forwards between her flat and the car parked two roads away in the *bloody* drizzle with bags-for-life full of presents and stuffing all those presents into the car. But it had never broken down before.

Obviously, if she hadn't got a parking ticket last time she double-parked outside her flat she *would* have tried to start the car before she filled it to the brim with presents and suitcases, because she'd have tried to drive it round to the flat, and then she'd have found out sooner that the engine was just going to splutter over and over again during the dozens of times she turned the key in the ignition, sometimes coming tantalisingly close to making a proper revving sound, but never actually starting.

And, *obviously*, if she'd known she was going to break down on the twenty-third of December when all seats on all trains to anywhere near the Cotswolds were booked solid other than a few incredibly expensive first-class ones, she would either have booked a reasonably priced seat a long time ago or gone for premium car breakdown cover.

But she had *not* checked and she *had* filled the car and there was no chance of anyone coming to fix the car for *days*, if not *weeks*, and she did not have an affordable train ticket and *what was she going to do*? She didn't want to spend Christmas by herself in London. She didn't want to spend *all* her disposable income for the next six weeks on one return train ticket for a ninety-mile journey. If she did manage to go, she *did* want to take all the presents she'd bought for her mum and Autumn and everyone else. And some clothes and toiletries. So cycling wasn't an option even if she was fit enough to cycle all that way and even owned a bloody bike.

What was she going to do?

Coach. There were coaches.

She got her phone out and googled. No. There were no seats on any coaches to anywhere vaguely near home before the twenty-seventh.

She really wanted to stamp her foot.

She did stamp it. Ow, ow, ouch. She'd stamped it far too hard. Owwwwww. Now she'd probably broken a metatarsal or something. Ow.

Right. Deep, deep breaths. First she was going to text Sasha and her mum and tell them that she would not be joining them for the Melting Bishop Christmas tree walk at 2 p.m. today, and then she was going to unpack the car and while she unpacked she was going to try to think of a solution.

A message from her mum pinged through just after she'd lugged her third lot of presents back into the flat.

Everything will be fine. Going to work something out and will come and get you by car by end of today. WE WILL RESCUE YOU. Love you. LOOKING FORWARD TO SEEING YOU LATER xxx

Evie sniffed. She *really* wanted to get home today and even though she was going to be twenty-eight tomorrow she was going to have to let her wonderful mum do a big round trip to London and rescue her.

Her phone rang as she was typing out a *thaaaaaank youuuuuu* reply. Sasha.

'I have a solution,' Sasha said without any hellos. 'All sorted. Don't move. Just be ready. Dan's coming to pick you up because he's driving home today almost past where you live and it makes perfect sense. I'm going to send you his number now and yours to him and you're *sorted*.'

'Oh, wow. Does he *mind*?' And also, was South Wimbledon really on anyone's way to the Cotswolds?

'Course he doesn't. You'll be company for him on the journey and I've Google-Mapped it and I really don't think it's that much of a detour for him. Anyway. I'll see you later. Got to go now. Have a good journey.'

'Thank you so much, lovely Sasha. Can't wait to see you.'

'Me too and nothing to thank me for. See you later.'

It was the perfect solution. Dan was always good company.

Right. She'd unpacked slightly under half the contents of the car so far. Should she leave things half-and-half as they were, or have them all in one place to make it easier for Dan, and in that case should she put everything back in the car or bring the more-than-half of her stuff back to the flat?

She wondered if Dan had a girlfriend at the moment. Nothing to do with her, of course. Yes, she was single, and yes, she'd love to meet someone nice and not boring but at the same time very sensible and tidy, and yes, she and Dan had made that pact and it had kind of felt like they'd sealed it with that kiss, and she'd thought about it every time that she'd ever seen mistletoe since, but in reality, of course, nothing was ever going to happen between them. Which was totally fine. She lived in *London*, and there had to be literally about a million men in approximately her age bracket here, so there were a lot of fish in the sea.

Anyway. Focus. The suitcases and the presents. It would be easier for Dan if they were all in one place and it would be better to bring them back to the flat because she didn't need to have her car broken into on top of everything else.

By the time she'd schlepped backwards and forwards five more times between the car and her flat with overflowing present bags and her wheely suitcases, she'd broken two of her nails and had had to strip down to a vest top and was *still* slightly sweating. Hauling luggage around was a very good workout; her arms and lungs were both going to be in better condition after this. Right now, though, she maybe needed just to have a very quick shower and maybe also put some more make-up on before Dan arrived.

He rang her doorbell just as she was blotting her lips on loo paper having decided that she'd gone a step too far with all the lip gloss she'd applied on top of her lipstick. She did a final blot and *thank goodness* glanced in the mirror again as she made her way out of the room. She had a bit of the loo paper stuck to her lower lip. Very close shave. She pulled it off and reapplied just a bit more gloss, and then some more, didn't blot this time, and made her way to the door.

'Hello,' Dan said. And there was that gorgeously infectious smile. Whenever she hadn't seen him for a while, the smile always hit her with surprising force, right to her stomach. Evie licked her lips, just to check that she definitely didn't have any more paper stuck there. Which of course she didn't, because she hadn't blotted again. And...

what had she been thinking? Who licked their lips when someone said hello? Really, who?

'Hello. Hi. Lovely to see you,' she said. Oh, God, she was over-helloing straight after lip-licking. Why did this suddenly feel awkward? 'Thank you so much for the lift. I hope it isn't too much out of your way. Sorry Sasha press-ganged you into it.'

'Hey, no need to say sorry, and it'll be nice to have the company. Where are your bags?'

'Right here. There are quite a few. Do you think they'll all fit in?'

'Wow. That *is* quite a few. But, yes, I think so. I mean, I might not be able to see out of the back window at all and the suspension might break and you might have to cuddle some of those presents – what *is* that enormous one, by the way? – but I'm sure it'll be fine.'

'I could leave some behind?'

'*Joking*, you muppet. We'll get them in, it'll be fine. Not joking about the really big one, though – what *is* it? And the other nearly-as-big one?'

'The biggest one is the biggest teddy you've ever seen, for Autumn, and the other big one is a little desk for her. In a box.'

'How old is she now?'

'Five. She's very keen on writing and colouring in, hence the desk, and she still loves teddies.'

'Cute. How's she enjoying school?' Dan picked up two bags in each hand while holding the wrapped teddy.

'She's loving it. She has *so* much to tell me every time we speak. Really sweet.' Evie picked up one bag in each hand. 'How are you *doing* that with the bags? Aren't the handles hurting your hands?'

'Nope. I'm a man of steel. Although I'd be very keen to get these into the boot *quickly*. I've double-parked right outside.'

*

After only two trips – Dan proved he really was made of steel when it came to carrying bags of presents, and also lucky when it came to parking wardens, because he hadn't got a ticket – they had everything in the car and were setting off.

'So Sasha told me you moved to London late summer?' Dan asked as he put the car into gear. 'That must have been a huge change?'

'Yep. Massive. Although long overdue, really, given that I'm about to be twenty-eight. And it isn't like I've moved to the other end of the country. I've already been home several times to see Mum and Autumn. In my car, which has never broken down before.'

'That's any kind of appliance or electrical item for you. They save their worst performance for when you need them the most. My boiler broke down last Christmas during that week when it was below zero the whole time and British Gas couldn't get to me for several days, because apparently half of the rest of London also had broken boilers.'

'That sounds chilly.'

'Yes, unbelievable. But luckily I live in a very small flat with basically only three very small rooms and a shower room and I managed to get some very efficient fan heaters, so all was well within a few hours.'

'Lucky. So whereabouts do you live? Sasha said Fulham?'

'Yep. In a tiny flat above a busy restaurant, but it's mine – other than being mortgaged to the hilt – and it's a great location. Walking distance to work.'

'So you must feel kind of like a Londoner now,' Evie said. Dan had been to university in London and had just stayed. 'I still feel a little bit, like, *woah*, about the traffic, the Tube, all the *people*, the noise. I mean, it's great, because, you know, the restaurants and the shops and the theatres and the cinemas, just everything, and it's all *open* all the time, and I'm having a lot of fun, and I'm lucky because I have some university friends living nearby plus the teachers at school are lovely and there's a lot of social stuff amongst the staff, but it's a *big* change. Okay, and that sounded ridiculously country bumpkin and underlined *exactly* why it was time for me to finally live by myself.'

Dan laughed. 'Yeah, I can imagine. And, yeah, it's been a long time now that I've been here. I can't totally imagine living in the countryside as an adult. Shit, maybe it's time for *me* to make a change.'

'Where would you go if you *were* going to leave London?'

'Literally no idea. I'm too busy to ever think.' The car in front of them turned out. '*Finally*,' Dan said, edging forwards, right up to the junction.

'Yeah, I can imagine. It took me years to decide where I was going before I finally moved out of Mum's.'

Dan put his foot down for a very cheeky right turn onto a main road.

'Woah,' Evie said, holding onto the side of her seat.

'Woah?' Dan said, eyes focused on the traffic as they waited at a roundabout. 'That was nothing. You never get anywhere in London if you wait for big gaps in the traffic.'

He screeched out onto the roundabout between a bus and a Range Rover and Evie said, 'Woah,' again.

'Really?' Dan said.

'Yes, really.' Not *really* really. The strange thing was that he was definitely quite an aggressive driver but at the same time you felt like he was a very safe one. He had his shirt sleeve rolled up and his forearm and hand looked *great* on the gear stick. So great that if you thought about it, it definitely gave you stomach flutters. And, really, *what*? This was embarrassing, even just as a thought that he definitely wasn't going to know about. 'So do you have a Christmas playlist for the journey?'

Dan shook his head, his eyes still focused on the road ahead. 'Nope.'

'Well then,' Evie said, 'you're going to be *so* grateful to Sasha for suggesting that you give me a lift. And to *me* for having only the best playlist *ever*.' Maybe she was being a *teensy* bit over-excitable just in case he'd noticed her lusting after his *arm*, for God's sake.

'Okay. Are you going to talk me through it or are you going to surprise me?'

'I mean, I'd *like* to say I'm going to surprise you, but it's a Christmas playlist. How surprising could it be?'

'I'm pretty sure there are some weird Christmas songs around.'

'Yeah, I don't love the weird ones.'

'Do you like *bad* ones, though?'

'No, I don't. All my choices are very, very good.'

'Okay, hit me with your list.'

'Actually, first I want to know what you think I have on it. What do you think my top three Christmas songs are? And what are your top three Christmas songs?'

'Hmm.' Dan whizzed through some lights very much on the turning-to-red part of amber and Evie yelped. 'Seriously. You have to drive like this if you're going to get anywhere. Right. Yours. "Do They Know It's Christmas?", "Last Christmas" and I'm going to go out on a limb and say that you have some actual carols in there. And for mine, tricky. Hmm. Maybe "Merry Xmas Everybody", because that always gets a party going. I do like "Do They Know It's Christmas?". I'm struggling to think of three that I like. Maybe that old Kirsty MacColl one. Or "I Wish It Could Be Christmas Everyday". I don't know really.'

'Interesting,' Evie said, wishing that she had something unusual and cool in there. She pressed play and 'Driving Home for Christmas' started.

'Nice,' said Dan, nodding in an appreciative way, and tapping the steering wheel in time to the music. 'I like a song that describes exactly what you're doing. Good choice.'

'Thank you,' said Evie. 'I am indeed a song-choosing genius.'

The second song was 'Do They Know It's Christmas?'.

'Get in,' said Dan, grinning.

Within a few bars they were both belting the words out, going for some serious a cappella extras at the end.

The third song to come up was 'Hark! The Herald Angels Sing'.

Dan shook his head. 'So predictable. But also so good.'

And then they both really went for it, Evie with some extreme soprano notes and Dan some very deep ones.

'We're *amazing* singers,' Dan said a couple of songs later.

Evie nodded. 'We really are.'

If she was honest, she'd have to admit that right now she was really glad that her car had broken down. This was a lot more fun than driving home by herself.

Chapter Nineteen

THEN – CHRISTMAS 2019

DAN

Evie's playlist moved on to 'Last Christmas' and Dan laughed out loud.

'It's very satisfying to be right,' he told her. '*So* predictable. But you can't beat cheesiness at Christmas.' She'd already started singing along to this one. She was *good*. She'd been like this at Lucie's wedding too, now he thought about it. Excellent on lyrics. 'Do you know the words to all songs ever or have you just listened to these ones a lot?'

'I've got to say, I *am* good with lyrics. I was *really* bad at remembering a lot of stuff at school, like languages and sciences, things like that, but I've always been able to remember songs. I always used to wonder whether the reason that my French vocab and chemistry facts wouldn't stay in my head was that it was already full of lyrics. And I wish there'd been a song-lyrics GCSE.'

'They actually should have a popular music GCSE.' Dan indicated right, moved into the outside lane and speeded up. '*Finally* we can go at a normal speed. The traffic's insane today.'

'Everyone's going home for Christmas,' Evie said. 'And so are we. I'm actually *so* excited. I can't wait.'

Dan smiled and shook his head slightly. Still so ridiculously uncynical.

A few minutes later, 'Mistletoe and Wine' came on, as they were slowing down for another traffic jam.

Dan felt himself go slightly rigid. And he was staring straight ahead. Was that normal? Yes, it was normal. You always looked straight ahead when you were driving. God, he was behaving like a child. Surely he could act naturally around Evie when the words *mistletoe and wine* were mentioned. It was years since that time they'd made their pact under the mistletoe and kissed. It had been a fantastic kiss, but, again, it was years ago, and a one-off, and he'd seen her a fair few times since then without thinking about it. Why had it come into his head now?

They were stationary now. He took a sideways look at her. She was staring straight ahead too.

It wasn't often that you could get to just look at someone's face in repose but at close quarters. He loved the curve of her cheek.

After a few seconds, she turned to look at him, perhaps sensing his eyes on her.

And said nothing. And nor did he. They were looking at each other and Cliff Richard was singing the cheesy song to end all cheesy songs and they were just… looking. And, certainly in Dan's case, remembering.

Evie swallowed visibly. And Dan swallowed too.

God, she was beautiful. And sweet and funny and lovely and kind. And still gazing at him. As he was at her.

Just the two of them. With all the opportunity in the world right now to say whatever they liked to each other.

It felt like this could be a big moment. One of those moments where you chose which course your life might take. Was that fanciful? Probably. But… She was take-your-breath-away gorgeous and she was fantastic company.

It was easy to imagine being around Evie a *lot*. Being *with* her. And it was easy to hope that if he made the first move she might be interested.

Except he couldn't do this. It would be a killer if things went wrong in a relationship with someone like Evie. It would hurt too much. And, realistically, they would go wrong. So many relationships did. Especially his.

Evie was biting her lip now. *God*.

No. Better never to go there again.

'Such a cheesy song,' he said, putting the car back into gear and crawling forward a few metres.

An hour and a half later, the village church's spire came into view as they rounded a bend in the road.

'Seeing the church always makes me feel like I'm home,' Evie said between verses of 'O Come, All Ye Faithful'. 'Mum always said that, when I was little, if we'd been on a long journey and she'd wanted me to sleep and I just *wouldn't*, I'd always nod off just as we saw the spire. And then she'd have a nightmare when we got home and I was sound asleep and she wanted to get me out of the car. Autumn's exactly the same.'

'Interesting. A family habit of falling asleep in the car at the wrong time. Question is, are you going to nod off now?' Dan said.

'What?' said Evie. 'Sorry, missed what you said, think I was asleep.'

'Ha.' Dan smiled at her and changed down to third gear to round a sharp corner. Despite some serious Christmas traffic and several lengthy hold-ups, this journey had gone very quickly. He couldn't remember a drive he'd enjoyed so much. 'How long are you staying? I'm going back to London on the twenty-seventh. You're very welcome to a lift back if you're going back then?'

'Thank you so much. I'd have loved to have done – think how many more songs we could have got through – but I'm staying until the second, and then I'm going to go back and power through a big pile of marking and lesson prep before term starts. Are you working over New Year?'

'I'm actually not. First year for a long time that I'm not working either Christmas or New Year. I'm in on the twenty-eighth and twenty-ninth and then I'm flying out to New York on the thirtieth for a long weekend with some friends from med school.'

'Wow, that's exciting.'

'Yeah, I'm looking forward to it. We're going to do the whole tourist thing. The Statue of Liberty. Skating at the Rockefeller Center. Times Square for New Year's Eve. The works.'

'Perfect. I say that like I know New York; I've never actually been. I'd *love* to go. I'd love to go to America full stop, in fact. Sasha and I have been talking about organising a US trip with our old gang from school for all our thirtieths. Two years to plan it, so hopefully it will actually happen.'

'You should definitely do that. And what are you doing for New Year this year? The usual?'

'Yup.' Evie and Sasha and various other friends nearly always spent New Year's Eve in the Duck and Grapes pub in the village.

A wave of nostalgia so strong that it felt almost physical washed over Dan. Youth. The pub. The landlord had let them drink in there from when they were fifteen as long as they only had a pint of shandy. Lots of friends. No worries, just a lot of chat and laughter. Until Max's accident.

And they'd arrived in the centre of the village.

'I love the green,' Evie said. 'It gives me a thrill seeing it every time. We're so lucky to have grown up in such a chocolate-box perfect village.'

Dan glanced over at Evie and thought about the time they'd sat on the bench on the green late at night and then kissed on her doorstep.

He looked away and manoeuvred the car into her lane, stopped outside her mum's cottage and turned back to her. She was gazing at him, biting her lower lip slightly again. Beautiful. God, he was remembering that kiss again. He was supposed to have parked that memory. Her eyelashes fluttered a little as they looked at each other.

Eventually, Dan realised that the car was still running and pulled his key out of the ignition.

'Thank you so much for the lift,' Evie said, sounding a little husky.

'Not a problem.' There was something about being inside the car, just the two of them. So intimate.

Dan cleared his throat and Evie's mum tapped on the window and he and Evie both jumped.

Evie's mum pulled the passenger door open and enveloped her daughter in a huge hug. Then Autumn ran out of the house and joined in with the hugging.

'We should unpack the car,' said Evie. 'We're holding Dan up.'

'Really, not a problem,' Dan said.

'No, we should let you go. I think this drizzle's going to turn into heavy rain and that won't be fun for either of us with the unpacking.'

Evie and her mum and Autumn took armfuls of presents and Dan hefted all the remaining bags out and deposited them just inside Evie's mum's front door.

'I think that's everything,' he said.

'Thank you again, *so* much.' Evie's smile really was beautiful. 'Total knight in shining armour.'

'No, thank *you*,' he said, meaning it. 'I enjoyed the singing. Happy birthday for tomorrow.' He hoped he'd see her again soon. Hard to imagine not enjoying her company.

Chapter Twenty

NOW – MAY 2022

EVIE

Evie's hands were bordering on sore from clapping and her face was bordering on sore from smiling. Thank goodness her school had an inset day today so that she'd been able to make it to Autumn's Year Two Robin Hood play.

The applause eventually started to die down and her mum said, 'Did you definitely get it all on video?'

Evie nodded. 'Yes, every minute. She was perfect.'

'I know. I can barely speak.' Her mum dabbed a tissue to her eyes. Autumn had had a starring role *and* had played a short violin solo – genuinely not that screechily – at the beginning.

'And now you can all go and say a quick hello to your family and friends before you get changed,' Autumn's class teacher told the children. 'Slowly and quietly,' she yelled, as they all stampeded towards the audience and two of Robin Hood's merry men tripped over their bows and went flying.

Autumn sprinted towards Evie and her mum and they swung her up together for a big three-way hug.

'You were literally the best Maid Marian I've ever seen in my whole life,' Evie told her. 'And violinist.'

'It was fun,' Autumn said. 'Where are we going to go for dinner?'

'I'm going to take you to Cirencester for pizza, just the two of us for a special treat,' said Evie. 'Mummy's got stuff to do.' Their mum was packing up her newly ex-partner Richard's stuff and leaving it on the doorstep. Evie couldn't understand why her mum constantly chose obvious bastards like Richard when she had lovely friends like Grant.

'But you said we were going to have dinner with Richard,' Autumn said to Evie's mum. 'And he said he was coming to the play.'

'He was busy,' Evie's mum said. Busy forever more, apparently. 'I don't think we're going to see him a lot any more.'

'But he said he had a present for me for doing the play.' Autumn's little face fell. Evie *really* loathed Richard in that moment. She'd loathed him already for being the last – or more realistically latest – in a long line of men who'd hurt her mum, and it was even worse that he'd broken a promise to a seven-year-old. And been so nice to her when he was around if he wasn't expecting to stay around. No-one should have their heart broken, but especially not a child.

'I'm not sure we're going to see him again, darling,' their mum said. Oh, God, it looked like her eyes were swimming again. Yep, she was sniffing and pulling her sunglasses out of her bag.

Evie really hoped that her mum wasn't going to get upset again right now. She'd spent a lot of the last couple of days crying over Richard, a lot of it on the phone to Evie on Wednesday evening, and in person last night when Evie had arrived after her drive over from London. If Evie was honest, she wasn't just annoyed with Richard, she was fairly pissed off with her mum too, however unreasonably. Evie knew from personal experience that it was unsettling and unpleasant as a child watching your mum in and out of relationship after relationship, and she hated seeing Autumn experiencing the same.

'Big night last night, Jenny?' said one of the other mums, indicating the sunglasses and chortling a bit. 'Still recovering nearly twenty-four hours on?'

'Yep, exactly,' Evie's mum said in a slightly wobbly voice.

'Did you say you needed to get going?' Evie asked, to save her mum from the chat.

'Yes, I did.' Her mum shoved the sunglasses on further. 'Lovely to see you, Zara.'

Evie's mum wore her sunglasses all the way out of the dark church hall and through the church grounds in grey drizzle and up the road to Evie's car, before finally taking them off as they got into it. If Evie ever saw Richard again, she'd be tempted to punch him. Thank goodness she was here to cheer up her mum and Autumn. Her mind went to Matthew. He might not be winning any prizes in the excitement stakes, but she couldn't imagine him ever upping and leaving out of the blue. He was dependable, safe. Everything she'd ever wanted. Like the way he'd given her a key to his flat so soon. Lovely. She'd never used it, in fact, and she wouldn't like to move in together yet, but she appreciated the sentiment a lot.

Evie dropped her mum in front of the pub in Melting and then drove down to the church and round the green and off towards Cirencester. She paused to turn right onto the Fosse Way and looked at Autumn in her rear-view mirror. She'd been remarkably monosyllabic the whole time since they'd dropped their mum.

'You okay, Autumn?' she asked.

'Yes,' Autumn said, and turned her face to the side so that her hair was hanging over it and Evie couldn't see it.

Evie's throat was quite sore by the time they arrived at the pizza restaurant, from maintaining a flow of chirpy conversation in the face of total silence from Autumn. It was beyond bizarre. Her little sister was normally incredibly – occasionally exhaustingly – chatty.

'You know something?' she said to Autumn when they were seated at a red-and-white-checked-tablecloth-covered table and had menus. 'When I'm upset about anything I find that the best thing to do is to tell someone who loves me all about it, and then I feel better. Are you upset about anything?'

Autumn didn't say anything but swung her foot and kicked quite hard.

'Ow,' yelped Evie. 'You kicked me.'

'I didn't mean to,' Autumn said. 'I meant to kick the table.'

'Why did you mean to kick the table?' Evie rubbed her shin.

'I want to come and live with you,' Autumn said.

'Erm. Why?'

Autumn aimed another kick and connected with the table leg this time. She winced but didn't say anything. Really not her usual behaviour.

'Why, Autumn?' Evie repeated.

'Have you seen Mummy crying?'

'Yes.'

'I don't like it when she cries.' Autumn kicked again.

'Oh, Autumn.' Evie wanted to *kill* their mum. This hadn't been okay when Evie was little and it wasn't okay for Autumn now. 'Come and sit on my lap for a minute.'

'I can't. We're in a restaurant.'

'It'll be okay. Come on.'

Autumn walked round the table and got onto Evie's lap. Evie wrapped her arms round her like she could shield her from the rest of the world like that.

'You know what,' Evie said into Autumn's hair.

'What?'

'Um.' Evie didn't actually know. What could you say to comfort a child when their mother cried? She'd never told anyone about it when she was little. In fact, she didn't really talk about it now either. 'Basically, yes, it does feel rubbish when your mummy's sad. But luckily, you don't just have Mummy, you've got me too, and I'm not sad, am I? So maybe if Mummy gets sad you can talk to me. But hopefully Mummy won't get sad again. And she's probably feeling much better now. It was probably just one of those things like how you kind of wanted to cry when you kicked the table too hard just then, didn't you?'

'I don't think she hurt herself. I think it was because Richard was mean to her.'

'Yeah. But she'll get better. She always does.' And then she'd fall for the wrong man again and Autumn would get upset again. 'Come on. Let's read the menu together. I bet you can't manage garlic bread *and* pizza *and* pudding.'

Evie did Autumn's bath and bedtime story when they got home, firstly because she adored her little sister and it was a pleasure, and secondly because their mum was still sniffling behind sunglasses.

'Are you staying all weekend?' Autumn asked.

'Yes, poppet.'

'Good. Mummy will probably have stopped crying by the time you leave.'

That was it. Evie kissed Autumn and went downstairs – angrily fast – and into the kitchen, where her mum was staring into a glass of red.

Evie walked across the room, took the glass out of her mum's hand and poured it down the sink and said, in a hiss, but quietly, so that Autumn wouldn't hear from upstairs, 'If you can't stop crying in front of Autumn, I don't think you should drink.'

'*What*? Who made you the tears and wine police?'

'Autumn wants to come and live with me because she hates you crying every time you argue with or split up with a boyfriend. And I hated it my whole childhood too.'

Her mum's head went back like Evie had slapped her and the colour literally drained from her cheeks.

'God.' All Evie's anger evaporated all at once. 'I'm so sorry. I can't believe I said that. Mum, I'm really sorry.'

'No.' Her mum shook her head, slowly, and got up and went upstairs.

Evie heard her close her bedroom door. Shit.

What could you do when you'd just told someone the truth and that truth was really unpalatable? Maybe nothing.

Her phone buzzed. She looked at the screen. Matthew.

No. She felt *terrible* right now and she didn't feel like just being normal and chirpy on the phone, but she couldn't tell him; he wouldn't understand. And that was the beauty of being with someone like him, in fact. He and his entire life experience were completely safe and sensible and unchaotic.

After a good couple of hours of watching crap TV that didn't take her mind off the situation, Evie went and knocked on her mum's bedroom door. There was no answer.

Right.

She sent her mum a text telling her she loved her and went to bed for an early night.

Evie was dragged out of a very deep sleep the next morning by strange, muffled music. Where was she? Gaaah, why was there a wall in her *face*? Oh, okay, she was at her mum's, in her bedroom there, her bed against the wall. And that noise had to be Autumn watching TV. Or probably some YouTube channel.

She squinted at the clock on the wall. Three twenty. What? Oh, it had stopped. It probably needed a new battery.

And then she remembered. Last night. She'd said those terrible things to her mum. And she hadn't been able to get to sleep for ages but then she'd actually slept very deeply, which felt like something to be ashamed of. What if her mum had been tossing and turning all night, really hurt?

She rolled over and looked at her phone. Eight twenty-five, not three twenty. Okay, she was going to go and apologise.

She hauled herself out of bed, wrapped herself in the dressing gown that lived on the back of her bedroom door, and went downstairs to the kitchen.

'Morning.' Her mum was dressed in black Lycra and no make-up and had her hair up in a high ponytail. 'Hope you slept well. I was waiting for you to wake up to keep an eye on Autumn so that I can go for a run.'

'You what?' Evie gaped. The last time she could remember her mum going for a run was a New Year's Day when Evie was at uni and her mum's man of the moment had been a fitness fanatic. Her mum had dumped him after their second run because, she'd said, their lifestyles were incompatible, and had taken her running kit to Oxfam in Cirencester to celebrate. She'd obviously bought some new running kit in the past decade. Or maybe not. Evie took a closer look. 'Are those leggings mine?'

'Yep. And the top. I got them out of your bedroom before you went to bed last night. I love you, Evie. I had a good long think yesterday evening. I'm so sorry for everything. I'm turning over a new leaf. I'm going to respect my daughters and myself. I don't need a man and I do need to go running.'

Evie stepped forward and held her arms out to her mum and they had a big, long hug, which might have involved a few tears on Evie's part.

When she'd dried her eyes, she said, 'I shouldn't have spoken to you like that. I'd never want to hurt your feelings.'

'It was true, Evie, and sometimes the truth hurts. And I was hurt. I am hurt. Because I see now that I could have been a much better mother to you.'

'No, you really couldn't.'

'Well, I could. And the first thing I'm going to do is go for my run, to start demonstrating a healthy lifestyle to Autumn.' She raised her voice. 'Autumn, darling, I'm just going for a run. Evie's going to look after you while I'm out. And next time, you and I can go together.'

Autumn came into the kitchen, stared at her mother and said, 'Weird,' with a really impressive sneer.

Within fifteen minutes, their mum was back, red-faced and sweating.

'Oh my *God*, Evie,' she panted. 'That was effing torture. Those sodding hills.'

*

Six hours later, Evie was finishing lunch in an Italian restaurant with Sasha while her mum and Autumn were having lunch at Grant's pub. Again, *why* had her mum and Grant never started going out?

Sasha smiled at the waiter who'd just taken their card payments for their pizza lunch, checked her watch and said, 'Fancy a little bit of retail therapy before we head back? I really want a cream polo neck jumper to wear with my new burgundy skirt for work days when I'm at the surgery.'

'Definitely,' said Evie. 'I think I need to buy something else for Matthew. A couple of small presents.' His thirty-fifth birthday was coming up on Friday and they were going out for a special birthday dinner that evening, and he was quite tricky to buy for – he was very conservative in his tastes – and it didn't feel like she had a good enough present yet. 'And we could have a look in that new shop in the arcade for something for us.' She really didn't need to feel guilty about the fact that it was *way* more fun shopping for herself, or for Autumn, or for her mum, or for Sasha or any of her other friends, than for Matthew. Apart from Priya, who had *the* most perfect flat and clothes in the world and was very stressful to buy for.

'Fab. What have you got him so far?'

'A shirt, which was outrageously expensive because it was the make he likes, but is also soooo boring.'

'I'm sure he'll love it. You have such great taste.' Sasha opened her handbag and took out a lipstick and a little mirror and applied several layers of bright-red creamy gloss.

'That's a high-risk strategy,' Evie said. 'If you're trying on cream jumpers with tight necks. Really hard not to brush them against your mouth.'

'Yes, but I can't not,' Sasha said. 'We might bump into Angus. And I do know that it's stupid given that I wake up next to him a lot, make-up free. And probably very unfeminist. But, you know.'

'You always look amazing, lipstick on or off,' Evie told her, trying not to think about the fact that Sasha's honeymoon phase with Angus had obviously lasted a lot longer than hers with Matthew had. She'd definitely dress up for Friday evening, of course she would, it was his birthday and they were going to a very nice restaurant, but if she was honest, she'd be more likely to apply lipstick because she was seeing a girlfriend – or her very critical Year Elevens – than because she might bump into Matthew. 'Didn't you just say Angus was working this afternoon? So he's going to have his arm up a cow somewhere several miles away?'

'Yep, but you never know. What if he has to pop into Cheltenham for something?'

Hmm. Maybe it was just that Evie was less self-conscious around Matthew because they'd met playing badminton, which wasn't a time when anyone looked glamorous, and they'd just gone from there. In fact it was probably a really positive thing that she felt so comfortable with him.

Fifteen minutes later they were in a department store in the middle of Cheltenham looking at men's socks.

'I'm scraping the barrel, aren't I?' Evie said. 'Buying socks. Even just as an extra little present to open.'

'They're only part of his present. I think it's a nice idea.' Sasha picked up some red ones. 'These are cool.'

'Yes, they are. I *really* like those.' Evie looked at them and tried to imagine Matthew wearing them. 'I think they might be a bit too bold for Matthew's taste.'

'I mean, they're *plain socks*,' Sasha said. 'Just red. It isn't like they've got willy pictures on them.'

'Yeah. No. I don't think they're quite right.' Evie moved over to the black socks. 'Actually, what about these?' She picked up some charcoal ribbed ones. 'These might make a nice change from black ones. Just a hint of grey, and ribbed instead of just normal flat.' The rib wasn't too noticeable. Actually, maybe it was a bit. No point buying something for Matthew that she knew he'd never wear. 'Maybe I'll just go for flat charcoal ones.' Dan's appreciation of the naughty socks she'd bought him for Secret Santa popped into her head. She pushed the thought away, hard.

'Good plan. Anything else?'

'Yep. A couple more small things.' Evie thought, for a while. 'I'm not sure what, though.'

'Okay. Smaller things. A book?'

Evie shook her head. 'He's very fussy about what he reads.'

'Okay. Wine?'

'No. He likes nice wine and a) I don't know anything about labels and b) I think he drinks quite expensive stuff. Maybe let's just shop for us now and if I see something I'll get it. And if not I'll Amazon-Prime something before Friday.'

*

At exactly seven thirty-five on Friday evening, as agreed, a taxi horn honked outside Evie's flat and she – armed with three wrapped presents, the shirt, the socks and a novelty-and-yet-tasteful kitchen timer that had seemed like a good idea when she'd bought it but less so now – let herself out of the house and hopped into the taxi that Matthew was waiting in.

'Happy birthday,' she said, kissing him on the lips.

'Thank you,' he said, smiling at her. She caught him dabbing surreptitiously at his lips with his fingers a couple of seconds later.

Hmm. How did Sasha manage to kiss Angus when she was so frequently fully lipsticked-up? Maybe Angus just didn't mind getting lipstick on his lips.

Evie pushed the thoughts away and snuggled against Matthew where he had his arm waiting for her resting along the back of the seat.

This was nice.

'So what have you been doing today?' she asked. 'How was your birthday golf?'

'Very good, actually. I tried out my new irons. Fantastic. I have an aged copper wedge, which has really improved my play. I've got a couple of funny stories for you from today. But tell me about your day first. How did the Year Ten parents' breakfast go?'

They were still telling each other about their days when they arrived.

'When would you like to open your presents?' Evie asked when they were sitting at the table.

'Now?' Matthew smiled at her.

She beamed back at him and handed the presents over.

'I love them,' he told her when he'd finished opening them, and leaned across the table for a quick kiss. 'Thank you. Great choices. You know me very well.'

Two courses, lots of chat and some laughter later, they'd downed a whole bottle of champagne and were halfway through a nice bottle of red and Evie was feeling very mellow.

'Want to come back to mine tonight?' she asked.

'Definitely.'

The next morning, Matthew woke up earlier than Evie would have liked, because he was meeting some friends. For a game of golf, obviously.

Josh was up early, too, Evie discovered when they made their way into the kitchen.

'You know it's Saturday?' she said. 'No work today.'

'Ha, hilarious.' Josh poured green juice into a glass. 'Fergus and I are meeting some friends of his at a stately home in Surrey for the day. He's in the shower. They have *babies*.' Fergus was his latest partner.

'Wow,' said Evie, gobsmacked. This was *so* not what Josh liked to do with his weekends.

'I know. And the amazing thing is, I'm slightly looking forward to it.' Wow again. Maybe Fergus was *The One*. 'What are you two up to?'

'I'm playing golf,' Matthew said, and launched into a golf anecdote. A lengthy one as it turned out.

The anecdote came to a sudden end when he looked at his watch and said, 'So sorry, I'm late. I'll tell you the rest later.'

He did have time for a lovely goodbye kiss at the front door. He *was* lovely. Evie walked back into the kitchen, smiling.

Josh coughed, 'Boring. Just saying,' on his way to the shower.

'Piss off,' said Evie. Not boring. Matthew was lovely, kind and sensible; and a strong interest in hobbies was no bad thing, surely.

Chapter Twenty-One

NOW – JULY 2022

DAN

Dan scrunched his coffee cup and aimed at the bin in the corner of the waiting room. In in one. Nice. He looked again at the large clock on the opposite wall. 3.30 a.m. Hopefully there wouldn't be too long to wait now. A lot of babies were born in the early hours. He remembered the midwives talking about it when he'd been on the obs and gynae ward as part of his rotation.

The baby might be a bit smaller than average because she was a couple of weeks early. He hoped she'd be okay. No, of course she would. No reason to panic.

Waiting was very stressful.

God, he was tired. And *that* was exactly the kind of thought that people always despised fathers-to-be for. Hannah was in the delivery room, labouring away, and had been doing so for a long while now, and his sole contribution was to stay up all night. He should really not even *think* that he was tired.

What if he nodded off, though?

He got his phone out and started scrolling through news feeds. It was definitely easier to stay awake when you had something to do.

*

What time was it now? 3.45 a.m. The minutes were barely even crawling by. Swiping through his phone wasn't helping. He put it back in his pocket and rubbed his eyes.

What was happening in there? He did understand why Hannah hadn't wanted him to be in the delivery room – they were still near-strangers really after their few weeks together in the autumn involving a lot of sex and huge ramifications – but he was the baby's *father* and he was a doctor and he'd have happily stayed up Hannah's head end, *obviously*, and he'd have liked to have *been there*. His own child was making its way out into the world and Hannah was labouring with her mother as birthing partner, and he was just sitting here on a tasteful grey crushed velvet sofa in the swish waiting room of the private maternity wing of his own hospital.

'Dr Marshall?'

Dan said, 'Mmph,' and sat up. A midwife was standing in front of him. 'Yes?'

'Your daughter was safely delivered half an hour ago. Three point four kilos. Seven pounds seven.'

'Oh. Wow.' *Wow*. His daughter had been born. Wow.

He sniffed and blinked hard because his eyes were suddenly damp. 'Could I see her? I'd really like to.'

The midwife nodded. 'Yes. Hannah's mum's gone home to get a little bit of sleep.' She indicated for him to follow her and started walking.

The baby was swaddled in hospital sheets and lying in Hannah's arms.

Dan moved automatically to the basin in the corner of the room to wash his hands, craning over his shoulder as he squirted the soap and rubbed it off.

Then he turned around properly.

There were people and noise in the room, maybe someone addressing him, but Dan didn't have the head space to work out what they were saying. He was walking towards the bed, towards his tiny little daughter.

Wow.

She had the most beautiful face he'd ever seen in his life. Just amazing. Perfect. There were really no other words.

'She's perfect. Could I hold her?'

Hannah didn't say anything but she held their baby out to him.

Dan took her and sat down in the chair next to the bed. 'She's perfect,' he said again. God, he wanted the *world* to be perfect for this little girl. He wanted no-one ever to be cruel to her, for her never to be unhappy in any way, for her never to be disappointed.

It was like his heart was going to burst with love and fear all at the same time. How could you love someone so fiercely so fast? He'd only been in the room for a couple of minutes.

He looked up at Hannah. He knew that she hadn't been seeing anyone else since they'd split up straight before she found out she was pregnant. And he was single. So he hoped they could spend some proper time together as a family.

'Thank you,' he said, suddenly overwhelmed by the miracle of women being able to grow babies. 'So much. For having her. Thank you.'

'She's worth it.'

'Yeah.'

They smiled at each other.

Dan looked back down at the baby and stroked her tiny hand.

'Do we have a name?' he asked. They hadn't discussed anything before the birth. Hannah had been too busy at work.

'Katie.'

He nodded. 'I love it. Katie. Wow.'

He didn't want to leave. Ever. He wanted to be around Katie as much as possible.

Katie was having a little wriggle in her sleep. Was it possible to actually melt with love for a person who'd only been born for less than an hour?

'I'd like to see her as much as possible,' he said. When was Hannah going to make her final decision on New York? She'd said recently that as they all got to grips with new hybrid working practices it still wasn't clear-cut where senior staff should be based. 'If that's okay. I mean, whatever you think. But I'd love to spend time with her.'

'Yes, of course,' Hannah said. 'I'd like that too.'

The thought of them leaving London, the *country*, was terrifying. What if he hardly ever got to see Katie? That would be devastating.

He was spiralling, he realised. But he just hated the fact that he had so little control over the situation.

He looked down again. Katie had a very symmetrical face. Maybe that was what made her the most beautiful baby ever born. She wriggled and gave a tiny mewling cry and moved her little head from side to side.

'She's rooting, isn't she?' said Hannah.

'I think so.' Dan nodded.

'Oh, God. Breastfeeding. What if I can't do it properly?'

'You'll be brilliant. I mean, you've just given birth to the most amazing baby ever. You *are* brilliant.'

'Thank you.' She smiled, a bit tearfully. 'Do you think a midwife would help me?'

'Definitely.'

When the midwife arrived, Dan said, 'So, I'm going to leave you to it.' He looked at his watch. 'It's five thirty. You must be exhausted. Would you like me to keep an eye on her while you get some sleep after you've fed her?'

The time that Dan sat with and cuddled and watched and marvelled at Katie in the visitors' room along the corridor from Hannah's room were possibly the shortest two-and-a-half waking hours he'd ever experienced. He now knew that you'd literally be able to watch a baby twenty-four/seven and not get bored. Well, not any old baby. *Your* baby.

At around nine o'clock, Julia showed up.

'Good morning,' she said. 'I don't want to intrude, so please do just tell me to go away if that's how you feel, and I also don't want to be rude, but you do look tired, so would you like me to take my beautiful granddaughter while you go and get some sleep?'

Dan didn't want to relinquish Katie but he had in fact now been awake most of the time for twenty-six hours. It would probably be better for everyone if he had a rest and came back later. He also needed to take a few minutes to tell everyone he knew about his daughter. Shout the news from the rooftops, basically.

'That's such wonderful news,' his mother said. He'd called her the second he left Katie. 'I can't wait to meet her. Tell me everything.'

At the end of the call, she said, 'Darling, I don't want to interfere, but I just wanted to let you know that I do think that for your sake you should probably tell your father, even if you don't really want to speak to him.'

Yeah, Dan had been thinking about that. 'I might text him,' he said. 'With a photo.'

'That's a good idea,' his mother said. 'Perhaps do it this morning? Do you think?' Yep, she was probably right. So right that he wasn't even annoyed that she was interfering so much. While saying that she didn't want to interfere. He'd include his father on the group text he was going to send to friends.

He called Lucie and Sasha to tell them in person, and then Max too. He always found it hard to talk to Max but that wasn't Max's fault and Dan would never want to hurt his feelings. By the time he'd finished the three calls, his ear was almost ringing from his siblings' loud excitement.

Going through his phone to decide who to include in his group text, he hesitated on Evie's name. It felt like she was someone who he should tell about such a big event. Given that he had her number. But at the same time… she wasn't exactly his friend; she wasn't even really an ex. Sasha would tell her, anyway. He carried on scrolling down without adding her to the list.

The congratulatory replies started flooding in pretty much immediately, obviously.

There was one from Max.

So many congratulations!!!!!! I was too overwhelmed on the phone to say that Greggy and I would love to visit SOON to meet my NIECE!!!!!! Today????? Let me know when would suit.

And one from his father.

Congratulations.

Quite a contrast. Dan bashed out lots of replies – other than to his father – and then put his phone on silent to grab some sleep.

Sasha was FaceTiming him when he stepped out of a fast shower after a three-hour nap.

'There's a group of us here having lunch,' she said. 'We had to phone and congratulate you again. My first niece! I'm putting the phone in the middle of the table so everyone can say hi.' She disappeared from view and was replaced by first a pepper pot and then a view of several faces, including Evie's, which gave Dan a jolt.

He said a lot of thank yous and then set off back to the hospital.

Becoming a father was mind-blowing.

Chapter Twenty-Two

NOW – AUGUST 2022

EVIE

'Are you all ready?' Tiff, the wedding boutique owner, poked her face out from behind the changing room curtain.

Lucie, Fiona, Evie and Dervla, Sasha's university friend who was the other bridesmaid, all nodded.

'Okay then, she's *coming out*.' Tiff pulled the curtain sideways and up, and Sasha stepped out.

'Oh my goodness.'

'Wow.'

'Gorgeous.'

'You look *amazing*.'

Sasha's dress was sixties-style simple in cut, in a warm ivory fabric, which set off her slim figure and strawberry-blonde hair and pale skin to perfection.

Fiona dabbed delicately at her eyes with a sparkling white handkerchief. 'My baby girl,' she said.

Evie could do with a tissue herself. It wasn't every day that you saw your best friend in her finished wedding dress for the first time.

'So, obviously,' Sasha said, 'I can't eat anything for the next ten days.'

'No, no, no,' Tiff said. 'Don't *stop* eating. We don't want a shrunken-bride situation. I don't want to be taking this dress in next Friday. I want you to stay exactly the same size until then. You wouldn't believe the number of women who over-shoot on their pre-wedding diets.'

'Okay.' Sasha nodded, eyes wide. 'Bloody hell. One more thing to worry about. I hadn't thought of that.'

'You'll be fine,' Lucie said. 'We've all been there. And it's always perfect in the end.'

'You will, darling,' Fiona said.

'You will.' Dervla nodded earnestly.

'Totally,' Evie said, feeling like a fraud. The other three all had actual being-a-bride-in-a-wedding-dress experience. All Evie knew was how *not* to be a bride. In the red knee-length dress she'd worn for her Vegas wedding. Oh, for goodness' sake. Her mind had wandered to Dan again. She should stop thinking about what had happened during their car journey after the quiz night, and seeing him at Sasha's wedding and wondering if he would get back together with Hannah, and focus on Sasha. 'Honestly, Sash, you'll be fine. You know you will. You always look amazing and you always weigh the same no matter what you eat.'

*

A week later, Sasha was saying, 'Oh my God, oh my God, oh my God. I shouldn't have carried on eating normally. Maybe it was that curry at the weekend. And bread. Too much bread. So hard to resist.' She took a deep breath. 'Okay, try again.'

Tiff pulled the two halves of the back of the dress in towards the centre, hard, and Sasha squeaked.

'Are you alright?' Tiff said.

'Fine.' Sasha sounded like she was being strangled.

'Are you sure?' Evie asked, worried.

'Totally fine.' She was so not fine. She was talking the way Evie's mum had when she'd had tonsilitis.

'Sasha, you can't breathe in for your entire wedding. It'll ruin the day for you. We've got to do something. Tiff, can we take it out a bit?'

'Well, we really don't have much time.'

'Could we add an extra panel or something?' Evie asked. 'Like down the sides? Would that be quicker?'

'But that would ruin my beautiful dress,' Sasha wailed.

'Laxatives,' Tiff said.

It wasn't the right time for weak jokes, but Evie laughed politely anyway, while Sasha sniffed.

'I'm not joking,' Tiff said. 'It's a tried-and-tested method.'

'Great,' said Sasha, 'I'll do that.'

'What? I really think that's a bad idea.' Evie didn't like being rude to relative strangers, but this was her best friend's *wedding*.

Tiff shook her head. 'It always works. Why don't you take the dress off, now, Sasha, and I'll get it all packed up for you?'

'You're actually suggesting that Sasha should take laxatives three days before her wedding? Strong enough ones to make her lose actual noticeable amounts of weight?' Evie said. 'What if they work too well? What if they keep on working? What if they're still working on Saturday? *During her wedding*? Also, I'm pretty sure it's not, like, medically advisable to use laxatives for weight-loss purposes? If anything, maybe just a strict diet for three days. But wouldn't it be a *lot* better to just let it out a bit *now*?'

Tiff shook her head again. 'Laxatives,' she said.

'Let's go.' Sasha pulled on Evie's sleeve.

'Could we maybe reconvene on Friday morning, Tiff, and if necessary let the seams out a tiny bit?' Evie said.

'There won't be time then.'

'Well, let's start now then,' Evie said.

'Laxatives,' Tiff said.

'Let's go,' Sasha said again.

'I'm going to get laxatives,' Sasha said the second they'd closed the boutique door behind them.

'No, Sash, you can't,' Evie said. 'Honestly, I do think Tiff's lovely—' she wasn't; she was a dragon in fluffy-wedding-boutique-owner clothing '—but I also think she's gone mad in this instance. It's like she's promoting eating disorders. It's a ridiculous suggestion. And *what if* you're still *going*, post-laxatives, *on Saturday*? It doesn't bear thinking about.'

'I can and I'm going to.' Normally, Sasha was one of the most reasonable people Evie had ever met, just one of the reasons that Evie loved her. 'Oh my *God*, Evie, this is a *disaster*.'

Evie pulled her into a hug. 'Listen. It's going to be okay.'

'My dress is too small. My beautiful, perfect wedding dress is too small. And the wedding is in two days and twenty-two hours' time. *How is that going to be okay*? I'm getting laxatives.'

'I think we should go back in and insist that Tiff take it out slightly,' Evie said.

'No. She clearly doesn't want to.' Several tears rolled down Sasha's cheeks. 'Let's go to the pharmacy.'

'There must be someone else we can talk to about this,' Evie said.

'You *can't* tell Angus. Or Mum. Or anyone.' A lot of tears were pouring down Sasha's cheeks now. 'But maybe we should call Dan. He's a doctor. He'll know the best laxative to take.'

'Will he?'

'Yes, think about it,' Sasha sobbed. 'You probably get severely constipated people in A&E all the time. Let's call him. Could you maybe ask him for me?'

Evie really didn't want to speak to Dan because of their argument after the quiz night but she obviously couldn't let her best friend down in her hour of need. And, also, this was a crisis, and Dan was good in crises, and hopefully he'd talk Sasha out of the laxative idea and into the getting-extremely-firm-with-Tiff-and-letting-the-dress-out idea.

She took her phone out. He didn't pick up. Which felt like a bit of a relief, even though she could do with some anti-laxative backup.

'Hi, Dan,' she said into the phone. 'It's Evie. Sasha has a wedding dress emergency and she wanted to ask your advice about laxatives.'

They were in a queue in Boots five minutes later, waiting to talk to the pharmacist about laxatives, when Dan called back. Evie stared at the phone for a few moments, feeling her shoulders tense, and then picked up.

'Evie. Hi. Sorry I couldn't take your call immediately; I'm at work. What's the emergency?' Evie relaxed a little. There was something very comforting – as well as sexy, no, ignore that – about Dan's voice, and clearly they didn't need to mention anything personal.

'Basically, Sasha's wedding dress is a little tighter than expected…'

'Because I'm too fat,' Sasha said.

'Sasha looks gorgeous as always,' Evie said, 'but the dress is a bit small, and the seamstress is suggesting that Sasha take laxatives so that she can get into it, and Sasha thought that you might have some useful advice, being a doctor.'

'What?' Dan said.

'I'm not joking.'

'That's insane. No-one should be taking laxatives for dieting purposes. She could easily ruin her wedding day and her honeymoon. It's a ridiculous suggestion.' Hooray. 'Can't they change the dress?'

'Exactly. Would you like to speak to Sasha directly? Sasha, would you like to speak to Dan directly?'

'Okay.' Sasha sniffed.

'So I'm going to pass the phone to Sasha,' Evie told Dan. 'Obviously I know that you know this but a wedding dress is a *huge* deal for a bride and the wedding's on Saturday.'

'Yep, I'll channel my inner adult and not be mean to my little sister.'

'Thank you.'

Evie handed the phone to Sasha.

Whatever Dan was saying had to be good. Sasha was no longer crying; in fact, she was almost smiling.

'Thank you,' Sasha said. 'No, we'll do it. Evie'll be amazing. But if we need help from a third party we'll call you.' She handed the phone back to Evie.

'So what are we doing?' Evie asked. *Please* let Dan have prevailed common sense-wise over the laxatives.

'We're going to go back to the shop and *tell* Tiff that she has to let the dress out. We're going to be firm and she's going to do it. And then I'm going to weigh myself literally about every hour, to make sure that I don't change size any more. Dan offered to phone Tiff and speak to her for us, but I told him we don't need a man to fight our battles for us.'

'We certainly don't,' said Evie, *really* wishing that Sasha had let Dan make the call, because Tiff was actually quite scary.

'Exactly. We are strong women.' Sasha linked her arm through Evie's and started walking out of the shop. 'Let's do it.'

'Hang on.' Evie stopped just outside Boots's entrance. 'I need to google. I need some ammunition. Okay, got it. The Consumer Rights Act 2015. Come on. I'm going in.'

'No,' Tiff said, when they were back in the shop. 'Really, I don't think so. Please try the laxatives. Sasha, darling, I have it on great authority that several members of the royal family, and Hollywood royalty too, swear by them.'

Evie tried to imagine Tiff away and replace her with a naughty Year Seven. 'Well, more fool them, frankly,' she said. She squinted down at her phone screen. 'I'm so sorry, Tiff, but I'm going to have to quote the Consumer Rights Act. Section Ten. Goods have to be fit for particular purpose. Section Fourteen. Goods to match a model seen or examined. Section Twenty-three. Right to repair or replacement. I could go on.' She couldn't go on much further without scrolling down on her phone.

'Evie's a very senior Consumer Rights Act lawyer,' Sasha said.

'Yes, I am,' Evie said. 'And not taking the dress out would be a clear breach of Sasha's consumer rights. Which obviously you're aware of, and I know that you just have Sasha's best interests at heart.'

'Obviously,' said Tiff after a long pause, her eyes scarily narrowed, and voice like nails on a chalkboard, 'if you want me to take it out, I will do that. I was just thinking of you. I'm not sure you want that stress.'

'It won't be stressful, because we know you'll do a fab job,' Evie said. 'Thank you *so* much, Tiff. We're both going to recommend you to all our friends.'

'Very rich friends,' Sasha said. 'Who are all getting married very soon. Dozens of them. It'll be very much worth your while. Thank you so much. We're very grateful.'

'Not a problem.' Tiff looked like she'd just eaten a large slice of lemon when she'd thought she was getting orange.

Three hours later, Evie and Sasha were on the sofa in Sasha's flat, watching *My Big Fat Greek Wedding*, with glasses of water – Sasha wasn't touching alcohol with a barge pole before Saturday because of the empty calories factor – and big salads, dressing-free in Sasha's case.

'You don't want to avoid *all* calories,' Evie said. 'You can't *lose* weight now.'

'I might have a square of chocolate for pudding,' Sasha said. 'And a rich tea biscuit – low GI according to Google. Thank you so much for being with me this week. I'm *so* glad I'm getting married in the holidays so that you could be here in the run-up.'

'Me too. If I hadn't been you'd have had laxatives for dinner instead of salad.'

'You were *amazing* with Tiff.'

'I was really scared.'

'You didn't look scared. It was *so* cool when you started quoting the law at her. I mean, I actually believed you.'

They both sniggered and then Sasha said, 'Can I ask you something?'

'Mm, hmm.' It was going to be another question about Dan.

Sasha opened her mouth and Evie's phone rang. Good.

It was Matthew, calling from his Tenerife golfing holiday.

'I'll leave you to it and make us some coffee,' Sasha said and left the room.

'Hello,' Matthew said. 'I'm missing you. How's everything going with the wedding preps?'

Evie told him all about her day, not really including the conversation with Dan, though, because it felt a bit weird talking about him with Matthew. 'And how's your day been?' she asked when he'd finished agreeing that no way should anyone suggest that a bride take laxatives.

When he'd finished a – genuinely very funny on this occasion – golfing anecdote, he said, 'I can't believe I'm away for a whole ten days. I'm really missing you.'

'Me too,' Evie said, meaning it. His presence was very calming.

'Are you sure you're okay about seeing Dan and meeting Hannah this weekend?' Sasha asked as soon as she was back in the room after Evie and Matthew's call finished. One-track mind. It was literally about the fiftieth time she'd asked the question. Like Evie, while totally sober, was suddenly going to give a different answer from the other forty-nine times. Sasha wanted her baby niece to be at her wedding so Hannah had been invited, and if Evie was honest *of course* she didn't particularly want to spend time with Dan *and* the ex he'd split up with just before Vegas. But they were all adults and it would be *fine*.

'Totally. I mean, he split up with Hannah before we went to Vegas and so of course it was *fine* that he and I… you know… *fine*. And it's clearly *fine*, more than fine, wonderful, that he has Katie. You know, I'm really pleased for him, both of them. And of course it'll be fine seeing them together, *totally* fine. I mean, obviously.' She was *clearly* doing the protesting-too-much thing. Also, what was she thinking? What about Matthew? 'And, I mean, I'm with Matthew. Really, Dan and Hannah are nothing to do with me.' It was really bloody annoying, frankly, that Matthew couldn't make it to the wedding. 'I'm really looking forward to your wedding and to seeing you walking down the aisle looking utterly, utterly fabulous in your gorgeous dress and marrying your amazing fiancé.'

'And Hannah and Katie will probably only come to the ceremony and the first part of the reception, so they won't really be there much,' Sasha said.

'Exactly. But even if they were, I *really* wouldn't mind.'

'Good. If you're sure.'

'I am *totally* sure.' Ish.

*

'So this is *great*.' Two evenings later, Evie took another glug of her champagne and then put it down on a side table. It felt like to survive this evening happily she needed to be very drunk or totally sober. Drunk and Dan weren't a good combination, so sober it was. 'So exciting that the wedding's *tomorrow*.' She looked at Sasha's mother on her right and then at Sasha's father on her left. Neither of them had said a word for literally minutes. *Such* bad timing that Sasha's parents had arrived at the restaurant at the same time, and straight after Evie.

'I can't wait to see how the church looks in the morning when the florist's finished.' Evie paused. More silence. Right. 'And the cake's going to be delicious. Such a good idea to have different types of cake in each tier.' And more silence. 'I can never decide whether I prefer fruit cake or your basic Victoria sponge. Or chocolate actually. Especially Black Forest gateau. Delicious. Yep. Everything's going to be wonderful. I wonder where they're going for their honeymoon. So exciting that

Angus is surprising Sasha.' More silence. Christ. 'August's a wonderful time of year for a wedding.'

There was the sound of a spoon tinkling against a glass.

'If we could all take our seats, that would be great,' Angus boomed. Thank *God*. 'Sasha's done a seating plan.'

Evie smiled at both of Sasha's unsmiling parents, said, 'Wonderful,' and moved, fast, in the direction of the table, to start on the looking-for-your-name sideways-shuffle-and-peer thing that everyone was doing to find their place.

There were sixteen of them, eight men and eight women, and Sasha had alternated the sexes. She'd had quite a few constraints to work with, including having to put her father as far away from her mother and all four of his children and ex-mother-in-law as possible, as well as Angus's mother and grandmother, who were both firmly in the Fiona-supporting camp, so he'd been placed between Evie and Dervla, the other non-family bridesmaid.

One of Angus's younger brothers, Rory, was on Evie's other side. Evie was pretty sure that she was relieved not to be sitting next to Dan, given all the awkwardness, except for some reason she also felt a bit miffed.

Silly, of course. There was nothing wrong with Robert, other than the middle-aged-letch thing he had going on and the fact that he'd betrayed his wife and never apologised. And she didn't really know Rory, but he seemed like a lot of fun. She was totally going to have a great evening.

'Thank you so much,' Evie said to the waiter as he put her main course of ballotine of rabbit in front of her. She looked across the table at Sasha and made a sympathetic face as Sasha pointed between her very plain salad and Angus's steak. She'd had soup and no bread to start with while Angus had had foie gras with a lot of toast. It seemed like there was something in all of this wedding dress and dieting stuff that summed up a lot that was wrong between men and women. Although tomorrow Angus was going to be wearing a boring suit while Sasha was getting to wear *the* most beautiful dress. Yeah, not the time to be philosophising.

'This food's delicious. Almost as delightful as my dinner companions this evening,' Robert told Dervla and Evie. Honestly.

'You old flirt,' said Dervla, not really sounding that light-hearted.

Evie sneaked her umpteenth look of the meal at Dan, at the far end of her side of the squarish table. He looked a bit tired. And also gorgeously slightly rumpled. Apparently he'd come here straight from work via Hannah's flat to pick her and Katie up. He hadn't been able to make it to the wedding rehearsal this afternoon because one of his colleagues had been ill so he'd had to work on his day off. He glanced up and caught her looking at him – oops – and gave a half smile. Evie half-smiled back. She loved the way his whole face usually crinkled when he smiled and you felt like it was only the two of you in the whole world. That wasn't the way he was smiling now, though. Now, he just looked a little wary.

Rory nudged her arm. 'The waiter would like to know if you'd like more wine,' he said. Oops again. She'd been paying no attention whatsoever.

'I'd love some, thank you,' she said. Actually, no, she really didn't want too much to drink. 'Just half a glass, please. Rory, could you possibly pass the still water?'

*

Robert concluded a *long* anecdote about his own heroics – something to do with helping a charming woman and her cat – and said, 'I've had a lovely evening with you two ladies. It's a great shame that I don't have time to stay for dessert. I have to join Stephanie at a drinks party this evening.'

'Must be an important drinks party,' Dervla said. 'To take precedence over your daughter's dinner the night before her wedding.' Evie nearly choked on her water.

Robert glared at Dervla, and then patted his lips with his napkin. He pushed his chair out and blew kisses around the table.

'Wonderful to see everyone. See you at the church tomorrow.'

'Now that he's gone,' Sasha said to everyone, before the door had fully closed behind him, 'let's shake things up a bit. Women, let's be lazy and stay where we are. Men, you all move four places to your left.'

And suddenly Evie was sitting between Max's partner Greggy and Dan, and, again, she wasn't sure how she felt. Definitely suddenly happier and more full of anticipation than she should have been.

Chapter Twenty-Three

NOW – AUGUST 2022

DAN

Dan plastered a smile on his face and stood up to move his four spaces along the table, to what felt like a hot seat.

The last time he'd seen Evie had been in the car after the quiz night, and he wasn't sure where to go from there. Plus, he wasn't precisely sure why, but he didn't particularly like the idea of Evie and Hannah meeting tomorrow. *However*, they were adults, and this weekend was all about Sasha and they could absolutely behave normally.

'Hey, Evie,' he said, sitting down next to her. 'Good to see you.'

'Hello. Thank you for your help the other day.'

'Always available to offer advice on bodily functions. Sasha said that you were surprisingly fierce with the woman in the boutique.'

'Yes, I was very proud of myself. Turns out that someone telling your best friend to effectively poison themselves before their wedding makes you pretty angry.'

'Yeah, you sounded quite stern even on the phone to me, and I was pretty sure that I'd done nothing wrong. Sounds like everything's okay now dress-wise? I'm looking forward to seeing it tomorrow.' He suddenly wondered what Evie's bridesmaid dress was going to be like. This evening she was wearing a light-blue silky top and her hair up so that he could see the line of her neck, and, if he looked at her too much, he felt his throat go dry, which was insane, given that she had a boyfriend apart from anything else.

'The dress really is beautiful. And Sasha's going to look amazing.'

'Yeah.'

There was a slightly too long pause and then Evie said, 'I haven't congratulated you in person on the birth of Katie. So… congratulations!'

'Thank you. Yeah, it's huge being a father. I mean, obviously. Goes without saying. Yeah, she's amazing.' He should say more, keep the conversation going until it felt like any awkwardness from their last meeting had gone. 'I can spend hours just watching her. She can smile now, and it's like every smile is the most precious thing you've ever witnessed.'

Evie smiled, properly, at that and Dan found himself thinking that her smiles were pretty precious too, actually.

'I remember,' she said, 'from when Autumn was born. You get that feeling of immense, uncomplicated, almost slightly desperate, love, that you hadn't even known existed.'

'Yep. You'd do anything to protect them from the world.'

'Exactly.'

Dan looked along the table at his mother. And then thought about his father.

'Obviously not every parent feels like that,' he said. 'Like my father. Kind of him to grace us with his presence briefly. It's Sasha's wedding tomorrow, for God's sake, and he's buggered off.'

'He did come, though? Maybe he felt awkward being here because he isn't the most popular family member ever?'

'Or maybe he's a total arse.'

'Maybe a combination of all of those? Not to be rude about your dad.'

A waiter clapped his hands right behind them and Evie squeaked and then laughed.

'That was *loud*,' she said.

'Dessert orders,' the waiter said.

'Oops, I haven't chosen yet.' Evie picked up the menu.

'I have. I'm going cheese.'

'I really can't decide.'

'I actually think I know what you're going to have.' Dan had been at enough dinners with Evie over the years to be pretty sure that he knew what she liked. Of the available options, she was going to go sticky toffee pudding, after a *lot* of deliberation.

'Hmm. I don't think it's a compliment when someone implies that you're predictable.' She narrowed her eyes at him.

'Predictable in a very nice way.'

'Hmm.' She mock-pouted and, God, he felt something inside him actually lurch.

'What would you like?' asked the waiter.

'Could you come back to me last?' she asked. The waiter visibly blossomed in response to her smile. She sat back and stared hard at the menu and then at the wall opposite, like all the horse paintings hanging on it might give her pudding inspiration.

'Okay, yes, I've decided,' she said when the waiter finally came back to her. 'The lemon tart.' What? Maybe Dan didn't know her as well as he thought he did. 'No, sorry, sorry, sorry, I'm changing my mind. Sticky toffee pudding, please.'

'You sure?' asked the waiter, laughing with her.

'Yes, certain. Definitely.'

'I'm a genius,' Dan said. 'I *knew* you were going to go sticky toffee.'

'It was the caramelised popcorn on the side that swung it.'

'I knew that.'

Evie shook her head, smiling. He wondered if, like him, she was suddenly thinking about how well they knew each other in so many ways. And yet not in others.

When their puddings were placed in front of them, they both said in the same moment, 'Wow.'

'Those are *enormous* plates of food,' Evie said. 'I know now that I'm not going to finish mine, or we'll be having a bridesmaid-dress-too-tight disaster tomorrow morning. You have to stop me if I look like I *am* going to finish it. Because it does look delicious and I *will* be tempted and I don't want to have to consider last-minute laxatives.' She turned her attention to Dan's cheese. 'So instead of bringing you a cheeseboard so you could choose, it looks like they've just given you the *entire* cheese board.'

'Pretty much.' He had five massive wedges of cheese, two crackers and one grape on his plate. 'Good job I like cheese. I think I'm up to the challenge.'

Evie shook her head. 'You're going to have *weird* dreams tonight if you eat all of that.'

Dreams. Dan suddenly wanted to tell her about his nightmares. The one where he pushed Max into the road and Max got killed. The one where his father was a serial killer and Dan didn't tell anyone and more people got murdered. The one where he was at work and forgot everything he'd ever known. And the new one, the enormous wall in the Atlantic with Katie on one side and Dan on the other. God, he wanted to know what Hannah's decision about New York was going to be. And he wanted to tell Evie everything. He was pretty sure that if he did she'd listen and care.

No. He wasn't going to go there. He couldn't talk about the accident.

'Nope, I'm going to sleep very well tonight.' He cut a slice of blue cheese, put it on a cracker, looked up at Evie and thought about sleeping with *her*. Christ. What was wrong with him? Yes, they'd slept together in Vegas, but you could be around someone you'd slept with – and only once – without constantly thinking about it. And, as far as he knew, she still had a boyfriend.

'Is Matthew coming straight to the wedding?' he asked, and then immediately despised himself. It sounded truly pathetic asking about him.

'He's away on a golfing holiday.' Evie didn't meet his eye.

'Oh, right,' said Dan, trying not to feel pleased.

Evie looked up at him and their gazes snagged. And neither of them said anything.

'Can I interrupt?' said Greggy, turning towards them from Evie's other side. 'Evie, I hear there's a laxative story for you to tell me.' And the moment, whatever it was, was broken, definitely a good thing.

Fifteen minutes later, Sasha finished her fruit salad and stood up and said, 'No speeches this evening other than to say thank you all so much for being the most wonderful family and bridesmaids and best man, and my nearly-husband and I can't wait to see you at our wedding – *which is tomorrow* – and now you all need to go and get a very good night's sleep so that you can enjoy the day. Taxis will be here for us all in five minutes.'

Dan ended up in a cab with Evie, Max and Greggy going back to Melting.

'You take the front seat,' Evie said.

'No, you take it.'

'I'll feel guilty. Your legs are longer.'

'Evie, just bloody get in the back and close the door so that we don't all freeze,' Max said. Evie laughed and bundled in with Max and Greggy.

'So it's a big day for the three of you tomorrow,' Greggy said. 'Bridesmaid, walking the bride down the aisle, and doing the reading. There's a lot of responsibility there.'

'Way to make us all nervous,' Evie said. 'Honestly.'

They all laughed and joshed each other all the way back to the village. Dan was genuinely looking forward to the wedding now. There was something about having Evie and Greggy there that made things easier between Dan and Max.

Chapter Twenty-Four

THEN – JULY 2021

EVIE

'Are you joking?' said Evie. 'After months and months of only being able to see people outside, you want to have a picnic? Why can't we go to the pub for lunch?'

'We've been able to go inside a pub for two months now. You should be used to it.' Sasha stuffed Evie's picnic blanket into a beach bag. She was staying with Evie for the weekend, without Angus, who was away on a stag.

'You couldn't get a table for the first few weeks and I'm still *over* meeting outside,' grumbled Evie.

'It'll be really nice.' Sasha grappled with the Amazon parcel she'd had delivered to Evie's flat that morning and then triumphantly held up an orange circle. 'The boys will like it.' They were meeting Dan and Max and Greggy.

'Is that a frisbee? You had a frisbee ordered to my flat?'

'Yep. If you're going to do a picnic, do it properly. The food should be here in a minute.'

'You're having food delivered to my flat?'

'Picnic food. Because if I hadn't, you'd have wriggled out of it. I thought it would be nice.'

'It's freezing for July.'

'Wear a jumper.'

*

Two hours later, they were wearing jumpers, and jackets, sitting on the picnic blanket in the middle of London's Richmond Park, next to Max and Greggy, who were sitting on their own picnic rug.

'The deer are amazing.' Sasha angled her phone and took more snaps of the herd grazing only a couple of hundred metres away. 'Soooo gorgeous.'

'You know they cull them every year?' Max said.

Greggy nudged him in the ribs and Sasha told him to shut up. 'Bloody brothers,' she said.

'Speaking of whom,' Greggy said, 'there's Dan.'

Sasha sat up straight and waved her arms above her head, and Dan, in the distance, waved back.

Evie felt her heart quicken. She hadn't seen him for eighteen months since the car journey back to the Cotswolds that they'd shared the Christmas before lockdown. He was getting closer and she could see him better now. He was dressed in beige cargo shorts, a navy jumper and Adidas shoes, gorgeously, reliably conservative, just, so, *Dan*-like.

'Hey.' He'd wound up in front of them and was grinning down at them all. Evie felt her stomach dip as his grin widened. 'I would say sorry I'm late, but, bloody hell, the *roadworks*.'

'OMG,' Evie said, 'I know.'

'Although at least I had my phone to guide me. Was Sasha directing you?' Sasha had form on getting distracted mid-directions.

'Yup. We're still bickering about it. Right instead of left at a crucial point.'

'I got distracted by that man on the golden, feathery bike,' Sasha said.

'Famous around Wimbledon,' Evie explained.

'Interesting.' Dan caught sight of the open picnic bag. 'That's a serious-looking feast there, Sasha.'

'If you're going to do something, do it properly.'

Max and Greggy both stood up and the three men did a lot of hand-shaking. Dan looked pretty open and relaxed with Greggy but the second he turned to Max he visibly tensed slightly, his shoulders suddenly tauter and his jaw a little clenched. Evie had noticed before that Dan wasn't always at ease with Max. Obviously some brother thing. Maybe something to do with their father.

'Why don't we try out my new frisbee before we eat?' Sasha asked.

'Sure.' The others all followed her, Evie not *totally* up for it. The others were all a lot better at sport than she was.

'Yesssss!' she shrieked five minutes later, having just done an *amazing* catch, if she said so herself. 'And owwwwww.' A frisbee thrown from a distance was *hard*.

'Why's everyone better than me?' Greggy yelled. 'Evie, you said you were rubbish. But you *aren't*.'

'Okay. I'm going to show you.' Max jogged over to Greggy and positioned himself behind him and held his throwing arm. Greggy leaned backwards into Max and Max planted a kiss on his neck. Evie went off into a little fantasy about *Dan* showing *her* how to throw the frisbee. Max and Greggy were pressed right up against each other. She'd *love* to be pressed up against Dan like that.

Sasha shouted, 'Stop smooching and throw the frisbee,' and Evie looked away from Max and Greggy, and over towards Dan. He was looking at her, a half-smile on his face. She shivered, allowing herself to imagine, just for another moment, the feel of his hard body against hers. His smile grew, and she felt her own lips turning up in response. It was like all her nerve ends were responding to him even though he had to be at least twenty feet away from her.

'Evie,' Sasha screeched, and Evie turned just in time to avoid being decapitated by the frisbee that Greggy had apparently just thrown. Okay. That would teach her to lust after her friend's brother.

They ate a huge lunch and then lay back on the rugs, chatting lazily.

'I could stay here forever,' Max said. 'Although I wouldn't mind working some of those calories off. Footie?'

Greggy and Sasha both stood up. Leapt up, in fact. How could they do that on full stomachs?

'Definitely in a few minutes' time.' Evie might explode if she ran around right now. 'I might just carry on lying here for a bit. I ate a *lot* and I need more digestion time.'

'I'll join you in a few minutes' time too,' Dan said, sounding oddly formal. And there was that slight tension again.

The others wandered off towards the middle of the large expanse of grass they were next to. Evie suddenly felt really self-conscious, alone with Dan, and yet not alone because the others were all very much within sight.

He was lying on his side, facing her, propped up on his elbow. They were close enough to each other that she could see that he now had a couple of grey hairs at his temples, which just made him look even sexier. Neither of them was speaking and suddenly the silence seemed too heavy.

Evie sat up so that she was cross-legged and began to pick some of the daisies next to her. 'I haven't made a daisy chain for years,' she said.

'I don't think I've ever made one. How do you even do them?'

'You make holes in the stalks and thread them through.' Evie could feel Dan's eyes on her fingers as she threaded, and, God, it was like her *hands* felt self-conscious now.

'You're very good at that,' he said, his voice sounding deeper than usual. She looked up and caught him watching her intently, a lopsided smile on his face, and her heart properly squeezed and her mind went blank, too full of wonder at the gorgeousness and closeness of him to be able to operate normally. He'd definitely just said something. What had he said? That she was good at daisy-chain-making.

'Yes.' She nodded. 'It's incredibly difficult and I'm very gifted at it.'

Dan laughed. Such a nice sound. Very deep and rumbly and infectious.

'I think you should have a go,' she said, actually feeling slightly breathless.

'Okay.'

She passed the chain and a new daisy to him, and their fingers brushed, and, Christ, it felt intimate. She looked up from their hands to his face and their gazes caught, and Evie's breath caught in her throat.

Dan coughed slightly and said, 'So what do I do?'

'You make a hole here.' Evie leaned forwards and her hair fell into his face. 'Oops, sorry.'

'No problem.' His smile was slow and it felt like it held some kind of promise, which was mad, because of course it didn't really.

'And then you thread it through,' she said.

Dan took the daisies back from her and their hands brushed again. He lifted a finger and brushed her cheek.

'There was a small insect,' he said, his voice husky.

'Thank you,' Evie said, her voice pretty husky too.

His eyes had gone to her mouth, like they did the time they kissed outside her house. Oh, God. Every part of her was aware of him. If he actually touched her again she might jump a mile. Or melt.

Chapter Twenty-Five

THEN – JULY 2021

DAN

Dan's heart rate had picked up way more than playing with daisies warranted. Right now, he'd kill to be able to reach out and kiss Evie. But Sasha, Max and Greggy were right over there and of course neither of them wanted to kiss or anything else in front of them.

Evie moved herself backwards slightly, and glanced over her shoulder at the others, presumably struck by the same thought at the same moment.

'So now that you're a flower-necklace-making expert,' she said, 'maybe we should go and join in with the others.'

'Absolutely.' Dan didn't like doing any kind of exercise with Max, but just now it felt like the lesser of two evils. He jumped to his feet and held a hand out to Evie. Her hand fitted so well in his. He could ask her if she'd like to meet up some time, and he was pretty sure that, if she said yes, they'd have a great time together.

He was also pretty sure that he could get to like her far too much – maybe already did – and that there'd be huge potential to get hurt if they started something. Far too big a risk.

'Race you over there,' he said, indicating the others with his head.

'Are you *joking*?' Evie said. 'That is so unfair. I'd *smash* you if we had a race.' She started jogging *very* slowly. Dan laughed – you couldn't grow up in the same village as Evie and not know how much she hated running – and joined her.

'Yasssssssss,' crowed Evie half an hour later, dancing gleefully around the goal they'd made with jumpers.

'That was a total mis-kick,' Dan said from the middle of the goal, folding his arms across his chest.

'It was not,' said Evie, still dancing. 'It was pure calculation. Either I'm very talented or you're a rubbish goalie. Or both.'

Dan laughed and shook his head. What he *wanted* to do was join in with her ridiculous dancing, because it just looked so much fun.

Evie finally stopped the dancing and said, 'I think we might need to get going soon, Sasha, otherwise we'll be late for the theatre, unless the journey home's a *lot* shorter than it was on the way here.' She looked at the others and said, 'We're going into town to see *Hairspray*.'

'Wow,' said Greggy. 'How did you get the tickets? I hear they're like gold dust. I mean, are you sleeping with the producer?'

'Yeah, totally,' Evie said, and, even though he knew it was a joke and that her love life was nothing to do with him, Dan felt a stab of pure jealousy at the thought of Evie sleeping with anyone. Insane. 'Friends in *very* high places. No, it was a present from all the parents at school at the end of the year.'

As they packed all the picnic gear away, Dan reflected that this had been the most relaxed he'd been around Max for years. That would be the presence of Greggy, and also Evie.

They all wandered back to the car park together, chatting and laughing.

'So this is us,' said Evie, stopping in front of a remarkably clapped-out green Renault Clio parked expertly in a tiny space. 'You'll be astonished to hear that this is the car that broke down that time you gave me a lift to Melting.'

'I am astonished,' said Dan, laughing. Astonished that the car still worked at all. It made his own ten-year-old VW Golf look like a high-performance luxury sports car.

'This car,' said Evie, 'is remarkable. It's actually one year older than me. And still genuinely drives like a dream, occasionally.'

'Wow.' Dan nodded. 'I don't think I should say anything else because I don't want to offend you.'

'Honestly,' Evie said. She got her – very dented – boot open on the third attempt and she and Sasha chucked their blanket and picnic bag in. 'So it was lovely to see you all.'

She hugged and air-kissed Max and Greggy, while Dan hugged Sasha, and then Evie turned to Dan. They both hesitated for a moment and then simultaneously went in for a hug. If the other three hadn't been standing next to them, Dan would have really struggled not to bury his face in Evie's hair and inhale far too deeply.

She felt *good* pressed against him for the brief moment of their hug.

'Goodbye, then,' she said. He *really* wanted to ask her if she'd like to meet up sometime. But he *really* didn't want to get hurt or to lose Evie as a friend when things didn't work out.

'Bye,' he said. 'Great to see you. Ignore Sasha's directions on the way back.'

*

That evening, while Sasha and Evie were at their big theatre evening, as evidenced by a constant stream of Facebook updates from Sasha,

Dan had four friends – the maximum he could seat in his flat – over to watch the cricket.

'Good day today?' Zubin asked him.

'Yeah, it was actually. Picnic with my brother and his partner and one of my sisters and her best friend. Really nice day.'

'You getting a bit closer to your brother?' Zubin took the lid off a bottle of Corona. Dan had told him once, when they were at uni, that he'd felt awkward around Max since the accident, which was more than he ever told most people. He hadn't told him the full story, because he never told anyone the full story.

'Yeah, little bit.' Not really at all. Although today had genuinely been nice. 'What about you? See the kids today?'

'Yep. Took them to their football matches this morning and then swimming this afternoon. The little one's five tomorrow and I can't see him because his mother's taking him to her parents'. Bit of a killer, if I'm honest.'

'I'm so sorry, mate.' Dan squeezed Zubin's shoulder in sympathy. This was why you were better off not getting into romantic relationships. They caused a lot of hurt.

Chapter Twenty-Six

NOW – AUGUST 2022

EVIE

Evie gave one final tweak to Sasha's veil, and stepped back.

'Oh. My. Goodness,' she breathed, blinking away sudden tears. 'You look stunning. Fairy tale. So beautiful. Angus is a very lucky man.'

Lucie, Dervla and Dan all nodded and chorused their agreement.

'You ready?' Dan asked.

'Yes,' squeaked Sasha.

'Let's go then.' Dan held out his arm and Sasha took it.

Dan and Sasha stepped onto the centuries-worn Cotswold flagstone in the entrance of the church and through the doorway. Evie was overwhelmed for a moment by the idea of tradition – so many brides must have stepped over this threshold on their wedding day.

She, Lucie and Dervla followed as the now extremely elderly Mrs Bird from the village started thumping out 'Pachelbel's Canon'. There was a new, younger, arguably much more competent organist at the church now, who did most Sunday services, but Sasha had gone with nostalgia and Mrs Bird.

Wow. The florists and Sasha and Evie's mums and two of their friends from the village had done the most incredible job. The church was decorated beautifully with orange, purple and green flowers and leaves. And the pews were packed with beaming guests dressed to the nines.

And two of the guests, sitting in the back pew, were a very striking woman with a sleek black bob wearing a spectacular, very tailored-looking, scarlet dress, and the very cute baby she was holding. The baby had a shock of red hair and, given the way Dan and Sasha's heads had both turned in that direction, had to be Katie.

Evie had to fight really hard with herself to maintain her serene, perfect-bridesmaid half-smile and continue to look straight ahead. She really wanted to turn back round and *stare*.

If she was honest, she'd have preferred Dan's ex to be a little less beautiful.

Obviously, Evie was with Matthew and it wasn't that she was jealous of Hannah. She had no reason to be, after all. But, okay, she *was* a little bit jealous. And a little bit uncomfortable at being in the same place as her.

Shiiiit. Dervla reached out and grabbed Evie's arm as she nearly tripped headlong.

'Thank you,' she mouthed. The floor of the church was so uneven. She'd better start paying a lot more attention to where she was walking and think a lot less about Dan and Hannah.

Angus was standing at the front looking adorably anxious and proud at the same time. 'You look *amazing*,' he said in an extremely loud whisper to Sasha when she joined him, and the guests in the front few pews all laughed.

*

Fifteen minutes later, the service was in full flow.

Sasha, who Evie had been best friends with since they were both six years old, was getting married to her soulmate, *right now*. Laura, the vicar, was gloriously sarcastic. The service was lovely. Everyone was happy. This was literally the most wonderful wedding Evie had ever been to and she should be drinking in every moment of it. She should totally not be thinking very frequently about Dan sitting a few feet away as she stood near to Sasha during the ceremony, and the stunning Hannah sitting at the back.

Dan did look *good* in his tails and fancy tie, and he did have a particularly gorgeous twinkle in his eye today, but still; he shouldn't be occupying so many of her thoughts.

Max did a beautiful reading about love and then Angus's grandmother, who was French, did one *in* French, which also sounded beautiful and which Evie was pretty sure had something to do with boats. Odd. She'd have to ask someone who spoke more than GCSE French about that later.

Evie got shivery goosebumps during the hymns, though if she was honest it was more from Dan's baritone a few feet away from her than the familiar and deeply meaningful words.

It was obviously because Dan was right behind her when Laura did the you-may-kiss-the-bride thing that Evie's mind leapt to when she and Dan had had their kissing-straight-after-the-marriage-ceremony moment. She'd tried really hard all year not to think of that. And now she was feeling it right to her stomach.

Anyway, time to pull herself together and proceed out of the church with Angus's best man, a very nice man called Seb, who had a lot of hair and a kilt.

The photographer was a very enthusiastic man named Kev, who, in his quest to produce the perfect wedding portfolio, wasn't letting anyone off the hook, no matter how young, old, infirm, desperate for the loo (or a beer) or freezing cold (the temperature was about ten degrees below the August average but all the women were in summer dresses) they might be.

Evie stood up from arranging the hem of Sasha's dress for the photos and bumped straight into Dan, who was holding the auburn-haired baby.

'Oh my goodness,' she said. 'Is this Katie?'

'Yes,' said Dan, rocking her slightly and looking at her with *the* most gorgeously proud expression. 'Say hi to Evie, Katie.'

Evie said, 'Hello, Katie,' and Katie smiled at her, windmilled her arms and connected with Evie's necklace. She was like some kind of baby ninja; she had her fingers firmly wound in the necklace chain within no time at all and was pulling with surprising strength.

'Oh, my God, I'm so sorry,' Dan said while Evie choked a little. He prised Katie's fingers open and got the necklace away from her.

'Thank you.' Evie took a step backwards. 'I should have remembered that you should always keep a good distance from a baby when you're wearing any kind of dangly jewellery,' she said, hoping that no-one would realise the effect Dan's fingers briefly touching her chest just then had had and also that she wasn't sounding rude.

Katie had turned her attention to Dan now and had her fingers twisted in the knot of his tie.

'Wow,' said Dan, a little red-faced, when he'd disentangled himself. 'My daughter's got some serious strength in those fingers. Just going to shift her around a bit so that she can't reach anyone's neck attire.'

'Can you clap?' Evie asked Katie, clapping her own hands together.

Katie gurgled and swiped at Evie's hands. Dan and Evie both laughed.

'Bride's family and bridesmaids,' hollered Kev.

Evie found herself standing next to Dan and Katie in several of the photos. It felt like they were together in that moment, and it was hard not to feel like she was blossoming under the strength of that feeling.

'And this is the final one before the big one with everyone,' Kev announced. 'Friends and siblings of the bride.'

Hannah took Katie and now, somehow, Evie and Dan were squashed right up against each other within the group, so much so that Evie could feel Dan's solidity and the warmth of his body against her side. She wriggled a little to try to dispel the feeling of raised hair on the back of her neck. God, she was *so* conscious of him. She was wearing high heels, and if she turned towards him now, her mouth would only be a couple of inches below his.

'And a big smile from everyone in my direction,' instructed the photographer, pulling the kind of face a kindergarten teacher might pull to get very young children to laugh. Everyone laughed obligingly, and Evie felt Dan's warm breath against her forehead.

'And now everyone,' Kev shouted. Hannah brought Katie over to Dan and everyone piled in together. Evie had no option but to stay where she was, so now instead of being deliciously close to Dan like it was just the two of them together in a sea of people, she was clamped pretty much between Dan and his ex and their baby. Really not great.

Kev hadn't actually needed that many takes on his other photos but on this one he just would not stop snapping, so Evie held herself rigid, a fixed wide – possibly rictus – smile on her face, for what felt like a really long time.

Eventually, Kev said, 'And we're done. Cracking photo, everybody.' He clapped and all the guests joined in with the clapping too. Probably not so much because they were pleased with the photos but because *finally* they were going to a) be able to go inside – it was *so* cold for August; and b) get a drink. 'I'll be taking more,' he shouted over the clapping, which then stopped pretty abruptly, 'but mainly inside the venue.'

'Thank God for that,' Dan said in Evie's ear as the clapping re-started, and she smiled. And then felt really awkward because she could *feel* Hannah's presence on her other side. And thinking of Hannah and the fact that she was Dan's ex suddenly reminded her that she had a boyfriend and that she should therefore not be feeling this attracted to Dan.

It was so annoying that he could still have this effect on her. They'd crossed the friendship line and slept together and it was now clear that nothing serious would ever happen between them, and now it was just pissing her off, frankly, that her stupid feelings for him got in the way sometimes of her actual, real-life relationship with Matthew, who was safe, solid, lovely and very interested in her.

She should sneak a moment to text Matthew this afternoon, actually, for a quick catch-up to see how his holiday was going.

'I think we can go now.' Sasha lifted her skirt as she walked delicately back over the grass to the non-green-staining safety of the church's path.

'I'll round the guests up.' Dan turned round, clapped loudly and bellowed, 'Could everyone follow us over to the house now?' The reception was being held in a marquee in Sasha's mother's garden.

Max, standing next to them, did an incredibly piercing wolf whistle and a big beckoning motion with his arm, which arguably had a bigger effect than Dan's bellow, and they all started the walk round the green, rather than across it, to avoid ruining everyone's shoes.

Evie *really* didn't want to walk with Dan and Hannah. Fortunately her schoolfriend Millie was nearby, so she did an exaggerated *Hi, Millie* and hung back to walk over with her. Which gave her an excellent view of Dan walking with Hannah. They didn't look remotely lover-like, more just like old friends who were comfortable with each other, but they did share an intimate parenting moment when Katie did some particularly manic waving with her arms and Dan caught Hannah's eye and they laughed together. Any new partner of either of them would always have that to contend with.

'That is *so* sweet,' said Millie, sounding incredibly insincere. 'They aren't together, though, are they?'

'I don't really know.' Evie shouldn't have chosen Millie to walk with.

'I don't think they are,' Millie said. 'Tonight might be my night.'

Evie had to struggle not to snarl her reply. Which, again, was utterly ridiculous, because she was with Matthew, and Dan's love life was nothing to do with her.

'I'm just going to pop to the loo,' she told Millie, to escape her. That would give her an opportunity to text Matthew too.

She could see that he was typing his reply immediately. He was loving his holiday but he was really missing Evie. She was missing him too. Not *really* missing him but that was because it was a busy day.

Evie walked into the marquee and immediately saw Hannah and Katie with Dan, and suddenly just wanted to talk to her mum. She looked

around and saw her with Grant and Autumn. She could go over and
speak to them and calm down and then go and mingle.

On her way across the marquee, Mrs Bird waved her stick at her
and called, 'Evie.' Loudly. Her lung capacity didn't seem to have
deteriorated with age at all.

'Hi, Mrs Bird.' Evie sat down next to her. 'Your organ-playing was
amazing today.'

'I'll tell you a secret. I got a few of the notes wrong.'

'No way,' said Evie. 'No-one would ever have guessed.' 'Pachelbel's
Canon' had literally morphed for several bars into 'All Things Bright
and Beautiful', more than once.

'I think I cover it up well. A lifetime of experience. What you do
if you lose your thread is you just play something you're very familiar
with, just briefly.'

'Wow,' said Evie. 'Such a good idea.'

'Thank you.' Mrs Bird leaned towards Evie and patted her on the
knee. 'How are you feeling, dear?'

Evie leaned back a bit. Maybe it was because Mrs Bird's hearing was
failing a little that she always spoke at such high volume nowadays.
'Very well, thank you. How are you?'

'I'm very well. I *meant* how *are* you? It must be terribly awkward
for you being around Danny.' How had even Mrs Bird, who Evie was
pretty sure didn't have either a smart phone or a computer of any kind,
heard about the Evie-and-Dan thing?

Evie kept on smiling and said, 'Not at all. We're friends.'

'*Really*? After a messy divorce?' Mrs Bird practically yelled. She'd clearly
heard a very garbled version of the truth. 'And him now with a *baby*.'

It was taking an increasing effort, but Evie carried on with the
smiling, directing the smile both at Mrs Bird and around at the various

groups of people close to them who'd turned to look, and said, trying to pitch her voice loudly enough that the same people would hear, but not so loudly that she'd sound as though she was shouting, 'It wasn't a messy divorce. It wasn't a divorce at all; it was an annulment because it was just a silly evening, which meant nothing. You know, high jinks. You know, these things happen.'

'You must have been devastated, though, dear. After so many years.'

'It was less than twenty-four hours.' Oops, it really wasn't right to sound snippy with an elderly woman whose heart was in the right place.

'I'm not talking about your *marriage*, I'm talking about your *relationship*,' Mrs Bird fog-horned. Evie winced and tried really hard not to swivel her eyes around to see who'd heard. 'The divorce and then to find out that he'd got someone else pregnant.'

'We don't have a relationship,' she said, trying to chuckle light-heartedly. 'Anyway, how are *you*? Mum told me you went on a coach tour of Holland this year?'

'Yes, we went to see the tulips. They were absolutely splendid. Now, you and Danny. You've had a *very* long relationship. I remember the time when you woke me up canoodling on your doorstep in the middle of the night. When was that? A long time ago. I remember it because I was wearing my green and pink floral night-dress and I think I've had that about ten years. You must have been very young then. How old are you now? I know you're all career women nowadays, but I always thought you'd be one of the ones who settled down young and had children early. You must be so upset that Danny had a baby without you.'

'Ha,' Evie said. Bloody *hell*. 'Honestly, no. I love my job. I'd love to have children one day but my career's very important to me and having children really isn't the be-all and end-all.' Genuinely true. Not so true that she hadn't had feelings for Dan for a very long time, though. 'I'd love to see the tulips. Such beautiful flowers. Were they in lots of very long straight rows like vines and olive plants are when they're farmed?'

'Some in rows, some not,' said Mrs Bird. 'I hope you get over Danny soon.'

'Nothing to get over,' said Evie, squashing the sudden memory of the far-too-intimate dream she'd had about Dan last night. This was karma. She shouldn't have been dreaming about Dan; she should have been dreaming about Matthew. Although, again, everyone was allowed a secret fantasy that they'd never act on, surely.

'You're so brave, dear,' Mrs Bird boomed. 'It must be very hard for you to see Danny today.'

Mrs Bird was well-meaning and sweet and lovely and part of the fabric of Evie's whole life since she and her mum had been welcomed so kindly into village life twenty-five years ago. Wow, quarter of a century. Evie was incredibly fond of her, but right now she wasn't loving her. The nearby – and not so nearby, because Mrs Bird was *loud* – guests had been earwigging like mad. And a lot of them had their necks and eyes on stalks looking to see where Dan – *Danny* – was. Evie couldn't actually abandon Mrs Bird but she *really* wanted this conversation to end.

She took a deep, *deep* breath, and said, 'Mrs Bird, let me go and get you another drink.' And she could get herself something seriously alcoholic at the same time, and drink a lot of it, fast.

'Oh, no, dear, I'm fine, thank you. I don't like to drink too much while I'm out. My waterworks aren't what they were. Something you'll find out about when you're older. You should start doing pelvic floor exercises now, even before you have a baby. Tell me all about your fancy life in London. Do you and Danny live near to each other?'

How had Evie never realised until now that Mrs Bird was an actual demon? She sighed. You couldn't just abandon an elderly person and

Mrs Bird would be sitting by herself if Evie got up and went, but this conversation was not fun.

'I don't live near Dan,' she said. 'I live in Wimbledon in a flat with two friends, near a theatre and a cinema and lots of shops. About a mile from Wimbledon Common, which is lovely for walking on.'

'Mrs Bird, I'm so sorry to interrupt your conversation with Evie. I hope you don't mind, but Evie's needed for some bridesmaid duties.' Dan was standing above them, smiling. Evie honestly wanted to hug him. Except, who was going to talk to Mrs Bird?

'And I'd love to have a chat, Mrs Bird,' said Laura, the vicar. Hooray, hooray, hooray.

'Thank you *so* much,' Evie mouthed at Laura as she stood up.

'Where are your baby and your partner?' Mrs Bird lifted her stick and prodded Dan with it.

'Ex-partner,' Dan said. 'They've gone back to London. They just came for the ceremony and the first part of the reception. Katie, my daughter, is too young to stay for the rest of it, but we thought it would be lovely for her to be here for her aunt's wedding, even if she won't remember it.'

'She's in the photos,' Evie said.

'Exactly.'

'It's all very messy, isn't it?' Mrs Bird prodded them both with her stick this time.

'Mrs Bird, could I talk to you about planning for the harvest festival?' Laura said.

'I *love* you,' Evie mouthed over her shoulder at Laura as she and Dan made their escape.

'You've got to admire Mrs Bird's tenacity,' Dan said.

'I know.' They both whisked glasses of champagne from a passing waiter's tray and Evie took a big sip. 'Such a one-track mind.'

'Yeah, she wasn't going down the tulip discussion track.'

'I know. Which is ridiculous, because who doesn't love a tulip chat?'

Dan took a mini olive-on-bread canapé from an offered platter. 'You know, I don't think I've ever had a conversation about tulips.'

'I mean, I can offer you some tulip talk right now, if you like, because you have *missed out.*'

Dan laughed. God. Evie really hoped that one day she'd stop going squishy inside at the sound of his laugh and the way his eyes crinkled and, basically, just everything about him.

Chapter Twenty-Seven

NOW – AUGUST 2022

DAN

Later that evening, Dan leaned back lazily in his chair at the top table and watched Evie for a moment as she made her way across the marquee to visit the loos between main course and pudding. It was taking her ages to get there: she had to stop for so many chats. Dan didn't think she had any idea how much she lit up every room or conversation that she was in. And he was pretty sure that she had no idea how good she looked in that bridesmaid's dress. In fact, she acted like she never realised how good she looked on any given occasion.

Angus's mother, sitting next to him, coughed, and he nearly jumped. Shit, he'd been totally ignoring her. And Max, on her other side, had also got up to go somewhere, presumably also the loo. The two of them had been chatting away for pretty much the whole meal, which had meant that Dan had had the perfect excuse to spend the entire time talking to Evie without it looking like it meant anything. But now poor Helen looked a bit lost.

'This is a delicious meal, isn't it, Helen?' he said to her.

As he listened to her telling him about the cruise she and her husband had taken around the Balkans recently, it was a struggle not to keep looking over to see whether Evie was on her way back.

In the end, she came back with Max, who could hopefully take the reins on the Helen conversation again.

'So I had a really good chat with Max and Greggy outside the loo,' Evie whispered after she'd sat down, shaking her napkin out in her lap. 'They told me about getting engaged last month but not announcing it yet until Sasha's wedding's over. That's so lovely. So you're going to have another family wedding next year.'

'It is lovely.' Dan nodded. 'Greggy's perfect for Max.'

'Max has actually got the perfect life when you think about it.' Evie looked up at the waiter as he placed her dessert in front of her and said thank you with a big smile, which made the waiter nearly drop his tray.

'Got it?' Dan straightened the tray in the waiter's hands and turned back to Evie. She had *no* idea the effect she had on people. 'Yes, he and Greggy are perfect together.'

'Not just that,' said Evie, taking a small mouthful of her crème brûlée. 'Everything. His job. They're talking about adopting together. I always get the sense that he's so happy in his own skin.'

'Really? I don't think so.' God, he hadn't meant to sound so harsh. Evie was staring at him, her eyes wide open.

'I'm sorry?' she said.

Dan suddenly wanted to explain.

'How can he be happy in his own skin and in his job?' he said, doing his best to keep his voice low. Max was sitting only two seats along. 'He should have been a top athlete. A star. He was a great footballer and he was also on course to make the GB athletics team. The Olympics. And instead he walks with a limp and he's physio *to* that team, to people he used to *beat*.' And all of that was Dan's fault.

'But he's got a great career now and when he talks about it he's so animated, and he has so many plans for the future. And *so* many athletes and sportspeople get injured at a crucial moment and it's all over. If he hadn't had that accident it could easily have been something else. Like that girl Sasha used to play netball with who fell off a kerb and twisted her knee the day before her England trials and never got to play for England even though everyone said she was the best wing defence *ever*. And, even for the tiny number of people who make it to the top, elite sport doesn't last long. You need another career afterwards. And Max has a fantastic career.'

Dan shook his head. Evie was wrong. 'But all he ever wanted to do was get to the GB team. I ruined that for him.' God. What had he just said? He never talked about this. He looked down at the table, put a couple of sugar lumps into his cup and stirred his coffee very deliberately.

'*You* did?'

'The accident was my fault.' That was only the second time he'd ever said that out loud. He looked up from his coffee cup to see how Evie was reacting. She had her eyes fixed on his face and she looked… sympathetic. Well, that was the wrong reaction. She should be condemning him.

'Dan. I'm so sorry. What happened? If you'd like to say? I never heard exactly.' That was because no-one knew the exact details, not even Lucie and Sasha. Their mother had shut them all down and never talked about it.

He shook his head. 'You shouldn't feel sorry for me. You've misunderstood. It was *my* fault. We'd been drinking. We were jostling in the road. I gave Max a big shove and he tripped, and a car came round a

bend and hit him.' It was strange saying this out loud. Straight after the
accident, at the hospital, he'd told his parents. His father had told him
he was a moron and his mother had hugged him and said he should
never ever say again that it was his fault, because it wasn't. That was
the kind of thing that mothers said, and when you were little it helped,
but when you were sixteen, and you knew they were wrong, it didn't.
The one thing Dan had gained from what she'd said that day was the
understanding that she definitely couldn't deal with talking about the
accident. So he'd never mentioned it again.

He added another two sugar lumps to his coffee and stirred some
more. This time he couldn't look at Evie. He didn't want to see the
sympathy in her eyes change to condemnation.

'Oh my goodness.' Bizarrely, her voice had softened. 'Dan, you
can't think that that was your fault. Presumably you didn't know the
car was coming. Presumably he'd been shoving you too. Presumably
it was all good-natured.'

'No, it wasn't good-natured. We were properly arguing. About our
father and his affairs.' Dan looked up at Evie again. 'We were really
angry with each other. Max wanted to tell our mother and I didn't.
He was right, of course.'

'I'm not sure he was necessarily right – I don't think it would ever
be that clear-cut? She might already have known and not wanted to be
pushed into acting on it. And it would be unbelievably hard to hear
that from your child, surely. But more importantly, did you want to
injure Max severely?'

'Well, no, obviously not long-term. Not severely. But in that
moment I wouldn't have minded giving him a nosebleed. I absolutely
acted in anger.'

'Everyone gets angry sometimes, though. You clearly didn't want anything really bad to happen to him. Was he equally angry with you?'

Dan nodded but didn't say anything. He didn't really have his voice enough under control to speak.

My first point—' Evie tapped one of the fingers of her left hand with her right forefinger '—is that if you were equally angry and a bit drunk and you were shoving each other in anger next to a road then either one of you could have got injured in many different ways. Arguably you're both lucky that nothing worse happened.' She tapped another finger, hard. 'Secondly, to my eyes, Max is genuinely really happy in his life now, maybe happier than you seem to be right now. Maybe it was a blessing in disguise. Maybe life as a top GB athlete wouldn't have been for him. I mean, he loves his lazy weekends with Greggy and his social life and his cooking and his career and his curries. I mean, all sorts of things that he wouldn't have got to do if he'd been an athlete all the way through his twenties. Have you ever talked to him about it?'

'No.'

'Maybe you should. Maybe you'd discover that I'm right.'

Dan added two more lumps of sugar to his coffee and did some more stirring. 'I guess you do have a point,' he said. Really just for something to say, because he didn't know what he thought about what Evie had just said. If she really did have a point. While she was talking, it had sounded like it made sense. Except he *knew* that it didn't. He *knew* that it was his fault.

'You're trying to work out the flaw in everything I said, aren't you?' Evie said. 'You think I'm wrong but you can't work out why?'

Dan twisted his mouth, gave his coffee another stir, and nodded.

'I don't think I'm wrong,' Evie said. 'And I think it's really important to talk about things that upset you, otherwise they eat away at you.'

'I don't actually know what I think now,' Dan said, round a sudden very large lump in his throat. He took a big drink of his coffee to hide his face because it felt like his eyes might be glistening. 'Oh my *God*,' he said.

'Coffee really sweet and really cold?'

'*So* disgusting. I'm almost gagging.'

Evie sniggered. 'I think you put about eight sugar cubes in there. Want one of those chocolate truffles to take the taste away? They're quite bitter. I'm just going to say one more thing about the accident. Talk to Max. Tell him what you told me and *listen* to his answer. Anyway.' She reached for the plate and handed it to him. 'Funny how dark chocolate's more addictive than the sweet stuff even though it isn't even that nice.'

'I think it's the caffeine content. And something like theobromine. I read about it recently.'

As happy chatter bubbled around them, and Dan and Evie's conversation meandered from chocolate and tastebuds through favourite books to great film adaptations, thoughts about the accident and Max chugged away at the back of Dan's brain.

When they stopped talking to clap while Sasha stood up to give the first speech, Dan said under cover of all the noise, 'Evie, thank you. For your pep talk. I think it might have made sense.'

'Hey. I *always* make sense.' She smiled at him. 'I really do think you should talk to Max about it.'

Dan looked at his older brother's profile. Max turned round and caught his gaze and grinned at him. Dan smiled back. Maybe he actually would talk to him.

Although… Yeah, it would be hard. And right now it was Sasha's wedding reception. Another time.

When dinner was over, Sasha hauled a supposedly reluctant Angus up onto the dance floor for the first dance.

'Oh my *goodness*.' Evie's jaw was literally on the floor. Most people's jaws were. 'Angus is *amazing*. He must have been having serious lessons. He's like a *Strictly* pro.'

'I know. Wow. Hmm. He's setting the bar high for the rest of us. The perfect excuse not to dance this evening, I think.'

'What? No. You *have* to dance. It's your sister's wedding. You can't let her down.'

Dan rolled his eyes but allowed Evie to draw him towards the dance floor when the first song ended and Sasha beckoned everyone over. If he was honest, he'd always had a lot of fun dancing with Evie in the past.

They joined a large group of enthusiastic dancers, including Max and Greggy, Lucie and her husband, and various friends and their other halves.

About five songs in, the band changed to a slow song, and, following Sasha and Angus's lead, everyone around them coupled up into waltzing stances. Dan looked at Evie. It would probably be stranger *not* to dance with her than to dance with her. He raised his eyebrows at her and held his arms out a little. After a moment's hesitation, she smiled at him and stepped forward.

And as soon as he was holding her close, it felt *good*. One arm round her waist, the other holding her hand, able to inhale her – frankly, seductive – scent, feel her gorgeous softness against him, he was overwhelmed with memories of their night in Vegas. Kind of wrong of him, given Matthew – currently playing golf, apparently all he ever did – but they were only dancing. It wasn't like he was going to act on his thoughts.

They danced slowly, languorously, closely, their fingers laced together, swaying in time to the music, not really talking, just enjoying the moment. Dan was enjoying it, anyway, and he was pretty sure that Evie was now, from the way that for a few seconds she'd held herself tense and at a slight distance, and then she'd relaxed right against him.

The next one was also a good one for slow dancing to.

It was a disappointment when the song ended and a very upbeat one – which made it kind of ridiculous to carry on with the waltz-ing – started.

They were still swaying together gently, when Greggy tapped Dan on the shoulder and said, 'It has to be my turn to dance with gorgeous Evie now. I think she deserves a partner who can pull some *serious* moves, and, if I'm honest, I'd have to call you a little conservative as a dancer.'

'Are you joking?' Dan said. 'I've been moving my feet and everything.'

Evie laughed and loosened her arms from where, Dan now realised, they'd still been round his neck. Dan reluctantly took his own arms from around her.

'Fancy some fresh air?' Max had popped up on the other side of them from Greggy.

'Yeah, why not?' Not really.

Dan couldn't resist looking over his shoulder as he and Max walked towards the marquee entrance, just to take a quick look at Evie and Greggy. He frowned as a man he didn't recognise held out his hand to Evie and gave her a quick twirl, and then relaxed when she shimmied back towards Greggy.

They smacked straight into a wall of freezing air the second they stepped outside the tent.

'Woah.' Dan's breath was visible in the air. 'That's fresh.'

'Yeah, great for clearing your head.'

'How come you need to clear your head?'

'Well, I don't really.' Max led the way towards the path that wound round the house. 'I just thought it would be nice to have a chat.'

'Okay.' Little bit weird.

'So I was chatting to Dad earlier.' Max stopped in the shelter of the porch next to the kitchen door. Oh, right.

'Great.' Dan could feel his shoulders growing tense.

'And I just wanted to say that I know that you can't bring yourself to speak to him really. And I totally get that. He treated Mum appallingly, for years, and obviously we aren't party to their conversations, but it doesn't seem like he's ever apologised properly. But he's our father and it feels like if we don't speak to him, we might suffer more than he does. And in fact do we actually want him to suffer? You know, the whole two wrongs don't make a right thing. He's our dad. And in some ways he was a good dad while we were growing up. And I'm feeling a lot better about things now that I've spoken to him. I'm going to meet him for lunch soon. Re-establish proper contact.'

Dan didn't want to re-establish contact and he didn't want to think about their father possibly having been a good dad at times. But as Evie had said about his parents, things weren't always black and white, were they? An image flashed through his mind of their dad bowling patiently to him and Max in the village cricket net for hours on end so that they could perfect their batting. And one of him joining in village carol-singing with great, good-humoured enthusiasm. And, further back, of him reading bedtime stories to Dan. There were so many memories. Some not brilliant – his father was definitely quite abrasive at times – but also a lot of good ones.

He shook his head and kicked his shoe against the wall of the house. What was it with this evening? Evie trying to get him to talk to Max and now Max trying to get him to talk to his father? Did everyone he knew think he had stuff he needed to talk about?

Nope. He wasn't talking.

'I can't,' he said.

'Okay. Fair enough. Just putting it out there,' Max said. 'So how are things with Evie?'

'There are no things with Evie,' Dan said, trying not to snap. Had Max and Greggy ambushed him and Evie on purpose to orchestrate this chat?

'Just, you know, every time I've ever seen you together, you seem to work so well together.'

Dan shook his head. 'She has a boyfriend. There's nothing between us.'

'Fair enough,' said Max, mildly.

Dan suddenly wondered what would happen if – in a parallel universe; he wasn't actually going to do it – he did talk to Max about the accident.

'What?' asked Max.

'Nothing,' Dan said.

When they got back inside, Dan saw that Evie was dancing with a smarmy-looking, boringly handsome man who he didn't recognise. All he wanted to do was dance with her himself, but obviously he couldn't just walk onto the dance floor and pull her away.

Maybe he'd get himself a drink. Yeah, he was a little bit thirsty. As he skirted the dance floor, he kept an eye on Evie. Just in case she looked like she wanted to stop dancing, that was all.

She must have felt his eyes on her, because she looked over and smiled right at him.

Dan stopped walking and smiled back at her.

She stood on tiptoes and said something to the man she'd been dancing with – Dan *really* didn't like the look of him, if he was honest – and wove her way across the dance floor towards Dan.

'Hey,' he said, still smiling, when she got to him. 'Drink?'

'That would be lovely. Dancing's hot work.'

They turned and started to make their way over to the bar, their steps falling in together.

'Max just told me that he's been talking to our father and he thinks I should too.'

'How do you feel about that?'

'I don't think I can. Definitely not now, anyway.'

'Maybe think about it in your own time? There's no hurry, is there?' Dan nodded.

'Want to dance again when we've finished our drinks?' he asked.

'Definitely. Although you have big shoes to fill now. Greggy's a *fantastic* dancer.'

Chapter Twenty-Eight

NOW – AUGUST 2022

EVIE

'Evie, your lipstick looks very nice.'

'Thank you, gorgeous Autumn.' Evie smiled at her younger sister, bouncing on Evie's bed. 'It's a new one. Maybe don't bounce *quite* so high, Autumn. You might break the mattress springs. Maybe don't bounce at *all*.' She leaned forward to get a better view of her eyes in her mirror and applied another coat of mascara carefully. She put the mascara back in her make-up bag and checked her fingernails. Yep, they still looked good from the manicure that she'd had with Sasha, Lucie and Dervla on Friday. She looked back into her mirror. Maybe just a little bit more eyeliner.

'Evie, you're taking a very long time to get ready,' Autumn said. 'Where are you going?'

'Just for a walk.' Evie put her eyeliner back in her make-up bag and patted her hair into place.

'A special walk?' Honestly. Now that Autumn was nearly eight you could have semi grown-up conversations with her, and that was lovely, but this was taking grown-up too far. Evie did not need her little sister to be this observant.

'Not really. Just a normal walk.'

'Who with?'

'Just a friend from the village.'

'Do you mean Sasha? But she's on holiday after her wedding.' Autumn tilted her head to one side and Evie smiled at her. Funny how you could *adore* a child while simultaneously really wishing they would *shut up*.

'Sasha's brother. Dan.' Evie tried to keep her face completely emotionless. Autumn was far too clever for Evie's good. She still wasn't quite sure why or even how Dan had suggested meeting for a walk today – they'd danced together for hours last night and, as everyone said their goodbyes, he'd made the suggestion – but she did know that she was having a hard time not smiling away just at the thought of seeing him. Which there was nothing wrong with. You weren't cheating on someone by going for a strictly platonic walk with someone else, and a lot of people had fantasy crushes, didn't they? That they'd never act on. Unless they were single and drunk in Vegas. And, frankly, if Matthew was going to play golf the whole time, she was bound to go for walks with old friends occasionally.

'Oh. But isn't Matthew your boyfriend?' *Seriously*. Bloody seven-year-olds and their questions. 'So how can Dan be your boyfriend too?'

'Dan isn't my boyfriend. He's just a friend. You know, like you're friends with Sammy at school.'

'Well, I'm actually going to marry Sammy. Are you going to marry Sasha's brother?' Thank God Autumn hadn't been old enough to hear about Vegas.

'*No*. You can go for a walk with a boy or a man without marrying them.'

'I *know* that.' Autumn practically tossed her head in scorn. 'I just wondered. Do you want him to be your boyfriend?' Maybe, in a fantasy world. But in reality, no. Dan clearly didn't want a relationship, and from Evie's side she wasn't sure she could really cope with being with someone who had so many unresolved issues. It felt like it would be similar to living with her mum's roller coaster love life. Evie wanted a solid relationship, like the one she had with Matthew.

'No. I have a boyfriend already, remember.' She lifted her wrist and said, 'Goodness, is that the time? I'm going to have to go.' She wasn't meeting Dan for another ten minutes but walking aimlessly around the village by herself for a few minutes would be vastly preferable to continuing Autumn's inquisition.

'Can I come with you?'

'I'm really sorry but we have plans to walk a really long way and, even though you're a very big girl now, I think it'll be too far for you. And, also, I think Mummy has plans for you.'

'What plans?'

'I don't know. Let's go and ask her. *Mum*,' Evie called as they went downstairs. 'I'm busy this afternoon and I can't look after Autumn and I know that you have plans for her.'

'I thought we could bake a cake together, Autumn,' said their mum, 'and then we're going to see Grant's new puppies. Going somewhere nice, Evie?'

'Just for a walk.' Evie pushed her feet into her boots and wound a scarf round her neck. Unbelievable how cold it was for the end of August. She'd turned into a soft urban-dweller, always expecting mild weather, after only a couple of years in London.

'She's going with Sasha's brother Dan,' said Autumn, putting her arms above her head so that their mum could tie an apron behind her back. Autumn was a seriously messy baker.

Their mum raised her eyebrows and said, 'Have fun. Tell me about it later.'

'Nothing to tell,' Evie said, grabbing her coat and heading for the door.

'Afternoon.' Dan was smiling, waiting for her under the tree in the middle of the green after she'd done a loop round the village. The permanently mistletoe-covered tree. She was back here bang on time, so he must have been early.

'Hello. How are you feeling today?' Should they hug? Cheek-kiss? No. She stopped a few feet away from him. 'Did you hear from Sasha this morning? I had a text from her a couple of hours ago just as they were boarding their flight.' They'd left first thing for their honeymoon.

'I had a one-worder – *Bali* – and a lot of exclamation marks. Sounded like she was happy with Angus's choice. This way?' Dan indicated with his head in the direction of the woodland and little river to one side of the village, Evie nodded and they started walking.

They were quite close to the cottages on the church end of the green now, so if anyone looked out of their front windows they'd definitely see them. Evie couldn't decide whether she more wanted no-one, particularly Mrs Bird, to see them and gossip, or *everyone* to see them and *know* that she was out for a walk with Dan, like she'd been lucky enough to land a dance with the coolest boy at the school disco. Basically, it was like she'd regressed a good fifteen years.

Oh, God, now she was really conscious of Dan. They were walking quite close to each other, but not touching, *obviously*, because why would they touch? Like, for what reason? No reason at all, clearly.

Woah, Evie had just swung her arm a bit too much and her hand had almost brushed Dan's and her heart had literally jumped as it happened. She'd gone *mad*. She was behaving like a lovesick teenager. And she had a boyfriend.

They turned the corner up the short lane that led to the church and then beyond into woodland. Why weren't they talking? Was this a companionable silence or was it awkward?

Oh, God, it was probably awkward.

'It's great weather today,' Evie said. 'Really nice. I love a sunny but cold day. Lucky for the photos that the weather turned before yesterday.' Seriously. A weather conversation. Scintillating.

'Yes, very lucky.' They'd got to a stile into a field. Dan pointed at the bushes at the foot of it. 'Those are some serious spider webs.'

'I love them in the winter covered in frost. Magical. I used to imagine that a winter queen with special powers made them.'

Dan laughed. 'I've just always thought they look nice. Clearly I have no imagination. Come on.' He climbed over the stile and turned and held his hand out for Evie.

She could totally have got herself over it and she had a vague feeling that she ought to tell Dan that, but no way was she passing up an innocent opportunity to hold his hand for a moment.

She was so conscious of the fact that she had her hand in his that she wobbled massively.

'Argh,' she screeched.

Dan reached his other arm up and caught her round her waist, which stopped her crashing down on top of him. He lifted her down and for what seemed like a very long moment after he'd set her on the ground held onto her. Evie's heart was hammering away, and she was pretty sure that it wasn't from the near-miss fall.

Her lips and mouth were very dry all of a sudden. She didn't want to lick her lips, though, because that was your cliché please-kiss-me-now action. Oh, God, she wanted him to kiss her now. He was looking at her with a small smile on her face. And she was smiling at him. And he was moving a little bit towards her. He was going to kiss her. He absolutely was.

He'd stopped moving. They were still standing there, Dan with his hands on Evie's waist and Evie with her hands on his upper arms.

She could just slide her hands up his arms right now and round his neck. She *knew* how good it would be if they did kiss.

They'd been standing like this for a really long time. Nothing was happening.

And, Christ, this was terrible. Matthew.

She let go of his arm, like it was scalding hot, and cleared her throat. 'Thank you,' she said. 'For catching me.'

'Not a problem,' he said, and let go of her waist.

'So which way shall we walk?' Evie said.

'I'm totally easy and I have all afternoon, so whichever way you prefer.'

'What about the circular walk via Little Bishop?' That was quite a long walk, which usually took a good couple of hours, but not the longest.

'Good plan. There's that great view over the Bishop valley on the way. It's only in the last few years that I've started to appreciate how lucky we are to have grown up here.'

'I know. It's gorgeous. But when you're sixteen, you're just pissed off that there's only one pub in the village and everyone knows how old you are and it's miles to the nearest clothes shops. Or whatever you're into.'

'Exactly.'

By the time they'd got to the viewpoint, Evie was puffing slightly – quite a lot, actually – from trying to pretend she was fitter than she was, and she was back in control of herself. They were just two friends out for a really nice walk.

'Little rest?' Dan said.

'Definitely.' She plonked herself down on a wide, smooth rock and began to unwind her scarf. 'That was *hot* work.'

Dan settled himself down next to her.

'Wow,' he said, as she kept unwinding. 'That's a long scarf.'

'It's very clever,' Evie said. 'Stops you having to wear loads of layers. You can have this longer or shorter or all sorts of ways, depending on how hot you are.'

'Genius,' Dan said, laughing. He reached over to take the scarf from her and their fingers touched briefly. Evie wasn't sure whether to let her fingers linger next to his, or snatch her hand away.

She watched, almost mesmerised, as Dan wound the scarf idly round his hands. His fingers were square, and strong looking, and *capable* looking, and *God*, you could really start fantasising about hands if you weren't careful. Looking now at his hands, she was really struggling not to think about all the sex in Vegas, if she was honest.

'Evie?'

'Mmm?'

'You okay? Lost in your thoughts?'

Oops. Yes. Thoughts about *him*.

'I was just thinking about the Frog,' she said, looking towards the pub in Little Bishop. 'My mum, your mum, Sasha and I set up a Melting village darts team once and we played in a league, and we had a match in that pub.'

'*Really*? I didn't know any of you were darts experts.'

'We aren't. I mean, you do improve if you play a *lot*, and we practised really hard for about two weeks, but you do kind of lose it if you don't use it, and we got bored. But we all always believed that we had world champion potential and it was only because we didn't invest enough time into it that we didn't make it big.'

'How did you do in the league?'

'Came bottom.'

'You were incredibly talented but everyone else had practised more?'

'That's right.'

They sat there in silence – definitely companionable this time – for a couple of minutes, and then Dan said, 'I used to play darts with my father sometimes. In my teens. In the pub. He'd buy me a pint and a packet of crisps and convince whoever was behind the bar that it was a meal so it was okay for me to be bought beer by a responsible adult, and we'd play darts or pool.'

Evie looked at him out of the corner of her eye. He was staring straight ahead, and twisting her scarf, hard, round his hands.

'Do you miss him?' she asked. She wouldn't have dared ask the question before yesterday evening.

Dan didn't answer for a second or two. Then he said, 'I don't even know.'

'I'm really sorry,' Evie said. 'It must be hard. I hope…' She stopped, to think. 'I hope you don't mind me saying this and I can't think of a good way of wording it, and obviously your dad's only in his sixties, but for your sake, not his, and not anyone else's, just your own, do you think you should try to re-establish contact in case anything ever happens to him?'

'Which it will. Taxes and death.'

'Yep. And, I hope you don't mind me saying, your mum's lovely, and I'm pretty sure that what she wants is for you to be happy, and she'd rather you talk to your dad and have a relationship with him than that you never speak to him again out of loyalty to her.'

'Yeah.' Dan paused and then said, 'You're very wise, Evie Green.'

'Yeah, course I am,' said Evie, thinking of all her un-wise relationships and the fact that she was seeing Matthew but sitting on top of a hill next to someone else who she had feelings for.

Should she split up with Matthew? No. She did care about him and they did get on well and it just didn't feel like Dan, with all his life issues – and apparent lack of interest in commitment – was right for her. Thinking about her mum, it was easy to see that romance with people like Dan wasn't good for you; and she couldn't let her feelings for him prevent her forever from having a meaningful relationship with someone else. Really, she should probably just avoid Dan for a while, once they were back in London living their separate lives.

'I might call him,' Dan said after a while. 'See if he wants to meet for a beer. Pretty sure I'm always going to think he's a bastard for what he did to Mum, but also, he was an okay dad in some ways. I mean, he obviously isn't pure evil. He was often a harsh parent but I'm fairly sure that, if I get in touch with him, he'll be pleased. And make time for me. Although, saying that, he left Sasha's pre-wedding dinner early.'

'Your dad's maybe the kind of man who's proud. And it was probably obvious to everyone there including him that he was spectacularly unwelcome, so maybe he thought it was for the best? A lot of things aren't really that straightforward, are they?'

'I hadn't actually thought of that. Too busy being angry. Okay. That's it. I'm going to call him later. Or text him, anyway. What about you? Do you ever think about your father, if you don't mind me asking?'

'Not much. I try not to, really. Mum has literally no idea who he was and the only thing she knows for definite about him was that he was mixed race and that his name rhymed with "ick". And I used to wonder and then I just stopped. It is what it is. I'm very happy being me and I love my family unit with Mum and Autumn. I had a great upbringing with a mother I know adores me and who's so lovely that people in the village like Mrs Bird who were initially disapproving of her lifestyle are now big fans of hers.' Her mother really was wonderful despite the chaos. Evie *had* had a great childhood. 'And I was lucky that school was multi-cultural and also had a lot of other kids from single-parent homes, so as a family we've encountered less prejudice than a lot of people do. And when you look at all the bastards that Mum's hooked up with over the years, including Jack, who *knows* about Autumn and yet has only met her twice, even though she's now nearly eight and *amazing* and a lot easier to look after than when she was a baby or toddler, chances are that my father was a bastard too and wouldn't have added anything to my life.'

'Sounds rational,' said Dan. 'Although these things aren't always rational, are they?'

'No, they aren't. But I genuinely have rationalised it and most of the time I've succeeded.'

Dan nodded. 'So, "ick"?'

'Yeah. Apparently she was pissed at the time, and they were in a club and it was noisy and she never really caught his name, but she's pretty sure it might have been Nick. Or Vic. Or Mick. But she definitely remembers "ick". And that was it. A one-night stand.' One reason that Evie wasn't so keen on them herself.

'That must be hard,' Dan said.

'I mean, yes, a bit, if I'm honest, but also, you know, it is what it is. A lot of people don't know their fathers.' Evie watched some rabbits playing on the hill opposite them. 'Anyway. If I ever want to look for him, at least I have "ick" to go by. I mean, "*ick*", for God's sake.'

'The pair of us,' Dan said. 'Shit father situations one way or another.'

'Mum sometimes says the "ick" was probably *Dick* or *Thick*.'

They looked at each other and sniggered a little bit, and then they both really laughed, for ages.

'Not even that funny,' said Dan, eventually. 'Come on.' He stood up and then took Evie's hand and pulled her to her feet. 'Scarf back on?'

'Yep. Feel that breeze.'

Dan looped the scarf round her neck and said, 'Lots of layers or only a couple?'

'More than a couple but not loads.'

'Okay.' Dan nodded, very seriously. 'Got to get it right. The beauty of an extremely long scarf.'

'Exactly,' said Evie, pleased. '*And*, because it's so wide, and yet soft, you can fold it too. A little bit pashmina-like.'

Dan looped it again round her neck. They were standing very close now, and he was holding both ends of the scarf.

'Like this?' His voice was slightly hoarse.

'Mmm,' said Evie. He had that look in his eye again. It probably mirrored how her own eyes were looking. Dan tugged a tiny bit on the ends of the scarf and Evie stepped forward.

He moistened his lips slightly. It felt like right now Evie had a decision to make about whether or not they would kiss. She was *soooo* tempted. But it was so wrong. And, even if she were single, Dan was the wrong person for her.

She smiled at him and pulled her scarf away and wound it once more round her neck and said, 'So I think that's the perfect amount of scarf winding,' and started walking.

Chapter Twenty-Nine

NOW – AUGUST 2022

DAN

Fair enough.

Dan smiled at Evie and shoved his hands in his pockets.

She was absolutely right to have broken the moment. What had they been thinking?

It was utterly ridiculous how deflated he felt.

She smiled back at him.

Yeah. Move on.

'There's a pheasant,' he said, pointing. 'Lot of them around at this time of year.'

After, really, a *long* nature conversation, they moved on to other topics, until it was like the near-kiss hadn't happened and things were back to normal, except for the fact that thoughts about Dan's father – and how much he liked Evie and how much he'd *stupidly* missed the boat because now she was going out with Matthew – were bubbling at the back of his mind. If he was honest, he'd also missed the boat because he'd been too scared, of having a disastrous relationship like his parents and of losing Evie's friendship completely and both of them getting hurt. Anyway, academic now; she was with Matthew.

'That was a lovely walk,' said Evie as they rounded the corner near the church onto the path round the green.

'It was.' He wanted to say that they should do it again sometime, but he wasn't sure how to word it. In case it sounded like a date or something. 'I think I'm going to text my father and suggest meeting up. Somewhere neutral. Not at his place. I'll let you know how it goes.'

'Good luck.' Evie smiled at him. 'I'll be thinking of you.'

'Bye then,' he said. Hug? Air-kiss?

Evie said, 'Bye,' and gave him another one of her smiles and started walking off round her side of the green. Stupidly, he felt bereft now, like he didn't want to go home.

Okay. He was going to text his father now, as he walked back round to the house. It felt like he'd promised Evie that he'd do it.

The reply came straight after he'd got inside the front door. It smelled as though his mother was making a beef stew. Loudly: there was a lot of clattering from the kitchen.

'Hello,' he said, putting his head round the kitchen door. 'How's your afternoon been?' His mother was loading the dishwasher. 'Let me do that,' he said, 'while you put your feet up for a minute. Can I make you a cup of tea?'

'No, no, no,' his mother said, batting him away from the dirty dishes. 'You work such long hours and you're here for a holiday. *You* sit down and *I'll* make the tea.'

'You've twisted my arm,' Dan said, smiling at her. There was no way he could read the text from his father when he was in the house with his mother; he'd feel like he was betraying her.

*

His mother popped out a couple of hours later to drop some home-made jam with Mrs Bird and a couple of other villagers. Dan waited until the coast was clear and then pulled his phone out. God, this felt awful. He was totally going behind his mother's back. It would actually have felt less like a betrayal if he *hadn't* waited until she'd had gone out.

Okay. His father was suggesting meeting tomorrow morning for a coffee in Cirencester.

What Dan wanted to do now was call Evie and ask her if he should go.

But since he was thirty-three years old and he and Evie were just friends who saw each other occasionally, that would be an odd thing to do.

So what was he going to do?

He was going to go. He was just going to go and meet his father.

*

'Hi, Dan.' Dan's father had arrived before him at their meeting place in Cirencester and he was standing outside looking unusually unsure of himself, his smile a little tentative and his voice not that confident-sounding. Like a shadow of himself. Had the prospect of meeting Dan done this to him?

'Hello.' What now? Should they shake hands? What would they have done in the past, when they were still speaking? Dan realised with a jolt that he didn't know, because he'd been holding his father at a distance ever since he first realised that he was having an affair, half a lifetime ago, when Dan was sixteen. 'How are you?' he asked.

'I'm well, thank you. You?'

'Yep, great, thanks. Shall we go inside?'

When they were seated at a table in the corner of the café – café was the wrong word; it was a very fancy tea room, of course, because his father had suggested it and he liked fancy places – his father said, still sounding like a muted version of his normal bombastic self, 'I was very pleased to hear from you.'

'I thought it would be good to talk,' Dan said. He'd spent all evening yesterday, eating dinner with his mother and some of her friends, knowing that he should prepare something to say today, and not doing it, because it had just felt too hard. So now he was floundering. What a muppet.

His father waited and then said, 'About anything in particular?'

'Yes,' said Dan. 'I think so.' He raised his eyebrows and smiled at the waiter who was hovering a few feet away. The waiter stepped forward and handed menus to them and then melted away. Dan opened his menu and blinked at the array of different teas on offer. He looked up at his father. They hadn't been on their own together like this for years and Dan never studied him closely nowadays. His father was actually showing his age physically. His face was pretty lined and his hair was completely grey now. Dan had a sudden wave of memory of maybe the last time they'd sat together like this, just the two of them. His dad had taken him out for dinner to a smart restaurant in Cheltenham a few days after he'd finished his GCSEs. That had been a great evening. 'I think I miss you,' he said.

His father nodded, very slowly. 'I know that I miss you,' he said.

Dan looked back at his menu. What now? Where were they going to go with this conversation? He gestured at the page in front of him. 'That's a lot of teas,' he said. 'I'm more of a plain English breakfast man.'

His father smiled at him. 'You never liked a lot of fuss. Like your mother, I suppose. Sasha would be the one who took after me with a liking for fancier things.'

Dan couldn't smile back. How *dare* he just talk about Dan's mother like that? In fact, why didn't he just *ask* him that question? Otherwise what was the point of being here? 'Do you not feel bad, talking about Mum so casually? You betrayed her. You betrayed all of us.'

His father's head shot up and he looked Dan right in the eye. Then he looked down again.

'Yes, I do feel bad,' he said. 'I made a choice and it hurt a lot of people.'

'Was it the right choice?'

'Probably not.'

Dan looked down. He was holding the menu very tightly.

'Why not?' he asked.

His father pursed his lips and then twisted them. 'I damaged my relationship with all of my children. And I feel that that probably damaged you. And children only get one father, whereas most people get more than one shot at love.'

'From where I was standing, it looked like you took a *lot* of shots at love,' Dan said. Maybe that had been rude, but it felt like his mother had only had the one shot. Dan was pretty sure that more than one man had been interested in her since his father left, and she kept them all at arm's length. 'And I think you destroyed something in Mum, as well as in me.'

His father nodded. 'I'd like to apologise,' he said, 'if that's possible.'

'Is it? Would you do the same again?'

His father pressed two fingers to his forehead for a moment. 'Now, looking back, I don't know. Your mother and I... we didn't have the best relationship. All my doing. I think therefore that by staying I'd have destroyed my relationship with you no matter what. I should really have left when you were all little, so that you didn't witness the deterioration of our marriage. I can never regret marrying your mother, of course, because we created four wonderful children together.'

'Right.' Dan suddenly really wanted just to leave. He stood up and pulled his wallet out of his pocket and put a twenty-pound note on the table. 'For our tea,' he said. 'I have to go. Thank you for meeting me.'

'We didn't even order,' his father said to his back. 'And I wanted to pay.'

Dan didn't turn round as he left.

He should have stayed. He should absolutely have stayed. Dan indicated left and pulled the car into a gateway in the narrow lane and took his phone out of his pocket. He sent one text to his father apologising for leaving so abruptly and thanking him for his time. And then he sent another to Evie to see if she was around to meet for a quick drink at some point today because he really needed to talk and she was the only person who knew about this.

*

'Hey, Evie.' Dan stood up as she walked over from the door to where he'd nabbed the sofa next to the pub's open fire. 'Thanks for agreeing to meet.'

'It's lovely to see you.' She smiled at him and started to unwind a scarf – a different one from the one that she'd been wearing yesterday – from round her neck. God, this was ridiculous. Due to the direction his mind was taking, watching a woman wearing a jacket over jeans and boots take a scarf off was feeling like he'd ventured into a strip club. How could *scarf* removal seem erotic?

'Can I get you a drink?'

'Just a lime and soda would be lovely. The party I'm going to this evening is a gin cocktail one, and I'm a bit of a lightweight nowadays…' She coughed and Dan tried to keep his face completely emotionless despite a wave of memories of Evie under the influence of cocktails washing over him. 'So I'm not going to drink now.'

'Very wise,' he said. 'Lime and soda it is.' He wandered over to the bar, astonished by how much he wanted to turn back round and drink in the sight of Evie arranging herself on the sofa.

When he was back at the fire with the drinks, he put hers on her side of the table in front of them and sat himself on the opposite end of the sofa from her, angling himself so that they could talk comfortably. This was awkward. It didn't normally take this much brain power trying to work out how to sit next to but not too close to someone.

'Not sure why I didn't just choose a table,' he said. 'Much easier to reach the drinks.'

'You know Sasha and I used to come here really early in the evenings – late afternoon really – *just* so that we could get this sofa? It's *the* best seat in *the* best pub,' she said. 'And here you are, dissing it, like one of the tables over there might be better. Honestly. No respect.'

Dan laughed and took a sip of his beer.

'So you said you met your dad? How did it go?' Evie sipped her own drink.

'Basically, he apologised for having messed up and having left but said, I think, that he never loved my mother so it would always have been awful and his biggest mistake was not leaving her earlier but he's glad he married her because of us.'

'Wow. That's quite honest. What did you say? And how do you feel?'

'I'm not sure how it made me feel. Not great. I walked out before we'd even had a drink and then I regretted it. Imagining being in his position, I suppose you can sympathise with realising that you'd married the wrong person. But I don't think staying and having a lot of affairs was the right thing to do. I think that was cowardly and it hurt a lot of people. He should have left as soon as he realised. Which he did admit, to be fair.'

'I suppose things probably aren't straightforward in practice. He probably hadn't realised that he'd fallen out of love with your mum before Lucie came along. And then a lot of people find things tricky when they have young children, don't they? And you can see why someone would feel too guilty or confused or whatever to leave a family with young kids.'

Dan nodded. 'Yeah, maybe I do kind of get that. It's harder to understand or forgive the affairs, though. Those were a choice. Falling in or out of love isn't.' Their gazes held for a long time, too long.

Eventually, Evie visibly swallowed and said, 'Adult relationships are different from parent-child ones, though. If it would be the right thing for you, I think your mum would want you to start seeing him again.'

'Maybe.' Dan thought about Katie and how he hoped beyond hope that she'd have good memories with both her parents as a child, and about Evie and how she'd never had the opportunity to meet her father. His father was an arse but he *was* his father. 'I might stay in touch with him.'

'Sounds like a good plan. For your sake as well as his. And, for what it's worth, there are far worse fathers than him. Jack can't even be bothered to pitch up for the textbook biggies, like Autumn's birthdays and Christmases.'

'Yeah. I'm sorry. And I'm sorry you've never had a dad around.'

'Honestly, I'm fine. My mum was and is always amazing. And this is about you and your dad, and I think you have to focus on the positives.'

'Yep. I'm thinking about birthdays now. I remember this one time when he took us camping for Max's birthday and we all thought it was the most amazing thing ever. Max and I were literally high-fiving. He nearly always made it home early for our birthdays. In retrospect, he must have blocked his diary out a long time in advance.'

'You know what I think,' Evie said. 'Maybe see your dad again, maybe don't, but *do* talk to Max about what you told me at the wedding. Sounds to me like a lot of your good childhood memories involve him.'

'That does sound quite wise again.'

'It is. As you know I'm *exceptionally* wise.'

'Yeah, maybe I will talk to him.' Maybe he would. 'Okay, enough about me. Talk me through what a wise woman's cocktail plans for the evening are.'

What felt like a very short time later, Evie checked her phone and said, 'Oh my goodness. I'd better go. I'm going to be late. I need to get ready.'

'You already look ready to me,' Dan said. He frowned and laughed. 'Sorry, that sounded ridiculous. I meant you look nice.' *Nice*. That was far too lukewarm for how Evie looked, which was gorgeous, frankly, whatever she was wearing.

'Well, thank you,' Evie said, 'but I *really* don't look cocktail-party-ready. I need to pull some kind of miracle out of the bag in the next half hour.'

'I think you look lovely,' said Dan, standing up.

'Oh my God—' Evie stood up too and started with her scarf arranging '—I sounded like I was fishing for compliments. I really wasn't.'

'No, you didn't. And it wasn't a compliment, it was a fact. Come on. I'll walk round your side of the green with you.'

When they got to Evie's mum's house, Dan really didn't want to say goodbye.

'I'd better go inside and get on with glamming myself up,' Evie said, rooting around inside her bag for her key. 'Found it.' She looked up at him and smiled. Dan swallowed. He loved the shape of her lips. 'So, bye then.'

'Bye.' He really wanted to ask if she'd like to meet up in London. Except she had a boyfriend and it would maybe sound odd. 'Hopefully see you sometime soon.'

'Yes, hopefully,' she said. 'Good luck when you speak to your dad again.' And then she whisked herself inside, and Dan had the strangest feeling that his fairy godmother had just disappeared in a puff of smoke. Though he doubted Cinderella had ever wanted to kiss her fairy godmother to high heaven.

God, he wished Matthew didn't exist.

*

A week later, back in London, Dan was in a pub in Islington with Max, just the two of them, and he was wondering whether Evie was actually wise or whether this was going to have turned out to have been a big mistake.

'Thanks,' Max said when Dan, back from the bar, put his beer down in front of him. Dan sat down on the stool opposite Max's, and Max raised his glass and said, 'Cheers.'

'Cheers.' Dan took a long sip.

'So you said you had something you wanted to talk to me about?'

'Yup.'

'So, fire ahead?'

'Okay.' Dan took another long sip and then said, 'I wanted to apologise again, as adults, about the accident.'

'What?' Max was just staring at him.

After a few seconds, Dan couldn't take the silence any more. He drank some more beer and then looked around at the bar. Maybe he should go and buy some crisps or something. Or just leave.

'Why are you apologising now?' Max asked, just as Dan was on the brink of standing up. 'It was so many years ago and you apologised then, a lot, and it wasn't your fault, so actually there was never any need for any apology.'

'It was my fault.' Dan partially relaxed back down onto his stool. 'I'm sorry.'

'Seriously. It wasn't your fault. It could have been either of us. We were both a bit pissed and we were half-fighting. And I'm cool about it now. It was half a lifetime ago. I'm happy now. You can't regret stuff that happened in the past if you're happy where you are now, can you? It all contributed to getting to that happy place. I can't actually believe you've brought this up now. Has this been eating away at you?'

'No,' Dan said. 'I mean, maybe a little.'

'God, Dan. *God*. Is this why I've always felt that you've kept me a little at arm's length? I thought you were just really busy with work, or it was something to do with Dad.'

Dan shook his head. And then nodded.

'Oh my *God*.' Max had spoken so loudly that the people at the nearest tables turned round to look at them. Max ignored them. 'I wish we'd had this conversation a long time ago. Just for the record, I properly love my life now. I've met the man of my dreams, not to sound too vomit-worthy, and we're getting married. I have a great job, which I might not have if I hadn't had the accident when I did. And I swerved a lot of pressure. I mean, I saw some of my friends develop real mental health issues from the whole selection thing. Constant stress. Like, even if you make it to the GB squad, do you make it to the Olympics, for example? And, if you do, what are the chances of you actually winning? As it is, I never failed at anything. I went out at the top of my game. Who knows, I might have peaked five minutes later and been dropped. Obviously I wasn't happy in the immediate aftermath, but I was never angry with *you*, and, you know, you have to be able to make the best of any given situation. I'm *really* happy with my life.'

'So. Wow.' Dan couldn't quite believe it. 'Is that all true?'

'Yes. One hundred per cent.' Max shook his head again. 'I'm so sorry that you've been holding this burden for so long.'

Dan couldn't speak. He couldn't even move his mouth into a smile. If he did disturb his features at all, tears might spill out, and he was a grown man and he didn't want to cry.

'Can I ask you something?' Max said. 'I was going to ask this anyway, but now feels like the right time.'

Dan nodded.

'Will you be my best man? And help me plan the wedding? We have less than a year until the big day and that isn't long.'

'Really?'

'Yes, really. Of course, really.' Max looked seriously offended.

'I'd be honoured.' Dan could barely squeeze the words past the lump in his throat.

'And I'm honoured to have you. Come here.' Max moved round the table and pulled Dan into a rough hug. 'Love you, brother.'

Dan's eyes felt far too full right now but his shoulders felt a lot lighter, like years of guilt and shame had just been lifted off.

If he could ever talk about this without blubbing like a baby, he'd have to tell Evie. He needed to thank her.

Chapter Thirty

NOW – SEPTEMBER 2022

EVIE

Evie was in the staff room with her friend Priya, feeling – like she did every September – both excited and shellshocked about the first day of the new school year, when she got a text from Dan. Her heart literally lifted at the sight of his name on her screen.

And now Priya was in full flow about three of her Year Tens having fainted during a fish eye dissection in the first lesson of the afternoon, which, to be fair, was a good story, but Evie was struggling to concentrate because she *really* wanted to read Dan's text. But not in front of anyone. Just in case it said, well, she didn't know what, but she was going to wait to read it.

She opened it between lessons.

Had beers with Max. Had the chat about the accident. All good. Incredibly grateful to you. Sending flowers to thank you. You in this evening between 6 & 8 for delivery? I have your address.

It was lovely that everything had gone well with him and Max, and lovely of him to send her flowers. Lovely.

If she was honest, though, she was *really* disappointed that he hadn't suggested meeting up again. They had so much fun together, and, if she was being even more honest, he made her heart flutter more than a little.

Which meant that it was actually a very good thing that they weren't going to see each other for a while. She wouldn't act on any feelings for Dan, but she didn't want to be disloyal to Matthew in any way, even just in her head.

Matthew was her partner and she was very lucky to have him.

This evening they were playing badminton and then going to the pub with the others from their little squad and she was really looking forward to it, and then on Saturday they were going for dinner near Wimbledon Common with Josh and his boyfriend Fergus – who he was still going out with after four months, his longest ever relationship – and she was really looking forward to that too.

*

Dinner on Saturday with Josh and Fergus was lovely.

As they were sorting out their jackets afterwards, Josh said in Evie's ear, 'Not so boring actually. I like him.'

'I like him too,' Evie said. 'Is that an actual admission that you were wrong?'

'Might be.'

'Ready to go?' Matthew asked Evie when they'd said goodnight to Josh and Fergus, who were going back to Fergus's. 'I thought we could take a walk on the common on the way back?' He was staying at Evie's tonight.

'Perfect,' Evie said. 'I like a walk after dinner. Helps you digest.'

They wandered along the road to the common, admiring the amazing houses they were surrounded by and talking about the nearest golf courses.

They came to a pond, and Matthew tugged Evie's hand a bit to bring her to a halt. He turned to face her and took both her hands.

This was nice. A kiss next to a moonlit pond. Or maybe he was going to point a constellation out to her. Nice. This felt like a romantic spot, a place for lovers. Nice. Although there were quite a lot of midges. Evie really wanted to pull her hands out of Matthew's so that she could swipe them away. Eurgh. She was pretty sure she was getting bitten.

'Shall we walk?' she said. 'Midges.'

'Oh. Right. Yes, of course.'

They wandered a little further into the middle of the common, away from the pond. Evie really hoped she wasn't going to end up standing in anything grim. A lot of people walked their dogs here.

Oh.

Goodness.

Matthew had stopped under a tree – which felt like it was going to prove to be another midge hotspot – and was kneeling down very carefully in front of her.

There was only one reason that she could think of that someone would kneel down like that.

She stood stock-still, quite frozen to the spot. This was just, God, what was it? It was unexpected, that's what it was. They'd only been going out for eight months. He was lovely, he really was, but this was *soon*.

He was still holding onto her hands and looking up at her in a very sweet way and clearing his throat.

'Evie Green,' he said. Oh, God. He was going to do it. Right now. He looked so sweet and earnest, and also very handsome. What was she going to *say*? 'Will you move in with me?'

Oh, okay, so this wasn't a marriage proposal. It was still a big deal, though. Huge.

Evie thought about how much she liked Matthew. Then she thought about her mum and all her messed-up relationships. And about her own failed romances. Matthew wouldn't let her down or be dishonest with her. He was solid. He was dependable. He was an accountant. He had a lovely, tidy flat. He was *so* much tidier than both Evie's mum and Josh. They had a nice time together.

Evie would miss Josh and Mia if she moved out. She'd have to move out one day, though. They couldn't live together forever. Maybe Josh would want to move in officially with Fergus soon.

'Evie?' Matthew's smile was faltering a little bit.

Evie cleared her throat. Clearly, she needed to give him an answer, and she needed to do it *right now*. This was huge, though. It required thought. Matthew looked very serious. It felt like the next step – and maybe quite soon – might be a very carefully thought-out actual marriage proposal.

She suddenly thought of the pact she and Dan had made all those years ago. And Vegas. Dan. It was ridiculous to think of him now. Her crush – because that's what it was – might as well be a crush on Ryan Reynolds or someone. It wasn't *real* and it didn't mean anything.

Real was lovely Matthew kneeling on the ground in front of her with a now very uncertain smile and a very anxious look around his eyes.

There was only one sensible answer.

Oh, but she wanted even just a fraction of the excitement and longing and fun she felt when she was around Dan.

She couldn't do it. All she could think about right now was Vegas.

Chapter Thirty-One

THEN – 23RD DECEMBER 2021

EVIE

Celine Dion impersonator (they hadn't been able to get tickets to actual Celine Dion) smashing 'My Heart Will Go On' – tick. Feather boas, glitter, glamour, the works – tick. Everyone around their table all dolled up to the nines – tick. Piles of chips waiting for them later in the casino after they'd been instructioned-up on how to play – tick. Plus a great menu and a tableful of cocktails. Basically, your perfect Vegas last-night-of-your-twenties evening just starting.

So Evie should really *not* be constantly trying hard not to look over her shoulder to check whether Dan had arrived. And she should accept that there was no way it would look anything other than odd to ask Sasha to check her phone to see if he was definitely still coming.

And, honestly, why did she even care that much? She hadn't seen him for several months and she was with her old schoolfriends and this was going to be a fab evening. Best thirtieth birthday dinner she could ever have hoped for.

Their waiter – a man called Joe sporting a floral cowboy outfit – salsa-danced himself over to them with another two jugs of bright pink and bright orange cocktails.

'Come on, birthday girl,' he said. 'Hit me with your order.'

'Okay.' Evie looked again at the starters section. 'I can't decide between garlic prawns and the quail's eggs on crostini to start with.'

'You gonna be spending any *quality* time with a partner tonight?' Joe asked. 'Because if you are, I'm thinking quail's eggs. Those prawns are *good*, I'm not saying they aren't, but they're very garlicky, you know what I'm saying?'

'I'd go eggs,' Anita said from across the table. 'I think tonight's the night to end your dry phase. There are a lot of nice men here.' There *were* a lot of men here, but they weren't necessarily all *nice*. Evie definitely wouldn't mind ending her dry phase, but she wasn't sure she wanted to do that with a one-night-Vegas-stand.

'I think eggs too,' Sasha said. 'You need to *get* some tonight. Eggs, eggs, eggs, eggs.' She started swinging her arms in a conducting motion. 'Eggs, eggs, eggs, eggs.'

'Sasha, we haven't even had our *starters* and you're chanting,' Evie said. 'Drink some water.' She was going to go with the prawns. She *wasn't* going to 'get some' tonight and she *loved* garlic prawns.

'Honestly, you sound like Dan,' Sasha tutted. Her gaze switched to beyond Evie's shoulder. 'OMG, Daaaaaaaan,' she screamed, standing up and pointing.

Evie turned round, her heart suddenly beating faster. It was totally okay to turn round when someone had *pointed*; it totally wasn't desperate-looking. And no-one would know that she was *really* hoping that it *was* Dan. Unless they saw the huge smile that she could feel spreading across her face, because it *was* him. Looking extremely Dan-like. No concession at all to the glitz of Vegas. He was dressed in straight-legged blue jeans and a bottle green needlecord shirt, teamed with Timberland deck shoes. Pretty much the same style of clothes that he'd been wearing every time Evie had seen him since forever. She felt her heart swell with the *niceness* of how solidly reliable he was.

People were looking at him as he walked across the room, because that did happen with Dan – there was something about the way he carried himself. He always seemed completely unaware of it.

When he reached them, Sasha made her way round the table and chucked herself on him with an enormous hug.

'Hey, sis,' he said, laughing. 'Good to see you too.'

'Sit here.' Sasha did some sleight of hand with chairs and cutlery and suddenly there was a free space right next to Evie.

'Great, thank you. Hi, everyone.' Dan nodded round the table and sat down. 'Happy birthday for tomorrow,' he said to Evie. 'And I'm honoured to be sitting next to the birthday girl. Pride of place. How's your evening going?'

'It's going very well,' Evie said, beaming. It had felt like a good evening before; now it felt *wonderful*.

'Welcome to our special new arrival,' Joe said, winking at Dan, who laughed and winked back, which made Evie want to throw herself into his arms, or something; *how* embarrassing to realise that you had *such* an immense crush on someone when you were turning thirty tomorrow and you'd known that someone for so many years. But equally *how* cool that he was here and was going to be sitting right next to her for the rest of the evening. Hopefully dinner was going to last a *long* time. 'I'm guessing you're *definitely* going quail's eggs now?' Joe said to Evie, indicating Dan with a lot of eye and eyebrow action. God, embarrassing. What if Dan thought she'd said something before he arrived?

She shook her head. 'We aren't, you know, like that,' she said. No, even more embarrassing. She should just have laughed and ignored what he'd said. 'But the quail's eggs do sound delicious and I will go for them. And for main I'll have the cod,' she said quickly, to try to stop any more garlic comments.

'Good choice,' Joe said, winking again. 'I'll come back to *you*, sir, when I've taken the ladies' orders and given you some time to look through the menu.'

'Thank you.' Dan opened the menu. 'So this is great,' he said to Evie, looking up. 'I've never been to Vegas before and so far it's *exactly* what I always imagined.'

'I know,' Evie said. 'Literally down to the Elvis impersonator who sat next to me in the bar earlier. Amazing sideburns and flares.'

'I'm very pleased to hear that,' Dan said. 'So how've you been?'

'You need a drink, Dan,' Sasha interrupted. 'And you need to drink faster, Evie.' She filled Dan's glass from one of the jugs and sloshed more pink cocktail into Evie's glass. 'Do you think we should play some drinking games?'

'Absolutely not,' said Angus, overhearing her. 'God. It's going to be carnage on Sasha's own thirtieth.'

'But fun,' Evie said.

'Are you ready to order now?' Joe had made it all the way round the table and was waiting in front of Dan, pencil poised above pad.

'Yeah, for my starter, I'm hesitating between the prawns and the pâté,' Dan said.

Evie held her breath. What was the point of her being un-garlicky if Dan was going to be garlicky? What? Where had that come from? What was she even thinking? There was definitely going to be no kissing between them. All that stuff had just been one evening in time. She was still holding her breath, though.

'I think I'm going to go pâté,' Dan told Joe. 'And ribs for main.'

Evie smiled and took another large sip of her cocktail.

'Grrrreat choice,' Joe said.

By the time they all had their starters, Sasha had them all going on a drinking game.

Evie downed half a glass while everyone shouted, 'Three fingers,' and said to Dan, 'Honestly. Your sister.'

'Your best friend. You can choose your friends but not your family.'

'I actually love Sasha so much.' The alcohol was leaving Evie with a warm, fuzzy feeling as it spread through her body. 'I'm very lucky to have her.'

Dan laughed. 'Me too.'

'Your turn.' Evie clapped as Dan started to recite the Fuzzy Duck rhyme.

It was a bad idea to drink a lot, and Evie definitely wasn't going to drink too much this evening, but these cocktails were delicious and she was feeling sooo relaxed and *happy* now.

Halfway through their main courses, Joe brought jugs of two different cocktails. They'd finished all the pink ones.

'They're blue and green,' Evie said. 'Unusual colours for drinks. Very… *bright.*'

Dan nodded, very seriously. 'Those *are* unusual beverage colours.'

'We need to try them.'

Dan nodded again. 'You're right.'

'I'm going to be thirty tomorrow,' Evie told Dan. 'That's a *big* one.'

'Yes, *although*, I hear that forty's the new thirty. So maybe thirty's the new twenty.'

'No.' Evie took a long drink of blue cocktail and then shook her head. 'I'm a lot older than I was when I was twenty. I'm ten years older.'

'Great arithmetic.'

'Thank you.' Evie leaned in towards Dan. 'I'm not just ten years *older*, I'm ten years *more experienced*.' She frowned. Had that sounded *weird*?

Dan smiled at her, like he was trying hard not to laugh. 'Congratulations?' he said.

'Are you laughing at me?' Evie drank some more. 'Because it's no laughing matter. Experience is important. I've learned a lot of things about life. I have a lot of wisdom I could impart.'

'Okay, hit me with some of your wisdom.'

'Well—' Evie thought; she was definitely a lot wiser than she'd been at twenty. 'I don't even know where to start. There are so many different areas of life. For example, there's work. There's exercise. There's relationships. Take exercise: when I was twenty I really believed that I'd like to play women's rugby and that I'd like to do an army assault course. I tried women's rugby when I was in my final year at university. Terrible. I'm not brave enough. And I volunteered for a cadet assault course at my last school. So bad. I thought I was going to die, covered in mud under a net thing. I cried in front of the Year Nines and I had to pretend it was because I had mud in my eye.'

'So your wisdom is if you cry at work pretend you have mud in your eye? Or never play women's rugby?'

'Both.'

Dan nodded. 'Okay. I'll bear all of that in mind.'

'Yeah, I think I have better wisdom than that.' Evie drank some more green cocktail. 'I'm gaining wisdom all the time. Right now, I'm learning not to drink blue things. That blue stuff was horrible. *This* is nice.' She pushed her glass of blue away and it wobbled a lot on the edge of the table and then spilled onto the floor. 'Well, look at that.' She pointed. 'That's amazing. It's disappeared.'

'It's a magic floor.' Dan was scrutinising the swirly carpet. He tipped a bit of his own blue drink onto the floor and nodded. 'Gone. Genuine magic.'

Evie drank some more of the green one. She tapped the side of her glass. 'That's *really* nice. You have some. You can share my straw.' She nodded approvingly while Dan drank. 'Well done. We should get some more drinks.' She looked up and then squinted down the table and round the room. 'Where's everyone else?'

Dan looked around. 'I think they're dancing. Over there, look.'

'Oh, yes. Maybe we should join them,' Evie said. 'This is our big birthday trip and tomorrow I'm going to be the birthday girl and I should probably be dancing with my friends.' She hiccupped. 'I need to make the most of the last night of my twenties. Maybe we should have some more green cocktail before we dance. It's very, very good. And then when we've had some more of it we should dance with everyone because dancing's fun and also it'll work off the drink.' She poked Dan triumphantly in his chest. His solid, muscly, *lovely* chest. 'And that is a wise plan. It's wisdom I have gained in my twenties. Ten years ago I didn't know all this wise stuff.'

Dan nodded very solemnly. '*So* wise,' he said.

They were halfway through their next green cocktails when 'Dancing Queen' started playing.

'Oh. My. Goodness,' Evie said, trying to put her glass down. Weird. It was like the table had moved. She tried again. 'There. Glass down. Anyway. As I was saying. OMG. It's like this is *our song*.'

'Totally. The ABBA wedding.'

'Exactly. We have to dance to this.'

'We do.' Dan pushed his chair back and it fell over. He turned round and frowned at it for a moment and then bent down to pick it up. He tried a lot of times but it didn't work. 'Something wrong with that chair,' he said. He held his hand out to Evie. She took it and they began to dance-wind their way through all the tables to the dance floor.

'Wait,' said Evie suddenly. 'We need to make you more Vegas.' Dan had the top button on his shirt undone, but it wasn't enough. She started to undo the next three. She was concentrating hard but it was really tricky doing buttons this evening. Dan tried to help her but he was rubbish at it too. Eventually she had them undone.

'Liking your hairy chest,' she said admiringly.

'Well, thank you. I like your chest too.'

They both kind of scrunched their faces and looked at each other for a moment, and then started to move towards the dance floor again.

When they got to it, Evie stood on tiptoes to say over the music, 'We should look for the others,' in Dan's ear. She didn't *want* to look for the others.

'Definitely,' Dan said, spinning her round and making no attempt to move further into the centre of the dance floor.

Two songs later, Evie was very hot and her stomach was churning a bit.

'I think I need to get some air,' she told Dan.

'Let's go,' Dan said, grabbing her hand.

'Woah,' said Evie as they left the building. 'That's *so* chilly. Why isn't Las Vegas hot?'

'It's December.'

'Oh yes. You're very good at months. It's December because it's my *birthday* tomorrow.'

Dan started to sing '*Happy birthday to you*' as they walked down the Strip.

Evie got her phone out to google the sights of Las Vegas. The Fountains of Bellagio and the High Roller were supposed to be somewhere around, but it was really difficult to work out what direction they were walking in.

'You're shivering,' Dan said. 'Come here.' He put his arm round her and Evie leaned against him. *Melted* against him if she was honest. 'That better?'

'Mmm?' Evie *loved* how their hips were bumping as they walked and how Dan's arm felt along her shoulders. She could smell his musky scent too. And if she glanced up she could see his strong jawline and cheek. So bloody sexy.

'You should have brought a coat.'

'I don't need a coat. I have a gorgeous man heating me up.' She stopped and pointed. 'Look. It's an actual Vegas wedding chapel. We have to check it out.'

Dan nodded. 'Important sightseeing.'

'*That* is one of the tackiest Christmas trees I've ever seen,' said Evie in delight, stopping outside the chapel. She looked up above the chapel entrance. 'And that is one of the biggest bunches of mistletoe I've ever seen.'

Mistletoe.

She looked at Dan and smiled. He looked at her and smiled too.

'Mistletoe,' he said. 'It's obligatory.'

Evie closed her eyes as Dan bent his head and kissed her. And, *God* that was good. His firm lips on hers, their mouths opening for each other, his arms round hers, hers round him, her hands on his back, his legs hard against hers.

They were pressed up against the wall of the chapel now, kissing and kissing.

'Remember,' said Dan, between urgent kisses, 'the pact we made. Under the mistletoe. Our fallback pact. We were young then.'

'Yes,' panted Evie. 'A lot… older… now.'

'We said your thirtieth birthday.' Dan ran a finger along her cheekbone and jawline.

'Mmm.' Evie couldn't really speak. Where else was he going to trace his finger?

A couple came out of the chapel and nearly bumped into them.

'Whoops.' Evie would have fallen over if Dan hadn't held her up. 'Your arms are very, very strong,' she told him, giving his biceps a little squeeze. 'Let's go and look inside.'

'You wanna get a licence, you only have a half hour. Closes at midnight,' a woman with a gigantic beehive hairdo and a pale-yellow pussy-bow blouse told them as they stood there, still with their arms round each other's waists.

'Do you work here?' Evie asked.

The woman nodded. Her hair didn't move.

'You have great hairspray,' Evie said. 'I'd like hairspray like that.' She leaned in towards the woman and pulled Dan in with her. 'I'd like to get married. I'd like to get a licence. This is Dan. I'm Evie. We have a pact. We made it under the mistletoe and we kissed just now under mistletoe.' She stuck her finger out to point at the mistletoe but everything was spinning a bit and she couldn't remember where it was. Never mind. It was irrelevant. The *point* was the *pact*. 'We're supposed to get married on my thirtieth birthday tomorrow if we're still single.'

'And are you both still single?' the woman asked.

They both nodded.

'So you need to get married, right now.'

'What's your name?' Evie asked.

'Susan.'

Evie turned to Dan. 'Susan's making a lot of sense.'

Dan nodded, looking really serious. 'She is.'

Forty-five minutes later, they emerged from the chapel, Evie holding their marriage certificate and a glass of sparkling wine, and wearing a gigantic beam.

She clinked her glass against Dan's and they both took a long drink.

'Look. We're back under the mistletoe,' she said, pointing.

Dan kissed the back of her neck and then moved the neckline of her dress down so that he could kiss along her shoulder.

'That is so good,' Evie told him, shivering. 'And you're my husband and I would very much like you to have your wicked way with me.'

'I would very much like that too.' Dan kissed the curve of her neck some more.

'Hotel's this way,' Susan called.

Evie opened her eyes and tried to focus. It was difficult, because Dan had his hands inside her dress and she had hers under his shirt and his stubble was grazing her face and her chest *so* deliciously.

'And get a *room*,' Susan yelled. 'This way.'

'Different hotel,' Dan said.

'No, you bought the honeymoon suite package. This way.'

Chapter Thirty-Two

NOW – SEPTEMBER 2022

DAN

Dan clapped Katie as she pulled the extending squeaky giraffe neck on her playmat over and over again.

'You're so clever,' he told her. His daughter was amazing in every way. Her smiles, her chortles, the way she held her arms out to be cuddled, her giraffe-neck pulling.

The doorbell rang and he tensed as the familiar wave of sadness washed over him. He hated saying goodbye to Katie each time. And there was the underlying worry that Hannah might decide to move to New York after her maternity leave. She'd been vacillating about it for months now.

'Hey, Hannah.' He used his best cheery tone. You wanted to be on good terms with your daughter's mother, however much you wished that she would just *bloody* tell you her plans.

'Hi, Dan. How's she been?'

'She's getting really good at pulling. Watch her go with that giraffe. I think she's definitely a lot more advanced physically than your average baby of this age. And mentally. She recognises so many people.' He might have to fake cheeriness around Hannah, but he didn't have to fake adoration of his daughter, and if there was one thing they agreed on, it was that she was literally the most perfect human ever born.

They sat at opposite ends of Dan's sofa and watched her for a minute or two, both clapping for her, while she gurgled and beamed at them.

Hannah suddenly stopped clapping and turned to face him and said, 'I'm so sorry, Dan, I should have told you immediately. About New York.'

God. Dan felt his face and stomach drop, like the joy had been sucked straight out of the day. Out of his life. He couldn't *bear* the thought of not seeing Katie regularly any more.

'I've decided not to go,' she said. 'I'm going to co-head the desk with someone already there, so I'll only need to visit from time to time. I just can't bring Katie up away from you, and my family. It wouldn't be right for her, and I don't actually think I could cope. I'd have to have at least two full-time nannies to cover my working hours.'

'Are you certain?' Dan said.

'Yes.'

'I'm going to be honest: I'm incredibly relieved. I'd have been devastated not to be able to see her regularly.'

'I know.' Hannah turned back round to Katie, who was still busy with the hanging giraffe. 'I'm sure she'd have been devastated too, growing up far away from you.' She turned back to Dan. 'I'm sorry it's taken me so long to work things out but I'm sure now that I can manage things remotely from here and just fly out there every month or two for a few days.'

'Not a problem,' Dan said. He really wanted to ask about formalising arrangements about how often he would see Katie going forward, but maybe now wasn't the time.

'So I'm thinking maybe we carry on like this for a while,' Hannah said – Dan had Katie one full day each weekend and for the occasional evening – 'and then once I stop breastfeeding you could see her a minimum of one evening a week and have her to stay over one night every weekend? And have her for at least a couple of weeks' holiday every year? Would that suit you?'

'Yes,' Dan said. 'Thank you so much.'

'No, thank *you*. You're an amazing dad.'

*

Dan was still in such a state of euphoria that he genuinely wasn't that pissed off that he was going to be seeing Evie *with* Matthew that evening. Angus had won a wine tasting for eight at a London wine merchant's, and he and Sasha had invited Max and Greggy (who they were staying with), Evie and Matthew, and Dan and Angus's brother Rory, who also lived in London, to join them. Dan hadn't really wanted to go, because of Evie and Matthew, basically, but he hadn't felt like he could say no, especially now that things were so good between him and Max, because he wanted to keep them that way.

He arrived about fifteen minutes later than the others, due to the longer-than-expected handover chat with Hannah, and walked in to see the seven of them sitting round a table, with one spare chair, for Dan, obviously.

Evie was telling an anecdote – something to do with spiders and her classroom – and she was gesticulating and laughing almost as much as she was talking. She looked gorgeous, as always. *God*, he'd messed up not asking her out when she was single.

He frowned. The man she was sitting next to really didn't look like the man Dan remembered as Matthew. It wasn't like Matthew was etched in Dan's mind but at the same time he did quite clearly remember talking to the two of them – and not enjoying it – and Matthew had definitely been tall and blond (and annoyingly handsome), and this man was shorter and dark.

'Hi, Dan. This is Jimmy, my flatmate,' Rory said. Looked like Matthew wouldn't be coming given that there were no more spare chairs. Excellent. Probably playing more golf.

Dan said hi around the table, trying not to smile too much at Matthew's absence.

An hour and a half later, they'd all shifted positions round the table and Dan was sitting next to Evie, who was completely ignoring the host – who'd been a sommelier at a couple of very fancy restaurants before setting up this business, and sounded like he really knew his stuff and was currently talking about vineyards in Armenia and Turkey – and was busy re-tasting the six different reds they'd tried so far.

'I always like the cheapest ones,' she said happily. 'Which I think you'll find is this one because it's the nicest.' She finished one of the glasses.

'Wasn't that the one he said was served in the Ritz Paris and is incredibly rare, like the grapes only develop once every twenty years and are trampled by foot by princes and unicorns?'

'Nope. I really like it, so I think you'll find it's Chateau Lidl at best.' Evie picked up one of her other glasses, took a sip and sucked her cheeks in. '*This* will be the expensive one. One mouthful of that and I can feel a headache coming on. Seriously. I know my stuff. I can rank them in order of price based on what I like.'

Their host raised his voice and said, 'So now I'd like to play a little game. I'd like you to rank them according to price. There's a prize for the winner.'

'Yessssss,' said Evie. 'Finally, my life skills come into play. I'm going to get them all right.'

'There's no way you will.' Dan closed his eyes and re-tasted all of his and started to arrange them in order.

When he'd finished, Evie looked at his and compared them to her own. 'You're rubbish,' she said. 'You've only got two right.'

'I'm genuinely quite good at this,' Dan told her. It was only fair to warn her. 'Currently *you* only have two right. You're welcome to copy me.'

'No way,' said Evie. 'I want that prize.'

'And let's go,' said their host.

Five minutes later, Evie was bowing and clutching her prize: a bottle of rosé. 'Six out of six,' she crowed.

'I'm genuinely impressed,' Dan said when everyone had finished clapping and she'd sat back down.

'Always works. Nicest the cheapest, worst the most expensive. I'm a very cheap date.'

'So what's Matthew up to this evening?'

'We split up,' Evie said.

'Oh, no,' said Dan, trying really hard to sound sincere. 'Are you okay?' He really wanted to ask what had happened.

'Yep, fine, thank you.' Evie gave him a small smile and said, 'So which was your favourite of the wines?'

They spilled out onto the road outside the wine merchant's at about eleven, all saying how much they'd enjoyed the evening.

'Tubing it home?' Dan asked Evie. Max, Greggy, Sasha and Angus were going back together to Max and Greggy's place in North London.

He was going to take the plunge. He should have asked her out at the beginning of the year, built on their night in Vegas. Maybe she'd be happy to go on a date with him now, maybe she wouldn't, but he should give it a shot. He could ask her on the way home.

'Yep. I think Rory and Jimmy are going to Wimbledon on the District Line too so we can all go together.'

'Great,' Dan said. Not exactly what he'd had in mind.

'Night,' he said to the other three, fifty minutes later, when the train stopped at Fulham Broadway. He could have saved himself a fair amount of time and left them at Earl's Court and not waited for the Wimbledon branch train, but he'd hoped the whole time that he might be able to chat to Evie, just the two of them.

Okay. He was going to text her instead. The worst that could happen would be that she'd say no.

Chapter Thirty-Three

NOW – SEPTEMBER 2022

EVIE

Evie's phone buzzed with a message *from Dan* as they pulled into Putney Bridge Tube station, two stops after Fulham Broadway where he'd got off. She took a quick peek at it.

He wanted to know if she'd like to go to the cinema next Saturday evening. *He wanted to know if she wanted to go to the cinema with him.* It had to be a date. A date. With Dan.

Well, *yes*, she wanted to go out with him. But *should* she go out with him? She already knew that there'd be a lot of potential for hurt in a relationship with him, and it didn't feel like he was the one for her long-term. But she *really* wanted to go on a date with him. A proper date after all these years.

She was busy next Saturday, and the one after. She *could* cancel her plans.

And that would be stupid. You shouldn't put your love life – *love life – he'd asked her out* – above your friends.

And if he was properly interested, he'd be happy to see her in three weeks' time.

'Evie, you're in a world of your own,' Rory said. 'It's our stop. Good job we're here or you might have ended up spending the night on the train.'

*

They met three weekends later. The cinema was within walking distance from Evie's flat, but she was running late. She'd spent too long deciding what to wear and arrived, at a bit of a run, a good ten minutes after the time they'd agreed. Dan was standing, hands in pockets, in the middle of the cinema's wide entrance, smiling at her as she hurried through the rotating doors. There was something very nice about the fact that, unlike all the other people waiting, he didn't have his phone in his hand.

'Hi,' she said, trying not to pant. She really needed to get fitter.

'Hello.' Dan's face crinkled into an even bigger smile. 'Been running?'

'Maybe.'

'You're wearing yet another scarf. In yet another very nice colour.' It was emerald-green. He gave the end of it a gentle tug and, honestly, Evie felt tingles everywhere. Unbelievable. He hadn't even touched *her*, he'd just touched her scarf.

She smiled back at him, definitely foolishly, and wondered if she was losing her mind.

'Scarves are very important,' she said. 'They frame a person's face. Hide wrinkles. Elevate an outfit.' Seriously. She might as well be talking about the weather. Ridiculous first-date nerves with someone she'd known forever.

'And also they're important for keeping you warm,' Dan said.

'I mean, that's a *very* secondary consideration.'

'So are you de-scarfing now or wearing it all evening? Bearing in mind that it's quite warm in here even though that's a secondary consideration?'

'Well, *fortunately*, I've come prepared and I'm wearing a jumper that I quite like, so I'm okay to take the scarf off.'

'Well, *phew*,' Dan said. 'I really like that jumper too.'

'Why, thank you.' She'd bought this cream jumper and another one – red – this morning and had spent far too long before she came out deciding which one to wear. Hang on. Had she taken the price tag out? She hoped so. 'I might just pop to the loo before the film starts,' she said.

The price tag was still there. She could feel it attached to the label. And it wasn't held on by a normal, thin plastic tag; it was on a cord loop, which she couldn't cut without scissors, which she didn't have. Why didn't she carry scissors? Actually, this was ridiculous. There was no need to panic. It wasn't like Dan was going to be looking inside her top, was it? And if he *did* happen to come back to her flat, she could pop into the bathroom and cut the price tag out then. Just in case for some reason she ended up taking the jumper off.

And standing in the middle of some very brightly lit loos that smelled of pine bleach and something grim, she had goosebumps all over thinking about what might happen later.

She moved closer to the mirrors. Did her lipstick look okay? Maybe she should have worn a slightly different colour. And was her hair looking alright? She gave it a couple of tweaks.

Okay. She was being ridiculous. Dan probably wouldn't notice her lipstick or her hair. He wasn't standing out there feeling like a gibbering wreck. He was just being normal. She was going to pull the tag off the loop and leave the loop itself and Dan would never notice and if he did – which, again, he wouldn't, because they probably weren't going to be removing clothes; oh, God, maybe they would – he'd actually never notice or he'd think it was just part of the label of the jumper and he'd never know she'd bought the jumper today just for this evening and everything was going to be fine and she just needed to *stop panicking*. It was strange, though, finally being on an official date.

She took some deep breaths and left the loos.

When she got back to the cinema foyer, Dan was next to the pick 'n' mix, holding a big stripy paper bag and an expression of extreme concentration.

'Oh, wow, sherbet lemons,' Evie said, pleased that her voice sounded normal and non-jittery.

'I know,' Dan said. 'I couldn't resist. I literally never eat sweets but these were calling out to me. I was just trying to work out whether to take a punt on what you'd like and go big on just a few of what are in my opinion are the best ones, or whether to get a little bit of everything.'

'We have to go big on just a few,' Evie said. 'Unless you have very bad taste in sweets and we can't agree.'

'No,' said Dan. 'If we can't agree, it'll be because *you* have bad taste.'

Fifteen minutes later, they were sitting in the middle of the second from back row of the auditorium, munching happily on the sherbet lemons, plus fizzy cola bottles and pineapple chunks, people-watching while they waited for the film to start. Evie honestly couldn't remember enjoying a cinema trip this much, even as a little girl. She had a what's-going-to-happen-this-evening fizz of anticipation inside her even bigger than the fizz from the sherbet lemons.

When the credits rolled at the end of the film and the auditorium lights came on, Evie saw that every seat was taken, which was weird, because it had felt like it was just the two of them for the duration of the film. Then she looked down and realised that she had both her hands clamped on Dan's forearm.

'I didn't know you were a screamer,' he said, grinning at her.

'Me! What about you? You gasped so much when that man leapt out with the knife I thought you were going to choke.'

'I mean, the whole cinema gasped at that point. Whereas the whole cinema did not scream when you did.'

'Quiet screaming, though,' Evie said. 'You gasped *really* loudly.'

They grinned at each other.

'Quick drink so we can recover from the screaming and gasping?' Dan said.

'Sounds like a plan.' Should she invite him back to her flat? Cue extreme stomach butterflies. 'There's a lovely wine bar up the road if you fancy it?'

As they pushed through the crowded bar, Evie almost wriggled with pleasure, feeling Dan's hand in the small of her back. It felt intimate, it felt like the promise of things to come later, and it just felt *right*.

Once they were sitting at a table in the corner, Dan with a bottle of beer and Evie with a glass of white, Evie said, 'So it's wonderful that you and Max sorted things out.'

'Yeah. Thank you, so much, again. We're in touch a lot more now. It's nice. He and Greggy are making progress with their wedding plans. By the sounds of it, they're going to make Sasha's wedding look almost low-key. You know he asked me to be his best man? I have the job of organising his stag, and he said he has no guidance other than he wants it to be unpredictable and spectacular.'

'Easy, then.'

'I know. So far I have no ideas beyond your bog-standard Ibiza or Prague trip, both on a budget. I need something original but not too expensive.'

'Hmm. Bingo?'

'That is original and also cheap, but maybe a miss on the spectacular front.'

'Hey. Have you been to Johnson's Bingo in Cirencester? Because that *is* spectacular.'

At midnight, when the bar closed, Evie was *so* not ready to end the conversation, and it seemed like Dan wasn't either.

'Can I walk you home?' Dan asked. 'For my peace of mind.'

'Yes, you can, and thank you,' Evie said. She really wished the bar had stayed open for longer because now it felt like she had a decision to make and she wasn't sure which way she wanted to go. She didn't want the evening to end now but she wasn't sure if she wanted to invite Dan in tonight, because it felt like they could be at the start of something big and like she needed to work out what she wanted. 'I'm quite tired, though.' Aargh. She could have worded that a *lot* better.

He smiled at her. 'I'm tired too.'

*

'This is a *great* location,' Dan said as they rounded the corner of Evie's road ten minutes later. When he'd dropped her off after the quiz, they hadn't been chatting about things like locations. They'd been arguing and apologising and then they'd nearly kissed.

'I know. There is a *slight* issue with Tube noise, and I have to keep my bedroom curtains closed at all times, because otherwise I'm literally eye-to-eye with passengers at a distance of only a few metres, but it's *so* cool to be so close to the centre of Wimbledon, which I never thought I'd manage on my salary. So lucky that Josh had a spare room. Well, spare boxroom.' She stopped outside the house. 'So we're here.' Should she, shouldn't she invite him in? 'I've had a lovely evening.'

'Me too.' Dan was planted in front of her, his hands in his pockets again, smiling down at her.

Evie drew a deep breath and licked her lips.

And then he bent his head towards hers, very slowly, and gave her the most fleeting of kisses on the lips.

Evie's heart was hammering against her ribs and she couldn't have moved if you'd paid her.

Dan's smile grew and then he leaned forwards again and Evie reached up to meet him and this time it was a proper kiss. They relaxed into each other, kissing, exploring, Evie's arms around Dan's neck, his around her and his hands wound gorgeously, sensuously in her hair.

'Excuse me.' Josh was doing an exaggerated cough right next to them. Fergus was holding his hand, trying to pull him away and shushing.

'Whoops,' Evie said.

'Whoops yourself, ooh-er,' Josh said, moving round them. He inserted his key in the door and pushed. 'You coming in?'

Eek. Decision time right here, right now.

'Um.' Evie still had her arms round Dan. She let go of him and stepped backwards, and he let go of her too. 'Yes, I am,' she said.

'We'll leave you to your *goodbyes*,' Josh said, with a lot of suggestive eyebrow waggling.

Evie waited until Josh had closed the door – with a bit of *hilarious* have-I-haven't-I reopening and closing of it – and said, 'So, goodnight, then.'

'Goodnight.' His voice was so deliciously gravelly. 'Do you…?' He cleared his throat. 'Do you fancy dinner soon?'

'I do, actually,' Evie said.

'Cool. Night.'

Evie let herself into the house and smiled all the way up the stairs to the flat.

Chapter Thirty-Four

NOW – OCTOBER 2022

DAN

Dan looked up at the – somewhat weird – orange, geometric clock on the far side of the café.

'That clock must be fast,' he said, pulling his phone out. 'Nope. It's right. I'd better get going.'

'Me too,' said his father. 'I'll get this.'

'My turn.' Dan put his wallet on the table.

'But I'm your dad and I'd like to get it.' His father raised his eyebrows. 'If you'll let me?'

Dan looked at him, and nodded, slowly. It felt symbolic. Like he was *letting* him be his dad again.

'Thanks,' he said. 'This has been good.' Domino effect. Evie had nagged him into talking to Max, and Max had nagged him into talking to his father.

'I wondered,' said his father, when he'd paid, and they were huddling in their coats in biting wind on the pavement outside, preparing to go their separate ways, 'if you'd like to go to the rugby at Twickenham with me next month. The England–Italy match. I have four tickets. I thought I could ask Max and Greggy too.' Right. Several hours together. Father/son bonding. It felt like a commitment.

It felt like it would be a great way of rebuilding their relationship.

'I'd like that,' Dan said. 'I'm not sure what weekends I'm down to work, though. Could you send me the date and I'll have a look and let you know?' If he got cold feet he could use work as an excuse. He didn't think he would, though.

*

Dan slapped aftershave on and then laughed at himself in his bathroom mirror. He couldn't remember the last time he'd shaved any time other than first thing in the morning. Normally, he took the view that if he was stubbly, he was stubbly.

Seeing Evie today felt special, though, like they were both acknowledging that they had a relationship and it could be going somewhere.

It was Wednesday evening, ten days since their cinema trip. They'd squeezed a coffee in, just outside Earl's Court station, on Sunday morning, but other than that hadn't managed to see each other, and they couldn't find a weekend time that they were both free for the next week and a half. This evening, though, they were both free, and they'd planned to catch the end of the day at a funfair currently on Wimbledon Common, and then go for dinner at a nearby pub that Zubin had recommended.

Just over an hour later, they were wandering hand in hand around the funfair.

'Okay,' said Evie, 'we don't have much time, so we need to prioritise. I *love* dodgems and, if I'm honest, I'll be disappointed if we don't do them.'

Dan nodded. 'Good call. I love a dodgem too. Also the shooting range.'

'Okay. I'm rubbish but I don't mind having a go.'

'That's good news for me. If I say so myself, I'm not bad, so I'll be able to strut some macho impressing-the-ladies stuff.'

'I will prepare to be duly impressed. Dodgems first? In case you win lots of stuff on the shooting range and it won't fit in the cars with us?'

Fifteen minutes later, Evie had just rammed two teenage boys, hard, for the umpteenth time, and was cackling away like a woman possessed.

'You're a *demon* at the wheel,' Dan said, impressed, as their cars bumped together and they were momentarily halted next to each other at the side.

'I know,' she said happily. 'Honestly, I was never like this before I started driving in London, but now I've started I can't stop. Next time I get in my actual car I'm going to have to remind myself that it isn't a dodgem. Anyway. Move. You're cramping my bumping style.'

At the end of their go, they got out of their cars, both staggering slightly.

'That's quite high impact,' said Dan.

'It is. Good job we're just going to be standing still shooting now. Time to recover. You'll have to show me how to do it.' Evie smiled at him and he felt it right to his stomach. He put his hand out and she put hers into his. They fitted perfectly together, like a jigsaw.

They also fitted together perfectly when he stood behind Evie and reached round her to show her how to use the air rifle. She wriggled slightly against him as they adjusted her hold and *God* that felt – he hoped – like a promise of things to come tonight.

He really needed to get a grip, otherwise he'd literally be panting right here in the middle of a fairground.

He leaned down and planted a kiss on the back of her neck and she wriggled even more.

'Porn,' yelled one of the boys that Evie had been ramming on the dodgems. Fair enough.

'Right,' Dan said to Evie. 'You ready?'

'I think so. You go first, show me how it's done.'

Dan did pretty well actually. Out of three shots he had two near misses and with the third won a mid-sized teddy, which Katie would definitely love.

'Wow,' said Evie. 'You're amazing.' Dan tried really hard not to preen like a peacock. 'Okay. My go.' She screwed her face up adorably, took aim and, squeaking as she did so, fired, and then closed her eyes.

'Evie!' Dan said. 'No way! Amazing.' She'd won the biggest teddy they had, which was genuinely not much smaller than her.

She opened her eyes and started jumping up and down, saying, 'Wow.'

The stall owner was looking part-annoyed, part-stunned. 'That's incredible,' he said.

'Talk about beginner's luck,' said Evie, when she'd finished jumping. 'Okay, I'm going again.'

On her second attempt she hit the second biggest teddy and on her third attempt she didn't bother with all the face-screwing-up and squeaking and just laughed and narrowed her eyes and shot the third biggest teddy.

'Oh my God,' Dan said. 'You're a complete hustler. Where did you learn and how have I never known this about you?'

'Army cadets and, clearly, the first secret of hustling is to keep your skill as secret as possible.'

'Well, wow. That was seriously impressive. You're my woman if I ever need a sniper. Ready to haul our booty off to the pub now?'

*

Two and a half hours later, Evie looked at her plate and the last mouthful of her sticky toffee pudding and said, 'I *really* want to eat that, but I'm *so* full.'

'You going to go for it?'

'I actually can't. I'm going to have to admit defeat.' Evie gestured at the panelled walls surrounding them. 'I love this pub. So much character. And such good food.'

'Yeah, me too. I'm going to tell Zubin it was a great suggestion. Shall we get the bill and I'll walk you home very slowly to try to work some of the pudding off?'

'Oh my goodness,' Evie gasped as they opened the door of the pub and a blast of freezing air hit them. 'You never think of London as being this cold. Especially in the autumn.'

'Good job we have the teddies to warm us and that you have one of your trusty scarves,' Dan said. This evening's one was a sort of coral colour and woollen. 'How many times are you wrapping this one?'

'As many as I can.' Evie shivered.

'Come here.' Dan put his non-teddy-holding arm round her shoulders and hugged her into him. 'Warmer?'

'Mmm,' said Evie. He couldn't see her face very well because her head was kind of nestled into his neck as they walked, but he'd definitely caught a glimpse of a big smile.

They wandered along like that, across Wimbledon Common, talking a little bit, about light stuff, until they stopped to cross a road, and then looked into some of the shop windows on Wimbledon High

Street, and then afterwards ended up holding hands instead, all the rest of the way down the hill and back to Evie's flat, still chatting, still about nothing serious.

They stopped outside Evie's front door. Dan looked down at where their fingers were laced together. Her hand really did fit perfectly inside his.

'I really enjoyed our evening,' he said. He'd be pretty keen for it not to end right here.

'Me too,' Evie said. She looked up at his face for a long time, and then said, 'Would you like to come in for a coffee?'

Stupid question. Dan would *love* to go in for a coffee. Except. Evie had hesitated for way too long there. It was like she thought she should ask him in but she wasn't totally sure about it.

'Are you absolutely sure?' he asked. Shit. That sounded like he thought they were talking about sex, which obviously he hoped they were, but maybe they weren't, maybe she was just genuinely *only* talking about coffee. 'I mean, you aren't too tired? Dodgems, hustling and eating a lot are hard work.'

She smiled at him and his breath caught.

Chapter Thirty-Five

NOW – OCTOBER 2022

EVIE

It was Wednesday evening and Evie had to be up at the crack of dawn tomorrow to help supervise Year Nine netball practice at seven thirty – just hideous – but she was still sure about inviting Dan in. They'd had an amazing evening so far and it felt like the natural next step.

'I'm very sure. I need a coffee to carry on digesting.'

'Then I'd love to.' His smile was slow and held a *lot* of promises.

Woah. Evie had just had a serious stomach lurch. He was coming inside. Thank God she was wearing matching underwear. Not that drinking coffee with someone meant that you were *necessarily* going to undress in front of them.

It would be seriously disappointing if no undressing happened, though.

They held hands all the way up the stairs to the flat, which was a bit cheesy, but felt really, really nice.

'So here we are,' she said, once they were inside. They weren't holding hands any more, because the front door was stiff and impossible to open without both hands plus a bit of a kick. Josh talked a lot about oiling it but never got round to it.

She took all the teddies and put them in an armchair.

'Thank you. This is lovely,' said Dan, looking around the room from where he was still standing, next to the door.

'It is. I fell on my feet big time being able to rent from Josh. And as I might have said a few thousand times before, I love the location. And I've almost stopped noticing when the whole building shakes because of the trains going past.'

Dan laughed. 'It's all about compromise. Same with my flat – it's such a luxury being able to walk to work but it's absolutely tiny. And smells very strongly of curry, from the restaurant downstairs, which I don't mind at all, because I love curry, other than when I'm trying to cook something different, like Italian, when you get a bit of a smell clash.'

They were standing on opposite sides of the room, Dan with his hands in his jeans pockets but his thumbs out, and Evie with her hands clasped together in front of her.

'So I'll put the kettle on,' she said. Mia was away this week on a work trip and Josh was staying over at Fergus's, as he did increasingly often because Fergus's flat was a lot closer to his office. So anything could happen right now and they wouldn't be disturbed.

'Great,' said Dan.

And then they looked at each other and Dan took his hands out of his pockets and Evie unclasped her hands and they moved towards each other and suddenly Evie had her hands on Dan's shoulders and his hands were cradling her face and they were kissing, urgently, madly, wonderfully, like the world might be ending.

They fell backwards onto the sofa, and *God* it was good.

Such a good call on the matching underwear.

Dan was kissing her everywhere and she was kissing him and between kisses she couldn't stop smiling and he was smiling too, and this was just *amazing*.

*

There was a very loud ringing noise. It sounded like Evie's alarm. It was her phone. *How* could it be her phone? It was the middle of the night. She was so tired. Her limbs were so heavy. And they were wrapped around Dan's limbs. She turned herself over and pressed Stop on her phone.

Woah. Her head was *so* fuzzy from lack of sleep. She didn't really want to turn back round and look at Dan. What if this was like Vegas and he was full of regret and couldn't get away from her fast enough? Although, really, that had been completely different. They'd been drunk then but sober last night. They'd *known* last night that they were on a date. Still, though.

Their legs were still tangled together. She started to inch away from him and then felt him reach an arm round her waist and pull her towards him. He moved her hair out of the way and kissed the back of her neck and her shoulder.

'Morning,' he said, his voice sleepy and deep. It sounded as though he was smiling.

Suddenly Evie really needed to see his face. She wriggled and twisted round.

And, yes, he was smiling. He was smiling very broadly, looking very contented.

'That was an incredible night,' he said. He ran his hand all the way from her thigh up her side and Evie shivered deliciously. 'What time did you say you need to leave for work?' he said, following his hand with kisses.

'Mmm,' Evie said. She had her hands on his hard chest and he had his hands and mouth on her and she was trying to think but it was really hard. 'I think early.'

'How early?' Oh, God, he was *skilled* with his hands.

'Mmm.'

Damn, damn, damn. So bloody late. Evie leapt from the cab almost before it had stopped, waved at Dan, and sprinted through the school gates.

'Morning, Miss Khera, morning, girls,' she shouted to everyone on the netball court. 'So sorry I'm late. My Tube train got stuck in a tunnel.'

'Miss, was that your husband in that taxi?' Delilah, one of the Year Nine girls, had just run in behind her. Evie sighed. Unlucky that someone had spotted her, given that she'd been fifteen minutes late. Lucky, though, that they'd only been that late. You could shave a lot of time off your morning routine if you missed breakfast and took a cab. Expensive, though.

'No,' said Evie, shaking her head and trying not to smile, 'just a friend.'

'OMG,' Priya – aka Miss Khera – said to her, when Evie reached the other side of the court. 'Your *smile*. Who *was* it in the taxi?'

'Honestly, just a friend who was going in the same direction.'

'Please. At seven thirty in the morning?' Priya said. 'I'm going to need details later.'

Evie rolled her eyes but it was hard not to smirk with extreme happiness. It really felt like this could be going somewhere.

Chapter Thirty-Six

NOW – OCTOBER 2022

DAN

'You look like you had a good night, mate,' leered the taxi driver as Dan paid him outside Wimbledon station.

'Yeah, we did actually,' said Dan, knowing that he was smiling stupidly and really not caring. He was probably going to smile stupidly for the rest of the day. He wondered if it was too soon to text Evie. He checked his watch as he walked into the station. Yep, it was only about fifteen minutes since they'd said goodbye. And she'd be busy with the netball practice. He should probably play it cool. Or at least wait until, say, another fifteen minutes had passed before sending her a text, which he was pretty sure would say something goofy, because he wasn't going to be able to help himself.

He was pretty sure he was in love.

He really hoped she'd be able to meet for a coffee again next week, because they couldn't get together properly until Sunday in ten days' time, because they both had a lot of work commitments and Evie was out with friends on Friday night and he had Katie staying over – for the first time – on Saturday night, and was meeting Zubin and some other friends for beers on Sunday evening.

God, he missed Evie already.

*

Dan's mother came up to London for lunch on Saturday, to spend time with Dan, she *said*, but he was pretty sure that her main motivation was – understandably – to coo over her youngest grandchild. She arrived laden with soft toys and books that she just happened to have spotted when she'd just happened to be passing a toy shop in Cheltenham the other day. If she carried on like this, Dan's flat was going to resemble a toy shop itself.

They took Katie out for a walk in her pram, after which Dan's mum gave her a bottle of Hannah's expressed milk before Dan put her down for her sleep.

'So what have you been up to the last couple of weeks?' he asked his mum as they ate curry from downstairs for lunch. 'Sorry I haven't had a chance to call much. I've been really busy with work and things.' Evie. He hoped he wasn't smiling too goofily at the thought of her.

'Jenny and I started playing darts again. We've been practising in her friend Grant's pub. I can't understand why she can't see that he's so obviously the man for her.'

'Maybe it's a very slow burn thing.'

'Incredibly slow burn. They met at Lucie's wedding and that was six years ago.'

'Yeah, that is a long time. What about you? Have you been out anywhere else recently?'

'Did Sasha say anything to you? She did, didn't she?' Nope, it had been Evie who'd mentioned that Jenny had told her that his mum had been asked out for dinner by a very nice architect friend. A seriously foxy silver fox, according to Jenny. 'I decided that I'm not ready to meet anyone again yet.' Five years since she and his father had split up and she still wasn't ready to go for dinner with someone. Dan was really going to struggle to ever forgive his father, no matter how many tickets to the rugby he offered him.

'There's no hurry about these things,' Dan said, feeling like he was floundering. This wasn't the kind of conversation you wanted to have with your mother. He shouldn't have started it. 'Speaking of nice meals, try some of the prawn biryani. Best one I've ever tasted.'

*

It was a huge wrench to hand Katie over to Hannah on Sunday afternoon. Dan was busy for the rest of the day, with laundry and some admin to do before he met his friends for their early dinner, but it still felt like he had a baby-shaped hole in his heart knowing that he wasn't going to see her again until Wednesday evening this week, and then only for an hour before her bedtime.

Presumably as she got older it wouldn't seem so bad, because he'd get used to it, and teenagers and adults didn't live in their parents' pockets, but right now it really felt like he and Hannah were both missing out not getting to live full-time with Katie.

He was halfway through ironing his work shirts for the week, still not in the best of moods, when a message came through from his father. He hoped Dan wouldn't mind but he was going to have to take some important colleagues to the rugby instead of him and Max and Greggy.

He was *so* pissed off.

Hurt, he was hurt.

He was in his mid-thirties and he'd been hurt yet again by his own father. It wasn't the rugby – they could watch that on TV if they wanted to see it – it was that in his father's eyes rebuilding their relationship was apparently less important than sucking up to some colleagues.

He should say something.

Nope. He wasn't going to stoop to that level. He was just going to ignore him.

Nope. He wasn't going to do that either. He was going to be polite and move on. He sent a *No worries* message and stared at the wall opposite for a long time until he heard a strange noise from the iron and realised he'd left it flat on top of his favourite blue shirt and burned a hole in it. Marvellous.

God, family relationships were shit.

You wanted to stick with just friends. Friends didn't hurt you.

Chapter Thirty-Seven

NOW – NOVEMBER 2022

EVIE

Evie woke up latish the following Sunday morning and lay under her lovely warm duvet for a few minutes, regrouping.

Sunday. *Dan.* They were meeting at two thirty at Portobello Market. And then they might go for a walk and grab an early dinner, *or*, say, go back to one of their flats and have afternoon sex. *So exciting.* It was a week and a half since she'd seen him, and she couldn't wait.

She'd thought they were going to meet quickly during the week but he hadn't been able to get away from work in the end, and he'd been fairly monosyllabic with his texts over the past few days, but that was understandable given the full-on nature of his job.

Right. She was going to get out of bed now and this morning she was going to paint her toenails, pop to the shops for some nicer coffee, just in case they came back to her flat and got as far as actually having a cup of anything, and maybe buy some fresh flowers for the sitting room, change her bedsheets, and finish some marking.

Honestly, she actually felt like *squealing* in excitement about the day ahead.

What was she going to wear this afternoon? Maybe her new jeans with a loose top over a camisole.

Evie had just got home with the coffee, some flowers and a nice new scarf for herself, plus a book that Dan had been saying that he wanted to read that had just come out in paperback, when her phone pinged.

It was a text from Dan. She balanced all her shopping in one hand and swiped her phone. Probably a *Looking forward to seeing you* message. Only a couple of hours now until they were meeting.

Evie, I'm so sorry but I think we should maybe cancel this afternoon. I'm worried things are going too fast for both of us. I'm so sorry. Dan x

Evie dropped her phone on the sofa, dumped the flowers in the sink, plonked the coffee, book and scarf on the work surface, and sat down hard on the sofa next to the phone.

She read the message again and sniffed and scrubbed her eyes.

Bastard. Or not a bastard. Yes, a bastard. If he wanted to dump her, fair enough, his prerogative, but by *text* for fuck's sake. He could have had the courtesy to bloody call her at the very least.

She went into her bedroom, closed the door behind her and sank onto her bed. Then she lay down and rolled onto her tummy and cried, a lot, for several minutes. And then she just lay there, feeling truly bereft.

Her phone rang a few minutes later, while she was still lying there doing nothing. She ignored it. There was no-one she could bear to talk to right now.

It kept on ringing, stopped and restarted. And again.

Oh, God, what if this was the actual worst day of her life and something terrible had happened to her mum or Autumn. Or Sasha. She picked it up and looked at the screen.

It was Dan. God, it was *tragic* the way her heart leapt when she saw his name on her screen, because maybe he was calling to say his text had been a mistake, and then plummeted again, because of course he wasn't.

Whatever, she might as well speak to him. Just in case.

'Hi, Dan.'

'Evie, hi. I'm sorry. I just… I'm sorry. I'm scared and I don't think I can do this and I wanted to tell you in person. I'm sorry.'

Right. No. She couldn't talk to him right now. It hurt too much.

'Thank you,' she said. 'I've got to go.'

Evie's mum phoned straight after Dan had ended the call.

'I'm so stupid,' she wailed as soon as Evie swiped green. 'Alex has apparently been sleeping with three different women at the same time.' Alex was her latest OMG-he-might-be-the-*One*. After her longest ever period – a good six months – on the no-men wagon, she'd fallen off about a month ago. 'He wasn't serious about any of us. What's wrong with me? I always read too much into things. Like I believe what I want to believe. And you're my daughter and I'm your mother and you don't need to hear this about my life. And I'm going to be okay. I'm going to go to the cinema with Grant this evening and cry on his shoulder. Tell me about you. How's your day going?'

Evie's day was going pretty similarly, actually. She'd been believing what she wanted to believe about Dan. She was just like her mum. Not surprising, really.

In the same way that it was really bloody obvious to everyone except Evie's mum that Grant was the man for her, it was probably obvious to everyone but Evie that Dan was *not* the man for her.

The one difference between her and her mum in this instance was that she hadn't really told anyone about her and Dan. Not even Sasha. Maybe she'd subconsciously worried that something like this would happen.

*

A week later, Evie had just trudged home from the supermarket with her groceries, after an entire week of trudging, basically, because the whole of life felt like a bit of a chore with Dan definitively not in it, when she got a message from Matthew. It was out of the blue; they'd only spoken once since they split up, to give each other some belongings back. Their split had been amicable, but Matthew had seemed very hurt and had said he didn't want to stay in touch, which Evie had felt awful about.

Did she want to join him for a charity quiz night the following Friday evening? Not really. Life felt too boring to be bothered to do anything. And she'd already done one quiz night this year. Two in the space of about nine months felt like overkill.

But, actually, she should snap out of this. She couldn't mourn her relationship – such as it had ever been – with Dan forever. He clearly wasn't the right person for her. She didn't want to end up like her mum. Maybe Matthew was her Grant. Maybe this was a sign. She was going to go.

*

The quiz night had been better than expected – it was actually really nice to see Matthew again, and there'd been a musicals round *and* a seventies music round, both of which Evie had shone in – and now she and Matthew were wandering along the Broadway in Wimbledon together in the direction of both the station and Evie's flat.

They came to the little junction where they'd say goodnight if Matthew wasn't going to come back to Evie's flat with her: decision time.

Matthew was lovely. Matthew wouldn't hurt her. And if you ever needed someone to answer golf questions at a quiz night he was a complete legend. In fact, their general knowledge was completely

different. You could say they had little in common, *or* you could say
that they complemented each other perfectly.

'Would you like to come back for a coffee?' she asked.

'I'd love to.' He smiled at her and took her hand.

When they rounded the bend in her road, Evie saw a man sitting
on her doorstep. Maybe Josh was locked out again. It had happened
once or twice before. Although wasn't he out with Fergus this evening?
God, she hoped they hadn't split up.

Goodness.

Total stomach-lurching realisation.

It wasn't Josh. It was Dan.

'Evie.' He stood up. 'And Matthew.' His voice was remarkably cold.
He looked pointedly at where they were holding hands. Matthew tried
to let go of Evie's hand and she clung onto his. 'I thought we ought to
talk. But apparently you've wasted no time.'

'Apparently I've *what?*'

'Wasted no time,' Dan repeated, enunciating very clearly.

'Are you *joking?*'

'No.'

Matthew pulled his hand a bit harder, and Evie clung on a bit
harder. No way was Dan doing this.

'Goodnight, Dan,' she said.

'I'd like to talk,' he said.

Matthew said, 'If you're alright, Evie, I think I should probably
leave you to it.'

'Okay,' Evie said and reluctantly let go of his hand. 'Thank you for a
lovely evening, Matthew. I'm so sorry about this.' She gestured at Dan.

'Don't worry.' Matthew looked almost as miserable as she felt.
'Goodnight.'

Evie looked at Matthew's disappearing back, and then back at Dan. His jaw was clenched and he actually looked like he wanted a fight. She looked down, and, yes, his fists were clenched too.

'Excuse me,' she said. 'I'd like to go inside. I can't open the door with you standing there.' She wanted a fight too. How *dare* he say that she'd wasted no time. How *dare* he. But, also, had he, maybe, come to tell her that he loved her and he was ready for a relationship?

'Could we talk?' he said, not moving.

'Do you mean so that you can apologise for being a hypocritical arse? I mean, "wasted no time"? Are you *insane*? Frankly, I could have slept with a hundred people in the past twelve days and that would be *nothing* to do with you, because, *if you remember*, you told me that you "couldn't do this". And it isn't like you didn't leap into bed with me in Vegas straight after getting Hannah pregnant, is it?'

Dan stared at her for a really long time, his jaw still clenched, while Evie hoped desperately that he was going to tell her that he was sorry and he loved her and wanted to be together and that he'd manage to say it convincingly enough that she'd be able to believe him and forgive him for all his arsery.

Eventually, he said, 'I'm sorry. Really sorry. That was unforgivable. Yes, I was being a hypocritical arse. For the record, as I think I mentioned before, Hannah and I split up a good couple of weeks before Vegas. And for some reason that feels very different.' Maybe because he and Evie loved each other and from the sounds of it he and Hannah hadn't? 'Yeah, I'm sorry.' He looked at the key in her hand. 'I'm sorry. I'm in your way. Goodnight.'

He watched her open the door, and then, as she went inside, off he buggered. Off he bloody buggered. Arse. *Arse*.

And Evie went upstairs and cried even more than she had before.

Chapter Thirty-Eight

NOW – NOVEMBER 2022

DAN

He was so ashamed of himself. What was wrong with him? How could he have said that?

Dan reached the end of Evie's road and turned round. Maybe he should go back. Apologise properly. Explain that the reason he'd lost it was that he'd gone there to tell her he loved her, and then when it had become obvious that she was out for the evening he'd started torturing himself with the worry that she'd be out with someone else. And she had been. And he *knew* that Matthew was wrong for her.

But she was right. It was none of his business what she did.

Except he wanted it to be his business.

He started walking back towards her house and then stopped.

Better if he phoned her first maybe.

She didn't answer. He tried again. Still no answer.

Maybe that was for the best. He was hurting so much right now it felt like proof that loving someone was, basically, horrible.

He turned back round and started walking towards the station.

*

Saturday, a week later, Dan rolled his eyes at the ringing sound and didn't budge from the sofa. That was the third time in about three minutes that his doorbell had gone. You'd think whoever it was would have realised by now that he wasn't going to answer it. If it was a delivery they could leave it downstairs in the restaurant like they normally did and he could pick it up later. He lifted the TV remote and increased the volume.

His phone pinged. It was Max. Apparently he was outside and he was coming in.

'Afternoon,' Max said about ten seconds later.

'I should never have given you a key,' Dan said.

'How are you doing?' Max asked, sitting down in Dan's armchair.

'I'm fine. Just having some downtime.' Downtime thinking about how monumentally he'd cocked things up with Evie. He'd been trying very hard not to think about her and had slightly been succeeding until this morning when Sasha had mentioned Evie and Melting and Christmas in a text.

'You don't look fine.'

'I'm completely fine.'

'Bro. It's three o'clock in the afternoon and you're in your underpants watching *The Simpsons*.'

'I like *The Simpsons*.' In moderation. He'd definitely overdosed on them this afternoon.

'How's Evie?'

'I don't know.'

'I think you need to speak to her.'

Dan *really* shouldn't have given Max a key. What was even the point when he lived on the other side of London?

'I don't need to speak to her.' He increased the volume of *The Simpsons* even more. 'Nothing else to say.'

'Ever told her you love her?'

Dan put his hands over his face and sighed loudly.

'Remember when you didn't want to talk to me?' Max said. 'Did it *help* to talk?'

'Oh my *God*,' Dan said. 'So many questions. That was different.'

'How was it different?'

'Well, for a start, you didn't hate me.'

'She probably doesn't hate you. Do you hate her?'

'No.' Dan suddenly really did want to talk. 'Kind of still angry with her because she got back together with Matthew so soon after we split up. But, as she pointed out, that's incredibly hypocritical and just wrong and it's entirely up to her what she does because we aren't together. Basically, I behaved really badly and I'm not sure she'd be interested in talking to me.'

'I don't think you have anything to lose if you tell her you love her. You have to be brave and fight for what you want sometimes.'

'I don't even know if I do want her,' Dan said. Max stared at him. 'I'm scared of getting hurt,' he said.

'What, because it would make you deeply miserable if you split up?' Max was still staring at him, like he was stupid.

'Yes.'

'And what are you now? Deeply happy? You idiot. Take happiness where you can find it.' Max lunged for the remote and turned the TV off. 'Come on. Get some trousers on. Let's go out.'

'Seriously,' Dan grumbled. It would probably be nice to go for a walk or something, though. He hadn't exactly been enjoying himself sitting here. It felt like there might be something in what Max had said. Maybe he'd think about that later. 'I'm picking Katie up in an hour.'

'I'll come with you. If that's alright?'

*

When Dan, Katie and Max got back to Dan's flat, Max sang some nursery rhymes – painfully tunelessly, although Katie loved the singing – before standing up to leave.

'Think about what I said,' he told Dan before picking up a beaming Katie and plonking a big kiss on her cheek. 'See you soon, Kitty-Kate. Tell your daddy to think about what I said.'

It was starting to feel like Max was right and Dan *should* talk to Evie. When, though? And how? He could ask her if she wanted to meet up over Christmas. And she might not want to. Or he might mess up and not say things right. And, also, now he wanted to talk to her, he wanted to do it immediately.

Maybe an old-fashioned letter would be the way to go. But, no, a letter would be too slow. He'd send her an email. This evening. Maybe both an email *and* a letter.

Chapter Thirty-Nine

NOW – DECEMBER 2022

EVIE

Evie shivered, pulled her coat more tightly around her and dug her chin into her scarf. Bloody December. Bloody train station platforms with their wind tunnel effect. Bloody South Western Railway with their reduced timetable because there'd been a leaf or a snowflake on a train track in the past week. She was going to turn to ice while she waited for the train following the one that she'd hurried to catch but which had been cancelled, and then she was going to have to *sprint* at the other end to meet her friends at the cinema before the film actually started.

Stupid idea to go touristy and go to a fancy cinema in Mayfair in the first place. Stupid idea to go out full stop.

What she'd really like to do right now was go home and have a hot bath, get into her pyjamas and watch junk TV all evening. And wallow again a tiny bit, or maybe a lot, about Dan.

Obviously, she shouldn't wallow. She'd already spent far too much time being miserable. She should be grateful that she was living in an amazing city at the moment and that she'd met some great new friends at work, and enjoy a night out in the middle of London with people she liked. It would be nice to go home for Christmas, though, to her lovely, familiar village and her mum and Autumn and old friends. And maybe wallow a bit more.

Her phone buzzed. She pulled it out. Checking her emails would be something to do while she waited. Although her hands were going to freeze now while she swiped. She should get some touch-screen gloves.

She had an email from Dan. With the subject line *I love you*. Her heart lurched.

She kind of wanted to open it immediately, but she also kind of didn't. It felt… too much. Maybe he had something to say that would make everything feel better, but maybe she'd just feel even worse afterwards.

She pulled her phone in against her chest and stared straight ahead.

There was a lot of screeching of brakes and movement of people. Her train was coming. She'd better get on it.

She stumbled into a seat near the door, still holding her phone against her, and then moved the phone out in front of her and looked again at the unopened email.

It was like her whole body and brain were too stunned to open it. *I love you* was a strong phrase.

She put her phone down on her lap, turned it over and looked out of the window at rail-side buildings illuminated by street lights. Not *the* most scenic view. Better than thinking about Dan, though.

Oh, for God's sake. She was being ridiculous. If she didn't read it now, she'd think about it the whole time and wonder and wonder and ruin her evening. Better to *know* what he had to say.

From: Dan Marshall
To: Evie Green
Subject: I love you

Hi Evie,

I never told you how much I love you. I've written a letter that I'm going to deliver to you tomorrow.

I love you (and I miss you).

Dan

He loved her.

Wow. She didn't know what to think.

What was his letter going to say? Another *I love you*? Or more?

When would he deliver the letter? And did she want to read it?

His life seemed so *messy*. Could she deal with that, if he wanted them to be together? She did love him. She *really* loved him, which she'd never told him. But was that enough?

After that awful evening, when she'd effectively lost both Dan and Matthew for good, to her shame she'd thought very little about Matthew, because any feelings about him had been eclipsed by the utter devastation at the loss of her soul mate in Dan.

'Arriving at Waterloo.' Oh, *shit*. She'd missed her station. She should have got off at Vauxhall to switch to the Underground. Actually, she could just get on the Jubilee Line to go to Green Park. The station was heaving, though, and the Jubilee platform was a really long walk from here. Maybe she'd get a taxi. It felt like she deserved a little treat to cheer herself up after the shock of Dan's email.

In a *far* too expensive black cab – there was already eight quid on the clock and they'd barely moved; she'd just have got the Tube if she'd realised there'd be such a long queue at the taxi rank and it would cost this much – she texted her friends to let them know that she'd had a train issue but that she'd be there any minute. Bit of a fib if she was honest, because the traffic looked solid.

'Who you meeting at the cinema?' the taxi driver asked her.

'Some girlfriends.' Evie smiled at him in his rear-view mirror, feeling guilty about the fact that she *really* didn't want to talk to him.

'What film you going to watch then?' Christ. Evie just wanted to *think* right now.

Forty-five minutes later, she'd made it into her seat in the auditorium just as the ads finished and the trailers started. She hadn't had any time to buy any chocolate or popcorn, which was obviously a good thing given that this was right in the middle of the Christmas over-eating season, but she did still feel cheated.

She and Dan had chomped their way through a *lot* of sweets when they'd been to the cinema together.

She looked at Priya, sitting to her right, as Dan had been when they went to the cinema.

Priya was lovely.

She wasn't Dan, though.

Evie reached down to her bag and sneaked her phone out and into her pocket. When everyone was really focused on the film, she could re-read his email without disturbing anyone. Maybe she could look at it now while people were watching the trailers.

'Are you having a laugh?' The man behind her, who'd been rustling his popcorn bag *really* annoyingly loudly for the past five minutes, poked her in the shoulder. 'Put that away. I can't watch a film with a phone light below me.'

'Are *you* having a laugh?' Priya had turned round and was glaring at him. 'Looking at a phone's a lot less disruptive than eating really loudly right behind people. And kicking the chairs in front.'

'Sshhh,' said about twenty people around them.

Evie said, 'Sorry, everyone,' put her phone back in her bag and hunched down in her seat.

'Waiting for you to apologise too,' Priya told the man behind them.

Evie screwed her face up and hunched further down. The man kicked both their chairs, hard, and crunched *disgustingly* loudly on some more popcorn.

Priya got her phone out and turned the light on and waved it above her head.

Evie put her hands over her face.

An hour later, Evie sneaked a look at her watch during a very brightly lit scene. There was about an hour to go. The film wasn't bad, actually. Except for the fact that it was a drama involving a sexy doctor and Dan was a sexy doctor – although red-headed and rugged as opposed to dark and suave – so it was very hard not to keep thinking about him.

Snippets of different conversations with Dan were replaying in her head now.

She really wanted to know what his letter said.

She did not want to sit through the rest of this film.

Maybe she could go out to the foyer and wait there.

She whispered to Priya, 'I'm going to pop outside for a few minutes,' and half rose to go.

'Sit down,' growled the popcorn-and-kicking man from behind.

'Stand up if you want to,' hissed Priya.

'I'm fine,' whispered Evie, hunching in her seat again.

'Sshhh,' said several people.

Honestly. What if she'd just wanted to go to the loo?

Finally, the – to be fair, very good – film finished, and everyone watched and cheered the credits, for, honestly, *ages*, and then they made their way out to the foyer.

'Such a shame that it's too late for a drink,' Claire, one of Evie's friends, said.

Evie nodded. 'I know. Next time.' It was actually *such* a good result. She really wanted to go home and get on with obsessing about Dan in peace.

They all hugged goodbye and the others left Priya and Evie, who were going back to Vauxhall together.

'This looks interesting.' Priya stopped Evie in front of a large poster advertising the next *Star Wars* film and started reading out the names of the actors in it. Weird. Priya didn't strike her as a *Star Wars* fan.

'Haven't heard of any of them,' Evie said. 'Do you *like Star Wars*?'

'Kind of.' Priya did the same in front of the next poster, which was advertising the new Disney film. That one did have a lot of famous actors in it.

'This is going to be either a mega hit or a mega flop,' said Evie, 'with all these people in it.'

Priya didn't reply. Evie looked round to see why not. It turned out that she had her back to her and was talking to a man, who looked a lot like the popcorn-kicking man. She was gesticulating like mad. Evie really hoped she wasn't going to start a *fight* or something.

She was talking very animatedly.

Evie started obsessing about Dan again. When would his letter arrive?

She looked up. Priya was walking towards her brandishing her phone.

'Got a date,' Priya said.

'What? Who with?'

'The man who was sitting behind us.'

'No way.'

'You got to seize your opportunities when they present themselves. Life's short and he's hot. There's a fine line between hate and love.'

Hmm. There was maybe something in that.

*

Evie made sure that she was out all day Sunday because she did *not* want to sit around for hours waiting for Dan to deliver his letter only for him not to turn up.

She got home late afternoon from a long walk on the common with Mia to discover an envelope with 'Evie' written on it in decisive-looking navy handwriting on the front door mat. Her heart started racing just at the sight of it. It had to be Dan's letter.

'Cup of tea?' Mia asked.

'Cool, thanks,' Evie said. 'I'll be there in two minutes.' She went straight into her bedroom and closed the door and sat down on her bed to open the letter.

*

Dear Evie,

I don't really know where to start other than to say that I love you and I'm so sorry for messing up.

I love everything about you. I love the way you throw yourself into every dance. I love that you're such a loyal friend. I love that you're a fairground hustler. I love your sense of humour. I love talking to you. I love that you can't help yourself tidying up around people. I love YOU. (And you're gorgeous but I'm not sure if it's acceptable to say that in writing.)

I messed up. I got scared. As you know, I spent a lot of years seeing my mum get hurt by my dad and being hurt by him myself. I realised that I'd fallen in love with you and I got scared that loving people was dangerous, in that there's so much potential for pain.

I realise now that in trying to protect myself, and you, I've just ended up hurting us both.

I'd love to try again.

Obviously you might not feel the same way.

But I wondered if you'd like to meet for a walk in Melting next week?

All my love,
Dan

Evie re-read the letter and then folded it up very carefully and put it back in the envelope, and then put the envelope on her bedside table.

She knew what he meant when he said that loving people was dangerous, because of the potential for hurt, because that was exactly how she felt about loving him. She didn't want to be like her mum, involved in a series of messy relationships and frequently devastated. But Dan wasn't like the men that her mum tended to hook up with.

It probably wouldn't hurt to meet him for a walk.

Chapter Forty

NOW – DECEMBER 2022

DAN

'It's the village carol singing this evening,' Dan's mum said, handing him the cup of tea she'd made him while he unpacked his car.

He looked at her. Village carols were a big thing and the date was arranged weeks in advance. She was very over-nonchalantly putting biscuits on a plate for him.

'Did you happen to forget to mention them to me on purpose so that I wouldn't postpone my arrival until tomorrow?' he said.

'Well, obviously,' she said, laughing. 'But since you're here, you might as well come if you have no other plans?'

Dan rolled his eyes at her but said, 'I'd love to.' He did not particularly love carol singing and he did not love the interrogation about every minute aspect of his life from people like Mrs Bird – if you sang carols for her she *would* chat to you on her doorstep for ages – but he did love his mother and he knew she'd love him to go.

He wondered if Evie would be there. They'd had a brief text conversation in response to his letter, and had agreed to MEET for a walk tomorrow, but he didn't know what else she was doing over Christmas.

*

Evie, Jenny and Autumn turned up a few minutes after Dan and his mum had joined the others under the mistletoe tree in the middle of the green, just as Dan was starting to think that they wouldn't be coming.

Evie – looking gorgeous in a beret-style hat and scarf – gave Dan a small smile and put her hand up in a half-wave greeting but stayed on the other side of the group of about twenty people and began to talk very animatedly to Autumn. Sasha and Angus turned up shortly after them, and Sasha wanted to say hello to both their mum and Dan *and* Evie, which forced Evie and her mum and Autumn somewhat in Dan's direction, but Evie still managed to stay far enough away from him that they couldn't speak.

As they made their way from house to house singing all the old favourites, Dan was reminded several times of carols he and Evie had sung in the car together that time, and when he was nearish to her in the group, heard snatches of her clear voice ringing out. She was *good* on the high bits in 'Hark! The Herald Angels Sing'.

When they got to Mrs Bird's house on the corner, Dan manoeuvred himself to the back of the group so that, hopefully, she wouldn't see him and start with one of her interrogations. He looked round to see Evie fairly close to him, having clearly had the same thought. He smiled at her and she smiled back, and they just stood there, smiling stupidly, for ages.

Eventually, Dan took a step towards her and said, 'So…' and then Autumn popped up, having wriggled through the others, and said, 'Evie, I'm cold.'

Evie looked down at her and then at Dan, and then said, her voice sounding a little bit odd, 'Shall I take you home for some hot chocolate and a snuggle to warm you up?'

'Yes, please.'

'Why don't I take her?' Jenny's friend Grant stepped forward.

'That's really kind,' said Evie, 'but, honestly, I'm very happy to. I'm going to enjoy our hot chocolate.' Maybe she was glad of the excuse to get away from Dan. Or maybe that was really self-obsessed of him and she really did want hot chocolate now, or she wanted to give her mum and Grant the opportunity to spend some time together. Everyone had been waiting – in vain – for years for Jenny and Grant to realise that they were the perfect couple. Evie took Autumn's hand and said, 'Come on. Night, everyone. Sing your hearts out for us. Happy Christmas in case we don't see you.'

And then off they walked up the lane, and Dan felt ridiculously disappointed even though he knew he was seeing her tomorrow for their walk.

*

Dan clapped his hands together and stamped his feet. It was a lot colder than it had been yesterday evening and it now looked like the forecasters were right and there was a very good chance that there was going to be a white Christmas. Evie would have to be well scarfed-up in this weather.

What if she didn't turn up?

She *would* turn up.

He checked his phone. She was three minutes late.

God, maybe she actually wouldn't come. No, Evie would never do that. Probably just busy choosing which scarf would be the best for this exact temperature.

Seriously. He was smiling just thinking about her. He shouldn't smile. At best, they were going to have a lot of talking, sorting things out, to do. There was a good chance things wouldn't work out between them.

Right. He was going to walk round the green while he waited.

One full lap. He *really* hoped she was coming.

Nearly a second full lap. But maybe that was her coming round the corner of her lane. Yes, it was.

'Hey, Evie.' He started to walk towards her over the green, grinning as he went, even though maybe things weren't going to be okay. It was just so good to see her.

'Hi, Dan.' God, he loved her smile, even when it was only a small one as it was at the moment. He hoped the smile was going to grow.

'It's great to see you,' he said, when they got close to each other. 'I like your scarf.' It was a nice pale-blue colour and very soft-looking.

'Thank you. Good to see you too.'

'Shall we walk? To keep warm? The path by the stream?'

'Lovely.'

Dan really wasn't sure of the etiquette in this kind of situation. Go straight in with what he wanted to say or attempt a bit of small talk first? So far, it was all a bit weirdly polite.

'Probably going to be a white Christmas,' he said.

'Yeah. I think so. Pretty sure you used to be cynical about white Christmases.'

'Not all white Christmases,' Dan said, pleased that Evie remembered that conversation. So did he. 'Just ones when it's fifteen degrees and it would take a miracle for snow to fall. Rational, not cynical. Today it's bloody freezing and every so often we're already getting a flurry of snow.'

'And the weather forecast said it's going to snow in the Cotswolds on Christmas Day.'

'Exactly.' Dan nodded. There was a bit of silence. 'Not sure whether we'll get a white New Year, though.' So lame to be continuing with the weather chat, but he felt *really* awkward right now. He wasn't sure how to start the conversation they needed to have, and he wasn't sure what to say to make sure it went okay.

'Probably not.'

'Now who's being cynical?'

Evie laughed.

They rounded the corner by the church and started down the path that led to the stream. Dan suddenly didn't want to waste any more time. But he didn't want to run the risk of being interrupted during their conversation, and he could see the vicar, Laura, in the distance. She held up a hand and waved, and they both waved back. And he carried on saying nothing and so did Evie.

A few minutes later, they were wandering along by the stream, and definitely alone.

'So,' Dan said. Oh, God, no. Now he was panicking. Although, she'd agreed to meet him after his letter. She wouldn't have done, surely, just to tell him she didn't want to talk.

He was just going to dive straight in. 'You know when we made our mistletoe pact,' he said. 'I think I always knew, even then, that I wanted to be with you. I mean, yes, it was a joke, but there was something there. And the same when we got married in Vegas. Again, yes, we were drunk and it was a stupid thing to do, but from my side I don't think I'd have done it if I hadn't actually wanted to be with you. But I always thought that we couldn't be together, because it was too scary. Because if you love someone you can both get hurt. But it really hurts *not* being around you. I love you, Evie. I'm so sorry for having messed up and got scared.'

He stopped talking and waited.

And nothing. For ages. Oh, God.

He couldn't even see Evie's face properly because they were walking next to each other and she was all wrapped up in her hat and scarf.

Then she said, 'I love you too. I think I always have.'

Yessss. *Yessss.*

He really hadn't expected her to say that.

'Wow,' he said. He stopped walking and Evie stopped too. 'Can we try again?'

Evie looked at him for what felt like another near-eternity, and then she began to smile. And Dan's heart began to beat a lot faster.

'Yes,' she said. 'Let's take it very slowly. One step at a time. Nothing scary.'

She took a step towards him. He put his arms out and she moved straight into them and, very slowly, his eyes on hers the whole time, he lowered his lips to hers. He was pretty sure that she was wrong about nothing scary. It would always be scary when you loved someone this much. But good-scary, rather than miserable-lonely.

*

A long time later, they were still there, and cold wet stuff was falling on them.

'White Christmas,' Evie said. 'Just for us.'

Dan smiled at her. 'Come on. Let's walk.'

They walked along hand in hand, stopping fairly often to kiss. It was a great walk. No, better than great. Perfect.

They stopped again for another kiss under the mistletoe tree in the middle of the green.

'I'm pretty sure Mrs Bird's watching,' Evie said eventually.

'I don't care,' Dan said. He kissed her again. 'I love you, Evie Green.'

Epilogue

NOW – ONE YEAR LATER

EVIE

'Come here.' Evie's mum held out her arms and Evie stepped into them, cautiously, for a non-squishy hug. They'd spent a long time getting ready this morning and they didn't need a crushed dress or ruined hairdo disaster at this point. 'You look beautiful, Evie.'

'You look beautiful, too, Mum.' Evie blinked away sudden tears. This was huge. Well, obviously. Getting married to the right person was, ideally, a one-off, for life.

'And me,' said Autumn.

'Yes, of course you too,' their mum said.

Autumn, looking fairy-tale gorgeous in her bridesmaid's dress, did a big pirouette and then ran in for a group hug.

'Careful,' screeched Evie and her mum in unison and they all held hands in a little circle instead.

'I love you,' Evie's mum told her daughters.

'Love you too,' they both said.

'Right. Ready?' Evie's mum finished smoothing Evie's dress where Autumn had creased it slightly, and then held her arm out.

'Wait.' Evie rearranged her mum's jacket from where it had been knocked lopsided. 'There. Yes. Ready. Deep breaths all round.' She blinked back yet more threatened tears – thank goodness for waterproof mascara – and took her mum's arm and checked over her shoulder that Autumn was in position behind them, and they started walking down the aisle, to a very shaky organ performance from Mrs Bird of Wagner's 'Bridal Chorus'.

Sasha, Lucie, Fiona and another couple of friends from the village had done an amazing job of decorating the church in holly, ivy, berries and twiggy things for the perfect Christmas wedding backdrop.

The church was rammed with guests, all glammed up in *Bridgerton*-themed outfits, put together with a fair amount of historical inaccuracy but a lot of enthusiasm, many of them wearing hats made by Evie's mum, who'd been in millinery overdrive for the past few months, and all beaming at them as they processed past.

And there was the groom, turned to greet them, his face splitting into the most gorgeous grin.

'You look stunning,' he mouthed as they arrived at the front of the church. He didn't look bad himself in his tight Regency trousers, shirt, waistcoat and jacket.

Evie felt happy tears pricking her eyes *again*. This mascara had cost a fortune, but it was going to have been worth every penny if she didn't end up with panda rings on her face by the end of today.

'I love you,' she whispered to her mum, and then let go of her arm and took her seat on the front pew next to Autumn, while their mum moved to stand next to her about-to-be-husband, Grant, and Laura, the vicar, began the service.

Evie looked over at Dan, looking very handsome as a slightly reluctantly garbed Regency gentleman, sitting on the other side of

Autumn and holding a wriggling toddler Katie, and smiled at him.
She felt like her heart was going to burst with joy watching her mum
finally make it official with the only man Evie had ever met who she
thought could make her mum happy. And it was even better having
Dan here to enjoy the day with.

*

Six hours later, Sasha did a massive yawn, patted her tummy and said,
'I've got to go to bed now. Pregnancy's really hard work when the
baby's pressed up against your lungs *and* down against your bladder.
Where are the kids?'

Sasha was eight months pregnant and exhausted, and had volunteered to babysit Autumn and Katie in Evie's mum's house while all
the adults partied in the marquee in Sasha's mum's garden. Evie's mum
and Grant had been planning to organise the reception themselves in
Grant's pub until Sasha's mum had insisted that she *wanted* to host her
best friend's reception, and surely Jenny and Grant *didn't* want to do a
busman's holiday pub evening. Sasha's mum was staying with her new
partner, Doug, the architect who'd asked her out a good year ago, and
who she'd eventually started going out with on Valentine's Day this
year, and Evie's mum and Grant were staying in Sasha's mum's house
tonight before going on a Christmas honeymoon tomorrow, while Evie
and Dan looked after Autumn.

Evie wasn't *totally* sure that Fiona had bargained for full-on *Bridgerton*, but once she'd got her head round it, she'd embraced it, like all
the guests had.

When Dan got back from settling Katie in her travel cot in the
cottage, Evie was in the middle of a square dance partnered by Grant's
brother. She caught sight of Dan on the other side of the marquee and

got the little heart flutter she always got when she saw him after any time apart, even after a year very much together.

When the dance ended, they threaded their way across the floor to each other, beaming away, like there were no other people around them, and Evie walked into Dan's arms as the band struck up a waltz.

The party finally wound up at around one thirty. Evie and Dan watched Mrs Bird accept the offer of a walk across the green with her Zimmer frame and Albert Fox, the elderly neighbour she'd spent the entire evening dancing with.

'Look at those two. Seems like it's never too late for love to blossom.' Dan looped his arm round Evie's shoulders and pulled her in towards him and kissed her.

'I know. It's like there's something in the Melting water. First my mum and Grant, then your mum and Doug. And now Mrs Bird and Albert.'

'I want us to grow old together,' Dan said as they began to stroll across the night-frosted green themselves.

'Me too,' Evie said, going all warm and fuzzy inside. It felt like it might be time for her big question.

'Pitstop on the bench for old time's sake?'

They sat down close together, Dan's arm still round Evie's shoulders, and her hand resting on his thigh.

'You fancy making it official us living together?' he asked. They'd spent almost every night together for the past year, which had been amazing. 'I've loved this year. Big things, like just being with you, and smaller things, like eating more healthily and sleeping well. I feel like we're good for each other.'

She turned to look at him and then nodded slowly. It definitely felt like it was time.

'I would,' she said. Dan smiled at her and her warm, fuzzy feeling grew. 'In fact,' she said, '*I* have a big question for *you*. I was thinking we could go for a reprise of Vegas. But for real this time. And maybe not actually in Vegas, because it would be lovely for all our family and friends to be there.'

'Evie Green, are you asking me to marry you?' His grin was *gorgeous*, and face-splitting.

'Dan Marshall, yes I am.' She was grinning like nobody's business herself now, because he was clearly going to say yes.

'I'd love to.' He leaned his head towards hers and they shared a long, lingering kiss, before Dan drew back. 'While we're asking big questions, I'm also wondering if you fancy trying to give Katie a little sister or brother in the next year or two.'

Evie was going to explode with warmth and fuzziness now. 'Yes, I actually would.' She squeezed his thigh and snuggled further against him.

'Imagine what we'd have thought all those years ago when we made that pact if we could have seen ourselves now on this bench,' Dan said.

'We'd have thought we were old. When I was twenty-two, I thought *thirty* was old.'

'I love you,' Dan said. 'Pretty sure I always did, even then.'

'Me too.'

And then they kissed and kissed again under the mistletoe.

A Letter from Jo

Thank you so much for reading *The Mistletoe Pact*. I really hope that you enjoyed it!

If you did enjoy it, and would like to keep up to date with all my latest releases, just sign up at the following link. Your email address will never be shared and you can unsubscribe at any time.

www.bookouture.com/jo-lovett

I loved writing Evie and Dan's story.

I had a lot of fun with the whole 'Did one or both of them actually mean it?' idea of a fallback pact, and how that might play out over the years as people mature and develop, maybe with a little help from a surprise Vegas wedding…

I also really enjoyed spending time with my characters in London and the Cotswolds, both places that I know and love.

And I love Christmas, so I've been very happy to have an excuse to immerse myself even more than usual in all things festive!

I hope the story made you smile or laugh, and that you loved Evie, Dan and their friends and families as much as I did!

If you enjoyed the story, I would be so pleased if you could leave a short review. I'd love to hear what you think.

Thank you for reading.
Love, Jo xx

 @JoLovettWrites

Acknowledgements

Thank you so much to the wonderful team at Bookouture. I owe huge thanks to Lucy Dauman, who is unfailingly lovely and makes incredibly insightful comments. Thank you also to Celine Kelly, who is also extremely lovely and whose comments also always make perfect sense. And thank you so much as well to Jennifer Hunt, Rhianna Louise, Donna Hillyer, Becca Allen, Sarah Hardy, Kim Nash and all the in-house team for all your amazing input – it's so much appreciated.

Bookouture is often described as a family, and it includes many hugely supportive authors, one of whom is Kristen Bailey, who I need to thank for a lot of fab advice, support and parenting chat!

Big thanks to many of my friends but in particular Dave MacLennan and Emma Kipps for answering a lot of (stupid) questions about doctors – any mistakes are very much mine.

And thank you as always to my family, including my sister Liz, who is an amazing friend. My husband, Charlie, is also an amazing support (and I think genuinely likes my rom coms!). And my children have been wonderful as I've written this book – in and out of lockdown and self-isolation, without too much fighting! Sometimes they argue all day, and other times they say truly gorgeous things – a couple of days ago my (usually boisterous) eleven-year-old gave me a big hug and told me that he was very proud of me for being an author – *so* cute. Thank you! (And sorry that you're all still eating too much pasta when I'm busy writing.)